Table of Contents

Preamble

764 4th Day of the seventh moon

Today, I finally gathered the courage to speak, to tell my lady what I have been holding in my heart for too long. I could feel my words ready to spill over the moment we reached the grove, that hidden place where she meets with him. The man whose world is so vastly different from ours, whose presence has stirred something fierce within her, something I can no longer ignore.

When she asked me to bring a letter to him, I took a deep breath and let it out, saying the words I never thought I'd dare to say: "My lady, you can't do this. It's against tradition. Our worlds—they aren't meant to blend like this. You know what the others say."
She looked at me, her gaze soft but unyielding, her resolve clear as daylight. "I know," she replied, her voice barely a whisper. "But I can't resist him. He has captured my heart and my soul. No one has ever made me feel this way."
I wanted to protest, to remind her of the risks, of the whispers that would follow if they were discovered. But there, in the soft light of the grove, her face glowed with a mixture of joy and sorrow that I had never seen before. Her love for him was unmistakable, like a beacon shining through the mist, and I sensed my resolve waver. I had never seen her so completely given over to anyone or anything, and I knew that nothing I said could change her heart.
"He sees me," she continued, a rare vulnerability in her tone. "Not for what I can give him or what my name means, but simply for who I am. It's as if he knows every part of me, the parts I've hidden even from myself."
And what could I say to that? How could I deny her something so precious? Yet, a part of me aches with fear, knowing that this love, as powerful as it is, comes at a cost. Their union would defy every rule our people have lived by, and the weight of that knowledge presses on my heart like a stone.
Still, I find myself unable to stop her. Each meeting with him deepens her bond, and I am left to stand beside her, guarding her secret with all the loyalty I can muster. And so I will continue, even as my own worries grow, because if anyone deserves happiness—even one shadowed by risk—it is her.
As I returned to the shadows to watch them, I knew I would protect her secret, even if it meant breaking the traditions that bind us. After all, if love can make my lady this radiant, then perhaps, just perhaps, it is worth the risk.

764 19th Day of the Seventh Moon

I could scarcely breathe when she told me. Her words seemed to float on the air, delicate and dreamlike: "He has asked me to marry him... and I shall bear his child."
My heart clenched, though I forced a smile, nodding as if this were the joyous news I'd been waiting for. But deep inside, jealousy twisted like a thorn. I have watched their love bloom from the shadows, have carried letters sealed with promises and sweet words. And in doing

so, I've become a witness to the passion that consumes them, a passion that I can't help but feel a part of and yet am forever distant from.

I could see the joy in her eyes, a light so radiant that it made the grove seem brighter. She spoke of him with a warmth that melted all her worries, her fears, and even the whispered doubts from our kin. But there, too, was something else—a sense of purpose, as though in carrying his child, she had become part of something far greater than herself.

And what of me? I am her handmaid, her confidante, but I am also simply a shadow in their world. The closeness I once felt with her seems to slip further each day, as if the very fabric of her life is stretching away, leaving me on the edges.

I confessed as much to her, or at least a part of it. "Are you certain this is what you want?" I asked, trying to sound steady, trying not to let the ache in my heart show.

Her smile softened, though she nodded without hesitation. "More certain than I have ever been. His love has become my anchor, my guide. And now, with a child on the way, our union will be bound by something eternal."

I nodded, biting back my sorrow and swallowing the envy that threatened to spill over. She deserves happiness, doesn't she? And if this is the path she has chosen, then who am I to wish otherwise?

But the thought remains. I once imagined myself a part of her world, intertwined with her life as much as her shadow. Now, I am reminded with every passing moment that her heart belongs to another, that her future is one I can only witness from a distance.

i am bound to her service, yet i feel as if I am slowly losing her. The words stay locked within me, but the pai lingers, as the moon rises tonight, I wonder what lies ahead for her...and myself.

Prologue

The chamber pulsed in rhythm with something ancient—something alive and ravenous.

Heavy vines writhed along damp stone walls, thick and serpentine, their thorned lengths slick with sap that glistened like fresh blood in the lantern's wavering glow. The air was thick, oppressive, laden with moisture, moss, and an undertone of rust and iron—an unsettling scent that hinted at darker deeds buried deep within the stone. Shadows pooled in every corner, restless, watching.

At the heart of the chamber sprawled the bloom, monstrous and unnatural. Its petals spread wide, lush and blood-red, quivering gently, breathing softly, almost whispering. Tendrils curled at its base, coiling impatiently, grasping blindly at empty air. It was beautiful in a horrifying way, captivating yet repulsive, a fusion of grace and menace.

Within its trembling embrace, the captive struggled.

Green-skinned, lean yet strong, he fought with a savage desperation born of instinctive terror. Sweat streaked down his slender frame, mixing with dirt and blood, silver fur rippling down the center of his back and along tense, wiry limbs. His small tusks jutted defiantly as he snarled and spat curses in a guttural tongue, his claws gouging uselessly at the thick vines that bound him tighter with each furious thrash.

Beside him crouched the smaller of his captors, lithe and lean, his narrow face split into a cruel grin. He jabbed a clawed finger into the prisoner's side, chuckling low at each growl he elicited.

"Still has some fight left," he murmured appreciatively, almost affectionately. "You chose well."

Across the chamber, his companion—a massive beast with broad shoulders and a scowling face etched by countless scars—grunted dismissively. Blood still trickled down his arm, the wound fresh from the last failed trial. "It won't matter soon," he muttered darkly. His gaze flicked toward the older woman who stood silently over the bloom.

She was unlike them—human in appearance, but unsettling in her stillness. Her long, white hair fell around her shoulders, tangled and damp with sweat from the humid cavern air. Her thin, lined face was sharp with intensity, her eyes cold and calculating. Between her pale fingers, she rolled a vial of thick violet liquid, its contents glowing faintly in the flickering light.

"Hold him steady," she commanded quietly, unnecessarily. The vines obeyed her unspoken will, binding the captive even more tightly, pulling him inexorably toward the hungry bloom.

The prisoner struggled harder as fear blossomed in his eyes, but the vines drank in his panic greedily, tightening until his movements slowed. His breath turned shallow, strained.

With deliberate care, the woman tilted the vial. The viscous liquid spilled onto the bloom's roots, disappearing instantly. The entire chamber shuddered, the ground heaving as if it had just inhaled deeply. Shadows lengthened, candles flickered, and the bloom quivered as though waking from slumber.

Instantly, the captive began to change.

A primal scream ripped from his throat—raw, wrenching, full of pain. Bones cracked audibly, shifting beneath his skin. Muscles twisted and bulged unnaturally, rippling under flesh that stretched taut and painful. Silver fur spread rapidly, thickening, darkening as claws elongated and teeth sharpened. His face contorted, jaw lengthening with an audible snap.

"Now, that's something different," the smaller beast whispered in awe, eyes glittering with dark delight.

At the back of the chamber, silent in shadows, the observer watched impassively. He had seen this too many times to be moved—but something cold settled deeper within him nonetheless. Something like dread.

The woman murmured softly, chanting in an ancient language. Her hands traced invisible symbols through the air, each gesture deepening the transformation, coaxing it forward, molding flesh and bone to her dark design.

But then—

Something twisted, went horribly wrong.

The captive's body spasmed violently, his eyes bulging, mouth opening in a soundless scream. The bloom recoiled, its petals shrinking back, edges turning black as if burned. The vines loosened in panic, recoiling from the suddenly limp form.

"No," the woman hissed, her voice brittle with frustration.

The prisoner collapsed, shuddering uncontrollably, silver fur rapidly blackening. He drew one last, rattling breath—then lay still, chest unmoving.

For a long moment, silence held sway. Then the corpse twitched, spasmed grotesquely, and jerked upright, its head turning sharply, eyes now wide and vacant, mouth filled with rows of warped, unnatural teeth.

In an instant, the larger beast moved. With brutal precision, he grabbed the malformed creature by the neck and snapped it viciously, the sound echoing sharply off stone walls. The corpse fell to the ground again, truly lifeless now.

"You fool," the woman snarled, fury radiating from her small frame. "You killed it."

"It bit me," he grumbled dismissively, brushing fresh blood from his wound.

The smaller beast shrugged, amused. "Make another. Plenty more where he came from."

The woman's cold eyes narrowed. She looked to the chamber's entrance, speaking sharply. "Bring the next one."

Another captive was dragged in, muscular and defiant, clearly a warrior—older, battle-scarred, his eyes unafraid as he stared directly at the woman. "Bloodfang tribe," the smaller beast remarked, grinning as he pushed him forward. "Meaner. Stronger."

The woman considered carefully, appraising her new subject. "This one will hold," she murmured finally.

She took a new vial—crimson and violet entwined, pulsing faintly like a heartbeat—and poured it upon the roots. Again, the bloom awoke. Again, flesh reshaped itself in agony. Yet this warrior did not scream, only grunted through clenched teeth, enduring silently.

When it was done, his new, feral eyes met hers. She saw defiance, hidden carefully beneath obedience. Her pulse quickened with satisfaction—and caution.

The observer saw this, too. He saw recognition flash in those altered eyes, a consciousness hidden behind the beast. A silent rebellion waiting for a single moment.

He had seen this too many times, indeed.

Slowly, silently, the observer stepped forward, finally breaking his silence.

"You should be careful," he said, his voice low and smooth as silk. "You may not fully understand what you're creating."

She turned sharply, glaring. "I know precisely what I'm doing."

His lips curved into a faint, unsettling smile. "Do you?" His dark gaze flickered once more to the transformed warrior, then back. "Because when the war starts, I doubt you'll be the one in control."

Without another word, the observer stepped outside into the cold night. The bloom behind him pulsed hungrily, the woman's whispers resumed, and another transformation began.

Standing beneath the starlit sky, the observer opened his palm. A blood-red rose blossomed gently from his skin, thorned and vibrant.

He stared thoughtfully into the dark woods beyond.

The woman thought herself the master, the beasts believed they were building an army. But the observer knew the truth—a truth he'd learned bitterly through ages of suffering and battles long past.

He crushed the rose softly in his hand, thorns biting into his skin.

"Wars never truly end," he murmured, watching the blood trickle between his fingers. "They only repeat."

Then he vanished silently into the waiting dark.

The night wrapped around him, cool and damp, clinging to his cloak like the ghost of forgotten memories. He lingered at the cavern's edge, watching the shifting darkness within the trees, his heartbeat steady despite the turmoil within. At his feet, the crushed rose lay broken, its dark petals already wilting, lost in the shadows.

"You hesitate."

The voice emerged softly from the gloom—steady, calm, aged by time and burdened by wisdom. He did not flinch. He recognized the voice immediately, a figure whose approach was always silent, his presence felt long before it was seen. From the shadows, an older man stepped forward, pale eyes gleaming beneath heavy brows, his worn cloak blending seamlessly into the night.

"Perhaps caution is justified," the observer replied, his voice low, careful. "Not long ago, we stood on opposite sides of the battlefield. Now here we are, allies plotting from the dark."

The old man moved closer, standing beside him, eyes fixed thoughtfully toward the faint lantern glow from within the cavern. "War forges strange alliances. Necessity binds even the most unlikely souls."

The observer cast him a wary glance. "Are you certain this is what you want? I've watched her closely for months now. She was formidable during the war, yes, but her powers have only grown since then. The creatures she commands are mindless fools, but even fools can become dangerous. If we allow her to continue unchecked, what was once weak will rise as a force to be reckoned with—and Sergora will fall. Your homeland will be destroyed."

For a long moment, the old man did not respond. Instead, his gaze lifted, drawn toward the distant stars shining above the jagged silhouette of mountains. When he finally spoke, his voice carried a calm, almost soothing tone—a storyteller weaving ancient threads.

"Did I ever tell you the true story of Sergora's rise? Long before it bore its current name, long before the Thorin Pass became a bloodied battlefield in our recent wars, Sergora stood firm. Its land has passed hands more times than memory serves: first shaped by the Vek'smed, then nurtured under the careful watch of the Slivdhe, and even once ruled by the muckspawn tribes who wandered freely beneath these very trees." He paused, letting the weight of his words linger in the cool air. "Yet all were swept aside when the first human kings arrived. Sergora is older than us all, and more resilient than we care to admit."

The observer shifted impatiently, irritation and uncertainty edging his tone. "I don't need your history lessons. I lived through the last war—I fought alongside the Sliver Fang and against him in equal measure. I watched comrades die in the Thorin Pass, defending the very ideals Sergora represented. But I fear if we permit her twisted creations to thrive, Sergora itself will become a barren land of thorns, ruled by shadows."

The older man finally turned, fixing his pale, piercing eyes directly upon the observer. "Yet here you stand, hesitating, still uncertain if this is the path to take."

The observer clenched his jaw, eyes hardening. Another faint scream echoed from deep within the cave, twisted and raw. His voice grew cold, guarded. "I have faced abominations before—monsters forged in desperation, like the Sliver Fang. I watched that beast rage beyond control, an experiment turned disaster. I've no desire to see another such horror unleashed on the world."

The old man nodded slowly, expression grave. "The Sliver Fang was a tragedy—a weapon that never should have been forged, a tool turned uncontrollable. But history, my friend, is built on mistakes. Each war teaches lessons we refuse to remember. Perhaps this woman and her beastly experiments are our reminder."

"And what of her hidden master?" the observer pressed, voice dropping to a whisper edged with suspicion. "She is powerful, yes, but something darker guides her hands. Something I cannot see clearly. Tell me—what shadow does she serve?"

A faint, knowing smile curled the old man's lips. "She serves but a shadow indeed, a puppet herself. Her master is nothing compared to the true power behind all of this—the power we ourselves serve."

A chill deeper than the night's embrace settled over the observer's shoulders. "Who, then? Who truly pulls the strings?"

The old man did not reply immediately. Instead, he turned again toward the silent forest, his voice gentle yet heavy with the weight of centuries. "Every age believes itself special, each war unique. Yet time flows in circles, history repeating itself endlessly. Sergora is merely the stage upon which old battles play anew."

"I tire of your riddles," the observer growled softly. "Speak plainly. Do we move against her now, or wait until Sergora is reduced to ash?"

The older man exhaled slowly, shaking his head with quiet resignation. "We watch and wait, for now. When the time comes, we will strike—not merely for Sergora, but for something greater."

"Greater?" the observer questioned, voice wary, uncertain.

"For a balance that must be restored. For truths lost to arrogance and forgotten pride." The old man turned fully, stepping back into the shadows, his figure blending easily with the night. "You must understand, this land—Sergora—is only the beginning. Once it falls, as it inevitably will, others shall follow. And each fall will ripple outward until the entire continent is reshaped. Only then can a new era rise from the ruins we create. All of this pain, this darkness—is for the greater good."

The observer stood silent, watching the old man fade from sight, words echoing painfully in his heart.

"Go now," the old man's voice echoed back to him, drifting from the darkness. "Observe her carefully. Be the warden you truly are. If you're clever enough, you might even learn a few of her tricks." He paused, tone sharpening. "Though you hardly need them—I can sense your power, boy. You cannot hide your bloodlust. It lingers in you, just like it did in your mother."

At the mention of his mother, the observer's breath caught sharply, a startled gasp slipping free before he could stop it. He turned quickly, his eyes narrowed to sharp points, searching vainly for the old man's figure in the dark. But only shadows stared back at him.

The old man chuckled softly, the sound drifting farther away. "I go to prepare. See you when it all begins."

The observer stood still for a long moment, tension coiled tight within his chest. Finally, he turned back toward the cave, fingers flexing anxiously at his sides. He knelt down, picking up one last fallen petal from the crushed rose at his feet, turning it slowly in his fingers. He had seen countless wars, stood on many battlefields, and watched kingdoms rise and fall. Every conflict promised peace yet delivered only more conflict, more suffering.

"Wars never truly end," he murmured softly, bitterness tinging his voice. "They merely repeat."

With that, he dropped the withered petal, grinding it beneath his heel, and followed the old man's trail into the darkness—uncertainty still clinging to him like a shadow he could never escape.

Chapter 1: Meeting In Marsh

762, 9th Day Of The Fifth Moon

"My father despises them, calls them no better than the mountain folk—'using women in war, sacrificing dignity for strength.' Yet I cannot deny there is beauty in it. Their grace on the battlefield is like poetry in motion, bodies flowing with a purpose that defies his narrow expectations. I could swear I even saw one reciting lines of verse before the battle. Strange, these people, but perhaps not so different from us.

At least they carry themselves with dignity, more civilized than the creatures in the marsh. The marshfolk—filthy, wild things—lack all grace, skulking about in the muck, their movements crude and their ways barbaric. My father may rail against these warriors, but I'd much rather face them than those creatures who know only how to survive in filth and shadow."

The marsh hung thick with mist, heavy and damp as it clung to the village nestled within. The early morning air was cool against Tala's skin as she stepped out from her family's hut. The soft glow of dawn barely pierced the dense fog that wrapped around the huts and crooked paths like a shroud. Villagers moved like shadows, their figures blurred and ghostly in the haze.

The village was a labyrinth of stilted huts woven from reeds and driftwood, their thatched roofs sagging under the weight of moss and creeping vines. Narrow walkways, slick with moisture, connected the homes above the murky waters below. Small fires flickered within, casting warm glows that fought against the encroaching mist. The air was rich with the scent of damp earth, mingling with the tang of herbs hung to dry beneath eaves.

Tala wandered through the winding paths, her small fingers trailing along the rough bark of the wooden fences that lined the way. The fences were adorned with charms made from bone and feather, clattering softly in the faint breeze. She noticed that the usual morning bustle was subdued; voices that were typically loud and hearty were hushed, murmuring in tones that piqued her curiosity.

She caught sight of a group of elders huddled together near the communal fire pit. The elders were a formidable sight—weathered faces etched with deep lines, eyes sharp beneath heavy brows. Intricate tattoos spiraled down their arms, telling tales of battles fought and victories won. Their garments were adorned with beads and carved bone, clinking gently as they moved. Their heads bent close as they whispered among themselves, the firelight casting flickering shadows across their solemn expressions.

She approached casually, pretending to adjust the straps of her satchel. As she neared, the elders glanced up, their conversations abruptly halting. One gave her a tight-lipped smile, his tusks protruding slightly over thin lips, before they dispersed, moving away into the mist with the shuffling gait of those burdened by unseen weights. Tala frowned, a knot of unease tightening in her stomach. It wasn't like the elders to avoid her so deliberately.

Continuing down the path, she saw her friends gathered near the well. Relief washed over her; perhaps they would know what was happening. The well was encircled by stones slick with algae, its rope and bucket worn from years of use. But as she approached, they exchanged glances and quickly scattered, their webbed feet making soft slapping sounds against the damp wooden planks. They mumbled excuses about chores that needed attending, eyes avoiding hers. Tala stopped short, confusion giving way to hurt. Why was everyone acting so strangely?

Determined to find answers, she headed toward the market square. The square, usually alive with the vibrant colors of swamp flowers and the rich aromas of fresh catches, was eerily quiet. Stalls made from woven reeds stood half-empty, the merchants behind them staring off into the distance or speaking in hushed tones. Small clusters of villagers spoke in low voices, their faces serious and creased with worry. As she walked by, conversations ceased, and eyes turned away from her, focusing intently on the ground or distant, unseen points in the mist.

Frustration mounting, Tala decided to hide and listen. She slipped behind a stack of woven baskets near the edge of the square, crouching low. The baskets smelled of the dried fish and herbs they once held, and their rough fibers prickled against her skin. The voices of two women drifted toward her.

"Dei samlast i kveld," one whispered, her voice barely audible. *"They gather tonight."*

"Ja, langt inne i myra," the other replied, glancing over her shoulder, her large, luminous eyes reflecting the muted light. *"Yes, deep in the marsh."*

Tala leaned forward, straining to hear more.

"Kva trur du dei vil gjere?" *"What do you think they will do?"*

The first woman shook her head, worry etched across her features. Her fingers fiddled nervously with a pendant made of carved bone hanging from her neck. "Eg veit ikkje, men det er ikkje godt." *"I don't know, but it can't be good."*

Their conversation was cut short as a man approached, and they fell silent, moving away swiftly, their cloaks swirling around them like the mist itself.

Feeling a mix of intrigue and concern, Tala made her way toward her father's tent. Surely he would have answers. The tent stood apart from the others, its entrance flanked by totems carved with ancestral symbols and decorated with feathers that fluttered gently. But when she arrived, the door flap swayed gently as if recently disturbed. She hesitated before stepping inside.

"Da?" she called softly, her voice barely more than a whisper.

Silence greeted her. The interior was dim, lit only by the embers of a dying fire. His ceremonial cloak, usually hanging proudly on the wall, was gone, as was his staff carved from ancient driftwood. Tala's heart skipped a beat. He would never leave without telling her.

She exited the tent, her pace quickening as she sought out the village guards. Spotting two standing watch near the boundary, she approached them. The guards were imposing figures, their bodies adorned with armor fashioned from overlapping scales of marsh creatures. They held spears tipped with sharpened bone, and their eyes were vigilant beneath helmets adorned with tusks and feathers.

"Kvar er høvding Arak?" she asked, trying to steady her voice. *"Where is Chief Arak?"*

The guards exchanged uneasy glances. One's grip tightened on his spear, the knuckles of his webbed hand turning pale.

"Han gjekk tidlegare. For dagen," one replied, avoiding her gaze. *"He left earlier. For the day."*

"Kvifor fortalde han meg ikkje?" *"Why didn't he tell me?"*

The guard shifted uncomfortably, the armor plates rustling. "Han hadde det travelt." *"He was in a hurry."*

Tala's unease deepened. The guards' usually stoic faces betrayed a hint of anxiety—a flicker in their eyes, a tension in their jaws. Something was definitely wrong.

Determined to uncover the truth, she decided to observe the villagers unnoticed. She slipped into the shadows, moving silently along the less-traveled paths where the wooden walkways gave way to soft, spongy earth. Her bare feet made no sound against the moss and damp soil. From behind a cluster of tall reeds, their thin leaves whispering with the slightest breeze, she watched as the villagers went about their tasks, their conversations hushed and eyes wary.

As dusk approached, the sky above turned a deep indigo, and the mist seemed to glow with an ethereal light. She noticed the chieftains preparing to leave. Gruk'thar strode purposefully toward the edge of the village, his massive form cutting an imposing silhouette against the fading light. His armor was adorned with the tusks of great beasts, and a heavy axe hung at his side. The ground seemed to tremble slightly with each of his steps.

Rak'tan slipped through the shadows, his movements swift and silent like a hunting serpent. His eyes, narrow and piercing, scanned his surroundings constantly. A cloak made from the scales of a giant swamp lizard draped over his shoulders, and a collection of daggers glinted at his belt.

Bea'ranti moved with silent grace, her footsteps barely disturbing the damp earth. Her long hair was braided intricately, woven with strands of silver and small charms that tinkled softly. She carried a bow carved from dark wood, its surface etched with runes, and a quiver of arrows fletched with crow feathers rested against her back.

They were leaving without her father. Panic and determination surged within her. The chieftains' departure felt like a foreboding omen, a shadow stretching over her village. She couldn't let them go without knowing what was happening.

She waited until they had disappeared into the marsh before following at a safe distance. The fog thickened as she ventured deeper, the familiar paths giving way to treacherous ground where roots snaked across the earth and pools of dark water reflected the sliver of moon above. The damp air clung to her skin, and strange sounds echoed around her—the distant croak of unseen creatures, the rustle of leaves stirred by movements just beyond sight. But she pressed on, driven by the need to uncover the secrets being kept from her.

Finally, a faint glow pierced the mist ahead. She crept closer, careful to stay hidden behind the twisted trees and dense underbrush. The trees here were ancient, their gnarled branches reaching out like skeletal arms, draped with hanging moss that swayed gently. The chieftains had gathered around a roaring fire in a small clearing. The flames cast a wild, flickering light, illuminating their stern faces and casting deep shadows that danced across the surrounding swamp.

Gruk'thar, Chief of the Boar Tusk Tribe, stood at the center of the circle, his massive frame illuminated by the flickering flames. His skin was a deep shade of mossy green, marked with swirling tribal tattoos that seemed to dance in the firelight. Two large boar tusks were mounted on his armored shoulder plates, and his helmet was adorned with curved horns, giving him an imposing presence. His voice boomed over the others, commanding attention.

"Lat møte starte!" he snarled, his fierce green eyes scanning the assembled chieftains. *"Let this meeting come to order!"*

The chieftains fell silent, eyes glinting with suspicion and impatience. Kraggor, Chief of the Stonetooth Tribe, stepped forward. His skin was a rich olive green, and his powerful build resembled that of a great bear. Thick muscles bulged beneath armor crafted from heavy hides and reinforced with stone plates. His helmet bore the likeness of a bear's head, with carved stone teeth lining the front, giving him a fearsome appearance. He slammed his massive fist down on a nearby tree stump, causing it to crack.

"Kva vil du, Gruk'thar? Me har ikkje tid for prat," he growled, his deep voice rumbling like distant thunder. *"What do you want, Gruk'thar? We have no time for talk."*

Gruk'thar's gaze hardened, eyes narrowing like a predator sizing up its prey. "Fienden kjem. Me må slå tilbake." *"The enemy comes. We must strike back."*

Another chieftain, Vruk'tal of the Thunderhoof Tribe, snorted, his muscular arms crossed over his chest adorned with intricate tattoos depicting storms and lightning. His skin was a vibrant emerald green, and his helmet was adorned with antlers resembling those of a stag, symbolizing his tribe's connection to the wild. "Alltid ein fiende. Kvifor bry oss no?" *"Always an enemy. Why bother now?"*

Gruk'thar growled deep in his throat, a rumble that seemed to resonate with the earth itself. "Dei brenn skogen vår. Tek folket vårt. Vil de la dei?" *"They burn our woods. Take our people. Will you allow it?"*

A murmur rippled through the circle. From her hidden vantage point, Tala's heart pounded. She had heard whispers of villages disappearing.

An older chieftain, Chief Fjellhorn, stepped forward. His skin was a weathered jade, and impressive horns made from mountain goat antlers adorned his helmet, decorated with bones and small trinkets that clattered softly with his movements. His eyes were as cold and steady as the stone peaks his tribe called home. "Me kjempar som alltid. Kva er nytt?" he spoke gruffly, his voice like gravel shifting underfoot. *"We fight as always. What's new?"*

"Ikkje nok lenger," Gruk'thar snapped, his fist tightening around the haft of a heavy axe etched with ancient symbols. "Me må samle stammane. Vere ein styrke." *"Not enough anymore. We must unite the tribes. Be one force."*

Silence hung heavy. The chieftains exchanged glances, some nodding thoughtfully, others frowning in skepticism.

Zra'ka of the Webshroud Tribe stepped forward. His skin was a pale, almost luminescent green, and his armor was crafted from woven spider silk and metal, shimmering in the firelight. Tiny spider charms hung from his gear, and his helmet featured slender, curved spires resembling spider legs. His eyes, dark and piercing, reflected the flames. "Kvifor skulle me følgje deg?" he challenged coldly, his voice a whisper that cut through the night like a blade. *"Why should we follow you?"*

Gruk'thar bared his teeth, his tusks gleaming menacingly under the shadow of his horned helmet. "Fordi eg leiar. Vil de heller døy?" *"Because I lead. Would you rather die?"*

A tense pause followed. Begrudgingly, Zra'ka inclined his head ever so slightly. "Greitt. Kva er planen?" *"Fine. What's the plan?"*

Gruk'thar's tone was blunt, leaving no room for dissent. "Me angrip først. Overraskar dei. Viser styrken vår." *"We strike first. Surprise them. Show our strength."*

The chieftains grunted in agreement, some pounding fists into open palms—the sound like distant thunder echoing across the marsh.

"Når?" Urshak of the Crowfeather Tribe asked sharply. Draped in a cloak adorned with black feathers, his skin was a deep forest green. His helmet was topped with crow feathers that ruffled in the night breeze. His sharp features were accentuated by tribal markings resembling beaks and talons.

"Ved daggry. Samle krigarane. Vere klare," Gruk'thar declared, his gaze sweeping over them like a storm front. *"At dawn. Gather the warriors. Be ready."*

With unity declared, Gruk'thar's gaze moved among the gathered chieftains, shifting to practical command as he delved into the state of their lands.

He turned to the next chief. "Og du, Rak'tan? Korleis held Owlbeak?" *"And you, Rak'tan? How fares Owlbeak?"*

Rak'tan, a sinewy figure with a cunning expression, tilted his head. His skin was a muted sage green, and his armor was adorned with owl feathers. His helmet featured stylized owl wings sweeping back from the temples. His eyes, large and unblinking, gave him an eerie presence. "Kven hindrar oss? Ingen." He sneered, casting a disdainful glance around the circle. "Mine er sterke. Me treng ingen hjelp." *"Who hinders us? No one. Mine are strong. We need no help."*

Gruk'thar narrowed his eyes but let the slight pass. "Venomfang, rapporter." *"Venomfang, report."*

Vark'nal of the Venomfang Tribe stepped forward, his movements smooth and deliberate. His skin was a dark, swampy green, and his armor was scaled, resembling that of a serpent. His helmet bore the likeness of a snake's head, fangs bared. His eyes were narrow slits that glinted in the firelight. "Byene kjem nærare, øydelegg våre marker. Meir gift trengs." *"The towns come closer, ruin our fields. We need more poison."*

Gruk'thar's expression hardened. The encroachment of the eastern towns was a threat to them all, one that poison alone might not repel.

Urshak nodded solemnly. "Treng høgare tre. Byen ser meir," he said, his feathered cloak rustling like wings. *"Need higher trees. The town sees more."*

The chiefs murmured in agreement. The marsh was more than their home; it was their shield, its dense foliage and towering trees essential for concealing their movements.

Finally, Gruk'thar turned his gaze on a figure directly across from him. "Korleis landet ditt, Bea'ranti?" *"How are your lands, Bea'ranti?"*

Bea'ranti, Chief of the Wolffang Tribe, met his gaze with eyes as sharp and cold as ice. Her skin was a deep hunter green, and her armor was crafted from dark leathers and furs. A wolf's pelt draped over her shoulders, and her helmet bore stylized wolf ears. She exuded a fierce grace, every movement deliberate. "Treng fleire krigarar," she replied, her voice cutting through the humid air like a chill wind. "Bazel stengjer vegen, austfolket plagar oss." *"Need more soldiers. Bazel blocks the path, eastern villages trouble us."*

Rak'tan of the Owlbeak Tribe leaned forward, his sharp, beak-like features twisted in amusement. "Kvinne svak. Eg leier, inga trøbbel." *"Female weak. I lead, no trouble."* he sneered.

Bea'ranti didn't flinch. Her icy gaze locked onto Rak'tan, letting the silence hang thick between them. When she spoke, her voice was as cold as the northern winds. "Eg høyrde unge slo deg." *"I heard a child beat you."*

The other chiefs shifted uncomfortably, but Bea'ranti's eyes never wavered, daring Rak'tan to challenge her again.

From her concealed vantage point, Tala held her breath, every word of the exchange pulling her deeper into the web of intrigue. She could not look away, even as Rak'tan's eyes narrowed, his jaw tightening like iron. Chief Gruk'thar stepped between them, his voice heavy with authority.

"Ho rett. Eg høyrde rykte, Rak'tan." *"She's right. I heard rumors, Rak'tan."* Many chiefs chuckled, nodding.

"Ikkje barn, trente ungdomar væpna, klare – eg tok ned ein." *"Not children, trained youths armed, ready – I took one down."*

Rak'tan growled, pulling a skull from beneath his cloak. "Blad skar djupt, hans fall gjer meg sterk." *"Blade cut deep, his fall makes me strong."*

With a swift, defiant motion, Rak'tan tossed the skull into the flames, the sickening crackle of bone resonating through the marsh. He eyed the laughing chiefs, their eyes widening in silent approval.

Tala stifled a gasp, her heart pounding. This was no simple meeting; it was a contest of wills, growing more dangerous by the moment.

Bea'ranti's gaze never faltered, her resolve like stone. She stood formidable, her twin daggers gleaming at her sides. "Du, feig for ungane." *"You, coward before children."* she spat, stepping forward with the ferocity of a wolf. Gruk'thar barred her path, his booming voice reverberating through the air.

"Stopp no, eller Bogsmal kjem!" *"Stop now, or I call Bogsmal!"*

Rak'tan's grin widened, firelight casting sinister shadows across his face. "Bea'ranti, Bogsmal! Du skjemmer meg!" *"Bea'ranti, Bogsmal! You dishonor me!"*

Tala's stomach twisted in knots. A challenge had been issued. She knew what was coming, yet she couldn't move, trapped by the tension that hung thick in the air.

Bea'ranti's response was swift and certain, her voice as sharp as her daggers. "Eg tar Bogsmal!" *"I accept Bogsmal!"*

The marsh seemed to grow colder around Tala, the fog closing in as if the very land sensed the storm about to be unleashed.

Gruk'thar's voice cut through the humid air like a blade. "Så, rygg! Bogsmal er erklært!" *"So be it. Step back! Bogsmal has been declared!"*

His proclamation rang through the marshlands, silencing even the insects that had droned on moments before. Tala pressed herself deeper into the shadows, scarcely daring to breathe.

"Rak'tan sier han er vanæret av Bea'ranti!" *"Rak'tan claims he has been dishonored by Bea'ranti!"* Gruk'thar's booming voice echoed through the crowd. "De kjemper her nå. Kun død gir løsning. Vinner tar stammen." *"They shall duel here and now to settle this affront. Only death shall bring resolution. Winner claims the tribe."*

Tala's pulse quickened as the marsh fell silent, thick with expectation. She watched, unable to look away, as the two chieftains prepared for a deadly duel that would decide more than their honor.

Around the fire, the Muckspawn warriors stirred, forming a broad circle, sloshing through the muck to mark the perimeter of the arena. Tala shrank lower, melding with the cold, damp earth beneath her. Her heart pounded like a war drum as Bea'ranti and Rak'tan stepped into the ring, faces etched with grim resolve.

"Stríð—dauða eller heiður!" *"Fight—death or honor!"* Gruk'thar's voice echoed once more. "Blod í bog! Sigur får heiður; fall går til myra." *"Blood in the bog! The victor claims honor; the fallen joins the marsh."*

The marsh itself seemed to stir at his words, steeped in memory of too much bloodshed. Tala sensed it in her bones, the land reacting to the battle that was about to begin. She held her breath.

Bea'ranti stood poised, daggers ready, calm and focused. Rak'tan, across from her, radiated fury, his movements sharp and vicious. Tala knew that neither would show weakness.

Rak'tan struck first, a roar slicing through the misty bog. His blade slashed through the air, but Bea'ranti evaded with a deadly grace, countering with a swift strike of her own, her blade grazing Rak'tan's arm. They circled each other, every blow met with a precise parry.

The marsh bore witness to their clash, the only sounds the splashing of feet in the muck, the clash of steel, the rhythm of their breathing.

Rak'tan's strength faltered, his swings slowed, growing desperate. Sensing her moment, Bea'ranti seized the opportunity. With a calculated maneuver, she threw him off balance, leaving him exposed. Rak'tan wavered, his breathing ragged. Then with a final, guttural growl, he lunged forward in a desperate attempt to reclaim control, his blade slicing through the air one last time. But Bea'ranti was ready. She sidestepped, her movements precise and unyielding. With a deadly grace, she drove one dagger deep into his chest, piercing through his armor, her strength holding firm as he gasped in shock.

The world seemed to hold its breath as Rak'tan's body tensed, his eyes wide with fury and disbelief. He dropped to his knees, his blade slipping from his grasp and sinking into the marshy ground beside him. The fog thickened, curling around him as if welcoming him back into the earth.

Bea'ranti's voice cut through the silence, low and steady, her words carrying an icy finality. "Din tid er over, Rak'tan. Myra tek deg tilbake." *"Your time is over, Rak'tan. The marsh takes you back."*

With a wet, strangled gasp, Rak'tan slumped forward, his body sinking deeper into the muck as the marsh claimed him. Bea'ranti withdrew her dagger, watching with calm detachment as his lifeless form was swallowed by the earth, leaving only ripples and shadows in the murky water.

The gathered chiefs stood in reverent silence, eyes fixed on Bea'ranti. In that moment, her authority was unchallenged, the strength of the Wolffang Tribe apparent in the quiet fury of her victory.

Gruk'thar broke the silence, a slight nod of respect in his gaze. "Ho leiar med styrke. Dei som tviler, ser no." *"She leads with strength. Any who doubt, see now."*

The other chiefs exchanged uneasy glances, acknowledging the weight of his words. Bea'ranti, with her cold poise and deadly efficiency, had proven herself a force to be reckoned with. Vark'nal, of the Venomfang Tribe, lowered his gaze in a rare show of humility, while Urshak of the Crowfeather Tribe gave a begrudging nod.

Gruk'thar turned to address them, his voice a low rumble. "Ho har vunnet. Wolffang vil bli høyrt." *"She has won. The Wolffang shall be heard."*

The chiefs muttered their assent, a reluctant respect settling over the gathering.

From her hiding place, Tala let out a silent breath. She'd witnessed more than a mere fight; she'd seen the power struggle that would shape the future of the marshlands. Bea'ranti's command was absolute now, a truth no one present could deny.

Bea'ranti's gaze swept over the assembly, her voice sharp and direct. "Vi går saman. Stammen vår er ein, ikkje delt." *"We go together. Our tribes are one, not divided."*

A ripple of surprise passed through the crowd. The Muckspawn tribes rarely worked in unity; each guarded its territory and traditions. But under Bea'ranti's command, the marsh was shifting, and the chiefs seemed to understand the weight of her call.

Gruk'thar's voice echoed in support, his booming authority reinforcing her words. "For myra. Ikkje for oss, men for våre land." *"For the marsh. Not for us, but for our land."*

A rumble of approval rolled through the circle, the chiefs slamming fists to their chests in a united gesture of solidarity. They would fight together, bound not by individual tribe but by their shared duty to the marshlands.

"For myra!" Gruk'thar bellowed, his voice carrying through the night. *"For the marsh!"*

"For myra!" the chieftains roared in unison, their voices blending with the fog and shadows, a primal declaration of loyalty.

Gruk'thar grinned, his tusks gleaming in the flickering firelight. Tala watched as all the chiefs began to plan for the dawn, their heads bent together in intense discussion. Armor clinked softly as they gestured, outlining strategies and marking the ground with symbols. The atmosphere buzzed with a fervor she hadn't felt before.

Was this the beginning of a new age or the downfall of her people?

Hidden among the twisted roots and dense foliage, Tala felt a chill run down her spine. The unification of the tribes was unprecedented, a turning point that could either save or doom them all. The chiefs' voices grew softer, but their determined expressions spoke volumes.

She knew she had to act quickly. With her father absent and unaware, it fell upon her to bring him this dire news. Careful not to draw attention, she slipped away into the mist, the weight of the night's revelations heavy on her young shoulders.

Chapter 2: The Path to Sergora

777, 18th Day Of The Eleventh Moon

A missive arrived from my wife's kin today. They claim they have my son's Thirst under control, that his anger will be "tempered." Yet I fear they may quench more than his rage. Both his fire and restraint have their uses; I need a general, not a mere soldier. I fear what is to come.

Mira says these visions are the result of my bond with my wife—a gift of her kin, a sight they've bestowed upon me. She calls it a blessing, but I wonder what kind of gift shows only shadows, images of battles and faces unknown. It weighs on me like a curse, as though each vision presses the coming storm nearer.

The afternoon sun cast a dim, unwelcoming light over the narrow chamber where Ky'len and Izell stood before Lord Dareth, Ky'len's father. Bazel, their home, was a city of strict discipline and unforgiving expectations, where wealth and influence held sway over titles and crowns. The city wasn't governed by a single ruler but was controlled by a powerful council of merchant lords, each vying for dominance. Trade deals, mercenary contracts, and ruthless alliances defined Bazel's hierarchy, and Lord Dareth stood among the highest, his wealth built on mercenary contracts and ruthless trade.

As one of Bazel's most influential lords, Lord Dareth's authority rivaled that of any king's. His gaze flicked between Ky'len and Izell with the unyielding sharpness of a blade, his expression as cold as the stone walls surrounding them.

"You don't have a choice in this, Ky'len," he said, his voice low and unrelenting. "Old King Tor'valis is allowing our people back into his lands, and I need you to find out why. Secure our status there. Or else, boy."

Ky'len clenched his jaw, but he didn't dare argue. He glanced at Izell, who looked equally serious, though a gleam of eagerness flickered in his friend's eyes. Izell caught his glance but kept his mouth shut, instinctively knowing better than to speak out of turn with Lord Dareth.

"What exactly do you want us to do, my lord?" Ky'len asked, choosing his words carefully.

Lord Dareth leaned back, studying him with a sharp, appraising look. "Keep your eyes open. Listen to what's not being said, not just what's spoken. Find out what Tor'valis truly wants, why he's allowing our people back in after years of exile. And, Ky'len"—his tone dropped, carrying an edge that Ky'len knew too well—"don't disappoint me. There's more at stake than you realize."

Ky'len fought the urge to retort. Instead, he nodded, keeping his expression impassive. "We'll do what we can, Father."

Lord Dareth's lip curled slightly, a trace of condescension in his gaze. "You'll do more than that. You'll do what's needed."

With that, Lord Dareth turned and left the room, leaving Ky'len and Izell alone in the silence that followed. For a moment, neither spoke, the weight of the command settling over them like a shadow.

Izell finally broke the silence, his voice low and light-hearted. "Not exactly the warm send-off I imagined."

Ky'len sighed, running a hand through his hair. "He wants us to play spies, to sniff out whatever Tor'valis is hiding. We're squires, Izell, not informants."

Izell shrugged, his eyes brightening. "We're squires, sure. But you know he'll expect nothing less than success. Besides, it might be… fun," he said, a grin breaking through. "Think about it —getting away from here, maybe learning a thing or two while we're out there. And look at it this way, you can get away from him for a while…"

Ky'len gave him a half-hearted smirk. "You really think so?"

"Of course!" Izell's eyes sparkled with a hint of mischief. "Think about all the training drills we've had—repeating the same moves over and over. Out there, we might even learn some new sword moves, pick up a few tricks we'd never hear about in Bazel." He clapped Ky'len on the shoulder. "C'mon, Ky'len. This could be exactly what we need."

Despite his misgivings, Ky'len felt a flicker of excitement. Izell's words held a certain appeal. Leaving Bazel, the expectations, and his father's endless commands behind—even for a while —was tempting.

"Maybe you're right," Ky'len said finally, a slight smile touching his lips. "Maybe there's something out there worth learning."

"Now you're talking!" Izell grinned wide, his energy infectious. "Whatever happens, we'll face it together. And who knows? Old Tor'valis might even surprise us."

Ky'len rolled his eyes, though he couldn't help a laugh. "I'll believe that when I see it."

As they walked through the streets of Bazel, the city's sharp structure loomed around them. Tall stone walls framed the streets, adorned with banners bearing the crests of Bazel's most influential merchant families. Narrow alleys and twisting roads crisscrossed through tightly packed buildings, where merchants bartered and haggled, and mercenaries roamed, each eyeing the other with a wary respect.

Around them, the hum of conversation shifted. As Ky'len passed, people glanced his way before hurriedly averting their eyes, their voices lowering to murmurs.

"Lucky boy, getting out of this city," one merchant whispered to another as they stacked crates. "Imagine, away from the lords' reach."

"Aye, maybe that old king is better than what we've got here," his companion replied with a scoff. "Lord Dareth and the others...they've got their grip tight on everything. And who suffers? Us. Maybe we could use a change."

"But don't go thinking King Tor'valis is soft," someone else muttered. "They say he's ruthless, fought through the entire war without backing down."

"Nah, that was Sliverfang who took down twenty men single-handed!" the first voice argued. "I heard he was like a ghost on the battlefield."

"Sliverfang or not," the other man said with a shake of his head, "any man who dares open his borders after all this time has got to have something up his sleeve."

Ky'len's jaw tightened, but he said nothing, quickening his pace as the murmurs trailed off behind him. He was used to the rumors, the comments just low enough to avoid catching his ear but never truly hidden. He felt Izell's curious glance but kept his eyes straight ahead, his scowl hardening with every step.

As they approached the city's edge, a rider on horseback, oblivious in conversation with a passing vendor, brushed past Ky'len, nearly pushing him off balance. Instinct flared, and before Izell could intervene, Ky'len grabbed the edge of the rider's cloak and yanked, sending the man tumbling off his saddle and into the dust.

"Watch where you're going," Ky'len growled, his fists clenched and his gaze dark.

The rider scrambled to his feet, his face paling as he registered who had thrown him. Stammering, he muttered a hasty apology, eyes darting between Ky'len and Izell, and quickly mounted his horse, riding away with a fearful glance over his shoulder.

Izell let out a sigh as he watched the rider disappear into the distance. "Come on, Ky'len," he said softly, resting a steadying hand on his friend's shoulder. "You can't keep letting them get to you."

Ky'len's glare softened as he took a deep breath, unclenching his fists. "He nearly trampled me. I wasn't just going to stand there."

"I know," Izell replied, his voice calm. "But we're about to get far away from all this. No need to carry it with you, right?"

For a moment, Ky'len didn't respond, his gaze drifting down the road where the rider had gone. Slowly, he let out a grudging sigh. "Fine. But next time, he'd better watch himself."

Izell chuckled, clapping him on the back. "That's the spirit. Save your energy for something that matters."

The two of them continued, passing the last of Bazel's walls as the crowd thinned. Voices faded into murmurs behind them, and Ky'len felt the tension begin to lift, leaving only the open road and a world waiting beyond Bazel's stone grip.

As they left the city behind, Izell shot Ky'len a grin. "Finally. No more routines, no more sharp eyes watching every move."

Ky'len managed a small smile, feeling the weight of his father's presence fall away with each step. With Izell beside him, he felt a flicker of something unfamiliar—hope for the journey ahead, and maybe even a sliver of freedom.

The night was quiet, thick with the scent of damp earth and distant woodsmoke. Stars winked above, hidden at times behind thin clouds, casting a faint glow over the camp. Ky'len and Izell were set up just off the road with a small caravan bound for Sergora, the travelers eager for the safety of city walls after endless, open roads.

The campfire flickered, casting a soft orange light on the faces of travelers who murmured in low voices or drifted to sleep. Ky'len sat by the fire, absentmindedly sharpening his sword, his gaze distant as the edge of the blade caught and reflected the firelight. Beside him, Izell leaned back against a log, yawning as he stretched his arms above his head.

"Think we'll reach Sergora tomorrow?" Izell asked, his voice low, as though unwilling to disturb the peace.

Ky'len nodded without looking up. "Should be close. We'll reach it by afternoon if the road's clear."

But as he spoke, a soft rustling in the shadows caught his attention. He stilled, his hand tightening on his sword hilt as his gaze flicked toward the dark edge of the campfire's reach. The faint crunch of leaves grew louder, and then, without warning, a guttural cry echoed through the night.

Figures surged from the shadows—muckspawn, hunched and twisted, with matted fur clinging to their limbs and eyes glinting with a feral hunger. They moved with unnatural silence, descending upon the caravan like predators closing in on their prey.

One of them, larger and more menacing than the rest, wore a tattered cloak adorned with owl feathers. He led the attack, his gaze fixed on the caravan's wagons, where supplies were packed tight. His presence was chilling, almost spectral, in the shifting firelight.

With snarls and grunts, the muckspawn fell upon the caravan, toppling crates and ripping through the travelers' belongings with savage glee. A young squire, barely older than a boy, lunged forward, his face pale but determined as he raised his sword to meet the muckspawn leader's gaze. But before he could even lift his blade, the feathered creature knocked him down with a brutal swipe, sending him sprawling to the ground.

The boy gasped, clutching his side, wide-eyed with fear as he tried to scramble back. But the muckspawn leader loomed over him, raising a jagged blade that gleamed cruelly in the firelight.

Izell's face darkened, and with a fierce shout, he rushed forward. "Get away from him!" He closed the gap between them, his sword flashing as he swung at the muckspawn leader. The creature twisted, hissing as it sidestepped, narrowly evading the blow. Izell followed, his strikes coming faster, each one forcing the creature back.

Ky'len was beside him in an instant, his blade cutting through the air as he drove back another muckspawn that lunged toward the wagons. His strikes were a blend of precision and raw power, pushing the muckspawn back step by step. The creatures snarled and snapped, but Ky'len and Izell held their ground, forming a tight defensive ring around the caravan.

The muckspawn leader, undeterred, darted back toward the wagons, his cloak of owl feathers trailing behind him as he moved with unsettling speed. He dodged past Izell's reach and lunged toward a wagon, where a young woman clutched a child, her face white with terror.

With a furious shout, Ky'len charged forward, bringing his sword down toward the muckspawn leader. Their blades met with a clang, grinding against each other as they locked eyes. The creature's yellow gaze gleamed with a cruel intelligence, and a twisted smile curled across his face as he pressed back against Ky'len, his strength formidable.

Izell struck from the side, aiming for the creature's shoulder, but the muckspawn twisted away, the sword grazing him but doing little harm. With a mocking laugh, the creature danced back, his cloak swirling around him as he slipped just out of reach, moving with an unnatural agility that taunted them both.

"Hold still, you coward!" Ky'len spat, his voice rough with frustration. He lunged forward, only for the muckspawn leader to evade him once more, slipping back into the shadows beyond the firelight's reach.

The creature paused, his eyes glinting with a silent challenge before he turned and vanished into the trees, the owl feathers on his cloak swaying in the dark.

Ky'len stood frozen, his chest heaving, his sword still raised as he stared after the retreating figure. Around them, the remaining muckspawn scattered, their snarls and hisses fading as they disappeared into the night, leaving only the bodies of the fallen and the wreckage of the caravan.

Izell sheathed his sword, his face set and grim as he approached the young squire, who was being helped to his feet by another. The boy's face was pale, his hands trembling as he nodded his thanks, his eyes still wide with the shock of near death.

Ky'len clenched his fists, scanning the shadows, his frustration simmering. "We should have taken him," he muttered.

Izell placed a hand on his shoulder, his gaze steady. "Next time. We'll be ready."

Ky'len shook off Izell's hand, striding toward the edge of the camp, his eyes still fixed on the darkness where the muckspawn leader had disappeared. He could still see the flick of owl feathers, the creature's taunting gaze before he vanished.

Izell joined him in silence, watching his friend's tense posture before speaking. "It's done, Ky'len. They're gone. We did what we could."

Ky'len didn't respond, his gaze still hard, but finally, he turned back toward the campfire, his hand resting on the hilt of his sword. "If we see him again," he said quietly, "he won't get away."

Izell nodded, his expression resolute. "Then we'll be ready."

The two squires returned to the fire, where the travelers and other squires had gathered, their faces a mix of relief and lingering fear. But Ky'len's thoughts were still on the muckspawn leader, the feathers swaying in the firelight, and the defiant grin that had marked his escape.

The next day, they journeyed on. The road was rougher now, carved with the grooves of countless wagons and worn-down boots. The forest thinned as they moved closer to civilization, though the shadows between the trees still made Ky'len glance back now and then.

When Sergora finally came into view, rising in the distance like a stone crown atop the valley, Ky'len felt something stir within him. A renewed determination—or maybe just the exhaustion of having somewhere safe to land. The city's high walls loomed like a promise: safety, order, something unshakeable.

Even so, he couldn't shake the image of those yellow eyes, watching him from the woods. The owl-feathered muckspawn was gone, for now, but not forgotten. It would not dare approach Sergora. Not with guards on every wall and steel lining every gate. And yet... he couldn't help but feel it was still near. Waiting. Hunting.

Izell, sensing the weight in his friend's silence, bumped his elbow against Ky'len's shoulder. "Remember, Sergora's got guards and gates," he said with a half-grin. "Not even muckspawn will come sniffing around these walls."

Ky'len gave a short nod, but his mind lingered elsewhere—on feathers in the dirt, on the breathless chase through the woods, on a fight they barely survived.

They joined the line of travelers at the gate, pressing forward between traders, peasants, and cloaked figures too quiet to trust. Sergoran guards stood tall in polished armor, inspecting wares and names with cold efficiency. Ky'len and Izell passed through with little notice, just two more young squires in the flood of humanity.

Inside, the city was alive.

The scent of baked bread and sweat clashed in the air. Horses clopped over cobblestone.

Children darted through alleyways and under carts, laughing. Merchants cried out, shoving fabrics, spices, and smoked fish toward uninterested hands. A smith's hammer rang in the distance, iron meeting iron in rhythm with the pulsing heart of the city.

As they moved through the market, Ky'len slowed near a wooden post hammered with parchment—Sergora's notice board. One freshly pinned poster stood out among the faded ink.

"Muckspawn Sighted Near Northern Trade Road. No Deaths Confirmed. Five Silver for Verified Reports. No Compensation Without Witnesses."

Izell scoffed. "Seems the merchants would rather stay safe and keep their gold. Pay for stories, not for solutions."

Ky'len stared at the ink a moment longer. *Five silver for fear,* he thought bitterly. Not enough to fight a monster. Not enough to stop it.

He turned away, but another poster snagged Izell's attention. Bright red ink, bold letters— boastful, like everything in Sergora.

"Sergora's Annual Tournament!

Test Your Skill!

All Fighters Welcome!

Glory,Gold, And Favor Await!"

Ky'len's eyes locked on the words. His heart thudded harder than the smith's hammer.

The tournament. Of course. His father had spoken of it often—of champions rising from nothing to become names whispered by lords. It wasn't just sport. It was power. It was recognition. *It was a way to matter.*

The command still echoed in his mind: *Secure our status.*

It wasn't a suggestion. It was a test. One he could not afford to fail.

Izell nudged him again, grinning. "Thinking of entering?"

Ky'len's jaw tightened. He nodded once. "We both should. A good chance to see how we measure up."

Izell raised a brow but didn't argue. He never did when Ky'len got like this—sharp-eyed and clipped, like a drawn blade. "Then let's find the sign-up tents before the crowd gets stupid."

As they made their way through the winding stone streets, the mood of the city began to shift. Beneath the noise and trade, there was something simmering—excitement, yes, but also unease. Murmurs of missing livestock near the outer farms. Of strange claw marks near the eastern watchtower. No one spoke too loudly about it, and no guard confirmed it. But the tournament came at a perfect time—just enough spectacle to distract from fear.

At the edge of the training fields, tents had been erected—bright banners snapping in the wind. Squires in leather, mercenaries in chain, and even a few proud nobles milled about, signing names, testing their weapons, boasting loudly.

Ky'len stepped forward. His name would be written here. His story would start here.

And if the owl-feathered beast dared to follow them—Let it come.

He'd show it, and everyone else, what the son of Bazel could do.

Chapter 3: A Cloaked Bargain

771, 18th Day Of The Fifth Moon

Today, I signed the peace treaty with the mountain men. It was not without difficulty—each negotiation was like walking a narrow ledge above the abyss, neither side willing to yield too much. Their leader, Orin, was wary, and I can't blame him. The scars from our past conflicts still linger.

But we have to move forward. This treaty means stability for our people, a chance to stop the endless cycle of raids and retaliation. I pray the promises made today will hold, that both our lands might know something other than war. Only time will tell if this is truly the dawn of peace, or just another fragile truce.

A rustling sound jolted Tala from her trance. Twigs cracked faintly behind her, and she pressed herself harder against the damp earth, willing herself to become invisible among the tangled roots and swamp grass. The marsh stood eerily still; the usual chorus of night creatures was silent, as if holding their breath. The chieftains, mid-chant around the flickering bonfire, fell into sudden silence. Their glowing eyes turned in unison, narrowing as they fixed their collective attention not on the aftermath of battle strewn before them, but on something—or someone—lurking in the shadows beyond the firelight.

Tala's pulse quickened as she followed their gaze. A figure glided through the darkness, her steps whisper-quiet despite the treacherous, sodden terrain. Emerging from the mist, the woman wore a cloak and hood that seemed untouched by the mire clinging to everything else. Her presence commanded the air, thickening it with a cold, electric energy that prickled Tala's skin and sent a shiver down her spine.

Who was she? No human dared venture this deep into the marshlands, especially not alone and unguarded. Yet here she was, moving with ethereal grace, halting at the edge of the chieftains' circle. When she spoke, her voice was low but unyielding, each word crisp in the heavy air.

"Jeg kommer på vegne av min herre. Han trenger deres ferdigheter. God betaling venter." "*I come on behalf of my master. He requires your skills. Good pay awaits.*"

A ripple of unease passed through the Muckspawn chieftains—fierce warriors who feared little, now eyeing this stranger with a mix of suspicion and cautious reverence. Tala's heart pounded. Whoever this woman was, she wielded a power that even they acknowledged.

Gruk'thar, ever the brute, stepped forward, his massive form casting a long shadow across the circle. His voice was a rumble of distant thunder.

"Hva er oppgaven? Hva vil herren din ha fra oss?" *"What is the task? What does your master want from us?"*

The woman remained unfazed. Reaching into her cloak, she produced a small, rune-etched chest, its intricate carvings faintly glowing in the firelight. When she opened it, vials of dark liquid pulsing with a malevolent aura were revealed. A chill ran down Tala's spine as she watched, her mouth dry.

"Disse," the woman murmured, her voice barely above a whisper yet slicing through the silence. "Disse er fra min herre. De bærer mørk magis kraft. Drikk, få styrke, hurtighet, makt som ingen annen." *"These are from my master. They hold dark magic's power. Drink, gain strength, speed, power like no other."*

The chieftains leaned in, eyes gleaming with a dangerous mix of curiosity and desire. Yet alongside that hunger, Tala noticed flickers of hesitation. Clawed hands twitched but did not reach out. Gruk'thar snorted, his voice grating like stones grinding together.

"Hvorfor hjelpe oss, skjøre menneske? Vi er mange, sterke." *"Why help us, fragile human? We are many, strong."*

His tribe echoed in agreement, guttural murmurs reverberating through the night air. The chieftains exchanged wary glances. Dark magic was not unknown to them, but it was a path fraught with peril—a double-edged blade that could just as easily turn on the wielder.

The woman's hood dipped slightly, her ice-blue eyes glinting beneath the shadowed cowl.

"Menneskene forakter dere. Stammer kjemper over små jordbiter. Min herre tilbyr dere herredømme. Ta disse flaskene, og dere vil knuse dem. Ta tilbake deres forfedres land." *"The humans scorn you. Tribes fight over mere scraps of land. My master offers you dominion. Take these vials, and you will crush them. Reclaim your ancestral lands."*

A heavy silence settled over the circle. Tala could feel the weight of her words sinking into the chieftains' minds, sowing seeds of temptation. Yet doubt lingered. Bea'rainti, her voice as calm as it was sharp, broke the silence.

"Hva krever du av oss for denne mørke kraften?" *"What do you demand of us in exchange for this dark power?"*

The woman's smile was thin, devoid of warmth.

"Bare det dere allerede er tilbøyelige til—å ødelegge menneskene. Jeg tilbyr dere seier, en måte å slutte å flykte ved synet av byvaktene." *"Only what you are already inclined to do—lay waste to the humans. I offer you victory, a means to cease fleeing at the sight of the town guards."*

The chieftains bristled at the insinuation of cowardice, muscles taut with restrained fury. Before any could retort, Vark'nal of the Venomfang Tribe stepped forward, eyes narrowed.

"Vi stoler ikke på deg. Mørk magi har alltid en pris. Hvorfor skal vi ta imot gaver fra en ukjent herre?" *"We do not trust you. Dark magic always has a price. Why should we accept gifts from an unknown master?"*

The woman laughed softly, a sound that sent chills down Tala's spine.

"Dere undervurderer hva som står på spill. Fiendene deres styrker seg mens dere nøler. Men hvis dere ikke ønsker makt, så..." *"You underestimate what is at stake. Your enemies grow stronger while you hesitate. But if you do not desire power, then..."*

She began to close the chest, turning as if to leave. Vark'nal growled, his pride wounded.

"Vent! Vi har ikke sagt nei. Jeg tar dem bare." *"Wait! We have not said no. I'll just take them."*

He reached out abruptly, attempting to snatch the vials from the chest. But before he could touch them, vines burst from the ground, twisting around his wrists and ankles, immobilizing him. His eyes widened in shock as he struggled against the bindings.

"Hva slags trolldom er dette?" he roared. *"What kind of sorcery is this?"*

The woman laughed again, the sound echoing eerily through the marsh.

"Du utfordrer meg, og likevel kjenner du ikke mine krefter? Kanskje du trenger en påminnelse om hvem som tilbyr, og hvem som mottar." *"You challenge me, yet you do not know my powers? Perhaps you need a reminder of who offers and who receives."*

Vark'nal strained against the vines, but they only tightened, cutting into his skin. The other chieftains took cautious steps back, their earlier bravado fading.

Gruk'thar's gaze hardened.

"Slipp ham løs. Vi vil høre mer." *"Release him. We will hear more."*

The woman regarded them coolly.

"Valget er enkelt. Ta imot min herres gave og bli uovervinnelige, eller bli værende i gjørmen, glemt og svake." *"The choice is simple. Accept my master's gift and become invincible, or remain in the mire, forgotten and weak."*

She snapped her wrist, and the vines released Vark'nal, retreating back into the earth. He stumbled forward, gasping for air, eyes filled with a mix of fear and rage.

Urshak, the eldest among them, spoke hesitantly.

"Hva vil skje med oss hvis vi nekter?" *"What will happen to us if we refuse?"*

The woman's eyes flickered.

"Da vil tiden vise. Men vit dette: Muligheten kommer ikke igjen." *"Then time will tell. But know this: The opportunity will not come again."*

A heavy silence enveloped the clearing. Tala knew the chieftains stood at a crossroads. The temptation of power was palpable, but so was the fear of the unknown.

Gruk'thar exchanged glances with the others before nodding slowly.

"Vi aksepterer tilbudet. For våre stammers fremtid." *"We accept the offer. For the future of our tribes."*

A murmur of agreement spread among the chieftains. The woman smiled, satisfied.

"Et klokt valg." *"A wise choice."*

As she distributed the vials, Tala felt a sinking feeling in her chest. She had to warn someone—anyone—about what was about to happen. Without a sound, she retreated into the shadows, her thoughts racing with desperate urgency.

As Tala began to withdraw, a new presence emerged from the shadows. She froze as a hulking figure stepped into the flickering light—a Muckspawn unlike any she had seen before. Mutt.

Tala had heard the tales: a legend among the Muckspawn, feared for his might, ostracized for the same reason. Even Gruk'thar narrowed his eyes, growling, "Hva bringer deg hit? Du har ingen plass her med oss høvdinger." *"What brings you here? You hold no place among us chieftains".*

Mutt's grin, sharp and feral, sent a shiver down Tala's spine. "Ingen plass? Du tar feil, Gruk'thar. Jeg har kommet for å ta min rett." *"No place? You are mistaken, Gruk'thar. I've come to claim my right."*

The chieftains exchanged uneasy glances. Vark'nal, never one to retreat, sneered and stepped forward. "Du? Ta lederskap? Du er bare et beist—en tankeløs brute uten stamme." *"You? Claim leadership? You're nothing but a beast—a mindless brute with no tribe to your name."*

Mutt's grin widened, revealing jagged teeth. "Bogsmal! Jeg tar dere alle. En for en eller alle samtidig. Det betyr ingenting for meg." *"Bogsmal! I'll take you all on. One by one or all at once. It matters not to me."*

The challenge hung in the air, thick with the promise of violence. Tala's heart raced, every instinct screaming for her to flee, yet she couldn't look away. The other chieftains stirred, some sneering, others chuckling darkly, each warrior emboldened by the defiant glare in Mutt's eyes. They called to each other, rallying in guttural shouts, emboldened by the scent of blood.

Vark'nal lunged first, his eyes blazing with fury, and Mutt met his assault with terrifying swiftness. As Vark'nal bared his teeth in a snarl, Mutt's hand shot out, gripping his throat and lifting him as though he weighed nothing. Vark'nal's limbs flailed, his claws desperate to find purchase, but Mutt's hold was unrelenting. With a mighty swing, he hurled Vark'nal to the ground, his fists crashing like thunder. The chieftain's skull shattered with a dreadful crack, his body falling limp in a pool of blood as a hush fell over the marsh.

Yet the silence was fleeting. Gruk'thar roared like a storm, his cry a rallying call for the others. He charged forward, his massive frame moving with the ferocity of a beast, claws slashing through the air. The other chieftains cheered, their voices mingling in a frenzied chorus as they banged their weapons against the ground, creating a rhythm to Gruk'thar's assault.

Mutt stepped forward, unfazed, his movements fluid and lethal as he met Gruk'thar with equal might. Their clash reverberated through the marsh, each blow a savage testament to their strength. Fists collided, each strike ringing out like a war drum as the marsh trembled beneath their fury. Mud splattered and clung to their limbs, yet neither relented, their roars filling the air as they wrestled for dominance.

Gruk'thar, though formidable, began to falter. His breath came ragged, his strikes slower. Mutt's wrath, honed by years of exile, had become an unstoppable force. With a final, crushing blow to Gruk'thar's chest, he sent the chieftain sprawling, his form falling motionless to the ground. The marsh fell silent once more, the other chieftains looking on, their faces painted with awe and terror.

One by one, their resolve wavered, and Mutt stood alone amidst the fallen. He looked to each of them, bloodstained and unyielding, daring any to step forward and challenge him. His victory was undeniable, and the chieftains knew then that Mutt's reign would not be easily contested.

As the last echoes of Gruk'thar's fall faded, fear rippled through the remaining chieftains. Moments ago, they had roared with bloodlust; now, they recoiled, their bravado crumbling in the shadow of Mutt's ruthless strength. His sharp eyes flicked from one chieftain to the next, daring any to step forward.

Kar'vash, a wiry figure, glanced nervously toward the edge of the marsh, hoping to slip away. But Mutt saw the fear in his eyes. With brutal speed, he lunged, grabbing Kar'vash by the shoulder and slamming him to the ground in a single, fluid motion—a warning to any who thought of fleeing.

"Feiginger, tror dere kan rømme? Ingen nåde." *"Cowards, think you can run? No mercy."*

Another chieftain, wide-eyed with terror, bolted into the undergrowth. Mutt caught him in seconds, dragging him back through the mud. The chieftain's pleas for mercy were silenced with a single, crushing blow.

The remaining chieftains exchanged glances, their defiance crumbling into reluctant submission. Once-proud stances slumped, each knowing they could not match Mutt's brutal strength. Some knelt, others stood with heads lowered, avoiding his gaze.

Mutt's voice boomed through the marsh.

"Trodde dere var ledere? Se nå. Myrsrotter." *"Thought you were leaders? Look at you now. Bog rats."*

Frak'thor, an elder, lifted his head. His voice shook.

"Vi følger. Du befaler." *"We follow. You command."*

Another chieftain joined, stumbling over his words.

"Mutt... du har vunnet. Vi er dine.""*Mutt... you've won. We are yours."*

A murmur of reluctant loyalty spread among the chieftains, each voice giving in, bending to Mutt's will.

Mutt's slow, dangerous grin spread across his face.

"Dere er mine nå. Kjemp. Drep. Hele myra skal vite." *"You're mine now. Fight. Kill. The whole marsh will know."*

The chieftains muttered their agreement, fear mingling with respect. Under Mutt's reign, the marsh would soon tremble.

Tala's heart pounded as the hooded woman emerged once more, rising from the marsh. Power rippled off her; her cold smile was chilling to the bone.

"Du har bevist deg, gammel venn. Stammene vil følge deg nå, som det er skrevet." *"You have proven yourself, old friend. The tribes will follow you now, as it is destined".*

Mutt turned to face her, his expression enigmatic.

"Hva nå? Hvilken oppgave gir du meg?" *"What now? What task do you give me?"*

Her voice was like silk, smooth and almost tender.

"En gammel kriger av stor legende—en mann med stor styrke. Min herre har stor interesse i ham. Ta ham med til dypet av skogen, uskadd. Hans forfølgere vil komme for ham. Knus dem, bryt deres ånd, men la dem leve." *"There is an ancient warrior of great legend—a man whose prowess is well known. My master has taken a peculiar interest in him. Bring him to the deep woods unharmed. His pursuers will come for him. Cripple them, break their spirits, but leave them breathing."*

Mutt nodded slowly.

"Jeg vil gjøre som du sier. Men merk dette: Jeg leder nå disse stammene, og deres skjebne er min å forme.""*I will do as you command. But mark this: I now lead these tribes, and their fate is mine to shape."*

The woman's smile was unnerving, cold and calculating.

"Selvfølgelig, Mutt. Men vit at din skjebne allerede er flettet sammen med min. Sammen skal vi bringe kongerikene til kne." *"Of course, Mutt. But know that your fate is already entwined with mine. Together, we will bring kingdoms to their knees."*

Her words hung in the air like an ominous prophecy.

Tala lingered in the shadows, watching as the woman disappeared into the mist, leaving Mutt standing tall, the newly crowned overlord of the Muckspawn. The others scattered, their heads bowed in submission. A heavy sense of dread enveloped the marshes like a suffocating fog. Mutt had seized his throne through bloodshed and brute force, but the true ordeal had only just begun. Now he had to keep the tribes in line. He had them under his command, but at what price?

A shiver coursed through her at the thought. The ancient one would fall, and the tribes would rise, but something more sinister gnawed at her spirit—something far more dreadful than mere warfare. The air grew colder, heavier, as if the very marshlands sensed the impending shadow.

She swallowed hard, steeling herself against the oncoming storm. Under Mutt's reign, the Muckspawn would become an unstoppable force. Their savage instincts had always been a menace, but now? Now they had power, a purpose, and a dark force propelling them forward. This could not be allowed. She had to take action, to warn those who could still stand against this scourge.

With one last glance at the grim assembly, Tala melted into the night, her footsteps whispering over twisted roots and through the fog. Her heart pounded, each step taking her farther from immediate danger but closer to the burden she now bore.

The night was far from over. A tempest was brewing, and its weight pressed heavily upon her.

By the time she reached her village, the marshlands had given way to familiar terrain, but she did not slow her pace. Her dad had left earlier that day to meet with old allies and had just returned—a fortunate turn of events.

As she hurried toward the firelit tent where Chief Arak would be, two guards stepped forward, blocking her path.

"Tala!" one of them barked, his face stern. "Hvor har du vært? Faren din vil ta skinnet ditt for dette." *"Where have you been? Your dad will have your hide for this."*

"Jeg må snakke med ham—det er viktig!" Tala shot back, trying to push past them. *"I have to speak to him—it's urgent!"*

They stood firm, towering over her. The other guard's hand reached out, grabbing her arm. "Du venter til møtet er ferdig. Du vet bedre enn å avbryte—" *"You'll wait until the meeting is over. You know better than to interrupt—"*

A flicker of suspicion ignited in Tala's mind. The guards exchanged a quick glance—one that did not go unnoticed. "Hva er det dere skjuler?" she demanded. *"What are you hiding?"*

"Ingenting som angår deg. Gå tilbake til teltet ditt." The guard's grip tightened. *"Nothing that concerns you. Go back to your tent."*

Tala twisted sharply, yanking free of his grasp. "Jeg har ikke tid til dette!" Without another word, she ducked low and slipped between them before they could react, her heart racing as she dashed toward her dad's tent.

"Stopp henne!" one of the guards shouted, and the sound of pursuit followed close behind.

She burst through the entrance to find her dad seated at a table laden with maps and scrolls. Across from him stood Yvonne—the fierce-looking woman with piercing green eyes—and A'nara, a Slivdhe whose ethereal presence was unmistakable. Arak looked up, relief crossing his face upon seeing her.

"Tala! Jeg er glad du er tilbake." *"Tala! I'm glad you're back."*

"Dad!" she gasped, cutting through his words. "Jeg har sett noe farlig—stor fare kommer." *"Dad! I've witnessed something of great peril."*

The guards stormed in behind her, but Arak held up a hand to halt them. His expression shifted from relief to concern. "Forklar deg." *"Explain yourself."*

"Mutt... han har tatt ned høvdingene. Han er konge nå, med en hettekledd kvinne som leder. De planlegger å angripe menneskene og Vek'smed. Alle uten rød ring av torner er mål." *"Mutt... he has taken down the chieftains. He's a king now, with a hooded woman leading. They plan to attack the humans and Vek'smed. Anyone without a red ring of thorns is a target."*

A heavy silence filled the tent. Yvonne and A'nara exchanged grave looks. Arak's eyes narrowed, his hand gripping the edge of the table.

"Er du sikker på dette?" he asked quietly. *"Are you certain of this?"*

She nodded emphatically. "Jeg så det selv. Vi må handle nå!" *"I saw it myself. We must act now!"*

The guards shifted uncomfortably at the entrance. Tala turned to face them. "Dere visste det, gjorde dere ikke? Dere prøvde å stoppe meg fra å advare ham!" *"You knew, didn't you? You tried to stop me from warning him!"*

Chief Arak's gaze hardened. "Er dette sant?" he demanded of the guards. *"Is this true?"*

One of them hesitated before replying, "Vi... vi fikk ordre om å holde informasjonen tilbake inntil videre." *"We... we were ordered to withhold the information for now."*

"Hvem ga dere disse ordre?" Arak's voice was cold. *"Who gave you these orders?"*

Before they could answer, the guards exchanged a quick look and lunged toward Tala, drawing their blades. "Vi kan ikke la henne forstyrre planene!" *"We can't let her disrupt the plans!"*

Yvonne moved with lightning speed, stepping between Tala and the advancing guards. "Ikke på min vakt!" she snarled, unsheathing a slender sword. *"Not on my watch!"*

A'nara raised a delicate hand, her eyes glowing with a soft luminescence. A shimmering barrier of light materialized, halting the guards in their tracks.

"Hva er dette?" one guard shouted, pounding his fist against the barrier. *"What is this?"*

A'nara's voice was calm yet firm. "Jeg foreslår at dere trekker dere tilbake. Dette er deres eneste advarsel." *"I suggest you stand down. This is your only warning."*

The guards hesitated, their faces reflecting both fear and anger.

Chief Arak drew his own weapon, stepping forward. "Forrædere i vår midte. Dette er uakseptabelt." *"Traitors in our midst. This is unacceptable."*

The guards glanced at each other, realizing they were outmatched.

"Dere forstår ikke hva som kommer. Mutt vil lede oss til seier!" one guard spat before retreating. *"You don't understand what's coming. Mutt will lead us to victory!"*

As they fled the tent, the barrier dissolved. A'nara exhaled softly, her glow fading.

Arak turned to Yvonne and A'nara. "Takk, mine venner. Deres hjelp kommer i rette tid." *"Thank you, my friends. Your help is timely."*

Yvonne nodded. "Vi kom så snart du ba oss møte deg. Det ser ut til at situasjonen er enda mer alvorlig." *"We came as soon as you asked us to meet you. It seems the situation is even more serious."*

Arak looked at Tala, his eyes filled with both worry and determination. "Tala, du må gå og advare landsbyene og Vek'smed. Jeg vil samle de allierte jeg kan før jeg drar til Vek'smed." *"Tala, you must go warn the villages and Vek'smed. I will gather what allies I can before heading to Vek'smed."*

He placed a firm yet gentle hand on her shoulder. "Jeg elsker deg, min datter. Nå gå, vær modig." *"I love you, my daughter. Now go, be brave."*

Tala felt a swell of emotion but steeled herself. "Jeg skal ikke svikte deg, dad." *"I won't fail you, Dad."*

Suddenly, shouts echoed from outside. The guards had returned, reinforced by others loyal to Mutt.

"Der er de! Ikke la dem slippe unna!" one shouted. *"There they are! Don't let them escape!"*

Arak glanced at Tala and her companions. "Gå nå! Jeg vil holde dem tilbake." *"Go now! I will hold them off."*

Tala's eyes widened. "Men dad—" *"But Dad—"*

He shook his head firmly. "Ingen diskusjon. Dette er din oppgave. Jeg elsker deg. Nå løp!" *"No discussion. This is your task. I love you. Now run!"*

Yvonne grabbed Tala's arm gently. "Vi må dra." *"We have to go."*

A'nara nodded, her eyes already glowing as she prepared to aid Arak. "Jeg vil styrke hans forsvar." *"I will strengthen his defense."*

Arak smiled gratefully at A'nara. "Takk. Nå gå!" *"Thank you. Now go!"*

As Tala, Yvonne, and A'nara rushed out the back of the tent, they caught a glimpse of Arak standing tall, weapon in hand, facing the approaching adversaries.

The last thing Tala heard was her dad's battle cry as he charged forward to meet the enemy, giving them precious time to escape.

They sprinted into the forest, the sounds of clashing weapons and shouts fading behind them. The night enveloped them, and the trees provided shelter as they moved swiftly through the underbrush.

Tala's heart ached, but she knew her dad was buying them time. With newfound resolve, she pressed on, determined to warn the Vek'smed and fulfill her mission.

Chapter 4: Old Friends And New

Strange dreams haunt me. Visions of a land beyond, both familiar and foreign, whisper of things not yet done, a quiet urging that lingers even as I wake. It is as if the stones themselves remember a story that I am only beginning to understand. Each night, I see fragments—a forest's roots plunging deep into darkened soil, the veins of the earth spreading like hidden rivers, reaching to connect lands and lives far beyond my knowing.

This land, so often taken for granted, is part of something greater than my own dominion or even my ancestors' wildest dreams. My place within it has only begun to take form, a shadow on the edge of an ancient purpose. I see now that power is not always found in the sword or throne but in the roots of things, the blood of the earth itself. Power lies in the silent, unseen forces that shape our world, the ancient promises etched into rock and soil.

I begin to realize that if I am to lead, I must honor what is buried as much as what stands above. Perhaps I am meant to become a steward of something enduring, something elemental. The echoes of this truth are in every tree, every stone—reminders that my role is less a right and more a responsibility.

A'nara tugged her hood lower over her eyes, her steps cautious as they moved through the crowded streets of Grey Leaf village. She had learned long ago that her ears, though not as sharply pointed as others of her kin, could still draw suspicion from unfriendly eyes. The humans of Seragora were wary of outsiders—suspicion ran deeper than just a glance, and A'nara had long since mastered the art of blending in. Even Tala, for all her curious energy, seemed more subdued as they made their way toward the village outskirts, where they would find more safety.

The village felt fuller than usual today. Families and refugees were spilling out of homes and into the streets, huddling close together, their belongings piled high in carts. A'nara saw a few people casting wary glances their way. Tala, walking beside her, was better at hiding her heritage, but the tension in the air made them all stand out.

Yvonne walked a few steps ahead, her green eyes scanning the streets with practiced ease, her movements calm and sure. The human woman moved as if she belonged, but there was a sharpness to her gaze, something A'nara had seen in warriors who had lived through more than their share of battles.

"Hvorfor landsby så full?" "*Why's the village so crowded?*" Tala asked in hushed Muckspawn as they passed a group of villagers. Her Common wasn't strong, and she was always more comfortable in her native tongue with the three of them were alone.

"Flyktninger." *"Refugees"* Yvonne replied without turning. She answered in Muckspawn as well, surprising A'nara at first. It wasn't the language itself, but how easily the human woman slipped into it. "Rykter spre seg om uro i Seragora. Alle dra til feiring." *"Word's spreading about something stirring in Seragora. Everyone's headed to the celebration."*

Tala's brow furrowed, her green skin barely noticeable beneath the shadow of her own cloak. She kicked a stone as they walked, her frustration evident in the small gesture.Trygt?" "I*s it safe?"* she asked.

Yvonne finally glanced back at her, her expression softening a bit. "Tryggere der enn de fleste steder. Men jeg ville ikke stole for mye på folkemengden." *"Safer there than most places. But I wouldn't trust the crowd too much."*

Yvonne looked down at Tala, her voice low. "Du snakke Common? Vi bør bruke det her." *"You speak Common? We should use it here."*

Tala nodded, though hesitant. "Yes… I speak. Not… not well."

A'nara watched Tala's brow furrow as worry washed over her, the tension in her friend's face drawing A'nara's attention like a beacon. She knew that look—the weight of memories replaying behind Tala's eyes, sharp and unforgiving. A'nara could almost feel the echoes of the battle cries and clash of steel through Tala's silence, sensing how each step away from the fight must feel like a betrayal to her.

Tala's fingers clenched the fabric of her cloak nervously, a subtle tremor that did not go unnoticed. A'nara reached out instinctively, her hand brushing Tala's arm in a small gesture of reassurance. "He is a great fighter, Tala. Do not doubt it," A'nara whispered. But even as she spoke, she noted how Tala's eyes darted back over her shoulder, searching for one last glimpse of her dad, the formidable Chief Arak, who had urged them to flee.

When Tala finally spoke, her voice was tight, broken, and laced with her native tongue. "But… mange of them. Too many," she said, her Common stilted and strained under the weight of her worry. "Dad… alone. Alone with fiender "*enemies.*" The raw fear in Tala's voice made A'nara's heart clench.

Yvonne, who had been leading the way, turned at the sound, her sharp eyes softening as they landed on Tala. "Your dad has faced worse and prevailed," Yvonne said, her voice strong and certain, carrying a calm that only years of experience could bring. "Arak does not fall easily, and he would not have sent you if he didn't think he could hold them."

A'nara watched as Tala's lips pressed together, her inner struggle palpable. Her gaze flickered with doubt and dread, the image of Arak standing alone against the Muckspawn undoubtedly haunting her. Yet, Yvonne's words seemed to seep through that heavy fear, sparking the faintest glimmer of hope. Tala took a shaky breath, the motion small but telling, trying to draw strength from their reassurances even as the worry settled stubbornly in her chest.

A'nara kept her hand on Tala's arm a moment longer, silently willing her friend to believe in the strength they all knew Arak possessed. "Vi må gå, Tala," she whispered, her voice steady. *"We must go, Tala."*

Tala nodded slowly, though her eyes still shimmered with concern. "Ja… go. For dad," she murmured, more to herself than anyone else.

As they walked, A'nara shifted uneasily, glancing at the villagers who eyed them with suspicion. Tala recognized a few faces from past visits, but the welcome felt thin and wary. Her broken Common left them vulnerable to doubt, and Yvonne could see Tala's discomfort rising with every wary look.

They reached a quieter stretch of road near the village's edge, where Yvonne gestured them toward the shade of a large tree. Tala leaned against the trunk, her eyes intense as if ready to release a question long held back.

Tala looked up, her words rough with curiosity. "Hvordan kjenne far?" *"How know father?"*

Yvonne gave a soft chuckle. "Din far, Arak… hard å lese," she said, switching to Common. "Strong, fierce—more in him than others see. Not always war, no… not always battle."

Tala leaned in, curiosity brightening her gaze. "You… fight with him?"

Yvonne nodded, her eyes drifting to memories. "Yes, we fight… many times. But there is… one time, I remember best." She glanced at Tala. "Lenge før du ble født, long before you were born. Before… Thorrin War." She paused, a distant look in her eyes. "I barely knew him then, but one night… everything changed."

A'nara shifted, recognizing this story as one she'd heard before. She could see it playing out in Yvonne's green eyes.

Yvonne's voice softened, slipping back to Muckspawn for the harder words. "We were… dypt i skogen (deep in the woods). Arak was hunting something dangerous. En ulv, a wolf, big—huge—terrorizing villages near Vek'smed borders. Bigger than any wolf I seen, silver fur, måneskinnet. (moonlight.) Not just a beast, no… noe mer, nesten unaturlig." *"something more, almost unnatural."*

Tala's eyes widened, her broken Common mixing with her native tongue. "Wolf? Father… never say this. He… aldri fortelle meg." *"never tell me."*

Yvonne chuckled softly. "He wouldn't. Far din holder ting tett, keeps things close. Anything that looks weak—svekkelse," she added, "not good for him. For Arak, asking for help is weakness. But that night… no, we didn't see it that way."

She glanced at A'nara, who nodded, recalling the night.

"We were dypt i skogen *(deep in the forest)* when we found him," Yvonne continued. "A'nara, din bror, og jeg… vi reiste sammen." *"A'nara, your brother, and I… we were traveling together."* "Arak, he was tracking the wolf, but hurt—bleeding, tired. Too proud to ask for help. Struggling."

Tala's face was full of shock, but Yvonne continued, her voice lower, almost pulling them deeper into the memory.

"He didn't want our help. Too proud. But we wouldn't leave him to face it alone. Ulv var klok," she explained, "wolf was clever—almost thinking, like it knew him, led him through trees, wore him down, waiting to strike. When it did, I stepped in."

Yvonne rolled up her sleeve, showing a scar. "This… my reward. Ulv nesten rev armen min," *(wolf almost tore my arm)* "but A'nara's brother drew it off long enough to bandage it."

A'nara smiled faintly, remembering her brother darting through the trees, Yvonne's quick hands binding her arm. She was always quick in a crisis.

"Together, we brought it down," Yvonne said, her voice reverent. "Your father made the killing strike, but… no victory in his eyes. He saw it different. Sa at hjelpe hverandre, gjøre oss sterkere." *(Said helping each other makes us stronger.)* "It showed him… all races could be united."

Yvonne's gaze softened, her voice wistful. "Far din ønsket fred, Tala," *(Your father wanted peace, Tala.)* "Saw big picture. Knew fighting each other only weakened us. So… derfor snakker han ikke om det." *(that's why he doesn't speak of it.)* "In your people's eyes, to show need for others is svekkelse *(weakness)*. But to him… it was strength."

Tala stared in silence. "Why… he no tell me?"

"To protect you," Yvonne answered softly. "Ditt folk ikke verdsetter samarbeid," *"Your people don't value cooperation"* "they value only strength. But your father… he built bridges, long time. That night, just start. He, A'nara, her brother, and I… we brokered peace that united races during Thorrin War."

A new understanding dawned in Tala's eyes.

Yvonne smiled and clapped her shoulder. "He keeps much from you, Tala. Not because he doesn't trust. He… forbereder deg, (prepares you) just as he did then."

After a pause, Yvonne asked, "Didn't you say you had friends in Grey Leaf? We should greet them… warn them."

Tala nodded and approached the group of human children near the well, steps slow. Grey Leaf was human land; here, her true heritage was always hidden. Yet, these children had been different. Curious, but never suspicious. Today, though, something felt different, their chatter quiet, faces more serious.

"Tala!" a girl called, running over, though her voice was muted.

Tala crouched to their level, smiling warmly. "Hello, little ones," she said, the weight of their mission not entirely hidden. "I… I need talk. It viktig." *"Important."*

A'nara watched from a distance, feeling a quiet admiration for Tala. Even in tense moments, Tala made others feel safe. The children clung to her words, trusting her. A'nara could see it in their wide eyes—the way they looked at Tala like one of them, unaware of her differences.

These children didn't mind her covered skin, her accent. They asked no questions. They simply accepted her. Watching them, A'nara wondered how long such innocence would last.

She's good with them, A'nara thought, a faint smile crossing her lips. Better than I could ever be.

Tala knelt closer, her voice soft as she whispered warnings. A'nara saw Tala's care in every gesture, treating them as equals, despite their youth. It was kindness that came naturally, pulling A'nara into memories of her own childhood—one so different from the one these children knew.

The stone halls of her childhood home were cold, with a quiet tension that clung to every shadow and corner. A'nara felt it in her bones as she moved down the corridor, her small footsteps echoing softly off the polished stone floors. The walls were adorned with tapestries depicting battles of old—ancestors wielding swords and shields, their faces stern and unyielding. Flickering torchlight cast dancing shadows, making the embroidered figures seem almost alive. She had long known the weight of her father's disapproval; it followed her through every room, lingered on her every action—a silent judge over her shoulder.

As she approached the grand study, the heavy oak doors loomed before her like a gateway to judgment. She paused, taking a deep breath to steady herself. The scent of aged wood and the faint aroma of burning incense seeped through the cracks.

"A'nara!" Her father's voice cut through the silence, sharp and clear. She flinched, heart pounding. Hastening her steps, she entered the room, eyes lowered in deference as expected. The study was lined with towering bookshelves filled with ancient tomes and scrolls. Her father stood by the fire, his back rigid, hands gripping the stone mantel. The flames cast a harsh light on his chiseled features.

"Sen'tir vor ni'thal?" he said coolly, his tone as sharp as a blade. Late again, A'nara? His gaze bore into her, a mix of disappointment and irritation. "Den'tor hin, mara'thor din, aen'thal var'tor fin vor? Haenar var, haenar din, hin thor'en'tor din." Do you feel it, the shame you bring? This house, this name—they are weight, and you carry them.

A'nara's throat tightened, her palms damp with anxiety. She felt small under his scrutiny, every flaw magnified. Words were futile here; he would not listen.

"Ther'tor hin," he demanded, his voice cold and unyielding. Answer.

She lifted her gaze briefly, meeting his icy stare before lowering her eyes again. *"Velin, Vorin. Mara fin vor ni en mara."* I am sorry, Father. It will not be again. Her voice was barely above a whisper, each word carefully measured.

He turned fully to face her, his expression hard as granite. *"Thor'tir ni fin. Haenar mara hin ni fin'nor."* It must not be. This burden is yours to carry, unbroken. The finality in his tone left no room for further discussion.

Her brother, Aric, who had been standing silently by the door, stepped forward. Tall and composed, he bore the same sharp features as their father but softened by a gentleness in his eyes. His tone was calm, respectful, but steady. *"Vorin, fin mara var vor'en. Mara ienar vor din hin tal, en vor far haenar ni var hin vor."* Father, it was I who am at fault. I asked her for help, and time slipped away as I needed her aid.

Their father's gaze shifted to Aric, his eyes narrowing. *"Fin mara en vor?"* he asked, moving closer, his voice as cold as iron. You as well? *"Hin var din mara haenar, en hin mara var'thal din? Mara var hin en vor haenar?"* You carry this blood yet stumble so easily? Is that blood, then, wasted?

Aric met his gaze evenly, unflinching. He placed a steady hand on A'nara's shoulder, gently shielding her. *"Ni mara'vor,"* he said firmly, his voice calm and unwavering. It will not be. *"Ienar fin vor, en'tal thor."* I will see it done, as is proper.

A tense silence enveloped the room, broken only by the crackling of the fire. Their father's gaze lingered, a storm of unspoken words in his eyes, but he finally turned away with a dismissive wave. *"Vor thor din hin,"* he said, his words low but cutting. Leave me.

They exited swiftly, the heavy doors closing behind them with a thud that echoed down the corridor. The air outside felt lighter, but the weight of their father's disapproval still pressed upon them.

Aric turned to her once they were a safe distance away, offering a faint, reassuring smile that softened his features. The dim light of the corridor cast gentle shadows across his face. *"Velin hin far; thor hin mara'vor. Ni haenar var din hin thor."* Let him be, A'nara; he will rest soon. Do not take his burden as yours.

She nodded, though her heart was heavy. "Thank you, Aric. I don't know what I would do without you."

He squeezed her shoulder gently. *"Hin mara tor'vel var."* You are stronger than you realize. *"Din thor mara var fin thor'tir hin vor."* Do not let his words define you.

She offered a small smile in return. "I will try."

As Aric departed, A'nara wandered through the hallways, her footsteps leading her to the inner courtyard. The garden there was a sanctuary—a place where the rigidity of her family's expectations seemed to soften amid the blooms of wildflowers and the gentle trickle of *fountains.*

She sat on a stone bench beneath a willow tree, its branches swaying softly in the evening breeze. The scent of jasmine filled the air, mingling with the earthy aroma of the soil. Gazing up at the sky, she watched as the first stars began to twinkle against the twilight.

But even here, she couldn't shake her father's words, the weight of his gaze, the feeling that no matter what she did, she would never be enough. A tear slipped down her cheek, and she brushed it away quickly, as if the act of crying was yet another failure.

This was the world she knew—a world where love was earned, approval withheld as if it were a precious stone, one she would never truly hold.

It wasn't until Yvonne came into her life that she realized there could be another way.

She remembered that first day by the river with vivid clarity. The sun hung high in the sky, casting a warm glow over the landscape. The water flowed gently, its surface sparkling like a tapestry of diamonds. A'nara sat on a smooth boulder by the riverbank, her knees drawn to her chest, arms wrapped around them. The soothing sounds of nature did little to ease the turmoil within her.

She was so lost in thought she didn't notice the soft footsteps approaching. It wasn't until a shadow fell across her that she looked up, startled. Standing before her was a girl, perhaps a year or two older, with dark hair cascading over her shoulders and eyes the color of the forest after rain—deep and full of life.

"Velin thir mara," the girl said softly after a moment, her voice gentle yet sure. Silence is yours, along with peace. She tossed a pebble into the water, watching the ripples fan out. "Var fin'tor hin vor mara, aen en'thal hin vor far mara?" Why here, though, and why alone, with none beside you?

A'nara blinked, surprised not only by the girl's sudden appearance but by her use of Slivdhe, her people's language. It was rare for humans to speak it, and even rarer for one so young to do so with such fluency.

She hesitated, unsure of how to respond. "Ni mara tor." I... I did not expect company.

The girl smiled, a warm expression that seemed to chase away the shadows lingering around A'nara's heart. "Ther ni tal vor," she said, settling down beside her at a respectful distance. There are times when words are not needed. She leaned back on her hands, tilting her face toward the sun. "Ni velin Yvonne, aen hin vor mara vel thir." I am Yvonne, if you would have my company. There is quiet enough for two here.

A'nara studied her for a moment. There was an ease about Yvonne, a tranquility that was both intriguing and comforting. "Hin haenar fin mara vel." Your Slivdhe is very good, she ventured.

"Velin mara haenar fin. Ni ienar fin var fin'tor vor fin mar." Thank you. I find languages fascinating. They open doors to new worlds.

"Din folk tor hin var din haenar fin." Not many humans take the time to learn ours, A'nara observed.

"Var din fin'tor mara var tor." Perhaps they should, Yvonne mused. *"Var fin en fin'thal vor hin'thal."* There is much to be gained from understanding one another.

They fell into a comfortable silence, the sounds of the river and the rustling leaves filling the space between them. For the first time in a long while, A'nara felt a sense of peace.

From that day forward, Yvonne became her only true friend. They met by the river often, sharing stories and dreams. Yvonne would teach her songs from distant lands, and in return, A'nara shared tales of her ancestors, the legends that were woven into the very fabric of her people's identity.

One afternoon, as they waded in the shallows of the river, Yvonne turned to her with a mischievous grin. *"Tor'vel hin ni?"* Do you trust me?

A'nara laughed softly. *"Fin ni tor?"* Should I?

Yvonne extended her hand. *"Vor mara ni. Ni velin thor fin vor tor."* Come with me. There's something I want to show you.

Curiosity piqued, A'nara took her hand. They made their way through the forest, the canopy above filtering sunlight into a mosaic of light and shadow. The scent of pine and damp earth enveloped them.

After a while, they reached a clearing bathed in golden light. Wildflowers swayed gently in the breeze, and at the center stood an ancient oak tree, its branches stretching wide like welcoming arms.

Yvonne led her to the base of the tree, where a small hollow held a collection of trinkets—stones, feathers, a delicate necklace of woven grass. *"Velin mara fin var talor,"* she said softly. This is my secret place. *"Far din fin mara fin'thal, ni tor vor."* When the world feels heavy, I come here.

"It's beautiful," A'nara whispered, touched that Yvonne would share such a personal sanctuary with her.

Yvonne sat down, patting the spot beside her. *"Ther'tor hin, A'nara, var fin hin mara vel en fin vor?"* Tell me, A'nara, what do you wish for most?

A'nara settled beside her, considering the question. *"Fin'thal, ni velin. Var thor ni fin vor en'tir."* Freedom, I suppose. To choose my own path.

Yvonne nodded thoughtfully. *"Ni thor hin var din."* I understand that.

"What about you?" A'nara asked.

Yvonne gazed up at the sky, her expression contemplative. *"Ther'thal. Var ni, var hin ni mara."* Peace. For myself, for those I care about.

A'nara looked at her friend, noticing a hint of sadness behind her eyes. *"Hin thor fin var hin'thal fin var thor."* You speak as if you've known great turmoil.

Yvonne offered a small smile. *"Hin mara haenar fin vor ni tor."* We all have our burdens.

A'nara wanted to ask more but sensed it was not the time. Instead, she reached out and squeezed Yvonne's hand gently. *"Velin mara tor'vel fin mara fin var talor vor ni."* Thank you for sharing this place with me.

"Velin mara hin mara var tor," Yvonne replied. Thank you for being here.

As their friendship deepened, A'nara couldn't help but wonder more about Yvonne's past. One evening, as the sun dipped below the horizon, painting the sky in hues of orange and pink, she finally found the courage to ask.

They sat on the riverbank, the cool water lapping at their feet. *"Yvonne,"* A'nara began softly, *"mara ni tor hin var fin'tor var en hin haenar fin var thor?"* May I ask you something personal?

Yvonne glanced at her, a knowing look in her eyes. *"Hin velin tor haenar ni fin mara vel."* You wish to know how I speak your language so well.

A'nara nodded. *"Velin. Fin mara, en hin haenar fin vel tor var ni velin din fin'tor."* Yes. It's rare, and you speak it as if you were born to it.

Yvonne sighed gently, her gaze turning to the flowing water. *"Ni ienar fin var hin tor. Var haenar fin var'tor."* I learned because I had to. Circumstances required it.

"Var haenar fin?" Circumstances?

She hesitated before continuing. *"Ni'folk var fin en'thal, en fin din haenar vor fin'tor—velin fin, velin din. Mara ni velin, fin'thal fin'tor. Ni tor... var'ienar din hin haenar fin folk."* My village was on the borderlands, a place where our people and yours often met—sometimes peacefully, sometimes not. When I was young, conflict arose. I was... taken in by a family of your people.

"Var'ienar?" A'nara repeated, sensing there was more to the story. Taken in?

Yvonne nodded. *"Hin velin mara, ienar fin vor hin thor, hin haenar fin. Mara ni velin mara var fin en fin'tor, fin'thal var hin din."* They were kind, taught me their ways, your language. But I was always between worlds, belonging fully to neither.

A'nara felt a pang of empathy. *"Fin mara tor'thal var haenar."* That must have been difficult.

"It was," Yvonne admitted. *"Mara fin var ienar fin vor fin'thal var en fin'thal var tor en'thal."* But it also opened my eyes to the possibilities beyond divisions.

A'nara reached out, placing a hand on Yvonne's arm. *"Ni mara vel tor vor hin tor fin'tor var haenar."* I'm glad our paths crossed.

"As am I," Yvonne replied, her smile returning.

One evening, Yvonne's eyes sparked with mischief. The moon was full, casting silvery beams through the trees. "Vor mara hin tal'ri. Ni'tor vor val'thal en talir." Come. We step into shadows tonight. I wish to show you something.

Intrigued, A'nara agreed. They slipped past the estate's guards, moving silently through the woods like shadows themselves. The forest was alive with nocturnal sounds—the hoot of an owl, the rustle of leaves, the distant call of night creatures.

They arrived at a secluded glade bathed in moonlight. There, lying beneath the stars, was a great wolf with silver fur that shimmered ethereally. It was injured, a deep gash marring its side.

"Vor fin'tor ni?" A'nara asked softly, watching as Yvonne approached the beast with cautious steps. What are you doing?

"Ienar hin ther." I give help. *Yvonne knelt beside the wolf, her movements slow and non-threatening. "Mara'vor fin var'thor, A'nara. Hin en, fin ther."* Not all is battle, A'nara. Sometimes... we heal.

A'nara watched in awe as Yvonne whispered soothing words in Slivdhe, her hands hovering over the wound. The wolf's eyes followed her, wary but not hostile.

"Hin mara tor'vel?" A'nara whispered. You're not afraid?

"Fear clouds judgment," Yvonne replied softly. *"Compassion bridges gaps."*

A'nara felt compelled to assist. She gathered herbs from nearby, ones she recognized for their healing properties, and brought them to Yvonne.

"Velin mara," Yvonne said, accepting them gratefully. Thank you. *Together, they cleaned and dressed the wound, their hands moving in unison.*

As they worked, A'nara couldn't help but marvel at Yvonne's ease with the language, her knowledge of healing. "Mara vor'thor fin?" she asked quietly. How do you speak this way?

Yvonne paused, a shadow crossing her face. She looked at A'nara, her eyes reflecting the moonlight. "Vel hin mara var'thor far en'tir. Thor var en hin vor." Once, many spoke, and I listened. My own voice, it was not needed.

Understanding dawned in A'nara's eyes. "Hin ienar var fin'tor, var fin'thal." You learned by listening, observing.

Yvonne nodded. "Words hold power, but so does silence."

The wolf began to relax, its breathing steadier. A'nara gently stroked its fur, feeling a connection to this wild creature.

"Ienar hin'tal, val fin val'thor," Yvonne said, her voice barely above a whisper. To heal another, to know strength in stillness. She glanced at A'nara. *"Far din, folk din... var fin en fin'thal."* Your father, your people... they believe strength is in battle. She looked deep into A'nara's eyes. *"Mara'vor fin var, A'nara. Ther fin en hin talor, hin en'thor."* But true strength, A'nara, is here. In hands that heal... in care that asks nothing.

A'nara felt tears prick at the corners of her eyes. *"Ni velin tor var."* I think I understand now.

Yvonne smiled gently. *"Ni velin ienar hin velin."* I knew you would.

As dawn approached, the wolf rose, giving them a final, appreciative look before disappearing into the forest.

From that night on, A'nara felt a shift within herself. The world seemed different, full of possibilities she hadn't considered before. She began spending time in the infirmary, learning from the healers, absorbing all she could.

One day, as she tended to a wounded soldier, her father entered unexpectedly. He stopped short upon seeing her, his expression a mixture of surprise and displeasure.

"A'nara, vor fin mara fin thor?" he demanded. A'nara, what is the meaning of this?

She stood, meeting his gaze with newfound confidence. *"Ni ienar hin ther fin var haenar fin velin tor vor."* I am helping to heal those who have fought for us.

"Hin fin var en fin'thal, thor'en vor tor, velin haenar." Your place is in the training yards, preparing to lead, he retorted sharply.

"Vorin," she said evenly, *"fin mara var fin'thal tor. Ni velin fin vor en'tir hin vor."* Father, there are many ways to serve. I believe my path lies here.

His eyes flashed with anger. *"Hin mara tor fin, fin haenar din tor."* You defy tradition, our ways.

"Ni thor fin var ienar fin," she replied calmly. I seek to expand them. *"Var fin fin vor ther'en ther fin haenar var fin."* To bring honor through healing as well as strength.

He stared at her, a muscle ticking in his jaw. *"Hin mara tor'vel."* You are naive.

"Perhaps," she conceded. *"Mara ni fin mara var hin fin'tor fin velin."* But I must follow what I believe is right.

He turned abruptly, leaving without another word. A'nara released a breath she hadn't realized she'd been holding.

That evening, she met Yvonne by the river. The setting sun bathed the world in hues of gold and crimson.

"He did not approve," A'nara said, recounting the encounter.

Yvonne listened attentively. "Change is often met with resistance."

"I worry I have disappointed him beyond repair."

"Sometimes, we must choose our own path, even if others do not understand," Yvonne said gently. "Hin mara tor'vel, A'nara." You are brave, A'nara.

She sighed. "I don't feel brave."

"Courage isn't the absence of fear, but the willingness to act despite it."

A'nara smiled softly. "Hin mara vel tor var fin'tor." You always know what to say.

Yvonne chuckled lightly. "Not always, but I speak from the heart."

They sat in companionable silence, the sounds of the evening enveloping them.

"Will you tell me more about your past?" A'nara asked tentatively.

Yvonne nodded slowly. "I think it's time."

She spoke of her childhood—of being caught between two worlds, of loss and resilience. How she had learned to navigate life through observation and quiet strength.

A'nara listened, her heart aching for her friend. "Hin mara haenar fin var tor'thal." You have endured so much.

"And yet, here we are," Yvonne said with a soft smile. "Finding our way together."

"Ni mara vel tor'vel hin," A'nara said sincerely. I'm grateful for you.

"As am I," Yvonne replied.

In the months that followed, A'nara continued her healing studies, earning respect among the healers and those she cared for. Word of her skills spread, and even her father began to hear of the positive impact she was making.

One day, he approached her in the garden. "A'nara," he began, his tone less severe than usual.

She looked up from the herbs she was tending. "Yes, Father?"

"Ni haenar fin mara... var'ienar fin tor ni vor," he said, almost grudgingly. I have heard... commendations of your work.

She stood, wiping her hands on her apron. "Ni velin mara var fin en'tir." I am glad to be of service.

He regarded her thoughtfully. "Var fin mara fin vor fin'thal hin var hin'tor." Perhaps there is merit in your pursuits.

She sensed a softening in his demeanor. "Ni velin fin var haenar fin vor fin'thal var en fin'tor var hin vor." I believe we can honor our traditions while embracing new paths.

He nodded slowly. "Time will tell."

It wasn't a declaration of approval, but it was a start.

After a few more words with the children, Tala rejoined A'nara and Yvonne, the weight of their journey hanging over them as they prepared to leave the village behind. As they walked, Tala noticed Jeff, a simple man with a quirky sense of humor, crouched over a patch of herbs.

"Hi, Jeff! How young ones?" Tala called, waving.

He looked up, a playful grin spreading across his face. "Oh, they're great! But keep them away from my herbs—they think pulling weeds is some kind of game!"

Tala chuckled, "I keep them away. You good, Jeff."

With a last smile, she turned back to her companions, the brief exchange adding a moment of lightness to the tension that pressed upon her.

Yvonne dusted off her hands, catching A'nara's eye as she noticed faint streaks of red paint on Yvonne's fingers. Following her gaze, A'nara spotted small thorn-like symbols marked in red on several carts near the well.

Tala's brow furrowed as her eyes followed A'nara's. "You make thorn marks?"

Yvonne nodded, her expression purposeful. "Red thorns. It's an old way to keep trouble at bay —especially Mutt and his warriors. They know this symbol; it's a warning."

A'nara raised an eyebrow, understanding dawning. "So that's why we paused by the carts earlier."

Yvonne offered a small smile. "Yes. I've been marking spots around the village as we moved through. These people don't need to be caught up in this, and if Mutt's scouts see these thorns, they might think twice about causing trouble."

Tala glanced back at the marked carts, a mix of relief and surprise crossing her face. "You did not say."

Yvonne pulled her cloak close, giving a subtle nod. "No need. Just a precaution. Now let's go— we've got a long way to Seragora."

With that, they turned their backs to Grey Leaf, leaving the village protected by Yvonne's quiet vigilance as they pressed forward toward Seragora.

Chapter 5: Errands

763, 11th Day Of The Fourth Moon

"Today, I faced a warrior unlike any other—a woman, fierce and unyielding, her eyes sharp as her blade. We clashed in a fury, but there was something in her stance, in the way she fought. When the moment came to finish it, I hesitated. I let her go, her silhouette vanishing into the trees like a phantom. Father would call it weakness, but I cannot deny the respect she commanded. Perhaps it was foolish, but the honor she bore deserved that courtesy."

✳✳✳

The Kingdom of Palrazara had stood resilient through ages of strife and triumph, with its history etched into the very stones of King Tor'valis's imposing fortress. Nestled within the jagged expanse of the Western Bear Mountains, Palrazara wasn't just a realm; it was a symbol of unyielding strength and unity, forged in the crucible of war and tempered by the hard-fought serenity that followed. Fifteen years had passed since the cataclysmic Thorrin War, a conflict that nearly tore the kingdom asunder. This brutal struggle sprang from bitter enmity with the neighboring kingdom of Bazel, a former ally turned implacable foe. The origins of the feud had faded into the mists of legend—ancient disputes over territories, trade routes, and forgotten prophecies—but the wounds it inflicted remained raw for those who survived it.

Young Prince Tor'valis had led Palrazara's forces against overwhelming odds, his resolve galvanizing his people in their direst hour. The kingdom's elite warriors, known as the Valiant Few, had played a crucial role in changing the war's bleak course. These champions, each a master of their craft, had risen to the status of legends, their names honored and revered throughout the realm.

The peace that ensued was fragile, bought with the blood of innumerable lives and sealed with a treaty viewed with suspicion on both sides. Bazel, stinging from the sting of defeat, had withdrawn within its borders, nursing its grudges and simmering with resentment. The tenuous armistice had held for fifteen years, yet the people of Palrazara knew it could snap with the slightest provocation.

Now, as the kingdom approached the 200th anniversary of its founding, preparations for grand festivities were in full swing. The highlight of the celebration was the market bazaar, a grand assembly attracting merchants from the farthest corners of the world. For weeks, villagers had toiled to transform Seragora, the town nestled beneath the castle's shadow, into a vibrant hub. Banners bearing the royal crest fluttered in the crisp autumn breeze, and the air was filled with the enticing aroma of fresh-baked bread and spiced meat.

Seragora buzzed with anticipation. Traders from distant lands arrived with caravans laden with exotic goods—silks from the East, spices from the South, and rare gems from the North. The market was a place where fortunes were made and lost, and alliances were forged in the flicker of candlelit negotiations. Yet, beneath the vibrant veneer, a simmering tension festered.

In a gesture of goodwill, King Tor'valis had extended an invitation to Bazel, prompting mixed reactions. Some viewed it as an act of magnanimity, a chance to finally bury old grievances and forge a new path. Others saw it as a perilous risk, fearing that Bazel's presence might rekindle ancient hostilities. The nobles whispered in clandestine corners, their expressions grave with worry. The Valiant Few, now the king's trusted advisors, remained on high alert, ever watchful for any sign of treachery.

The memories of the Thorrin War lingered over the kingdom. The Muckspawn raids, once a terrifying reality, were now a distant memory, but the scars of war were not so easily forgotten. The kingdom's soldiers, though fewer in number, were seasoned veterans, their presence a constant reminder of peace's costly price. The castle's turrets were manned by archers with sharp eyes, ready to defend the realm from any threat.

In the days leading up to the bazaar, Seragora sparkled with unprecedented cleanliness. Villagers scrubbed the streets and adorned their homes with garlands of autumn leaves. The clang of swords and the swish of arrows filled the air as the younger generation honed their skills, eager to prove themselves in the upcoming tournament—a tradition honoring the kingdom's martial past.

Yet, even as the kingdom prepared for celebration, an undercurrent of unease persisted. The invitation to Bazel was a double-edged sword. Would they come bearing gifts, as a gesture of reconciliation, or concealed daggers, ready to strike when Palrazara's guard was down?

As the sun rose on the day of the bazaar, its golden light kissed the rugged walls of King Tor'valis's castle, casting long shadows over the lively town below. The people of Palrazara were determined to celebrate, to embrace the peace they had fought so arduously to achieve. But they did so with their eyes open, ever wary of the dark clouds still looming on the horizon.

Amidst Seragora's grand preparations, the kingdom's heart pulsed within the bustling marketplace. Merchants and artisans, each a master of their craft, worked tirelessly to ready their stalls for the bazaar. The market square, normally a quiet space where villagers exchanged goods, had transformed into a vibrant tapestry of colors and sounds.

The air was thick with the scent of spices and roasting meats. Cooks set up makeshift kitchens, with enormous pots of stew bubbling over crackling fires, and skewers of seasoned meat sizzling on open flames. Merchants, many who had traveled for weeks to reach Seragora, shouted to one another in a medley of languages, their voices rising above the clamor. Traders from the East draped their stalls in rich silks and embroidered fabrics that shimmered like water; jewelers from the South displayed glittering gems of every hue; and apothecaries from the North crowded their tables with jars of rare herbs and mysterious elixirs.

Marella's stall brimmed with color and sweetness. Golden-brown pastries, their flaky layers shimmering with sugar, sat in perfect rows. She moved with swift precision, her fingers gliding over each delicate creation as she adjusted them on the display. A warm smile curled her lips as she greeted a familiar face, her focus never wavering as her hands shaped a final pastry.

The crowd around her swelled, the scent of buttery crust and rich custard drawing more eager customers with each passing minute. A woman leaned in, whispered something that made Marella laugh, the sound light and inviting, much like the treats she offered.

Across the square, the hammer rang out in steady rhythm. Darius's hand gripped the iron tongs, lifting a glowing piece of metal from the forge, the heat radiating in waves around him. His arm moved with practiced power, each strike deliberate and unyielding, shaping the blade beneath his hammer. Sweat trickled down his brow, his weathered face impassive as sparks flew. His eyes, though fixed on the glowing metal, flickered now and then toward the passing crowds, catching bits of conversation about distant battles or unrest in Bazel. Without a word, he nodded at a villager holding a worn sword, gesturing toward his workbench. The clang of metal never stopped, but there was something sharp in his gaze—always listening, always watching.

But it was not just the merchants who were busy; the townsfolk, too, were preparing for the grand tournament to be held in the castle's courtyard. The tournament, a tradition as old as the kingdom itself, offered knights and commoners a chance to prove their combat prowess. For many, it was the highlight of the festivities, a spectacle drawing crowds from all corners of Palrazara and beyond.

In the clearing just beyond the market, swords clashed, the sharp ring of metal slicing through the humid air. Young men and women moved in a fluid rhythm, their blades flashing under the harsh sun as they sparred, sweat glistening on their brows. Sir Cedric paced among them, his weathered hand resting on the hilt of his own sword, eyes narrowing as he watched their every move. A silver streak cut through his grizzled hair, catching the light, but it was his voice that truly commanded attention.

"Aelric!" Cedric barked, his tone cutting through the practice like a sword through armor. "Your guard, boy! Are you asking for a blade in your ribs?"

Aelric, wide-eyed and panting, fumbled to adjust his stance, his knuckles whitening around the hilt of his sword. His opponent lunged again, and he barely deflected the blow, his left side still exposed. Cedric's frown deepened as he stepped closer, shaking his head. The young man stumbled back, cheeks flushed with both exertion and embarrassment, but his determination was clear in the way he gritted his teeth and tightened his grip.

Nearby, the soft *twang* of bowstrings followed by the *thud* of arrows striking targets marked the archery practice. Two sisters, their brows furrowed in concentration, pulled back their bows with perfect synchronicity. The arrows flew, straight and true, embedding themselves in the center of their targets. Their focus never wavered, hands steady as they reached for another arrow, the sound of combat fading to the rhythm of their aim and release.

On the sidelines, Leon stood with eyes wide, his wooden sword clutched in small hands. His black hair gleamed in the sunlight as he mimicked the older boys, swinging his toy weapon with fervor, dreaming of the day he'd take their place. His father's gift never left his side, and each swing carried with it the weight of his aspirations, though his blows met nothing but air.

Not far from the training ground, the rhythmic pounding of hooves thundered as knights practiced their charges. Horses snorted, their breath rising in clouds as they pawed at the dirt, eager for another run. The jousting arena gleamed, banners of the kingdom's colors fluttering in the wind. Lances lowered, knights aimed at the rotating quintain, a wooden target designed to test both strength and precision.

"Steady, Cormac!" Sir Cedric's voice rang out again, sharp but not unkind. "It's not about brute force, but control. Hit the shield, maintain your balance."

Cormac, a knight's son, clenched his jaw as he spurred his horse forward, lance leveled. This time, the weapon struck true, the quintain spinning as the force of the impact nearly unseated him. He clung to the reins, heart pounding, as he looked toward Cedric. The old knight gave a single nod—small, but filled with approval—and Cormac sat taller in his saddle, knowing that single gesture was worth more than all the applause in the world.

All around the kingdom, anticipation grew. The tournament was more than a display of skill—it was an affirmation of Palrazara's strength, unity, and commitment to the hard-fought peace. Beneath the excitement, there lingered a sense of unease, a collective breath held as they watched to see if fragile peace with Bazel would endure.

As the day of the bazaar dawned, Seragora came alive with sounds of preparation. Merchants finalized displays, blacksmiths polished wares, and knights readied for battle. Through it all, the eyes of Palrazara remained sharp, ever vigilant for signs that the past might yet return to haunt them.

Amidst the lively commotion, Razma balanced on the edge of a hay bale, his sea-blue eyes tracing the outlines of Seragora. His gaze wandered over the bustling market and finally settled on the knights practicing in the distance. Each clang of their swords struck a chord in him, echoing the dreams he held so close but always just out of reach. The wind tousled his brown hair as he sighed, shoulders slumping under the weight of his unspoken ambition.

"I just want to prove myself out there, make something of myself," Razma muttered, more to the wind than anyone else.

From behind, the sound of footsteps signaled his father's arrival. Belazar strolled into the stable, his long black hair swaying in time with his easy, teasing gait. His lips curled into a grin, belly bouncing slightly as he gave a playful nudge to a bale of hay, causing the horses to stir. "Maybe some noble girl will ask for your hand in marriage at this tournament," he joked, though his eyes, hidden beneath the humor, carried a history of harder truths.

Razma chuckled, a soft sound edged with impatience, and hopped down to soothe Cleo, his white mare. Her muzzle pressed into his palm, warm and familiar, grounding him in the present. "Easy, Cleo," he murmured, fingers stroking her soft mane.

The playful light left his eyes as his frustration resurfaced. "It's not funny, Dad. The tournament… it could be my chance to prove myself, to make real friends." His voice cracked, the weight of the words heavy with unfulfilled longing.

Belazar paused, the teasing smile slipping just for a moment. His fingers absently traced the scar beside his left eye, the mark of a past Razma had never fully known. The scar caught the light, glinting like a memory that couldn't quite be forgotten. His face softened, concern deepening the lines of his brow. "We don't have much, Razma," he said, his voice a mix of love and hard-learned wisdom. "There's strength in not fighting every battle. Do you really want to raise a sword that badly?" The question lingered, carrying the weight of something deeper, something Razma could only half understand.

Razma met his father's gaze, torn between youthful defiance and a growing understanding. A light laugh escaped him, more genuine this time. "When you put it that way... maybe not."

Belazar smiled, but there was sadness in it, a recognition of his son's need to find his own way. He pulled out a small pouch and handed it over. "Take Cleo and get some supplies. There's a bit extra for you."

Razma nodded, fitting the leather saddle onto Cleo with careful hands, the weight of his father's words hanging in the air like a soft echo. He ran his fingers through her mane, the shimmering silver moon pattern on her coat catching the sunlight. Cleo nickered softly, a comforting sound as Razma mounted her, eyes glancing back at his father one last time before setting off, the unspoken desires of both father and son carried with the wind.

The streets of Seragora bustled under the high noon sun, the cobblestones glowing golden, capturing both the warmth of the day and the vibrant energy of the marketplace. Razma tied his horse, Cleo, to a post near the edge of the square, pausing as the hum of the crowd washed over him. The mingling scents of spices, roasted meats, and freshly baked bread combined with the earthy aroma of produce stacked in colorful heaps, creating a tapestry of familiar comforts. Voices rose in a lively chorus—merchants haggling, villagers exchanging the latest news, and the laughter of children darting between stalls.

He moved through the crowd with ease, weaving through the masses with practiced familiarity. "Good morning, Marella!" he called to the baker, who stood behind a stall piled high with pastries. The heat from her oven lingered in the air around her, cinnamon and sugar swirling in the breeze.

Marella, a stout woman dusted in flour, grinned at him. "Morning, Razma! Sweetroll for the road?" She held out a warm pastry, and Razma's eyes lit up as he took it, savoring the sugary flakes that melted on his tongue. "Perfect as always, Marella. Thanks!" He waved, tucking the rest of the roll into his pouch as he continued through the bustling rows.

Everywhere he looked, familiar faces greeted him with warm smiles and friendly banter. Old Man Tavin, the spice merchant, called him over with a wave, proudly showing off a new blend from the South. Razma inhaled the rich, earthy scent, his mouth watering. "That's incredible, Tavin. I'll tell my father to stock up for winter stews."

The older man chuckled, patting Razma on the shoulder. "That's why you're my favorite, lad—always thinking ahead." Razma grinned, the spice's warmth lingering in his senses as he moved further into the market.

He spotted Ilona, the florist's daughter, arranging vibrant bouquets. "Morning, Ilona!" he called, admiring the bursts of color that brightened even the sun-drenched square. She blushed, her fingers fumbling with the flowers. "You should bring some home for your father. Brighten up that dusty old place."

Razma laughed, feeling a warmth spread in his chest. "I just might." But his gaze moved on, drawn to the clatter of wooden swords behind Garen's butcher stall. A group of teenagers sparred with wooden blades, laughter and shouts filling the air. Razma's fingers twitched, his imagination igniting as he pictured himself among them.

"Razma!" Garen's booming voice broke his thoughts. "Care to join? Show these lads how a real fight's done?"

"Not today, Garen. Errands call," he replied, though a hint of longing lingered in his smile. Garen chuckled knowingly, sending him on his way with a wink.

Razma returned to Cleo, patting her neck as he prepared to head toward his next stop. But as he untied the reins, a strange feeling tugged at him, a sense of something out of place. He glanced back at the crowded marketplace, and that's when he noticed them—the refugees.

They moved through the crowd slowly, in groups and alone, their faces drawn and weary, carrying bundles and leading small children by the hand. Razma's heart tightened, the excitement of the market fading as he took in the somber sight. These people had fled from somewhere, that much was clear, and each face held a story he could only begin to guess at. Some looked lost, others clung to one another, and a few appeared almost dazed, their eyes scanning Seragora as if they'd woken in another world.

Razma's gaze fell on a young boy about his age, clutching a torn bundle to his chest, his eyes wide with fear. Razma reached into his pouch, pulling out the sweetroll he'd saved from Marella. He stepped forward, offering it to the boy with a gentle smile. The boy's eyes lit up with a hesitant gratitude as he took it, nodding silently before disappearing into the throng of refugees.

As he turned to leave, Razma caught a glimpse of a small, cloaked figure lingering at the edge of the crowd. Beneath the shadow of the hood, he thought he caught a flash of green skin. He blinked, half-wondering if his mind had played a trick on him, but the figure remained, moving with purposeful slowness, slipping between the refugees as if hoping to remain unseen.

A chill ran through him. Could it have been…? No, he pushed the thought aside. His mind must have been playing tricks. With a last look at the marketplace filled with both familiar faces and the haunted, uncertain expressions of the refugees, he led Cleo away, threading back through the city streets.

The image of the green-skinned child, mixed with the weary faces of the refugees, lingered in his mind, and the market's warmth faded. The city seemed heavier, cloaked in the whispers of unknown threats, and Razma couldn't shake the feeling that something was coming— something that would reach him, and all of Seragora, soon.

The guard caught Razma's lingering gaze on the refugees and offered a half-smile, meant to reassure but tinged with weariness. "Don't worry about it, kid," he said, resting a hand on Razma's shoulder. "Go on with your day. City Watch will handle it."

Razma hesitated, casting a final glance at the huddled families, their faces drawn and weary, shadows in the corners of Seragora. He knew the guard meant well, but the weight of the refugees' plight pressed against him, impossible to ignore. With a reluctant nod, he forced himself to turn away, willing his feet to carry him back down the cobbled streets as if all was as it should be.

Yet, even as he walked, the once-bustling the marketplace seemed oddly subdued. The familiar warmth of Seragora now distant and somehow dimmed. Each step took him farther from the haunting faces he'd left behind, but he couldn't shake the feeling that something darker lay beneath the surface of it all. He drifted further along the narrow streets, the lively sounds fading behind him, replaced by the softer, muted murmurs of refugees settling into alleys and abandoned courtyards. Everywhere he turned, he could see the weary faces, the frayed edges of lives uprooted, and It felt as though shadows wove through the very stones of Seragora.

The city had always seemed unshakable to Razma—steadfast, a fortress where neither danger nor misfortune could reach him or those he cherished. But now, seeing these strangers—so much like him, yet so adrift—left him with a creeping sense of fragility. As he wove through the crowd, his eyes searched the sea of refugees for the green-skinned figure, but it was as if they had disappeared into thin air. With each step, he felt an odd pull, an invisible force drawing him toward the edges of his certainty, whispering that he was part of something far greater, something he couldn't yet comprehend.

Finally, he approached the east wall, where the guards had gathered in greater numbers, their faces marked by the same tension stirring within him. Some of them nodded in greeting, familiar with Razma and his father's position, though today their nods seemed strained and preoccupied.

One guard, a seasoned man with deep lines etched into his face, stepped forward and lowered his voice. "These refugees," he muttered, casting a wary glance to ensure no one was listening. "They're from the outlying villages. They say something's been driving them out, creeping closer by the day."

Razma swallowed, listening closely. "Do they know what it is?" he asked, though he wasn't sure he wanted the answer.

The guard shook his head slowly. "Rumors, mostly. Some talk of raiders, others… strange creatures, shadows that move on their own. Whatever it is, it's enough to send them running here."

Razma sensed the weight of those words settle in his chest. He'd heard tales of dark creatures lurking in the wild, beings that slipped through the night, but they had always been stories. Yet now, seeing the hollow eyes of the refugees and hearing the guard's grim tone, it seemed real— too real.

As he turned to leave, a flicker of movement caught his eye. There, at the far edge of the crowd, he spotted the green-skinned child again, their cloaked figure blending with the shadows as they slipped between two buildings. Razma froze, watching them until they disappeared, swallowed by the narrow alleyways. Part of him wanted to follow, but the guard's voice brought him back to the present.

Razma wandered through the winding streets, his mind only half-focused on the errands his father had tasked him with. As he neared the bustling square, the familiar clamor of clashing staves and spirited cheers caught his attention, and he slowed his pace. Just ahead, a group of boys, some older and some his age, were sparring in a sunlit clearing. Wooden staves cracked and clattered against each other in a rhythmic dance, each strike and parry like a conversation, bold and unrestrained. His gaze locked on Ky'len, the son of a minor lord, moving with the kind of ease and fluidity Razma only dreamed of achieving. Ky'len's strikes were swift, his parries precise, his face wearing the confident smirk of someone well aware he was admired.

Razma lingered at the edge of the square, his fingers twitching, aching to grip a staff and feel the weight of a challenge. He could almost picture himself stepping forward, the crowd parting just enough to let him join in. But the thought faded as he heard the whispers around him, voices weaving through the crowd with the unease that had settled over Seragora like a low-hanging cloud. Townsfolk cast wary glances between the refugees gathered near the square's edges and the Seragoran guards stationed nearby, their expressions a mixture of pity and suspicion.

"I heard it was Bazel's doing, sent these poor souls running," a woman nearby muttered to her companion, her voice laced with distrust.

The man beside her scoffed, shaking his head. "Bazel? That'd be too clean for this lot. It's the muckspawn, mark my words. Filthy creatures, always stirring up trouble. It's a wonder they're even allowed this close to the city."

As the older man spoke, he stumbled slightly as a child darted past, weaving through the crowd with practiced agility. Razma caught a fleeting glimpse—a flash of green beneath the child's hood, wide eyes filled with something he couldn't quite place, somewhere between fear and defiance. The boy's cloak billowed behind him, but before Razma could get a closer look, the child disappeared into the huddled masses of refugees, swallowed up by the crowd.

Razma's stomach twisted, the unease of the townsfolk seeping into him as he took in the scene around him. Families clustered together along the edges of the square, their belongings bundled close, guarded fiercely despite their worn, defeated looks. Children clung to their mothers' skirts, their faces weary but wide-eyed as they scanned their new surroundings. Seragoran guards, usually relaxed, stood stiff and vigilant, their eyes darting between the huddled refugees and the townsfolk casting wary, mistrustful glances.

A guard near him caught Razma's gaze, his face softening slightly as he placed a reassuring hand on the boy's shoulder. "Don't worry about it, lad," he said, his voice gruff yet kind. "Go on with your day. The City Watch will handle it." The guard's attempt at reassurance only highlighted the tension Razma felt, and he forced himself to nod, though his eyes lingered on the gathering at the square's edges.

He turned back to the sparring boys, but the excitement that had gripped him moments before had faded, the spark replaced by a heavy, gnawing sensation. A part of him longed to take up a staff, to join in the simple thrill of friendly competition. But another part of him, one he wasn't used to listening to, couldn't shake the sight of the refugees, their haunted expressions, the child's green-skinned face vanishing among the crowd. Razma hovered at the edge of the square, torn between the familiar pull of a challenge and the quiet weight of a city strained by shadows he couldn't quite name.

Razma lingered at the edge of the square, half-hidden in the shadows, his gaze fixed on the boys sparring in the open sun. The clatter of wooden staves echoed off the stone walls, filling the air with a rhythm that stirred something deep within him. His eyes followed Ky'len, the minor lord's son, as he moved with effortless grace, each strike and parry laced with the confidence of someone who had trained under the best. The boys cheered, their admiration clear, but Razma felt a familiar knot tightening in his chest—an uneasy mix of envy and longing. He could feel the weight of his own hands, empty, aching for a staff of his own. He wanted to be out there, wanted to show them that he was more than just a stable boy. As Ky'len deflected another blow with a smirk, Razma clenched his fists, the pull to step forward growing stronger. His heart pounded in his chest as he took a deep breath, gathering the courage to leave the safety of the shadows. It was time to prove himself.

With a deep breath, Razma stepped out from the shadows, the sun suddenly feeling too bright. His heart hammered in his chest as he approached the group, his voice steady despite the quickening pulse. "Can I spar with you?"

Ky'len turned slowly, a sneer curling on his lips as he looked Razma up and down. "You're not thinking of entering the tournament, are you?" His voice dripped with condescension, the kind that made Razma's fists clench at his sides.

"Throw me a staff, and I'll show you what a peasant can do," Razma shot back, the words tumbling out before he could stop them, his anger bubbling to the surface.

A smirk tugged at Ky'len's mouth as he nodded to Iszell, who tossed a staff toward Razma. The wooden weapon felt heavier in his hands than he expected, but the moment he gripped it, the familiar rush of excitement pulsed through his veins. The circle of boys widened, their eyes gleaming with anticipation as Ky'len took his stance, his movements deliberate, confident.

Razma swung first, the force of his attack driven by a surge of adrenaline. Ky'len blocked it with a fluid motion, the crack of their staves reverberating through Razma's arms. The impact left him momentarily stunned. He gritted his teeth and swung again, but Ky'len deflected every blow with ease, his smirk growing wider.

"Show him what Bazel can do, Ky'len!" jeered one of the boys from the crowd, stoking the fire of Ky'len's ego. His taunts came quick, sharp. "Having trouble, peasant?"

Razma's frustration boiled over, his grip tightening as he launched another strike. This time, the staff connected with Ky'len's shoulder. Razma's smirk mirrored Ky'len's earlier expression. "I didn't know you were the prince rat," Razma spat, his words stoking the embers of their rivalry.

Ky'len's eyes flared with anger. With a swift, powerful motion, he knocked the staff from Razma's hands, sending him stumbling back, his feet skidding against the rough cobblestones. Razma barely had time to react before Ky'len's staff was at his throat, the wood pressing against his skin.

"Royalty always wins," Ky'len sneered, leaning in, his voice low and dangerous. "We're smarter, faster, and better." The crowd buzzed, split between those cheering for Ky'len and those silently watching, unsure.

But Razma wasn't done. In one quick motion, he grabbed Ky'len's staff and swept his legs from under him. Ky'len hit the ground hard, the breath knocked out of him. Razma stood over him, catching his breath, his heart racing. "It appears you're not royalty after all."

Ky'len's face twisted with rage as he scrambled to his feet, his hand going to the sword at his hip. The metal glinted in the sun as he unsheathed it, his voice shaking with fury. "You've done it now, peasant!" The sword gleamed dangerously, a stark contrast to the playful sparring from moments before.

Razma's breath caught in his throat, panic rising. "Put the sword down! This isn't a fair fight!" He ducked just in time, Ky'len's blade cutting through the air where his head had been moments earlier.

"Ky'len, stop! You're going to kill him!" Iszell's voice cut through the growing chaos, his face pale as he pushed through the crowd, trying to pull his friend back.

"That's the point!" Ky'len growled, slashing wildly, the tip of his sword grazing Razma's arm as he stumbled backward.

Iszell broke free from the grasp of his friends, but before he could reach them, one of Ky'len's supporters hurled a rock. It struck Iszell in the temple, sending him crumpling to the ground, blood seeping into the dust as his vision faded.

Razma's mind raced as he watched Iszell fall, memories flashing before him in an overwhelming rush. His father's stories of battles, the evenings spent riding Cleo, the quiet moments of fishing with Iszell. His stomach churned as he braced for the killing blow.

But it never came.

Ky'len's roar of anger was drowned out by the sharp whistle of an arrow. It struck the ground between them, quivering in the dirt. Razma's eyes darted upward, where a masked figure perched on the butcher's roof, bow in hand. Another arrow zipped past Ky'len's head, forcing him to freeze in his tracks.

The crowd fell into stunned silence as Ky'len stood, rigid with fear. The masked figure drew another arrow, the tension in the air now thick and heavy, a warning in every drawn breath.

Razma scrambled to his feet, seizing the brief distraction. The masked figure landed gracefully between him and Ky'len, moving with the silent precision of a shadow. Their mere presence seemed to command the attention of the crowd, a calm authority radiating from them. "That's enough," they said, voice steady and controlled, cutting through the chaos like a blade.

"You alright, kid?" The figure glanced toward Razma, their piercing green eyes flickering with concern beneath the hood.

Razma's heart pounded in his chest, his breath still uneven. "I'm fine, but watch out!" he shouted, voice trembling as Ky'len charged again, fury and determination burning in his eyes.

"Not a good idea," the figure said coolly. With catlike grace, they sidestepped Ky'len's reckless swing. In one fluid motion, they twisted his arm behind his back, forcing a groan of pain from his lips.

Ky'len struggled, his voice shrill with desperation. "Get them!" he yelled, calling out to his friends. But no one moved. The crowd that had once jeered and cheered now stood frozen, wide-eyed and silent, watching the scene unfold with nervous anticipation.

The masked figure's grip on Ky'len remained firm, unyielding. "It's over, Ky'len," they said, their voice low but commanding. "And you're lucky it's not worse."

Ky'len's bravado crumbled as the figure slowly lifted their free hand, pulling back the hood just enough to reveal their face. For a moment, Ky'len's eyes locked with those piercing green eyes, and whatever arrogance remained within him vanished in an instant. His face turned ashen, terror washing over him as he realized who held him captive.

The crowd strained to catch a glimpse of what Ky'len had seen, their collective breath held as the minor lord's son collapsed to the ground, his sword slipping from his hand. He scrambled backward, eyes wide with fear. "No… it can't be…" he stammered, his voice barely a whisper, shaking as he tried to distance himself from the figure cloaked in shadows.

The square was deathly quiet now, the tension thick in the air. Every eye remained on Ky'len, watching as his fear unfolded before them. Whoever this figure was, they commanded fear, respect, and a power that none dared challenge.

"Leave," the figure commanded softly, the authority in their voice undeniable. Ky'len didn't need to be told twice. He scrambled to his feet and bolted, his friends quickly following, disappearing from the square as if chased by unseen specters.

As the masked figure turned back to Razma, their face once again hidden beneath the shadows of the hood, they offered a final piece of advice. "Next time, be more careful who you challenge," they said, a hint of a smile in their voice before they melted back into the crowd, leaving Razma standing alone, still trying to process what had just happened.

Chapter 6: Crossroads of Fate

779, 2nd Day Of The Fourth Moon

"The marshfolk came before me again, requesting more land—enough for their growing families, they said, though some in my council doubt their motives...My son is away, training or perhaps lost to the same thirst that plagues our bloodline. I miss him more than I care to admit. If he were here, would he speak for peace or push me toward force? I can only guess."

The marshlands were silent except for the occasional croak of a distant frog or the soft rustle of wind through the reeds. Chief Arak stood at the edge of the water, watching the sun dip low, casting long shadows over the land that had nurtured and sustained his tribe for generations. His mind was a whirlwind of strategies and scenarios, each playing out with the heavy burden of potential loss.

His daughter, Tala, had already departed to warn their allies, carrying with her the fragile hope of their entire tribe. Her journey weighed heavily on Arak, though he trusted in her courage. Now, as the fading sunlight painted the sky in shades of deep amber, Arak turned his thoughts to the pressing matters closer to home.

He stepped into the communal hut, lit by flickering torches that cast dancing shadows along the rough wooden walls. The faces of his most trusted advisors awaited him, solemn and tense. There was Grik'nar, the seasoned warrior whose scars told countless stories; Varuk, the cunning scout whose eyes missed nothing; and old Fenna, whose wisdom had guided Arak since he was but a young chief.

Fenna's fingers traced slow circles over the worn wood of the table, her touch light but deliberate. The fire crackled beside her, casting flickering shadows that danced across the hut's rough walls. Her gaze settled on Arak, steady and unshaken, though the weight behind it was unmistakable.

"Folk uroleg," she said finally, her voice quiet, yet heavy with certainty. *"People are restless."*

She let the words hang in the air, allowing their weight to settle. The marshlands were never truly silent, yet tonight, the usual murmur of insects and distant creatures felt distant, muted, as if even nature itself had paused to listen.

"Andre høvdinga krev makt. Mutt hogge dei som ikkje knele. Han kjem." *"The other chiefs demand power. Mutt has already slaughtered those who do not kneel. Soon, Arak, he will come for us."*

The fire crackled, the flames casting a golden glow on Arak's face. His jaw tightened, his expression unreadable, but the shift in his stance told them all he had expected these words—dreaded them. His fingers curled slightly against his thigh, tension settling into his shoulders like the weight of an old wound aching before a storm.

"Mutt er ikkje same." His voice was low, edged with something unreadable. "Han høyre mørke stemmer, ser berre makt." *"Mutt is not the same. He hears dark voices, sees only power."*

A pause. The fire popped, embers shifting in the hearth. Arak exhaled, slow and measured, though his hands betrayed him, balling into fists before relaxing once more.

"Eg frykte han no. Om me ikkje stoppa dette, folk døyr." *"I fear him now. If we do not stop this, our people will die."*

The silence that followed was thick, suffocating.

Then, Grik'nar moved.

His fist slammed into the wooden table, rattling the clay cups stacked near the edge. The force of the impact sent a shock through the room, but Arak did not flinch. Instead, he simply lifted his gaze, meeting the warrior's eyes across the fire.

"Då slåss me!" Grik'nar's voice was a growl, thick with anger. His broad shoulders tensed, his breath sharp as if barely containing the rage bubbling beneath his skin. "Ulveklo knele ikkje!" *"Then we fight! The Wolfclaw does not kneel!"*

The fire flickered, catching the shine of sweat on his brow, highlighting the sharp lines of the scars carved into his face from past battles.

"Me har blad, me har styrke!" *"We have blades, we have strength!"*

The words hung there, fierce, unyielding, a challenge in their weight.

The hut felt smaller, the air thick with tension. The flickering torchlight did little to soften the sharp edges of the conversation, the unspoken war already forming in the spaces between their breaths.

Arak did not speak immediately. He let the words sink, let the firelight dance between them. His expression remained unreadable, but the depth of his thoughts was clear in the measured breath he took before answering.

Arak held up a hand, his fingers worn and calloused, a silent command for stillness. The tension in the hut hung thick as swamp mist, but his gesture carried the weight of leadership. Grik'nar's anger still smoldered in his glare, but he did not challenge Arak further. The flickering torches cast restless shadows across the wooden walls, reflecting the unease in every face present.

"Nei, min ven." His voice was calm, but edged with the weight of truth. "Ein open kamp vil øydeleggja oss." *"No, my friend. A direct fight would end in ruin."*

He turned, letting his gaze settle on each of them, as if ensuring they truly understood the gravity of his words.

"Mutt har mange stammar no. Talet hans har vakse." *"Mutt commands many tribes now. His numbers have swelled."*

The crackle of fire was the only sound that followed.

"Dei ville slakta oss alle." *"They would slaughter us all."*

The truth settled over them like a heavy fog.

Varuk, who had remained quiet, shifted in his seat. He was not a man prone to outbursts, but the sharpness in his gaze revealed the thoughts racing behind them. He leaned forward slightly, his voice low, but keen as a blade drawn in the dark.

"Kva alternativ har me, høvding?" *"What alternative do we have, Chief?"*

His fingers drummed lightly on the table, though his tone remained controlled.

"Me kan ikkje berre venta på at døden finn oss." *"We cannot simply wait for death to find us."*

Arak inhaled deeply, the weight of his next words settling against his ribs. He measured them carefully, knowing they could not afford mistakes.

"Me må gå varleg." *"We must act delicately."*

His gaze darkened, shifting beyond the hut, beyond the present moment, toward the storm that was gathering on the horizon.

"Mutt ser oss. Han ventar at me knele eller kjempar." *"Mutt's eyes are upon us. He expects our obedience or our defiance."*

A pause. Then, his voice, quiet but firm as stone.

"Me gjev han ingen av delane. Ikkje enno." *"We give him neither—at least not yet."*

Fenna, ever the wise one, narrowed her eyes. She had known Arak for many years, had seen him weigh decisions with the same careful patience that defined his rule. She studied him now, searching for the plan she sensed forming behind his troubled gaze.

"Kva er planen din, høvding?" *"What is your plan, Chief?"*

Arak did not answer immediately. Instead, he reached into his cloak, his fingers brushing against the rough fabric before finding what he sought.

A parchment. Sealed carefully. Small, but heavy with purpose.

He held it out to Varuk, his expression solemn.

"Varuk, du må gå raskt og lydlaust—ingen kan sjå deg." *"Varuk, you must go swiftly and silently —do not be seen."*

Varuk's sharp eyes locked onto Arak's. He did not hesitate, reaching for the parchment with steady hands.

"Ta denne meldinga nord, til Bjørnebrekk-fjella." *"Take this message north, to Bear Creek Mountains."*

The flames in the hearth flickered as the words settled in the room.

"Vår allierte der vil forstå." *"Our ally there will understand."*

Varuk's grip tightened around the parchment. He did not question the task. He simply nodded, knowing what was required of him.

"Eg drar straks." *"I shall leave at once."*

Arak placed a firm hand on his shoulder, his grip steady, a silent show of trust.

"Vår overleving kviler på di fart og løyndom." *"Our survival hinges upon your speed and secrecy."*

He did not release him immediately. Instead, he locked eyes with the scout, willing him to feel the weight of this mission—not just for their tribe, but for all who stood against Mutt's growing power.

"Gå no, bror." His voice was softer now, but no less commanding. "Lat skuggane følgja deg." *"Go now, brother. And may the shadows follow you."*

Without another word, Varuk dipped his head and disappeared into the night.

The hut fell into silence, broken only by the muted crackling of torches. The air had shifted—not with relief, but with the quiet understanding that the pieces had begun to move.

Then—

A sound.

One heavy footstep outside.

Arak's blood ran cold.

It was deliberate. Measured.

The advisors hesitated, their bodies tense with the instinct to stand beside their chief. The firelight flickered against their faces, highlighting the wariness in their eyes. For a brief moment, the weight of their choices pressed heavily upon them.

But Arak's expression was resolute—unyielding. His gaze, sharp as a blade honed for battle, left no room for argument.

"Gå," he ordered, his voice low but firm. "Alle. Lat meg møta dette aleine." *"Go. All of you. Allow me to face this alone."*

Fenna's weathered hands clenched briefly at her sides, her sharp eyes lingering on Arak. She had guided him since he was young—had watched him grow into the leader before her now. And though her heart protested, she knew better than to challenge his command.

Varuk nodded once, silent as always, and disappeared through the rear entrance like a shadow swallowed by the night. Grik'nar lingered a moment longer, his fists tightening in frustration, but even he knew when to yield. One by one, they slipped into the marsh's embrace, vanishing into the deepening gloom.

Then, silence.

Alone now, Arak turned slowly, his breath steady, his expression unreadable. He stepped into the cool night air, the mist curling around his legs as though the swamp itself sought to keep him rooted in place.

And then, through the haze, a figure emerged.

Broad shoulders. A towering frame. Power coiled beneath scarred skin.

Mutt.

Once a brother-in-arms, now a ghost of what he had been. The remnants of their shared past clung to him like old blood on a blade—faded, but never truly gone.

The marshlands stilled.

The usual chorus of croaking frogs and chirping insects faded into a tense, unnatural quiet. Even the wind, which moments before had whispered through the reeds, seemed to hold its breath.

Arak did not move.

He knew this moment would come.

And now, it was here.

Heavy footsteps shattered the silence, careless and deliberate, splashing through shallow pools of water.

Arak did not immediately turn. He allowed a moment to pass, deliberately stretching the tension like a bowstring drawn taut. Then, finally, he pivoted slowly, facing the man he had once called an ally.

His expression was calm, almost welcoming—yet beneath that facade lay the tempered steel of a seasoned chief.

"Mutt." Arak's voice carried easily over the quiet marsh, low and steady. "Lenge sidan desse land kjende fotspora dine." *"It's been a long while since these lands felt your presence."*

His eyes flicked over Mutt's imposing form, the shadows playing along the deep scars that marked his skin.

"Du ser større ut no—eller berre eldre?" *"You seem larger now—or perhaps merely older?"*

Mutt halted abruptly, golden eyes gleaming beneath his heavy brow. Suspicion and wariness flickered in his gaze, but his posture remained relaxed—too relaxed, like a predator toying with its prey.

"Og du, Arak—trur framleis visdom gjer deg sterkare enn klør og blad?" *"And you, Arak—still thinking that wisdom makes you stronger than claws or blades?"*

A faint, deliberate smile curled Arak's lips.

"Visdom tente oss nok under Thorrin-krigen. Eller hugsar du annleis?" *"Wisdom served us well enough during the Thorrin War. Or perhaps your memory paints things differently?"*

Mutt offered a dark chuckle, though there was little humor beneath it. Bitterness shadowed his bravado.

"Eg hugsar godt nok." His voice was low, edged with something old and dangerous. "Du kjempa ved sida av meg, Arak. Me blødde saman, dreiv menneska til ruin—og likevel tvinga dei oss tilbake hit." *"I remember clearly enough. You fought beside me, Arak. We bled together, drove the humans back to the edge of ruin—and still they forced us back here."*

His lips curled, a sneer creeping into his voice.

"Me blødde for land som skulle vore vårt." *"We bled for land that should rightfully be ours."*

Arak lifted his chin slightly, his gaze unwavering.

"Vold vinn aldri varig fridom." His voice was measured, unshaken. "Fred krev tolmod, Mutt. Visdom." *"Violence alone has never won lasting freedom. Peace requires patience, Mutt. Wisdom."*

The marsh was utterly still, save for the slow ripple of water against the reeds.

"Sjå kva tolmod har gitt meg: menneska handlar med meg, respekterer meg." *"Look at what patience has earned me: the humans trade with me, respect me."*

Mutt's laughter rang sharp and hollow across the water, a sound that sent ripples through the marsh's stillness.

"Respekt?" He spat the word like a curse.

He took a slow step forward, his massive frame casting a long shadow in the dim torchlight.

"Du trur dei respekterer deg?" His teeth flashed in something between a grin and a snarl. "Dei ser deg som ein kvalp—tam, lojal, lydig." *"You mistake their contempt for respect. They see you as nothing more than a puppy—harmless, loyal, obedient."*

Arak's smile did not waver, but there was a new edge to it now, a sharpness hidden beneath his calm exterior.

"Kanskje." His voice was mild, but his eyes gleamed with something keener. "Men fortel meg, Mutt—korleis ser dei deg?" *"Perhaps. But tell me, Mutt—how do they see you?"*

A pause.

Mutt's expression darkened slightly.

Arak continued, his words slow and deliberate.

"Ein gal hund, trur eg." *"A rabid beast, I suspect."*

The fire crackled softly, but the marsh remained silent, listening.

"Farlig, men lett å kaste eit kjøtbein til." *"Dangerous, but easy enough to distract with scraps of meat."*

He tilted his head slightly.

"Ein som bit sine eigne ved fyrste teikn på svakheit." *"An animal that turns on its own at the first sign of weakness."*

A low, warning growl rumbled in Mutt's chest, his fists tightening at his sides.

"Varsam, gamal venn." His voice was dangerously quiet now. "Eg toler berre så mykje hån." *"Careful, old friend. Friend or not, there's only so much insult I'll tolerate."*

Arak's smile faded, replaced by something quieter—something almost mournful.

"Venn?" He echoed the word softly, the weight of it heavy in the air.

His voice was steady, but sorrow edged its way into his tone.

"Du mista retten til det ordet då du byrja å drepa høvdingar som ikkje bøygde seg for deg." *"You lost the right to use that word when you started slaughtering chiefs who dared disagree with you."*

Then, his tone shifted—quieter, heavier.

"Og du mista retten då du lét Tal'shira døy." *"And you lost the right when you let Tal'shira die."*

Mutt flinched. It was small—almost imperceptible—but Arak saw it.

"Ho ville ha kjempa mot dette. Ho såg håp, ikkje vald." *"She would have fought against this. She saw hope, not violence."*

Mutt's hands twitched, curling into fists. His lips curled back in a snarl, but something flickered in his eyes—something raw, something bitter.

"Tal'shira var svak." His voice was a growl, but there was a crack in it, deep beneath the surface. "Ho kviler no under myra, der veike høyrer heime." *"Tal'shira was weak. Now she rests beneath the bog where weaklings belong."*

Arak took a slow step forward, his voice calm but unrelenting.

"Var ho svak? Eller trudde du berre ikkje ho ville knele for deg?" *"Was she weak? Or did you simply know she would never kneel to you?"*

Silence.

Mutt's nostrils flared. His fingers twitched. His breath came harder now, nostrils flaring as though he was fighting the instinct to lash out.

Arak let the moment stretch, let the truth settle between them like the weight of a blade left undrawn.

Then, he exhaled softly, voice steady but cold.

"Du seier det, men du trur det ikkje."*"You say that, but you don't believe it."*

Mutt snapped.

His hand lashed out—not to strike, but to seize the space between them, his muscles coiled like he might choke the words from Arak's throat. He stopped himself just short, fists shaking, his breath ragged.

"Hald kjeft." His voice was raw, edged with something far more unstable than anger. "Du veit ingenting om ho. Ho var min syster. Eg såg ho for det ho var!" *"Shut up. You know nothing about her. She was my sister. I saw her for what she was!"*

Arak did not flinch.

He stood his ground, eyes never leaving Mutt's, watching the fury burn behind them."Og likevel let du ho døy."*"And yet you let her die."*

Mutt let out a snarl, his chest rising and falling fast, like an animal pacing its cage. His scars stood out stark in the flickering light, his muscles tensed, ready to snap—yet he did nothing.

Because Arak was right.

And they both knew it.

"Ho trudde på frede, men verda viste ho ingen nåde!" Mutt's voice cracked, the growl underneath it desperate now. "Ho var blind! Ho trudde at menneska og me kunne vera eitt, men dei let oss rotna i myra!" *"She believed in peace, but the world showed her no mercy! She was blind! She thought humans and we could be one, but they left us to rot in the bog!"*

His breath hitched, his teeth grinding.

"Ho levde i draumar, Arak. Draumar drep. Eg sparte ho frå det!" *"She lived in dreams, Arak. Dreams kill. I spared her from that!"*

Arak's voice did not rise, did not waver.

"Nei, Mutt. Du sparte deg sjølv frå ho.""No, Mutt. You spared yourself from her."

Mutt staggered back.

It was small, just half a step, but it was there.

Arak tilted his head slightly, gaze unwavering.

"Ho såg kven du var. Det er difor du hata ho." *"She saw who you were. That's why you hated her."*

For the first time, Mutt had no retort.

His jaw tightened, his breath came sharp, but no words left his mouth.

Arak had cut through him.

There was nothing left to hide behind.

For a moment, just a moment, it almost seemed like Mutt might say something else.

But then he took a step back, retreating into the shifting mist.

"Vel fort, Arak." His voice had lost some of its earlier confidence, but the threat remained. "Slekt kjøper deg berre så mykje nåde." *"Make your choice quickly, Arak. Family ties will only buy you so much mercy."*

And then, softer—softer than Arak expected:

"Og gi mi helsing til niesa mi." *"And give my niece my regards."*

Mutt disappeared into the night, swallowed by fog and shadow.

Arak stood there, unmoving, listening to the last echoes of his footsteps in the marsh.

Then, slowly, he exhaled.

War was now unavoidable.

But he had won something tonight. He had seen it, just for a second. Doubt.

Tal'shira's memory was still a wound Mutt could not close.

And Arak would make sure it never did.

Chapter 7: The Weight of Welcome

773, 19th Day Of The Twelfth Moon

"They speak of my son's thirst, a relentless hunger that unsettles even his mother's kin. I have seen it myself—the way his eyes darken with fierce resolve, a drive that seems to grow stronger each day. It terrifies even me, that raw, untamed intensity, yet in it, I see potential. Perhaps this thirst, so feared and misunderstood, can be honed, shaped—not suppressed but wielded as a blade to carve the future we strive toward. For years, my wife assured me it was impossible, a relic of lore with no bearing on the world we are building. But I see the small sparks in my children, glimpses of something ancient and powerful."

Ky'len and Iszell sat in their modest inn room, their staves propped against the wall, the faint sounds of Seragora drifting in through the window. Ky'len stared out at the city, memories twisting through him, making his chest tighten. The face he'd seen earlier—the ranger who had stepped in—haunted him, her gaze cutting through his thoughts like a knife.

Iszell tossed his pack onto the bed, sighing heavily. "These lands… so different from home." He leaned back, eyes drifting to the ceiling. "At home, those refugees would have been turned away, forced to move on. But here…" His voice trailed off, the memory of what they'd seen pressing down on him like a weight. "I can't get that boy's face out of my mind. The way he screamed…"

Ky'len clenched his fists, the memories of the battle on the road returning in flashes—steel against bone, feathers slicing the air, the terrified cries of people who had nowhere left to run. He could still feel the blood on his hands, the hollowness of knowing they hadn't saved them all. "I can't forget either," he said, voice tight. "We did what we could, but it wasn't enough. It never is."

A tense silence fell between them, their unspoken guilt settling like a shadow. Finally, Iszell spoke, his voice low and strained. "Bazel is all about power, isn't it? Money, status—who has the upper hand. They wouldn't see the value in saving those people. But here, people fight for more than coin. They fight for hope, for each other. And we did that, Ky'len. We fought for them, and it meant something."

Ky'len's jaw tightened, a dark shadow passing over his features. "My father only ever valued power. To him, mercy is a weakness. Growing up, I watched his anger consume him, turn him into someone feared rather than respected. Everything was a battle—a contest of dominance. Sometimes… sometimes I see it in myself. The way my temper flares, the way my blood boils. Today, when I nearly struck Razma… or back in Bazel, when I ripped that horseman from his saddle just for bumping into me…" His voice cracked, and he looked down, a tear slipping free

70

in anger and shame. "What am I becoming, Iszell? Who am I?"

Iszell's expression softened, his own eyes reflecting the weight of Ky'len's anguish. "But you didn't, Ky'len. You stopped yourself."

"Because of her," Ky'len whispered, eyes distant. "The ranger. She stepped in, and it was like she saw straight through me. She stopped me from making the kind of mistake my father would have praised. If she hadn't…" He trailed off, turning to the window, the thought too heavy to finish. The fear of becoming his father—unforgiving, merciless—gnawed at him, clawing at the edges of his mind.

"Ky'len, listen to me," Iszell said, his voice steady but urgent. "You're not your father. You came here to prove that—to them, to Seragora, and to yourself. This place gives us a chance to see that strength isn't only in battle. It's in choosing who we want to be."

Ky'len's eyes met Iszell's, a glimmer of hope surfacing through the doubt. "But what if that anger, that darkness, is part of me? What if I can't escape it?"

"We all have shadows," Iszell said firmly. "But they don't define us unless we let them. Today, you chose differently. That's what matters, Ky'len."

The room fell silent, the sounds of laughter and music from the common room below seeping in, almost mocking in their warmth. Ky'len took a shaky breath, the noise grounding him in the present.

"The people here have freedom," he said quietly, as if the thought had only just occurred to him. "Freedom to choose, to fight for more than power. Sometimes I wonder if we're meant to learn from them, not spy for Bazel. To see that there's more than one way to lead."

Iszell's smile was small but genuine. "Maybe we're here for both—to learn, to change, and if we must, to share the truth with Bazel. Not the version they want, but the one they need." He paused and added softly, "We don't have to spy on them, Ky'len. We can just be here and live in it, even if it's just for a little while."

Ky'len's gaze returned to the window, the city lights flickering like distant stars. "If we do that, we risk everything. My father… he'll see it as defiance, and he won't forgive it."

"Then we'll face that when it comes," Iszell said, resolute. "Together."

Ky'len's shoulders eased, just a fraction. "Together," he echoed, the word carrying a fragile hope. He glanced at Iszell, who nodded back, offering silent reassurance.

The image of the ranger's eyes stayed with Ky'len, a challenge and a promise that he wasn't alone in this battle with himself. As the night deepened and Seragora's life buzzed beyond their window, he felt the first stirrings of a resolve he hadn't known he possessed.

They were here to fight, but not just for victory or recognition. They were here to redefine themselves, to prove to Seragora, to Bazel, and most importantly, to themselves, that they could be more than the legacies that threatened to consume them.

With a calm resolve settling between them, Ky'len and Iszell understood that they were here to win, yes, but also to make their presence felt—to give their titles meaning beyond the weight of their fathers' expectations. As dawn approached and the air grew heavy with anticipation, they knew this tournament would challenge them in ways they had never experienced before.

Ky'len turned to Iszell, his expression clouded with a rare vulnerability. "It's just a dream, you know," he said quietly, the weight of doubt pressing into his words. "These people don't trust us. They never will. Our fathers, our uncles... our men killed theirs. The memories linger—fifteen years isn't so long to forget."

Iszell looked back at him, his eyes steady, reflecting a glimmer of hope. "We're not them, Ky'len. We're a new generation." His voice was firm yet filled with quiet conviction. "We're here to change that, to prove that things can be different."

Ky'len sighed, running a hand through his hair as he leaned back against the wall. "I hope you're right, Iszell. I really do. But right now? I'm hungry." He managed a faint grin, shifting the mood as he nudged his friend's arm. "Maybe a Seragoran barmaid will help improve things. Think they'll be as welcoming as you say?"

Iszell chuckled, his grin widening. "With your charm? I wouldn't bet on it. They'll see right through that noble act of yours."

Ky'len raised a brow, mischief lighting his eyes. "First to get a blush wins?"

Iszell's laughter rang out, infectious and light. "You're on, but I'm not holding back. Maybe a little Seragoran hospitality is exactly what we need to start this whole 'changing the world' thing."

As they descended the narrow stairs of the inn, their laughter mingled with the sounds of clinking mugs and lively voices from the common room below. The hum of conversation washed over them—a comforting sound despite the unfamiliar faces. The inn was bustling with travelers, soldiers, and locals alike, all drawn by the promise of the upcoming tournament. The tension of their journey and the weight of their thoughts seemed to ease with each step.

Ky'len's gaze drifted over the tables, catching a group of young Seragoran men laughing loudly, oblivious to the Bazel squires in their midst. He nudged Iszell with a playful grin. "Reckon they'll be blushing before they're done with us?" he whispered, eyeing the nearest barmaid, who was weaving gracefully through the crowded room with a heavy tray balanced effortlessly on one hand.

Iszell smirked, crossing his arms with mock confidence. "Blushing? Please. I'll have her swooning by the time her shift's over."

Ky'len laughed, their banter pulling him back into the moment. As the barmaid approached their table, setting down a pitcher and two mugs, she glanced between them with a raised brow.

"Look at you two," she said, folding her arms with a grin that hinted at amusement rather than shyness. "What brings Bazel's finest to our little city?"

"Just two simple squires here to enjoy your fine hospitality," Ky'len said smoothly, lifting his mug with a wink.

"Hospitality, huh?" She arched an eyebrow, her smile unwavering. "Well, you'll find plenty of it here. But don't expect any special treatment just because you're from Bazel. We Seragorans have our own way of doing things."

Iszell laughed, raising his mug in acknowledgment. "We wouldn't expect anything less."

As the barmaid moved to another table, Ky'len watched her go, his gaze thoughtful. Beneath the friendliness lay a wariness—a reminder that even in the lively warmth of the inn, old scars ran deep. Turning back to Iszell, he couldn't resist one last barb. "Guess that counts as a blush for me."

Iszell rolled his eyes, smirking. "Dream on, Ky'len. We've got all night. Besides, I'm just getting started."

The warmth of the inn grew with each passing minute, the initial tension giving way to camaraderie. Travelers exchanged stories, soldiers swapped tales of past battles, and the anticipation of the tournament buzzed like an undercurrent. The scent of spiced meats and freshly baked bread filled the air, mingling with the rich aroma of ale.

Ky'len and Iszell leaned into the atmosphere, their guarded expressions softening as they watched the mingling crowd. The laughter and chatter around them began to feel less foreign, more like a shared experience bridging the gap between their worlds.

It wasn't long before a group of older Bazel knights entered, their armor polished and crested with noble sigils. Their presence commanded respect and a hint of wariness; these men had seen the bloodier side of history, and their reputations were as sharp as their swords. One of them, Sir Alwyn—a grizzled veteran with silver-streaked hair and a scowl etched onto his face— caught sight of them.

"Well, look who we have here," Alwyn drawled, his eyes narrowing as he approached. "Ky'len and Iszell, the young hopefuls." The knights pulled up chairs uninvited, settling in with an air of entitlement. "Out of place, aren't you? Mixing with common folk."

Ky'len forced a polite smile. "Just enjoying the evening, Sir Alwyn."

Alwyn snorted, glancing around the inn with thinly veiled disdain. "Hardly the kind of establishment befitting Bazel nobility. But I suppose standards have slipped."

Iszell bristled slightly but kept his tone even. "We find the atmosphere refreshing."

Another knight, Sir Garrick—a broad-shouldered man with a sneer twisting his lips—leaned forward. "Careful, lads. Too much 'refreshment' might dull your edge for the tournament. Though perhaps that would be a mercy; wouldn't want you embarrassing Bazel with a poor showing."

Ky'len felt a flicker of irritation but maintained his composure. "We'll do our best to represent Bazel honorably."

"Honorably?" Alwyn chuckled darkly. "Honor doesn't win tournaments—skill and a willingness to do what's necessary do. Remember that."

The barmaid returned, placing fresh mugs on the table. Alwyn eyed her appreciatively, a predatory glint in his eye. "Well now, perhaps this place has its charms after all."

She ignored his gaze, turning instead to Ky'len and Iszell. "Will there be anything else?"

Iszell offered a friendly smile. "Not at the moment, thank you."

As she moved to leave, Alwyn grabbed her wrist firmly, his voice low. "Hold on, girl. Surely you can spare a moment for some honored guests."

She tried to pull back, her eyes flashing with discomfort. "I have other patrons to attend to, Sir."

Alwyn's grip tightened, his tone dripping with menace. "It would be unwise to refuse a request from Bazel's knights."

Ky'len's patience snapped. "Sir Alwyn, release her. Now."

Alwyn turned his gaze to Ky'len, a cold smile spreading across his face. "Careful, boy. You're treading on thin ice."

Iszell stood up, his eyes hard. "Let her go."

Alwyn released the barmaid's wrist abruptly, causing her to stumble back. She shot the squires a grateful glance before quickly disappearing into the crowd.

Garrick leaned in, his voice a harsh whisper. "You two forget your place. Acting like saviors won't earn you any favors here."

Ky'len met his gaze steadily. "We didn't come here to bully the locals."

Alwyn's eyes narrowed dangerously. "No, you came here with a purpose—a purpose your fathers entrusted to you. Or have you forgotten?"

Iszell's expression faltered slightly. "What are you implying?"

Alwyn leaned closer, his voice barely audible over the din of the inn. "Remember why you're here. This isn't a pleasure trip. You're to gather information for your fathers—valuable insights about Seragora. They expect results, not distractions."

Ky'len felt a chill run down his spine. The unspoken threat hung heavily in the air. "We're aware of our duties," he replied cautiously.

"Good," Alwyn said, his tone dripping with warning. "Because failure to deliver won't be taken lightly. Your fathers have little patience for disappointments."

Garrick smirked. "And we wouldn't want any... unfortunate reports making their way back to Bazel about where your loyalties truly lie."

Iszell swallowed hard, the weight of their words sinking in. "We're loyal to Bazel."

"See that you prove it," Alwyn hissed. "Now, stop wasting time with games and focus on why you're really here."

The knights stood up, Alwyn casting one last piercing glare at them before moving away to another table. The tension lingered, a suffocating cloud that settled over Ky'len and Iszell.

Ky'len clenched his fists under the table. "They're watching us," he murmured.

Iszell nodded, his face pale. "And they're expecting us to act just like them."

Ky'len's eyes hardened. "But we won't. We can't."

Iszell took a deep breath, trying to steady himself. "What do we do?"

Ky'len met his friend's gaze. "We stick to our path. We gather information, yes, but not in the way they expect. We can find a way to honor our duties without betraying who we are."

Iszell managed a faint smile. "Always the optimist."

"Not always," Ky'len admitted. "But I refuse to become what they want me to be."

They sat in silence for a moment, the noise of the inn fading into the background. The weight of the knights' threats pressed upon them, but so did a renewed determination.

Just then, the group of young Seragoran soldiers they'd noticed earlier approached their table. One of them, a lanky youth with a friendly smile, spoke up. "Mind if we join you?"

Ky'len glanced at Iszell before nodding. "Please."

The soldiers pulled up chairs, their initial caution giving way to curiosity. "We saw you stand up to those knights," the youth—Tomas—said. "Takes guts, especially among your own."

Iszell shrugged modestly. "We just did what we thought was right."

Another soldier, a stout girl with bright eyes named Lila, leaned forward. "Not all Bazel folk would do that. Most turn a blind eye."

Ky'len sighed. "Not all of us agree with how things are done back home."

Tomas grinned. "Well, perhaps there's hope for you yet."

They spent the next hour exchanging stories, learning about each other's cultures and experiences. The Seragorans shared tales of their training, their traditions, and their hopes for peace. Ky'len and Iszell listened intently, contributing their own perspectives cautiously.

At one point, Lila eyed them thoughtfully. "You know, if more people were willing to listen like you two, maybe we wouldn't be on the brink of war every other year."

"Agreed," Iszell said quietly. "We have more in common than we realize."

The evening wore on, and the initial tension eased into genuine camaraderie. For a time, the lines between Bazel and Seragora blurred, replaced by the simple connection of individuals sharing a moment in time.

As the inn began to empty, Ky'len felt a mixture of exhaustion and hope. The threats from Alwyn and Garrick lingered, but so did the encouragement from their new acquaintances.

"Thank you for giving us a chance," Ky'len said as they all stood to leave.

Tomas clapped him on the shoulder. "Thank you for reminding us that not all from Bazel are the same."

Lila nodded. "Good luck in the tournament. We'll be rooting for you—not too much, but a little," she added with a wink.

Ky'len laughed softly. "We'll take what we can get."

As Ky'len and Iszell made their way back to their room, the weight of the night's events settled over them. Once inside, Ky'len closed the door, turning to face Iszell.

"They're expecting us to spy," he said bluntly.

Iszell nodded. "And they made it clear there would be consequences if we don't."

Ky'len's jaw tightened. "We need to be careful. But I won't betray the trust of those we met tonight."

"Nor will I," Iszell agreed. "Perhaps we can find a way to fulfill our obligations without harming anyone."

Ky'len sighed, running a hand through his hair. "It's a fine line to walk."

"One we'll walk together," Iszell said firmly.

Ky'len offered a grateful smile. "Thank you."

They prepared for bed in silence, each lost in their own thoughts. As Ky'len lay down, staring at the ceiling, he whispered into the darkness, "I won't become like them."

From the other bed, Iszell's quiet voice replied, "Neither will I."

Chapter 8: A Tale of Two Bloodlines

764, 3rd Day Of The Third Moon

"Even across the field, her gaze cut through the clamor of war, piercing straight to my core—sharp and unwavering, like the spear she held. I'd heard tales of her people, fierce and different, but seeing her there, resolute among her kin, was something else entirely. A woman in battle—so foreign to us—yet she moved with a grace that defied all expectation, her strength natural, almost effortless.

In that moment, as our eyes met, it felt as though time itself slowed, something strange and unspoken stirring between us. It was almost mystical, like a force beyond the physical—though surely, that's just an old wife's tale. Nothing more."

Razma walked through the dispersing crowd, his thoughts still swirling with the events of the day. The mysterious figure who had saved him loomed large in his mind—who were they, and why had they intervened? The memory of Ky'len's terror-stricken face when he glimpsed the figure's identity lingered, raising more questions than answers.

As he made his way toward Dalmon's shop, Razma tried to piece together the day's events. The scent of wood smoke and freshly baked bread from a nearby tavern wafted through the air, momentarily distracting him. Snippets of conversation reached his ears as he passed, but his mind was too preoccupied to focus on them.

Finally, Razma reached Dalmon's general store, where the familiar scent of hay, leather, and dried goods welcomed him as he stepped inside. The shelves were lined with everything from tools to grains, and the soft creak of the floorboards beneath his feet signaled his arrival. Dalmon, a tall man with blond hair and a friendly smile, looked up from the counter where he was organizing a shipment of goods. To Razma, Dalmon not related by blood, was more like an uncle than a shopkeeper, his friendship with Belazar stretching back years before Razma was born.

"Razma," Dalmon greeted warmly, though his sharp eyes quickly noted the tension in Razma's posture. "What can I do for you today?"

Razma hesitated for a moment, shifting uneasily. Then, before he could stop himself, the words spilled out. "I got into a fight in the square—well, not exactly a fight at first. I asked Ky'len, the Bazel royal, to spar with me."

Dalmon's expression shifted, concern crossing his features, though there was a glint of pride in his eyes. "Ky'len, a royal from Bazel?" he repeated, setting aside the box he was unpacking. "Razma, you know better than to get mixed up with someone like him. Especially now, with things being so tense between Palrazara and Bazel."

"I wasn't trying to start a fight," Razma explained, frustration creeping into his voice. "I just wanted to spar, but it got out of hand. He pulled a sword on me, Dalmon. I thought he was going to kill me."

Dalmon's brow furrowed as he leaned back against the counter, crossing his arms. "A sword?" he asked quietly, his eyes narrowing in concern. "What happened next?"

"That's when a masked figure showed up," Razma continued, the memory still vivid. "They shot arrows at Ky'len and then jumped in and disarmed him like it was nothing. Ky'len looked terrified when he saw their face, but I didn't get a good look."

Dalmon paused, rubbing his chin as he processed Razma's words. "A masked figure, huh? And Ky'len was scared?"

Razma nodded. "He ran off as soon as they let him go. Whoever it was, they weren't just some ordinary person."

For a moment, Dalmon was silent, his face thoughtful as he considered the situation. "You're lucky, Razma. Sparring with a Bazel royal could've gone a lot worse. Things between our kingdoms are fragile enough without incidents like this. You need to be more careful."

Razma's shoulders slumped. "I know. It just... happened so fast."

Dalmon placed a hand on Razma's shoulder, his grip firm but comforting. "Look, you stood your ground against a royal. That takes guts. Even if it wasn't the smartest thing to do, your father would've been proud of that." His voice softened, the pride in his words unmistakable.

Razma felt a flicker of pride at Dalmon's praise, but the mystery of the masked figure still gnawed at him. "But why would someone like that help me?" he asked.

Dalmon shook his head, his brow still furrowed in thought. "That's a good question. Maybe it doesn't matter for now—just be thankful they did. Ky'len could've killed you, and that might've sparked something neither of us wants to see."

He looked Razma in the eye, his expression serious. "I'll keep my ears open, see if I hear anything. But until then, keep your head down. Whoever that masked figure was, they helped you today, but you don't know their intentions."

Razma nodded, feeling the weight of Dalmon's words. "Thanks, Dalmon. I'll be careful."

Dalmon gave him a reassuring smile, though the concern didn't fully leave his eyes. "Good. Now, what brought you to the shop today?"

Razma quickly explained about Mrs. Glendale and the horse feed he needed to pick up.

Dalmon chuckled softly, shaking his head. "Ah, Mrs. Glendale. Tough as nails, but she's earned it. Don't let her gruffness fool you—she's done a lot for this town, more than most people know. And she's been a good friend to your father too."

Razma scratched the back of his head, feeling sheepish. "She's mad at me for breaking her ink bottles."

Dalmon's chuckle deepened. "Well, can't say I blame her for that. But replacing them is the right thing to do. Just remember, Mrs. Glendale's heart is in the right place, even if she doesn't show it much."

Razma nodded, feeling a bit more understanding toward the old schoolteacher. "I'll make sure to replace them."

"Good lad," Dalmon said, his tone lightening again. "But listen—don't tell Belazar about the fight, alright? You know how he reacts to you getting into trouble, especially with everything that's going on between Sergora and Bazel."

Razma sighed, knowing Dalmon was right. "I won't. I'll just tell him I was running errands."

Dalmon nodded, satisfied with the response. "Good. Now, fifty copper for the feed, and the ink's on the house."

Razma smiled, grateful for Dalmon's kindness. "Thanks, Dalmon."

As Razma turned to leave, Dalmon placed a hand on his shoulder once more. "And, Razma, if you ever need to talk—about anything—you know where to find me. Don't carry all this alone, alright?"

Razma managed a small smile, the weight of the day feeling just a little lighter. "I won't. I promise."

Dalmon's smile widened, and he handed Razma a small piece of rock candy, just as he had when Razma was a child. "Take care of yourself, Razma."

Dalmon tossed him a rock candy, "for the story something to chew on"

Razma left Dalmon's shop, the rock candy in his pocket a small but comforting reminder of the warmth and care he'd found there. His thoughts were still churning, a maelstrom of confusion and curiosity, but talking with Dalmon had helped to ground him, if only a little.

As he made his way toward Mrs. Glendale's school, Razma couldn't shake the image of the masked figure from his mind. The way they had moved with such precision, the way they had commanded the situation with effortless ease—it was almost otherworldly. And Ky'len's reaction… the terror in his eyes was something Razma couldn't forget.

By the time Razma reached the school, the late afternoon sun cast long shadows through the quiet streets. He was relieved to find the place empty, the stern presence of Mrs. Glendale nowhere to be seen. He stepped inside carefully, the familiar scent of old wood and parchment welcoming him like a half-forgotten memory. As the door creaked shut behind him, he moved quietly to her desk, setting down the replacement ink bottle with a gentle clink.

The classroom was just as it had been when Razma was a student—rows of wooden desks neatly arranged, the faint remnants of chalk dust still lingering in the air. His gaze lingered on the chalkboard, where faded lessons remained scrawled in Mrs. Glendale's sharp, deliberate hand. He could almost hear her stern voice echoing off the walls, a steady force that had shaped so much of his understanding of the world.

One particular lesson came rushing back—about the Muckspawn, those green-skinned creatures who lived deep in the eastern Bear Mountains. He remembered Mrs. Glendale's description vividly, the way she had warned them, her voice full of caution and a hint of disdain. "They may be small and not particularly bright," she had said, her sharp eyes sweeping across the classroom, "but do not underestimate them. In large numbers, they are dangerous, and they defend their territory with a surprising level of cunning."

Back then, Razma had imagined the Muckspawn as simple, bumbling creatures, more nuisance than threat. But after hearing stories in the marketplace—stories of organized raids, of Muckspawn moving with purpose—he couldn't shake the feeling that there was more to them than Mrs. Glendale had let on.

His thoughts drifted to another lesson that had left a deeper mark—one about the Slividhe. Unlike the Muckspawn, the Slividhe were spoken of with a mixture of reverence and fear. Mrs. Glendale had described them as tall, elegant, and almost otherworldly, with their fine features and pointed ears. "They possess magic beyond our comprehension," she had said, her voice softer, almost as if in awe. "But don't let their beauty fool you. The Slividhe are formidable warriors, and their magic makes them a force to be reckoned with."

Magic. Razma's thoughts lingered on the word. In Seragora, magic was a rarity, something whispered about but seldom seen. Most feared it—few understood it. The occasional traveler with a minor spell or a wandering mage drew wary glances, and most townsfolk preferred to rely on steel and wit. The idea that the Slividhe lived in harmony with such power seemed almost mythical, like something from one of the old stories his father used to tell him by the fire.

As he stood there in the stillness of the classroom, Razma couldn't help but think about the masked figure who had saved him earlier. Their movements had been almost too fluid, too precise, like a warrior who had spent years honing their skills. Could they have been Slividhe? But what would a Slividhe be doing in Seragora, a town where magic was viewed with suspicion, and their kind was nothing more than a whispered legend?

The thought unsettled him. The Slividhe were reclusive, their population dwindling over the centuries to the point where some believed they had all but vanished. Children among their kind were so rare that they were cherished and protected with fierce devotion. For one of their kind to appear in Seragora, intervening in a human dispute, seemed almost impossible. And yet, the memory of those swift, decisive movements refused to leave his mind.

Razma shook his head, trying to dismiss the thoughts, but they clung to him like a shadow. He could still see Ky'len's terrified face, the way his bravado had melted the moment the masked figure revealed their identity. Whoever that person was, they weren't ordinary. And the more Razma thought about it, the more convinced he became that there was something far bigger at play—something he couldn't yet understand.

Just as Razma was making his way back from Mrs. Glendale's classroom, Jeff ambled by, flipping two fingers at the schoolhouse. "Gods, I hate that woman," he muttered, rolling his eyes and letting out an exaggerated sigh. Spotting Razma, his expression softened, and he flashed a wry grin. "Oh, hey, Razma! Off to story time? Better go now if you want a good seat—Old Man Vil'elm's got half the town turned out tonight."

Razma gave a nod, his mind still tangled in the web of questions lingering from his conversation with Mrs. Glendale. The rock candy Dalmon had given him felt small in his pocket, but comforting, a steadying presence as his thoughts strayed to the mystery surrounding the masked figure and Ky'len's fear.

The sun dipped lower, casting a warm, golden glow over the cobblestone streets of Seragora. The air was filled with the scent of blooming jasmine and the distant sound of merchants packing up their stalls for the day. Razma weaved through the throng of villagers, his footsteps light as he made his way toward the heart of the town square. Tonight, an unusual tension hung in the air—a mixture of anticipation and unease that quickened everyone's pace.

The square itself was a wide, open space paved with time-worn stones, surrounded by a circle of ancient oak trees whose leaves whispered secrets in the evening breeze. Lanterns hung from their branches, soon to be lit as dusk settled into night. At the center stood a raised platform, modest in design but commanding attention—a stage for storytellers, musicians, and any who had something to share with the community.

As Razma approached, he saw that a sizable crowd had already gathered, families spreading out blankets on the grass, children staying close to their parents instead of chasing each other as they usually did. The atmosphere was subdued, the usual chatter dampened by an undercurrent of fear. Razma found a spot near the front, settling down cross-legged on the cool grass. He glanced around, taking in the familiar faces—the baker and his wife, the blacksmith, the schoolteacher—but tonight, their expressions were marked by a wary caution.

A few rows ahead, a younger boy kept glancing back at Razma, his eyes fixated on the small bag of candies Razma held. The boy's clothes were patched and worn, his dark hair tousled. Noticing the longing in the boy's gaze, Razma caught his eye and offered a friendly wink. He reached into his bag and pulled out a few pieces of the hard, honey-flavored candies, holding them out in his open palm.

The boy's face lit up, but his smile was tentative, his eyes darting around as if afraid someone might see. He mouthed a silent "thank you" before quickly accepting the gift and turning back around, hunching his shoulders as if to make himself smaller. Razma felt a pang of sympathy, sensing that the boy's caution mirrored the general unease of the crowd.

The gentle hum of conversation faded as Old Man Vil'elm stepped onto the platform. He was a tall, slender figure draped in a cloak of deep green, the hood pulled back to reveal a face etched with lines that spoke of both hardship and joy. His eyes were a piercing blue, still sharp despite his years, and his silver hair flowed freely over his shoulders like a waterfall caught in moonlight.

He carried with him a staff carved from yew wood, topped with a small crystal that caught the fading sunlight and scattered it into tiny rainbows. As he took his place at the center of the stage, he tapped the staff lightly against the wooden floor, the sound resonating through the square and drawing the last of the murmurs to silence.

"Good evening, friends and neighbors," Vil'elm began, his voice rich and sonorous, carrying easily to the farthest reaches of the crowd. "Tonight, I bring you a tale of old—a story woven through the fabric of our history, a tapestry of courage and caution."

Razma leaned forward, his attention fully captured. He had always loved Vil'elm's stories, the way the old man could transport listeners to distant times and places with just the power of his words. But tonight, he sensed that this story would be different.

"This is the story of King Halazor and Queen Lyrieth," Vil'elm announced, his gaze sweeping over the assembled faces. "A tale from a century past, yet its echoes reach us even now."

A hush fell over the crowd, and Razma sensed a ripple of discomfort among the listeners. He noticed that a group of well-dressed nobles shifted uneasily, their expressions guarded. It was rare for stories involving magic to be told openly, especially given the fear that surrounded such topics.

"In those days," Vil'elm continued, "King Halazor ruled over Tantora—a kingdom vast and prosperous, its people thriving under the sun's benevolent gaze. Yet beneath the surface, a deep-seated fear gripped the hearts of the people—a fear of magic and those who wielded it."

At the mention of magic, Razma saw the younger boy clutch the candies a little tighter, his eyes widening with apprehension. The very word seemed to cast a shadow over the crowd, eliciting nervous glances and quiet whispers.

"The Slividhe," Vil'elm said, his tone reverent yet cautious, "were an ancient race, beings of magic and mystery. They lived apart from us, their ways steeped in traditions we did not understand. To many, they were figures of fear—misunderstood and mistrusted."

A noblewoman whispered sharply to her companion, her fan fluttering nervously. "Why is he speaking of them? It's dangerous to even mention their kind."

"King Halazor," Vil'elm went on, "was a man of great ambition. He sought to unite the kingdom, believing that only through understanding could the fear that plagued his people be dispelled. To that end, he arranged to wed Queen Lyrieth, a Slividhein outcast."

82

Murmurs spread through the crowd, a mix of shock and disapproval. "Foolishness," an elderly man muttered. "You can't trust those who dabble in sorcery."

"Lyrieth," Vil'elm continued, "was different from others of her kind. She believed that magic could be a bridge rather than a barrier. She sought to share her knowledge, to teach humans the ways of the Slividhe in hopes of fostering peace."

A few gasps sounded from the audience. Razma noticed the blacksmith crossing himself, a gesture of protection against dark forces.

"But the people," Vil'elm said, his voice tinged with sorrow, "were not ready to embrace such change. Fear took root, spreading like a poison. Whispers of dark magic and ill intentions turned admiration into suspicion, and suspicion into hatred."

Razma felt a chill run down his spine. He could see the tension in the faces around him, the way parents pulled their children closer.

"Lyrieth and Halazor were blessed with twins," Vil'elm said softly. "But what should have been a joyous occasion became a catalyst for further fear. The birth of children with Slividhein blood ignited rumors—tales of enchantments and curses, of powers that could not be controlled."

"They're abominations," a nobleman hissed under his breath. "Magic like that should be stamped out."

"Overwhelmed by paranoia," Vil'elm continued, "King Halazor succumbed to the fears of his people. He began to question Lyrieth's intentions, to doubt the safety of his own kingdom. Consumed by fear, he plotted to separate the twins, to hide any trace of magic from the realm."

The crowd was utterly silent now, the weight of the story pressing upon them. Razma saw the younger boy wipe away a tear, his small shoulders trembling.

"Lyrieth, realizing the danger, acted to protect her children," Vil'elm said. "She hid one twin among the Slividhe, hoping that in time, acceptance might grow. But her actions only fueled the people's fear. They saw her as a traitor, a sorceress who had ensnared their king."

"She should have been executed," the noblewoman whispered harshly. "Magic users can't be trusted."

"Tragically," Vil'elm said, his eyes reflecting a deep sadness, "the fear and hatred culminated in violence. Lyrieth was cast out, and King Halazor, tormented by regret, withdrew from the public eye. The kingdom fell into a state of distrust, the fear of magic tearing communities apart."

A heavy silence hung in the air. Razma felt a profound sadness, a realization of how fear could destroy lives and fracture societies.

"To this day," Vil'elm concluded, "the legacy of that time lingers. The fear of magic remains, a shadow over our hearts. But perhaps, by remembering these stories, we can begin to understand that fear only holds power if we allow it."

Before Vil'elm could continue, a stern-looking man dressed in official garb stepped onto the platform, his boots thudding heavily against the wood. He whispered urgently into the storyteller's ear, his expression leaving no room for argument.

Vil'elm's face tightened, a flash of frustration crossing his features. He turned back to the crowd. "It appears that my tale must end here tonight," he announced, his voice laced with resignation. "But remember this story, and consider what it teaches us about fear and understanding."

A murmur of disappointment and relief rippled through the audience. Some seemed glad the story was cut short, while others looked troubled, their thoughts visibly churning.

As Vil'elm was led away, Razma noticed several nobles whispering among themselves, their faces tight with disapproval. "This is unacceptable," one hissed. "Such tales incite unrest and undermine our traditions."

"Agreed," another replied. "We must ensure that these dangerous ideas are not spread further."

Razma felt a surge of indignation. Why were they so eager to silence stories that could promote understanding? He looked around and saw the younger boy slipping away, disappearing into the shadows as if he had never been there at all.

"Razma!" a familiar voice called out. He turned to see Dalmon hurrying toward him, his face etched with urgency. Dalmon was a tall, lanky man with sandy hair and eyes that always seemed to be calculating.

"Dalmon," Razma greeted him. "Did you hear the story?"

"No time for that," Dalmon said, glancing around nervously. "I need you to get a message to Belazar. Tell him that my sister has arrived, and... I have the book."

"The book?" Razma repeated, confusion creasing his brow. "Is everything all right?"

Dalmon grabbed Razma's shoulder, his grip surprisingly strong. "Just tell him, Razma. It's important. And make sure no one follows you."

"What's going on?" Razma pressed, concern growing.

Dalmon shook his head. "I can't explain now. Just go. Quickly."

Razma nodded, sensing the gravity of the situation. He watched as Dalmon pulled a length of cloth over something strapped to his back—a glimpse of polished wood and metal hinted at a staff or perhaps a weapon. Without another word, Dalmon disappeared into the thinning crowd.

Feeling a knot of anxiety forming in his stomach, Razma headed toward the stables where Cleo, his faithful mare, was waiting. The streets were quieter now, the lively chatter replaced by the distant chirping of crickets and the soft rustle of leaves. But there was an undercurrent of tension, as if unseen eyes were watching from the shadows.

As he saddled Cleo, Razma's mind raced. What was so urgent that Dalmon couldn't speak openly? And what was this book that seemed so important?

Mounting the horse, he urged her into a steady trot, the familiar path home unfolding before them. The moon cast a silvery light over the fields, illuminating the way but also casting eerie shadows that seemed to dance at the edges of his vision.

"Something's not right," he muttered to himself. The events of the day—the story, the nobles' reactions, Dalmon's urgency—all swirled together in his mind.

Upon reaching the small cottage he called home, Razma dismounted and patted Cleo's neck. "Good girl," he whispered, leading her to the modest stable beside the house. "I'll bring you some oats in a bit."

He approached the front door, noticing that a single candle burned in the window—a sign that Belazar was still awake. Pushing the door open, he stepped inside to find his father seated at the table, a map spread out before him and a quill in hand.

"You're back later than usual," Belazar remarked without looking up.

"Sorry," Razma replied, closing the door behind him. "I stayed to listen to Old Man Vil'elm's story."

Belazar's hand paused mid-note. "Vil'elm," he repeated, a hint of tension in his voice. "And what tales is he spinning these days?"

"One about King Halazor and Queen Lyrieth," Razma said carefully. "It was... unsettling. He spoke of magic and how fear led to tragedy."

Belazar's eyes flickered with concern. "Did he now?"

"Yes, but he was stopped before he could finish. Some official cut him off."

Belazar sighed deeply. "These are dangerous times, Razma. Speaking openly about magic is unwise."

Razma hesitated before asking, "Why do people fear magic so much? Is it really that dangerous?"

Belazar looked up, his gaze meeting Razma's. "Magic is a tool, like any other. It is the intent behind it that determines its nature. But fear... fear can twist perceptions. People fear what they do not understand."

"Do you fear magic?" Razma asked quietly.

Belazar was silent for a moment. "I fear the lengths to which people will go when driven by fear. Magic itself is not to blame, but the actions it may provoke in others."

Razma nodded, absorbing his father's words. "I ran into Dalmon. He said to tell you that his sister has arrived, and he has the book."

Belazar's expression tightened. "He told you this?"

"Yes. He seemed... anxious."

Belazar stood abruptly, his chair scraping against the wooden floor. "Razma, I need you to stay inside tonight. Lock the doors and windows. Do not open them for anyone unless it's me or Dalmon. Do you understand?"

"What's happening?" Razma asked, worry creeping into his voice.

"Just a precaution," Belazar said, forcing a reassuring tone. "There's been talk of unrest. It's best to be safe."

Razma hesitated, sensing that his father was withholding something. "Is there anything I can do to help?"

Belazar shook his head, offering a faint smile. "No, son. You've had a long day. Best you get some rest."

Reluctantly, Razma nodded. "Alright. Goodnight, Father."

"Goodnight, Razma," Belazar replied, his gaze lingering on his son for a moment longer than usual.

Razma made his way to his small bedroom, the familiar surroundings offering little comfort against the unease gnawing at him. He changed into his nightclothes and slid under the worn quilt, but sleep did not come easily. His mind buzzed with questions—the strange urgency in Dalmon's message, the unsettling tale told by Vil'elm, and his father's cryptic behavior.

He lay awake, staring at the ceiling, listening to the creaks and sighs of the old house settling into the night. The moonlight filtered through the thin curtains, casting pale patterns across the floor.

Some time later, just as he felt himself drifting off, a soft sound caught his attention—the quiet opening of a door. Razma held his breath, straining to listen. Footsteps padded lightly across the main room, followed by the faint creak of the front door closing gently.

Curiosity and concern propelled him out of bed. Moving silently, he crept to his window and peered out into the night. In the dim glow of the moon, he could just make out his father's figure heading down the path away from the house, a cloak wrapped tightly around him.

"Where could he be going at this hour?" Razma whispered to himself.

He considered calling out, but something held him back—a sense that whatever his father was involved in, it was not meant for him to know. Yet the secrecy only fueled his unease.

Returning to his bed, Razma lay awake for what felt like hours, his mind racing with possibilities. Was his father in danger? Did it have to do with the book Dalmon mentioned? And why all the secrecy?

Eventually, exhaustion overcame him, and he drifted into a restless sleep filled with fragmented dreams—of shadowy figures, whispered warnings, and a pair of eyes that glowed like emeralds in the dark.

Chapter 9: Shadows Of War

764, 18th Day Of The Tenth Moon

"My father knows I go to see her. He hasn't spoken of it, but I can see it in his eyes—disgust, simmering beneath the surface. Yet I care not. If he fears her people so much, maybe he is the one unfit to rule. His vision is limited, shackled by old ways and blind to the possibilities that lie ahead.

Perhaps it is time for a new era, one where fear does not dictate policy, where strength and wisdom from all sides are embraced. When I am king, I will usher in that rule, and his small-minded legacy will fade with him."

The grand chamber of Seragora's council hall was a place that breathed history, its very stones whispering tales of kings, betrayals, and uneasy alliances forged and broken. The vaulted ceiling arched high above, supported by massive, carved pillars that were as old as the city itself, adorned with reliefs of past rulers and legendary battles. The air carried the mingled scent of old parchment, polished wood, and the faint tang of burning candles that flickered in iron sconces mounted along the walls. The chamber's centerpiece, an elongated oak table, was a testament to the kingdom's craftsmanship, its surface polished smooth and dark as the night.

King Tor'valis stood at the head of the table, a silhouette of command and resolve. The shifting light from the stained-glass windows painted his features in shades of deep crimson and gold, casting him as both a monarch and a warrior weighed down by the crown. Silver strands wove through his dark hair—a reminder of the years spent holding Seragora together through storms of war and fragile peaces. His storm-gray eyes scanned the room, the silence deepening with each heartbeat as the lords and ladies settled into their seats.

Lady Kira, her emerald gown flowing like liquid silk, moved with an air of composed elegance. The jeweled embroidery along her bodice sparkled in the candlelight, and her auburn curls framed a face that could disarm and challenge with equal ease. Her hazel eyes, keen and ever watchful, glinted as she cast a sly, appraising smile around the room, a silent acknowledgment of the power plays always at work.

Lord Cedric dropped into his seat with a deliberate huff, the sound a brief disruption in the taut quiet. His dark hair, perfectly combed, emphasized the harsh lines of his face and the perpetual scowl that rarely left it. Cedric was known for his sharp mind and sharper tongue, attributes that both served and hindered him in court. He crossed his arms, his eyes narrowing at the king with an expression that spoke of skepticism more than loyalty.

Lord Alric, the seasoned warrior with a reputation for loyalty and strength, offered the king a respectful nod before seating himself. The light caught on his broad shoulders and the small scar tracing his left temple, a relic from battles fought in defense of the realm. His piercing blue eyes, clear and unyielding, reflected his unwavering allegiance to the crown.

Lady Seraphina moved with a serene grace that belied her sharp intellect. In her late forties, she was a figure of quiet authority, a mediator in moments of heated debate. Her raven-black hair, streaked with silver, was pinned back to emphasize her high cheekbones and deep green eyes. She wore a gown of deep violet, its simplicity underlining her role as the voice of reason. She exchanged a glance with Lord Martan, a subtle communication shared between those who had weathered many councils together.

Lord Martan, the elder statesman of the council, leaned lightly on his intricately carved cane. The years had etched deep lines into his face, mapping a lifetime of battles, diplomacy, and the wisdom that came with both. His neatly trimmed white beard framed a mouth often set in contemplation, and his eyes, though shadowed by age, gleamed with the fire of a mind still sharp and observant. He inclined his head to Seraphina as they shared the unspoken understanding of what was at stake.

Tor'valis cleared his throat, a deep sound that silenced the last of the murmurs. The room seemed to hold its breath as he began. "Esteemed council members," he said, his voice resonant and unwavering, "our villages are under relentless attack, and refugees pour into Seragora seeking refuge. We have a duty to these people—a duty that extends beyond our borders. Bazel may well become a necessary ally."

Lady Kira's eyes sharpened, her fingers drumming lightly on the table's polished surface. "An alliance with Bazel?" she echoed, her voice smooth but laced with doubt. "Your Majesty, after all they've done... The people haven't forgotten. Vil'elm's story has revived old wounds. Many still remember Halzor's betrayal two centuries ago, and the scars of the Thorin War are far from healed."

The light shifted as a cloud passed over the sun, casting the room into a brief shadow. Tor'valis nodded, acknowledging her concern. "Yes, Halzor's betrayal lies deep in our history, and the Thorin War is not so far behind us. But this peace is young, and we cannot let old grudges cloud our judgment. If Bazel faces the same threat, we may need their strength as much as they need ours. Now is the time to bridge gaps, not widen them."

Lord Cedric leaned forward, his expression as rigid as the armor he preferred to wear outside these chambers. "I watched that boy Ky'len spar," he said, his voice low and accusatory. "He fights with an intensity born of anger. I saw him grow reckless, nearly striking a fatal blow in his training. It's that same fury that concerns me about Bazel. The boy reflects their volatile nature."

A ripple of unease traveled through the room, the rustle of fabric and shifting postures betraying the tension. Before Tor'valis could respond, Lord Alric's calm, measured voice cut through the silence. "Yes, Ky'len did show anger," he agreed, "but he also showed restraint. I observed him closely—he had a chance to deliver a killing blow, yet he chose not to take it. That speaks of control and potential for growth."

Cedric's eyes narrowed further, his scowl deepening. "Restraint? I heard he nearly killed Belazar's son, and if not for some bystander's intervention, he would have done just that. Does that sound like the restraint we need?"

"Your temper is nothing to gawk at either, Cedric," came Lord Martan's gravelly voice, tinged with the weight of memory. His eyes, bright with recollection, settled on the younger lord. "I remember you as a boy—you were quite the angry one. We all have our youthful indiscretions."

A few scattered chuckles rippled through the room, breaking the tension like a pebble in a pond. Cedric's face flushed, and a flicker of embarrassment crossed his features before he clamped down on it.

Lady Seraphina's voice, gentle yet firm, followed. "We cannot judge an entire people based on the actions of one youth. Prejudice will only blind us to opportunities for peace."

Cedric opened his mouth as if to argue but closed it again, jaw set in silent defiance. The chamber fell quiet once more, the flickering light casting long, shifting shadows on the walls.

Tor'valis stepped forward, his voice deepening with conviction. "We cannot afford to squander an opportunity for peace because of old rivalries. The people of Seragora need hope, not more bloodshed over ancient feuds. We are fighting a new enemy, one that threatens all of us— Bazel included."

He straightened, and the weight of his authority settled over the room like an iron mantle. "I am asking each of you to open your keeps and your coffers to support the refugees. They need shelter, food, protection. This is not merely a question of charity but of survival. If we allow fear and suspicion to divide us, we invite ruin."

The king's gaze lingered on Cedric, who finally dropped his eyes, the defiance in them dimmed under the king's steady stare. A long moment passed, thick with unspoken challenges and reluctant acceptance. Cedric gave a curt nod, breaking the silence.

"Tomorrow," Tor'valis continued, his tone softening but no less commanding, "is not only a celebration but a commitment—to our people, to peace, and to this kingdom's future. The attacks we face are a threat to every man, woman, and child in Seragora, regardless of bloodlines or grudges. If Bazel faces the same enemy, they should be treated as allies, not adversaries."

Lady Kira sighed, a delicate sound that conveyed her guarded acceptance. "Your Majesty, I will do what I can to assist, but we must tread carefully. Public opinion is a delicate matter."

"Agreed," Lady Seraphina added, a touch of steel in her voice. "But we can influence public sentiment through our actions. Compassion and strength can sway hearts and minds."

Lord Martan tapped his cane lightly on the floor, the sound punctuating his words. "Perhaps we can organize a council of envoys to engage with Bazel diplomatically. Show the people we are taking calculated steps."

Tor'valis allowed a faint smile to break through the gravity of his expression. "An excellent suggestion, Martan. Your experience in diplomacy will be invaluable."

Martan inclined his head, a look of satisfaction in his eyes. "I am at your service, Your Majesty."

The final murmurs of agreement echoed as the lords and ladies began to rise, the scrape of chair legs on the marble floor breaking the silence. Tor'valis watched them go, the mix of relief and lingering concern etched into his features. The sunlight had begun to wane, and the warm, rich hues of dusk flooded the chamber, casting long shadows and deepening the silence that followed.

Lady Seraphina lingered, her expression softening as she stepped closer to the king. "Your Majesty, if I may," she said gently. "A public address could help ease the people's fears. Hearing directly from you could inspire the unity we need."

Tor'valis considered her suggestion, a thoughtful frown pulling at his mouth. "You may be right, Seraphina. Transparency could bridge the gap between the throne and the people. I'll prepare a speech for the festival."

She placed a hand over her heart, her smile warm and genuine. "I am glad to assist in any way I can."

"Your counsel is always appreciated," Tor'valis replied, a hint of gratitude in his tone.

Just then, the clack of boots heralded the approach of Lord Alric. "Your Majesty," he said, bowing slightly. "I'll coordinate the relief efforts for the refugees. My men are prepared to distribute supplies and provide security where needed."

Tor'valis reached out, clasping Alric's shoulder. "Thank you, Alric. Your dedication does you credit."

As Seraphina and Alric turned to leave, the echo of their footsteps mingled with the distant murmur of palace staff going about their duties. Cedric and Kira lingered outside the chamber, their whispers barely audible beneath the high ceilings.

"He's blind to the risks," Cedric muttered. "Trusting Bazel is a dangerous gamble."

Kira's eyes gleamed as she tilted her head. "Perhaps. But those who adapt survive. We should position ourselves wisely."

Cedric cast her a sidelong glance. "What are you suggesting?"

She smiled, the curve of her lips sharp and secretive. "Only that we keep our options open. Influence can be as powerful as any sword."

Cedric nodded slowly, the seeds of an idea taking root as they disappeared down the corridor.

The chamber, now empty, seemed to exhale, the tension lingering like a ghost. Tor'valis stood alone at the head of the table, staring out the arched windows where the sky blushed with the first stars of evening pondering the past. The city below, with its narrow lanes and crowded market squares, looked serene from this distance. Yet he knew that within the heart of Seragora, uncertainty stirred.

Sixteen years earlier, the citadel of Seragora was steeped in the cool silence of an early spring morning. Tor'valis, then thirty-four years old, stood in the antechamber of the royal hall, feeling the weight of the world settle on his shoulders like an iron cloak. The banners hanging along the walls still bore the frayed edges of war, their once-vivid colors dulled by dust and grief. The recent conflict, known as the Thorin War, had scarred not only the land but the hearts of those who called it home.

Tor'valis's dark hair was untouched by silver back then, and his storm-gray eyes, though always sharp, were filled with a restless energy. He wore a tunic of deep blue with silver embroidery at the cuffs, the royal crest emblazoned over his heart. This day marked the beginning of his reign —a day that he had not expected to come so soon. His father's rule had been marked by strength and decisiveness, traits Tor'valis admired and, in his private moments, doubted he could emulate.

Footsteps echoed down the corridor, and soon Lord Martan appeared in the doorway, his presence as solid and reliable as the stone walls that surrounded them. At forty-four, Martan's once-dark hair had begun to turn silver at the temples, and his face was lined with the stories of battles fought and alliances forged. Yet, there was an unwavering vitality in his keen blue eyes that spoke of experience and a mind that missed nothing.

"Tor'valis," Martan said, his voice deep and steady, carrying both familiarity and formality. "The council is waiting. Are you prepared?"

Tor'valis met Martan's eyes, his jaw clenched tight with a mixture of nerves and determination. "I thought I would have more time," he admitted, his voice low but clear. "I always imagined my father's shadow would guide me longer."

Martan's expression softened, though he remained as composed as ever. He stepped further into the room, the worn leather of his boots brushing against the stone floor. "Few are granted the time they wish for. You, like many before, must find strength in the unexpected. Your father's rule was his own; yours will be different. That difference is not a weakness, Tor'valis— it's what will define you."

Tor'valis turned to the tall windows, their glass panes cool against his fingertips. Below, the city stirred as merchants set up their wares and townsfolk moved with the tentative hope that came after the end of a long, brutal war. He watched them, feeling the responsibility of their lives press on him.

"Martan, tell me," he said, turning back to his mentor, "do you believe they will trust me, follow me, after everything?"

A small, knowing smile touched Martan's lips. "Trust isn't built in a day or a speech. It's carved out of every decision, every moment of doubt where you choose to stand firm for them. You earned respect during the war not because of your name, but because you led when the odds were against us."

A memory flashed in Tor'valis's mind of a storm-lashed night on the front lines, when he and Martan had stood together, swords drawn, their breaths mingled with rain and the shouts of battle. Martan had been there, always steady, always watching. That same unwavering gaze was on him now, a reminder that he was not alone.

Tor'valis drew in a deep breath, the tightness in his chest loosening just a fraction. "I will try."

Martan's smile widened, the crinkles at the corners of his eyes deepening. "You will do more than try. And when doubt returns—and it will—you know where to find me."

A horn sounded from the great hall beyond, a signal that the gathered nobles awaited their new king. Tor'valis squared his shoulders, the echo of his father's lessons blending with Martan's words to form a quiet resolve within him.

"Then let us begin," he said, stepping toward the heavy wooden doors.

Martan followed, his cane tapping rhythmically on the stone floor. As the doors swung open and the light from the grand hall spilled into the room, Tor'valis knew that this was the moment he would begin to carve out his own legacy, shaped by war, guided by wisdom, and carried forward by the unwavering trust of those who believed in him.

Back in the present, the memory faded like the dying embers of a fire, leaving King Tor'valis standing alone in the council chamber. The echoes of that day mingled with the whispers of the current council's voices that had just departed. He turned to the window, watching as the last of the day's light bathed the city in a golden glow, knowing that the weight he had carried since that day had only grown more complex.

The door behind him creaked open, and the familiar sound of soft footsteps filled the room. Raelle entered, her presence as warm and steadying as ever.

Tor'valis turned, the lines of worry in his face easing at the sight of her. For the first time that day, he allowed himself a moment of respite in her presence, knowing that whatever trials lay ahead, he would not face them alone.

He exhaled slowly. "The council is divided. Even with Martan and Seraphina's support, the path ahead is fraught with uncertainty. They cling to the past, unable to see the necessity of unity."

She placed a reassuring hand on his arm. "You carry a heavy burden, but you don't have to bear it alone. Perhaps it's time to remind them—and the people—that strength lies in solidarity."

He considered her words. "A festival is planned, but perhaps more can be done."

Raelle's eyes sparkled with inspiration. "What if during the festival, we honor not just the nobility but the common folk as well? Show that we value every citizen of Seragora. It might bridge the divide and foster a sense of collective identity."

A small smile touched his lips. "An excellent idea. Celebrating our shared heritage could reignite the unity we so desperately need."

She returned his smile. "And perhaps, in that spirit, the council will find common ground."

Tor'valis's tension eased slightly. "You always know how to find light in the shadows."

"Because I believe in you," she replied softly. "And in the goodness of our people."

They stood together, watching as the first stars began to emerge in the twilight sky. The kingdom stood on the brink of a new chapter, and the actions of a few would determine whether Seragora would fall into darkness or rise united against the coming storm.

In the days that followed, preparations were made. Alric organized aid for the refugees, Martan began diplomatic overtures with Bazel, and Seraphina assisted in planning the festival that would celebrate unity and hope.

But beneath the surface, currents of dissent swirled. Cedric and Kira continued their whispered conversations in shadowed alcoves, their true intentions veiled but potentially perilous.

As the kingdom moved forward, the choices made by its leaders would shape the destiny of Seragora and all who called it home.

Chapter 10: The Tournament Of Kings

771, 21st Day Of The Fourth Moon

"I miss my son, the absence of his laughter echoing through these days, yet the moments I spend with my girls are ever so lovely. This evening, as the sun set in a warm embrace over the meadow, my wife, our daughter, and I strolled through fields of wildflowers. Our little one danced among the blooms, her laughter mingling with the soft rustling of petals, her presence bringing a gentle warmth to the world around us. From a distance, Mira scrutinizes quietly, ever the dutiful shadow, reminding her ladyship and me to keep our manners in check."

Razma blinked awake to the dim light of dawn spilling through the small window above his bed. His head still foggy from sleep, he stretched and rubbed his eyes, feeling the warmth of the morning sun creeping in. The room was quiet, save for the soft rustling of the wind outside. He rolled over, reaching for his shirt draped over the chair, when something caught his eye—a folded piece of parchment resting on the edge of the table.

He sat up quickly, grabbing the note and recognizing the rough, familiar handwriting. His heart thumped in his chest as he opened it.

Hey, son,

I didn't want to wake you. I've gone into town.

I know I told you not to fight, but I entered you in the tournament, knowing you'd go ahead and do it anyway. Dalmon is waiting at the arena to help you get ready.

Be careful, and good luck. I'll be in late tonight.

– Dad

Razma stared at the note, his hands tightening around the paper. A surge of excitement coursed through him, followed by a wave of confusion. His father had always told him to avoid conflict, to stay away from fighting. Why now? Why the sudden change?

His thoughts flickered back to a memory from when he was younger. A man had come to their smithy, unhappy with the price of a horseshoe. Razma had watched, wide-eyed, as the man shoved Belazar hard, demanding a discount. But his father hadn't gotten angry. He hadn't pushed back or even raised his voice. He had simply smiled, given the man a discount, and gone about his work. Belazar had always been the calm one, the diplomat, the man who avoided confrontation at all costs.

So why was he letting Razma fight now?

Razma couldn't shake the question, but at the same time, the thrill of the tournament called to him. He hurriedly dressed, pulling on his tunic and boots before grabbing his belt. The tournament. His chance to prove himself—not just to the knights and nobles, but to Ky'len. The memory of Ky'len's sneering face still burned in his mind. Today, things would be different. Today, he'd show them all that he wasn't just a stable boy.

As Razma rushed out the door, the early morning breeze greeted him, cool and crisp against his skin. The streets of Seragora were already buzzing with activity, villagers preparing for the day's events. Bright banners and flags bearing the colors of both Seragora and Bazel fluttered in the wind, the anticipation of the tournament hanging thick in the air. The cobblestones beneath his feet felt more alive than ever as he made his way to the arena, each step bringing him closer to his destiny.

When Razma reached the outskirts of the tournament grounds, his nerves buzzed with anticipation. Dalmon stood waiting by the entrance, arms crossed, a knowing smile playing on his lips. Razma hurried toward him, his heart racing, a mix of excitement and uncertainty swirling inside him.

"Morning, lad," Dalmon greeted, clapping Razma on the shoulder. "Got your father's note, I assume?"

Razma nodded, swallowing the lump of nerves in his throat. "Yeah… I didn't expect this. He's always telling me to avoid fights, and now he's entered me in the tournament?"

Dalmon chuckled softly, shaking his head. "Ah, your father… there's more to him than meets the eye. He knows you, Razma. Figured you'd be down here fighting anyway, so why not give you a chance to do it properly?"

Razma managed a small smile, but the confusion lingered. "It's just… it's so unlike him. I've never seen him stand up to anyone. I remember once, when a man shoved him over the price of a horseshoe, and he just smiled and gave him a discount."

Dalmon's eyes gleamed with something unspoken. He leaned in, lowering his voice. "Your father's a complicated man, lad. There are parts of his past even you don't know about. I've got my own secrets, too, you know."

Razma looked at him, startled by the hint of mystery. "Secrets?"

Dalmon chuckled again, this time with a bit more weight to his voice. "Let's just say there's more to us than what you've seen so far."

Razma's curiosity burned, but before he could ask more, Dalmon stood tall, patting him on the back. "Now, enough talk. Let's get you registered. You've got a long day ahead."

As they made their way to the registration tent, Razma's nerves simmered beneath the surface. The clang of swords and the smell of leather and dust filled the air, the tournament grounds alive with the buzz of preparation. Knights, squires, and their entourages milled about, the vibrant banners of both Seragora and Bazel flapping in the wind above the arena.

But as they approached the table where the officials were seated, Razma's excitement dimmed. The registration officer, a burly knight with a permanent scowl etched into his features, barely glanced at him before shaking his head dismissively.

"No peasants," the knight said bluntly, not bothering to look up from his parchment. "The tournament's for knights and nobles."

Razma's heart sank. He hadn't expected to be welcomed with open arms, but the outright dismissal stung deeply. He was about to turn away when Dalmon stepped forward, his usual easygoing demeanor hardening into something more forceful.

"You'll let the boy fight," Dalmon said, his voice carrying a sharp authority.

The knight behind the table frowned, finally looking up. "And who are you to—"

"Dalmon," Dalmon interrupted, his voice calm but firm. "Owner of the largest supply house in Seragora. And this boy"—he placed a firm hand on Razma's shoulder—"is Belazar's son."

The knight's eyes flickered with recognition at the name, though he tried to mask his surprise. "Belazar's son or not, this is no place for peasants. The nobles don't take kindly to commoners in their tournaments."

Dalmon leaned in slightly, his gaze unwavering. "If you want to explain to Belazar why his son was turned away, be my guest. But I think you'd rather avoid that conversation. Besides, the boy's earned a chance. He's no troublemaker."

Razma blinked in surprise. He hadn't realized his father's name held any significance here, but the weight behind Dalmon's words suggested something far deeper.

The knight hesitated, glancing between Dalmon and the growing line behind them. After a long pause, he sighed and scribbled something on the parchment in front of him. "Fine. He's in," he muttered. "But don't expect any special treatment. If the nobles take issue with him, that's not my problem."

Dalmon grinned, clapping Razma on the back as they stepped away from the table. "You're in. Now, let's get you ready."

Razma's pulse quickened again, the reality of what lay ahead sinking in. He was officially part of the tournament, but now he faced a much bigger challenge—fighting in front of nobles who wouldn't hesitate to look down on him.

"Thank you," Razma murmured as they walked toward the preparation area. He hadn't expected Dalmon to stand up for him like that, and a wave of gratitude washed over him.

Dalmon glanced at him with a grin. "Don't thank me yet, lad. You've got a fight ahead of you, and these nobles won't make it easy. They don't like seeing someone like you in their ranks—so you'll have to show them why you belong here."

As they neared the preparation area, the sights and sounds of knights polishing armor, adjusting shields, and sparring filled the air. Razma stood tall even with the weight of there gaze, a few of the younger squires eyeing him with thinly veiled disdain. Unlike them, he wore no gleaming armor, just simple leather gear. But as much as it made him feel out of place, he held his head high.

"Don't let them rattle you," Dalmon whispered, handing Razma a wooden practice staff to warm up. "They may have the fancy gear, but it's your skill that matters in the ring."

Razma nodded, gripping the staff tightly as he tested its weight in his hands. His mind was spinning, caught between the thrill of the upcoming fight and the pressure of representing himself—and Seragora—against nobles from Bazel and beyond. He spotted Ky'len across the field, surrounded by his entourage. The sight of the smug Bazel royal sent a surge of determination through him.

As Razma practiced, the arena continued to fill with spectators. The air buzzed with excitement, the tension between the two kingdoms hanging thick like the heat of the afternoon sun. The tournament was about more than just sport—it was a stage for pride, politics, and rivalry. And Razma was about to step into the middle of it.

When his name was finally called, a hush fell over the crowd. He could feel their eyes on him as he entered the ring, standing opposite his opponent—a Seragoran knight with a gleaming breastplate and a sword that caught the light. Razma's heart pounded, but he refused to show fear. He gripped his staff tighter, his hands sweating.

The duel began with a clash of weapons, the sound of wood meeting steel echoing across the arena. Razma's movements were precise, his training with Dalmon serving him well. But the fight was far from easy. His opponent moved with the practiced ease of someone who had trained their whole life, and Razma found himself pushed to his limits, blocking strike after strike.

But then, with a quick feint and a swing, Razma saw an opening. He struck, his staff landing a solid blow to his opponent's shoulder, sending the knight stumbling backward. The crowd gasped.

Razma didn't wait. He pressed his advantage, moving with speed and precision. His strikes were sharp, and before long, his opponent was on the ground, disarmed.

A stunned silence fell over the arena.

Dalmon's voice echoed in his mind. *Show them why you belong.*

As Razma stood there, breathing heavily, he glanced toward the nobles in the stands. Some were watching with narrowed eyes, clearly displeased. But others… others looked impressed, nodding at him as if recognizing something they hadn't expected to see in a peasant.

He had done it. He had proved he belonged. But as he looked out over the crowd, he knew this was just the beginning.

As Razma exited the ring, his pulse still racing, he found a spot in the shade near the edge of the arena where Dalmon was waiting for him. Dalmon gave him a nod of approval, his eyes gleaming with pride.

"Not bad for your first match, lad," Dalmon said, clapping Razma on the back. "You kept your head, stayed focused. That's how you win fights."

Razma grinned, the adrenaline still humming in his veins. "I just kept thinking about what you said—prove I belong."

Dalmon chuckled. "Well, you certainly did that. Now, take a breather and watch a few of these other matches. There's still a long day ahead."

Razma settled down on the rough stone bench, the heat of the day pressing down on him as he tried to steady his breathing. He wiped the sweat from his brow and turned his attention to the arena, where the next match was about to begin. Knights in gleaming armor, squires at their sides, and the fluttering banners of the noble houses created a dazzling spectacle. Beneath the glittering surface, however, Razma could feel the tension—Seragora and Bazel, their rivalry woven as tightly into the tournament as the swords and lances.

The next round started with a clash of steel, a Seragoran knight facing one of Bazel's elite. The sharp, rhythmic echoes of their strikes rang out across the arena. The Seragoran knight held his own, but Razma noted the calculated brutality in the Bazel knight's movements—a stark reminder of the tension simmering between the two kingdoms. When the Seragoran knight's shield finally splintered under the relentless assault, sending him sprawling to the ground, the Bazel supporters erupted into cheers.

Razma winced at the shift in the crowd. The Seragorans muttered darkly, while Bazel's contingent shouted with triumph. The animosity grew thicker with each match.

Then, Ky'len's name was called.

Razma sat up straighter, eyes narrowing as the Bazel royal strode confidently into the ring. Ky'len moved with deliberate poise, his gleaming armor catching the sunlight and displaying the sigil of Bazel prominently. He carried himself with the assurance of someone who already knew the outcome.

"Uh-oh, here comes the Bazel bulldog!" Jeff's voice cut through the din, drawing a mix of chuckles and exasperated looks.

Ky'len's opponent, a Seragoran knight named Harrick, entered with a fierce focus. Razma had seen Harrick fight before and knew him to be skilled and disciplined. Yet, as the match commenced, it became clear that Ky'len wasn't just there to win—he was there to dominate.

The arena filled with the metallic symphony of blades, Ky'len's strikes precise and unrelenting. Harrick fought hard, but each time he adjusted, Ky'len was already a step ahead. Unease spread among the Seragoran spectators as the Bazel knight struck with calculated ferocity.

Ky'len delivered a blow that shattered Harrick's shield, sending him stumbling. The crowd held its breath as Ky'len raised his sword, the tip hovering menacingly close to Harrick's throat. The silence was deafening.

"Come on, show us some flair! Even my grandma's got more spark!" Jeff's call broke through the tension, eliciting nervous laughter and annoyed glances.

Ky'len's eyes gleamed with dark satisfaction, but he lowered his blade slowly, a smirk playing at his lips. The Bazel supporters erupted into cheers while the Seragorans exchanged worried looks. Razma clenched his fists. This wasn't just competition—it was humiliation, a display of Bazel's power over Seragora.

Match after match continued, but Razma's mind lingered on Ky'len's unsettling performance. The noble watched the other knights with casual arrogance, as if the rest of the tournament were a mere formality.

The announcer's voice boomed across the arena: "Ky'len of Bazel versus Sir Tomas of Seragora."

Razma's attention snapped back. Sir Tomas, a seasoned veteran of the Thorrin War, stepped forward. His name alone commanded respect. The crowd buzzed with anticipation.

Ky'len watched Tomas approach, his expression unreadable, but Razma saw a shift in his posture. This was a fight Ky'len intended to take seriously.

The match commenced, and Tomas moved with measured confidence, deflecting Ky'len's blows with ease. Unlike the brutal clashes before, this match was a dance of skill and experience. Ky'len pressed harder, frustration evident in the tightening of his jaw.

With a sudden flurry, Ky'len disarmed Tomas, his sword hovering inches from the older knight's throat once more. The crowd froze, breath held. Tomas met Ky'len's eyes with calm defiance, a silent acknowledgment of defeat.

"Come on, Tomas! Give him a wink and throw him off!" Jeff's voice rang out, half playful, half hopeful, prompting scattered chuckles.

Ky'len lowered his sword, stepping back with a smirk. The Bazel supporters roared their approval while the Seragoran spectators exchanged anxious glances. The tournament was no longer just a contest; it was becoming a statement.

Razma leaned toward Dalmon, voice low. "He's not just fighting to win, is he?"

Dalmon's gaze was grave. "No. Ky'len's sending a message. And if we're not careful, this tournament might just spark a fire between Seragora and Bazel."

Razma's eyes flickered back to Ky'len, who stood at the edge of the arena, basking in the cheers. The tension between the two kingdoms was no longer just brewing—it was about to erupt.

As the announcer called Razma's name for the next match, a wave of nerves tightened his chest. His opponent was Cyril of Bazel, a knight whose reputation preceded him. Cyril stepped forward, exuding confidence. His lighter armor and fluid movements were designed for speed.

Razma met Dalmon's steady gaze and received a small nod of encouragement. "Stay focused, lad. You've got this."

The clash began, Cyril's strikes swift and precise. Razma parried and blocked, each blow rattling up his arms. Cyril circled like a predator, exploiting every weakness.

"Don't drop that stick, Razma! It's not a mop!" Jeff's voice cut through the tension, drawing both laughter and irritated glances.

Razma kept moving, eyes locked on Cyril's rhythm. Amid the chaos, he found a pattern in the knight's attack: two high strikes, one low, then a feint. He gritted his teeth, waiting for the moment to counter.

Cyril lunged, blade slicing toward Razma's side. Razma spun away and, with a surge of energy, swept Cyril's legs out from under him. The crowd gasped as Cyril hit the ground.

"About time! Show him what you're made of, lad!" Jeff called, this time with an edge of pride.

Razma didn't hesitate. He stepped forward, aiming a decisive blow to Cyril's chest. The Bazel knight scrambled, but Razma's strike knocked Cyril's sword away, leaving him defenseless.

The Seragoran crowd erupted into cheers, their voices lifting Razma's spirits. For a moment, the arena felt like it was his.

"Razma of Seragora is victorious!" the announcer proclaimed as Cyril glared up at him, breathless and defeated.

"Keep your chin up, Seragora! That knight just needed a nap!" Jeff hollered, half-sarcastic and half-encouraging.

Razma caught Dalmon's approving nod, but the shadow of Ky'len's gaze from across the arena reminded him that his victory came with consequences.

Dalmon's smile faded slightly. "Ky'len's watching you now. Be ready."

Razma's pulse quickened. The tournament was shifting from sport to a test of resolve—and the real fight had just begun.

The semi-final match between Razma and Ky'len arrived, the air thick with anticipation. Ky'len's eyes glinted with something darker, a sharp contrast to his earlier arrogance.

"Last time, someone saved you," Ky'len said, voice low and threatening. "This time, no one's coming."

"Uh-oh, here comes the drama!" Jeff muttered just loud enough for nearby spectators, drawing smiles and nods.

Ky'len charged, and Razma's world narrowed to the clash of steel. The relentless strikes forced Razma to the edge of the arena, each blow a test of endurance. Pain shot through his ribs, the sharp memory of their previous encounter echoing in every move.

Razma's mind raced, searching for any opening. A glimmer of hope appeared when he noticed a hesitation in Ky'len's attack. Summoning his last reserves, Razma dodged and struck, catching Ky'len on the arm and buying himself precious seconds.

The crowd's cheers swelled, blending with the pounding of Razma's heart.

"Lucky shot, stable boy," Ky'len spat, eyes blazing. He lunged again, and this time, his sword hit Razma's staff with such force that it flew from Razma's hands. He stumbled back, defenseless, as Ky'len loomed over him.

"It's over," Ky'len said, voice cold.

But hesitation flickered in his eyes. The blade trembled as he realized just how far he had gone. With a snarl, he raised his sword again, but the crowd erupted in protest as the referee stepped in.

"Ky'len of Bazel is victorious!" came the declaration.

The cheers and boos mixed, but Razma lay on the ground, relief and defeat swirling within him. Ky'len's victory felt hollow, the unease clear in his retreating figure.

The final match between Ky'len and Aelric began under a cloud of anticipation. Aelric's calm confidence was a stark contrast to Ky'len's simmering frustration. Every move Ky'len made lacked the precision he was known for, the weight of his earlier actions dragging him down.

Aelric's control never wavered, exploiting Ky'len's weaknesses until a final, flawless move disarmed the Bazel knight. The crowd roared as Aelric stood victorious.

The cheers and boos merged, but Ky'len, now without his sword and dignity, stormed from the ring. Razma watched him go, understanding that this defeat was not just of steel but of spirit. The conflict between Bazel and Seragora was far from over, and the tournament had merely set the stage for what was to come.

Chapter Interlude: 1

Lord Darth swept into the Crimson Fang Guildhall, his cloak whipping the air with a snap that made even the torches sputter. Silence gripped the stone chamber as mercenary officers—

veterans who'd braved countless raids—stood rigid in the face of his icy rage. Darth had long honed cruelty and cunning into a lethal art, but tonight there was something more, an undercurrent of personal affront that charged the air with dread.

At the far end of the hall, six Crimson Fang captains hovered near a raised dais, knuckles whitening around sheets of parchment detailing the latest disaster: Muckspawn ambushes on Bazel's caravans, even those guarded by the Crimson Fang. Darth ascended the dais in a swirl of fabric and fury.

He paused at the top step, letting his gaze roam over them. Not a single throat cleared; not one dared speak. There was no doubt that Lord Darth would take this incursion as a personal insult. A hush as thick as storm clouds settled before he finally spoke.

"Tell me how it happened," he demanded, voice slicing through the stillness. "And spare no details."

A senior captain—his scar-laced face betraying more alarm than he might wish—stepped forward. "My lord," he began, glancing at the parchment in his trembling grasp. "Two dozen of our best accompanied the caravan. At dusk, the Muckspawn closed in: coyote-based, savage, organized. They tore through our lines in minutes." He swallowed. "Only three survived."

Darth's lip curled. "My soldiers, trained by the Crimson Fang, undone by swamp vermin? They dare believe we'll accept such losses?"

Another officer mustered the nerve to add, "The survivors said they fought bravely, my lord, but these coyote-kin vanish like ghosts, coordinate their attacks, and strike whenever they find the slightest crack in our defense. We… didn't stand a chance."

Darth's eyes glinted with a mix of cold fury and shrewd calculation. He had built his power by turning threats to profit, and he'd never let something as trivial as a savage foe stand in his way. He let the officers squirm under his glare a heartbeat longer before speaking again.

"They think they've humiliated the Crimson Fang?" He let out a humorless snort. "Fools. We'll show them what humiliation truly looks like." His voice dropped, laced with lethal calm. "But first, we control the story. Spread word that our men died after slaughtering a horde of Muckspawn. Let no one imagine it was an easy kill. No one laughs at my Fang warriors."

The captains nodded hastily, scrawling his words onto spare parchment. Darth's lip twitched into something resembling satisfaction—he refused to let rumors paint his men as easy prey, or to see the Crimson Fang mocked in taverns across Bazel.

Turning to the massive map unrolled on a central stone table, he stabbed a gloved finger at the swamplands. "Next, we force the council to meet our terms. If they want caravans protected from these coyote-fiends, the cost doubles. Immediately. If they balk, we pull every Fang blade from their routes and let them fend off the Muckspawn alone. Then they'll come crawling back, paying triple instead."

A restless stir rippled among the officers, a few exchanging quick glances. One took a shaky breath. "My lord, if the council refuses altogether, they might try cheaper mercenaries—"

"Let them." Darth sneered, flicking his eyes across the gathered men. "No other guild in Bazel is half as skilled as the Crimson Fang. If these Muckspawn are truly formidable, lesser sellswords will be torn to scraps. By then, the council will beg us to return—and we'll set any price we please."

Half the captains exhaled relief; the others wore grim smirks. Lord Darth was nothing if not consistent: cruel but unfailingly cunning. They had seen him exploit many a crisis, wringing gold and power from every shred of fear.

He shifted his stance, cloak brushing the table's edge. "But that's not all. I won't tolerate our men being picked off like novices. I want a squad to locate their lair—there must be a leader orchestrating these strikes. If necessary, we cut a deal. These Muckspawn can ravage Sergora or any rival region, and we'll do nothing to stop them. If they won't negotiate, we drown them in steel." His voice softened to a deadly purr. "Coin and cunning are the blades we wield. Steel is merely the final argument."

A short silence followed. Then one officer murmured, "Yes, my lord. We'll dispatch trackers at once. And the rumor about our men's valor—"

Darth's face hardened. "Yes. Speak of how valiantly they fought. Let Bazel believe the fallen took thrice their number of Muckspawn with them. The rest of you—off with you. We have an assault to plan, and new fees to collect."

They bowed, quickly dispersing to carry out his dictates. The flicker of torchlight played over the anxious lines in their faces as they hurried away.

Alone, Darth gazed at the scrawled reports left on the table, brow furrowing. For a moment, his anger receded, replaced by something like thoughtfulness. He reached out and tapped one parchment that listed caravans due to pass near Sergora. Sergora—where his grown son had gone, hoping to claim his own slice of victory or reputation. Or so Darth had let him believe, anyway.

"I hope my son can seize some glory in Sergora," he said to the empty hall, voice laced with wry cynicism. "Or at least the contingency plan I set in motion will secure my foothold there." He snorted quietly, half a sneer at the notion of paternal pride. Yet in his own hardened way, he did hope the boy would bring victory, or prove beneficial. Or he'd become another pawn, furthering his father's ambitions in that distant city.

With a snap of his cloak, he turned from the table and strode out of the guildhall's grand doors. Two guards saluted, but he waved them off with a flick of his hand. He left the antechamber behind, stepping into a deserted corridor lit by only a couple of wavering torches. The gloom stretched ahead, quiet except for the faint drip of water seeping through old stone.

There, beneath a small breach in the ceiling where moonlight filtered in, Darth paused. Casting a glance to ensure solitude, he lifted his right hand. An ornate ring glinted on his finger—engraved with runes said to be Slivdhe in origin. A relic he rarely revealed, believing it might open channels to forces outside mortal politics.

He spoke two words under his breath: "Ther'val suren." *I have a task for you.* The ring answered with a faint glow, pale lines of power dancing over the stones. Darth's thin smile returned. Whether employing black-market deals or forging alliances with savage bog creatures, he always sought an upper hand. If Sergora and Bazel thought him content to let petty hostilities hamper his empire, they'd soon learn differently.

The ring's glow ebbed, leaving shadows to reclaim the corridor. Darth closed his eyes for a moment, exhaling a tension he wouldn't show around his captains. He could nearly taste vengeance and profit in the air, and both set his heart pounding with anticipation. Muckspawn, council negotiations, rumors of heroic last stands—he would weave each into a tapestry that served him alone.

"No one kills my Crimson Fang and walks away unpunished," he muttered, voice low. "We'll see who ends up on top when the blood and gold are counted."

He stepped into the fortress courtyard, boots echoing on damp flagstones. The night loomed overhead, a swirl of cloud covering most of the moon. A faint hush clung to every corner, as though the wind itself feared to disturb his determined stride. A few mercenaries noticed him crossing the yard, catching the tight-lipped severity on his face, and quickly turned their attention to anything else.

Lord Darth slowed at the gates, glancing skyward. In the far distance, the faint call of coyote-like howls drifted over the wetlands. The sound triggered a fresh spike of anger—and, oddly, a grim kind of excitement. He thrived on turning enemies into assets or corpses, and he never minded shedding blood for the right payoff.

And if, by some chance, these cunning Muckspawn refused to bend?

His gaze fell on a watchtower torch sputtering in a gust of wind. He pictured the cunning raids, the slashed throats, the stolen wagons. No, there would be no forgiveness. Only a lesson taught with savage clarity. The rumor campaign would ensure the fallen Fang mercs died heroes, bolstering morale and fear alike. Meanwhile, the trackers would sniff out the Muckspawn stronghold. Cruel as it was, that was how he'd mold the world to his advantage.

A final flick of his cloak, and he resumed walking. "My son in Sergora must do his part," he thought aloud, tone dripping with the same mixture of indulgence and calculation he granted all his pawns. "Or my… contingency plan shall handle matters. So be it."

He vanished under the arches, cloak trailing like a dark banner. The shadows swallowed him whole, leaving behind only the echo of his boots on stone—and the unspoken promise that the Muckspawn, Sergora, and anyone else who stood in his path would learn the full, cruel wisdom of Lord Darth and his Crimson Fang soon enough.

✳✳✳

A hot midday sun cast sharp shadows across the dusty village road. Jeff, commonly known by the local children as "Franpa" (a playful mashup of *friend* and *grandpa*), leaned against the rickety gate to his herb patch. In one hand, a long-handled scythe rested on his shoulder, the other hand gesturing animatedly as he explained the difference between mint and wild nettles to a small cluster of wide-eyed kids.

"All I'm saying," he drawled, "is you can't trust just any green leaf to taste good in a stew, unless you want your tongue falling off. And I, for one, like my tongue right where—"

He broke off at the distant thud of raised voices. A few yards away, in an apple orchard near the edge of town, a Bazel soldier in scuffed armor was rifling through branches, stuffing apples into a half-full sack. Two other soldiers lounged nearby, arms folded with lazy arrogance.

A lanky boy, maybe fifteen, stood in front of them, anger etched into his features. "You can't just take them!" he insisted, voice cracking with the strain. "My father grew those—if you want apples, pay up!"

The soldier let out an exaggerated yawn, turning to bite into one of the red fruits. "We watch your father's caravans," he retorted around a mouthful of pulp. "He won't miss a few. Think of it as early payment."

The boy's cheeks reddened. "That—that's not how it works!"

One soldier snorted, and the biggest, scowling under a dirty helmet, flipped out a dagger. He pointed it at the kid's chest. "Don't like it? Complain to Lord Darth. Now clear off, or this orchard'll get a fresh coat of red."

Despite trembling, the boy stood his ground. "I'm not letting you steal—"

The soldier lashed out, slicing a shallow cut across the boy's forearm. The kid yelped, stumbling back clutching the wound. The soldier smirked, clearly relishing his small victory.

Jeff (or "Franpa" to the children who followed him) arrived in the orchard just as the tension peaked. He swung his scythe off his shoulder with an air of casual threat, stepping between the soldier and the bleeding boy.

"Now, now," he said, voice tinged with sunny mockery, "any reason you'd rather carve up a kid than carve up that apple?" His gaze flicked pointedly to the fruit in the soldier's sack. "Seems a little… cowardly, no?"

The soldier's narrow eyes zeroed in on Jeff. "Who the blazes asked you, old man?"

From behind Jeff, a couple of little kids piped up, "He's Franpa, and he knows everything about herbs!"

106

Jeff smirked, raising an eyebrow at the soldier. "You heard 'em. I'm Franpa—friend grandpa—take your pick. But what I really am is someone who hates seeing bullies swagger 'round, stealing what isn't theirs." He nodded at the dagger, still stained with the boy's blood. "And you're holding that blade all wrong, by the way."

The soldier's lip curled. "Shut it, old-timer, or I'll—"

"—Use that toy on me, too?" Jeff interrupted with a brusque wave of his hand, scythe shifting in his grip. "Go on, then. If you think you can handle a scythe-wielding herb man."

Flustered, the soldier lunged. But Jeff spun the scythe like a walking stick, hooking the soldier's wrist in a deft motion. The dagger clattered to the dirt. Before the soldier could recover, Jeff scooped it up, turned it expertly, and in the same breath, plucked an apple from the soldier's sack. With a single precise cut, he sliced off a crisp wedge and popped it in his mouth.

"Mmm," he said, smacking his lips. "Better for fruit than for flesh, wouldn't you say?"

The soldier's face darkened. The other two behind him looked uneasy—clearly not expecting a gray-haired gardener to disarm them. After a tense moment, the soldier snatched the dagger back from Jeff's outstretched hand, glowering.

"We'll be back," he snarled. "And we'll take what's ours without your meddling." His glare roamed to the boy, still pressing a hand over his bleeding arm.

Jeff lifted his scythe in a mock salute. "I'll keep some bandages ready for when you trip on your own bravado."

A sneer, a spit to the ground, and the soldier spun on his heel. The three of them stomped away, muttering curses about "nosy old men" and "fool brats."

Once they'd gone, the lanky boy sagged with relief, though shock still shone in his eyes. A few trickles of blood seeped from his forearm. A couple of younger children hovered by Jeff's side, wide-eyed. One tugged his sleeve. "Franpa, that was amazing!"

Jeff breathed a measured sigh. He turned to the kid, scanning the wound with a discerning eye. "C'mon, orchard hero, let's get that sorted. No sense letting you bleed out after all that trouble." He beckoned the group toward his herb patch.

In the late midday heat, the patch looked vibrant: rows of basil, rosemary, and tall, rustling mint. As the boy slumped onto a wooden stool near a small table, Jeff rummaged through a pouch, producing a tin of salve and a fresh cloth bandage.

"I knew they'd come for apples eventually," the boy muttered, wincing as Jeff rinsed the cut with a ladle of water. "But I couldn't just… let 'em do it. They watch Dad's caravans, sure, but that doesn't mean they can steal—"

"You did right standing up to them," Jeff said, voice firm but kind. "Those bullies rely on folks rolling over. But next time, maybe holler for Franpa first, yeah?" He shot the boy a crooked smile. "I've got a scythe and a wicked tongue; might keep you from losing an arm."

The boy managed a weak chuckle. "Didn't think… you were, you know, that good at…" He gestured vaguely, implying "taking on armed men."

Jeff applied salve with careful precision, ignoring the question's edge. "I'm old, not dead. Lord Darth's men have tried me once or twice, so I've picked up a trick or two." A flicker of shadows crossed his face at the mention of Darth, but he masked it with a shrug. "Anyway, arm up, kid, let me bandage you."

As he wrapped the cloth tightly, a younger child whispered, "Franpa, are you gonna chase those soldier jerks away with your scythe again?"

Jeff barked a short laugh. "If they're silly enough to come back? Sure." Then, rummaging in another pouch, he pulled out a cluster of dried leaves. "Here, orchard hero, chew a bit of this or mix it in water. Helps with pain, though it'll knock you out if you're not careful—makes you hungry as a starved wolf, too."

The boy eyed the leaves warily. "Um… okay, if you say so."

Jeff wagged a teasing finger. "No complaining when you wake at midnight, scouring the pantry for food. That's on you, not me."

The kids giggled, one of them chanting, "Franpa's magical munchies!"

Rolling his eyes, Jeff waved them off. "Yeah, yeah, laugh it up. Now, big fella,"—he addressed the orchard boy—"try not to get yourself slashed by any more incompetent cutthroats, okay? I like my orchard defenders in one piece."

The boy nodded, cheeks warming. "Thanks, Franpa… I—I appreciate it."

A faint gentleness lit Jeff's eyes. "Call it a discount orchard rescue plan. You owe me, oh, let's say two apples next harvest." He winked, grabbing his scythe and giving it a flourish. "Now scram before I think up extra chores for you and that scrawny arm."

The boy ambled off, pressing his new bandage and the herbal pouch close to his side. A soft murmur of appreciation trailed him, and a group of younger kids started up a raucous cheer for "Franpa." Jeff pretended to grumble, but his affection for them shone through, no matter how sarcastic his grin.

One of the kids tugged on his pant leg. "Franpa," she whispered. "What if that soldier comes back with more? Lord Darth's men are scary."

Jeff's mouth tightened, a flick of worry crossing his features. He patted the child's head. "They are, but you know what's scarier?" He touched the scythe's blade gently, letting the steel catch the sunlight. "An old friend grandpa who has no patience for bullies."

She giggled, reassured, while Jeff turned his gaze toward the orchard—toward the path the soldiers had taken. His usual snark crumbled for a moment, replaced by a hint of something more somber.

"The weather's changing," he muttered under his breath, so quietly only the breeze heard him. "Time for me to get started… yep, it'll be here soon."

Then, slipping on his well-worn straw hat, Jeff mustered his trademark grin, scythe balanced lightly on his shoulder, and ambled back to his herb beds, children flocking at his heels. He'd watch over them—and if the time came that more bullies arrived, well, he'd be ready with both barbed wit and a scythe's swing, friend grandpa or not.

Sunlight dripped through the canopy, washing the forest floor in patterns of emerald glass. Each golden-green beam felt like an invitation, calling Sialin deeper into Kynavar, the ancestral woodland of the Slivdhe. For a moment, it was easy to pretend she still belonged here—that no betrayals or rejections had steered her away.

She moved on silent feet, toes pressing the spongy moss so gently that not even a leaf stirred. Up ahead, the forest opened onto a small glade where two lithe figures with pale braids practiced advanced illusions, arcs of shimmering energy dancing at their fingertips. Their laughter rang out, bright and self-assured, enough to make the leaves tremble. Sialin's throat tightened at the sound; she remembered how easily that laughter had turned mocking when directed at her.

Her uncle stood close by, staff in hand, posture stern. His dark hair, streaked with age, framed sharp features that rarely softened. She watched him tap the staff lightly to adjust the blondes' stances, a teacher's pride in his eyes. He offered gentle corrections, the kind of praise Sialin had always craved. Something twisted in her chest—a dull ache of longing.

She forced her shoulders back, swallowing her nerves. She had skill too, maybe not as polished, but her magic could hold its own if he would just see it. So she edged closer, magic already stirring beneath her skin like a cresting wave. A faint luminescence seeped into the grass around her feet, turning it pale. Little motes of light flickered upward, dancing near her ankles like curious fireflies. *Look at me, Uncle,* she wanted to shout. *I can do this too—don't just ignore me.*

But he was intent on the pair with the pale braids—so-called stars of the Slivdhe future. When Sialin stepped within earshot, gathering the courage to speak, she caught him glancing her way —just for a heartbeat. Then his gaze flitted back to the twins' demonstration, as though she were an afterthought. Gathering her nerve, she cleared her throat.

"Uncle…" she began, voice uncertain.

He waved a hand, half-turning. "Not now, child," he snapped, eyes still locked on the illusions. "I have to get them trained. Can't you see I don't have time for your foolishness?"

The words struck like a slap. She felt them echo in her ribs, stealing her breath. Her swirling magic faltered, and the glowing motes around her feet dimmed. Her eyes burned with tears she refused to shed. Numbly, she nodded, though he'd already turned away, offering the blondes more tips about controlling the shape of their spells.

Sialin's stomach knotted, shame tightening her throat. She wanted to tell him she'd practiced a new technique, something more advanced than he'd expect. She wanted him to notice how far she'd come, to draw him away from those two who ridiculed her at every turn. Instead, he'd shut her down with a dismissive wave. She swallowed, tasting a bitterness that lodged behind her tongue.

She might've tried again—reached out, tapped his sleeve. But an old fear kept her silent. *He's never had time for me.* She stepped back, letting the glow fade from her ankles. The forest hushed around her, a silent witness to her heartbreak.

Then, something on her finger throbbed—a startling jolt that rippled up her arm. The world around her blurred, the glade and her uncle's harsh words fracturing into shadows. She gasped, staggering as Kynavar's warm light vanished in a disorienting rush.

She blinked. Torchlight replaced the forest glow, harsh and flickering against stone walls. Her ring, a plain band etched with faint runes, glowed insistently, as though summoning her from that memory. Heart pounding from the abrupt shift, she steadied herself against the corridor's rough-hewn wall.

"I have a task for you."

The voice—resonant, commanding—belonged to Lord Darth. Clanking armor and half-muttered curses filled the hall as mercenaries bustled past. The ring's vibration ebbed, leaving her with a sense of hollow longing at the back of her mind. Another rejection by her uncle… and now a new summons by a man who offered her something like approval, though it came in cold and cruel forms.

She forced a breath, letting the echo of Kynavar's heartbreak slip away. The only acceptance she had now was from Darth—and it was acceptance she had to earn. If she did well, he might toss her a nod of acknowledgment or a curt word of praise. It was better than nothing.

"Yes, my lord," she said, mustering a respectful tone.

He offered her a measured look, half-smirk and half-challenge. "I've heard good things about your scouting, Slivdhe. You'll keep impressing me, won't you?" The faintest curl of satisfaction touched his lips, only visible to someone desperate to see it.

Her chest lifted slightly with that scrap of affirmation. "I will." She nodded, letting her shoulders square. *I'll do what you want. Just watch me.*

A dry wind lashed the open plains, each gust stirring the tall grass into a restless tide. Sialin crouched behind a low rise, eyes flicking over the rolling terrain. She'd come to confirm rumors of Muckspawn—the coyote-based variety—prowling farther from their swamps than usual. If she succeeded, Lord Darth would be pleased, maybe even pat her on the shoulder or murmur "Well done" in that clipped way. She clung to that possibility like a lifeline, ignoring the old pang for her uncle's voice in a forest glade.

A rancid smell drifted by, twisting her stomach. It reeked of coyote but was shot through with a sour musk. She inhaled carefully, using Slivdhe-honed senses to locate the source. Somewhere beyond this grass, something inhuman lurked.

She summoned her light-based magic. A faint glow sparked in her veins; the grass around her feet dulled, color siphoned away. Her chest tightened with the cost, but if it granted her more speed, it was worth it. She pushed off, footsteps barely skimming the dirt. The world blurred around her—she soared in near-silence, eyes alert for movement.

A grating snarl shattered that hush. She whipped around, spotting short, scrawny silhouettes bounding through the grass. Each had patches of red-brown fur over greenish skin, no taller than her chest, but all glaring with cunning malice. A jolt of alarm flared in her ribs: these were no mere beasts. Her heart pounded, and she reminded herself—this is the proof Darth wants. She could practically feel his "Well done" in her ears if she survived.

A pair of them rushed her. She darted left, blade flashing, carving across a sinewy forearm. A shrill yelp rewarded her strike. Another coyote-kin hissed behind, snapping at her cloak. She twisted away, breath ragged. They were faster than expected, bounding on all fours with lethal agility.

One blindsided her, smashing into her ribs. She flew sideways, magic faltering as she landed. The moment her glow broke, the grass flushed back to green, color reclaiming the space. A gasp tore from her lungs. She scrambled to her feet, dagger in hand, scanning for a gap to escape. But the Muckspawn had formed a ring, each muzzle parted in a hungry snarl.

A wiry figure stepped forward—clearly the leader, his tufted fur bristling around an elongated muzzle. Sialin forced a brave front, though her limbs trembled. She raised her dagger in quivering hands.

"You… you've been attacking caravans." She managed the words between heaving breaths. "Those were Lord Darth's soldiers, right?"

He cocked his head, black eyes glinting with dark amusement. "All who cross these plains, by Master Mutt's command." A snapping bark turned into something that might be a laugh. "*We do not like prying.*"

She dared another spark of magic, but a flicker was all she got. The cost weighed heavy, and the coyote-kin sprang before she could gather enough to run. He swatted the dagger aside, the steel clattering uselessly in the grass. She lashed out with a kick, connecting with a smaller Muckspawn's flank. It squealed, but two more pinned her arms, claws raking her skin through the sleeves.

Her vision blurred with panic. *No no no, I have to get out of this… I have to bring Lord Darth the news…* But the ring of snarling coyote-faces closed in. She glimpsed the leader's twisted grin.

"Master said kill anyone who pries," he growled, muzzle inches from her cheek. Rotting breath made her choke.

"My… my lord," she gasped, mind spinning. "He'll—he'll pay you—"

"Gold?" The coyote-kin snorted, half-laugh, half-mocking. "We want something else."

Then came a flash of metal. She tried to twist away, but the pack pinned her limbs. A hot, biting sensation lanced across her throat. Warmth flooded down her chest in a horrifying rush. She coughed, breath sputtering, tasting blood on her tongue.

The coyote-kin howled, a shrill cry of triumph that rang in her ears. Her heart stammered, eyes wide, picturing a forest canopy that no longer wanted her, an uncle she still yearned to impress, a lord she'd hoped to please. *It's all… undone…*

Weakness devoured her. She felt the grass scratch at her back as she fell, staring up into the bright, uncaring sky. Blood pulsed out from the gash at her throat, spattering her clothes, the ground, the savage little Muckspawn who bristled overhead. She wanted to scream, to cling to life, but no air reached her lungs.

A final, ragged exhale rattled from her lips. *Uncle… Lord Darth… did either of you ever truly see me?* That question flashed in her mind, lost in a wave of numbness. The coyote-kin howled again.

Sialin's eyes slipped shut, the howls echoing in the emptiness. Her chest rose once, then fell, the fight draining away along with the brightness in her veins. The last color she noticed was the grass, returning to vibrant green, as though her magic had never been there at all.

Chapter 11: A Shadowed Victory

767, 24th Day Of The Seventh Moon

"Today, as we walked through the quiet glades, I felt the weight of our future—a life she now carries, a bond deep as roots. The whispers grow louder; the elders see her as a threat to tradition, a step beyond the boundaries they cling to. They fear what her people might bring, and their warnings remind me of my father's resentment—his loathing of anything unfamiliar, anything that challenges the old ways.

Yet, I am unwavering. She brings peace and purpose, a strength that holds steady against all doubts. Together, we will forge a new path. Still, in quiet moments, I wonder what might happen if her people turn against us, if old grudges resurface. But I cannot let those fears consume me. For our child, I hope for harmony; for us, resolve. Whatever lies ahead, we will face it side by side."

As the sun dipped below the horizon, casting a warm, fading light over the streets of Seragora, the sounds of celebration filled the air. Banners fluttered in the evening breeze, their deep reds and golds catching the last glimmers of daylight. The townsfolk gathered in the central square, their voices raised in cheer as they honored Aelric's hard-fought victory. Tables groaned under the weight of food and drink, the rich scent of roasted meat mingling with the heady sweetness of honeyed cakes and spiced wine. Musicians played lively tunes on fiddles and flutes, and children wove through the crowd with laughter that rang out like bells.

Aelric, the hero of the hour, stood tall, lifted high on the shoulders of his fellow knights. They shouted his name with admiration, their voices filled with pride. To them, he was more than a champion—he was a symbol of Seragora's resilience and strength in the face of Bazel's long shadow. Razma stood on the outskirts of the crowd, watching the revelry but feeling detached from it. The victory felt hollow, as if it were a veneer stretched thin over the simmering unease beneath.

Snatches of conversation drifted to his ears, whispers carrying a different kind of tension. "Did you see the way Ky'len fought? Like he wanted more than just a win," one man muttered, leaning against a lamppost, his eyes narrowed. His companion nodded, his face etched with concern. "There's something brewing with Bazel. Aelric's win will only fan the flames."

Razma glanced over at a group of knights from Bazel, standing apart from the celebration. Their expressions were unreadable, but the stiffness in their postures spoke volumes. He couldn't forget the way Ky'len had looked at him in the arena—like a storm barely restrained. The image sent a chill down his spine.

The festival around them continued, but there was a shift in the air. The laughter grew strained, the cheerfulness almost desperate. Scattered scuffles broke out among the crowd, quickly subdued but leaving behind an electric charge of tension. Razma could feel it, the way the jubilant atmosphere felt ready to snap. The crowd moved and shifted, like a restless sea, and beneath it, the unseen current grew stronger.

He was pulled from his thoughts by a firm hand on his shoulder. Turning, he saw Dalmon, his mentor and guide, standing beside him. Dalmon's expression was serious, a shadow of worry in his eyes despite the small smile he offered.

"You fought well today, lad," Dalmon said, his voice steady but subdued. "I know the win wasn't yours, but what you did out there—it means more than you think."

Razma nodded, though unease coiled in his chest like a living thing. "Thanks, Dalmon," he said, his eyes darting to the edges of the square, searching for something unseen. "But something doesn't feel right. It's like we're being watched, and not just by the people here."

Dalmon's gaze followed his, scanning the crowd with the practiced eye of a seasoned warrior. His jaw clenched as he caught sight of a group of Bazel knights muttering among themselves, their eyes darting toward Aelric with dark intent. "You're not wrong," he said, voice low and guarded. "This celebration is more than it seems. There's talk—whispers of what this victory means. Aelric's win is a point of pride, but it's also a warning shot. Bazel won't forget this day, and neither will their knights."

The older man's hand tightened on Razma's shoulder. "It's time for you to go home," he said, his voice taking on an edge of urgency. "You've done enough for today. If things turn, I don't want you caught in the crossfire."

Razma's eyes narrowed, confusion sparking alongside frustration. "But why now?" he pressed, the question dragging out the memories he tried to forget. He thought back to the day in the smithy when his father, Belazar, had been shoved by a customer over the price of shoeing a horse. His father had only smiled, his usual calm and gentle nature unyielding, even offering the man a discount. Razma had never understood that moment—why his father had refused to fight back.

Dalmon's expression softened, though there was something wary in his eyes. "Your father's a man of peace, Razma. But even he knows when it's time to let things run their course. Maybe he sees that in you now. Or maybe he's tired of keeping secrets," Dalmon said, his voice dropping to a near whisper. "I have secrets of my own, you know."

Razma felt the words settle heavy in his mind, opening doors he wasn't sure he wanted to peer behind. The questions piled up, but he knew this wasn't the time to ask. "I'll go," he said, finally tearing his gaze away from the square. "Thank you, Dalmon."

Dalmon's expression shifted, a glimmer of pride cutting through the worry. "Stay close to your father. Whatever comes next, you'll need each other."

As Razma turned to leave, weaving through the crowd, the sounds of celebration seemed to shift. The laughter and music morphed into a backdrop of nervous glances and whispered concerns. A man's voice rose above the din. "Mark my words—Bazel won't stand for this. We need to be ready." His words were met with nods, the shadow of unease spreading like smoke through the square.

He hadn't made it far before more voices reached him, this time calling his name.

"Razma!" A woman stepped forward from a cluster of townsfolk. It was Mara, the shopkeeper's wife, her cheeks flushed from the wine and excitement. She grabbed his hand, her eyes shining with pride. "You did good out there, lad. Had us all holding our breath, you did." She squeezed his hand, her warmth genuine. "You showed them Seragora's not just knights and lords. You showed them our spirit."

Her husband, a wiry man with a thin smile and a patched cap, nodded beside her. "Aye, lad. You fought like the best of 'em. Don't let anyone tell you otherwise."

Razma felt a blush rise to his cheeks, surprised by their praise. "Thank you, Mara. You too, sir. It means a lot," he said, dipping his head respectfully.

As he moved away, more villagers stepped forward, offering small nods, words of encouragement, or friendly claps on his back. Each gesture was like a spark, igniting a sense of belonging that Razma had long thought out of reach. Even if he hadn't claimed victory, his efforts had left a mark.

Then, from behind, a voice that carried the weight of both command and respect spoke his name. "Razma." He turned to see Sir Tomas standing there, his posture as strong and steady as ever. The older knight's expression was thoughtful, a glint of approval in his eyes.

"You fought well today, lad," Sir Tomas said, his tone deep and measured. "More than many would in your place, especially against one as relentless as Ky'len."

Razma swallowed, the memory of Ky'len's eyes, blazing with intent, making his chest tighten. "Thank you, Sir Tomas. I only tried to do what I could."

Sir Tomas's mouth quirked into a small smile. "Sometimes, that's all that's needed. Courage, resilience, and the strength to stand your ground—these are rare qualities. Your father should be proud, and so should you." The knight's eyes lingered on Razma for a moment, as if searching for something. "Keep that strength close. You'll need it."

Razma's heart swelled with the weight of the words, the approval of a seasoned knight more potent than he'd expected. "I will, Sir Tomas," he promised, his voice firm despite the turmoil within.

With a nod, Sir Tomas stepped back into the crowd, disappearing among the celebrants. For a moment, Razma stood there, feeling the mingled pride and unease twist within him. The crowd around him seemed brighter now, the faces more vivid, the shared pride palpable. Yet beneath it all, the tension hummed like a plucked string.

A light pat on his back brought him back to the present. Dalmon stood there, his eyes kind but shadowed with thought. "It's a fine thing, being recognized, but remember, lad," he said softly, "glory can be fleeting. The road ahead won't be smooth, but tonight—tonight, you've done enough."

Razma nodded, looking once more at the crowd. The townsfolk were still celebrating, their cheers for Aelric mingling with newfound respect for him. He allowed himself to feel it, to bask in the warm glow of belonging, just for a moment.

But as the festival carried on, the pockets of unrest became more apparent. A group of Seragoran soldiers cast wary glances at the Bazel knights gathered at the edge of the square. Words were exchanged, their voices rising just enough for Razma to catch snippets.

"We'll see who's boasting when it comes down to real battle," one Bazel knight spat, his hand hovering near the hilt of his sword. The Seragoran soldier across from him narrowed his eyes but said nothing, his jaw clenched in restraint.

Razma shifted, Dalmon's hand on his shoulder reminding him of the older man's earlier advice. He took a breath and turned toward the quieter streets that led home.

The noise of the celebration receded with every step, replaced by the soft chirping of crickets and the whisper of leaves stirred by a gentle breeze. The cobblestones of the main road gave way to the rougher path of the outskirts, where cottages sat nestled in the shadows of tall trees. Here, the night felt more profound, the quiet holding an edge that the noise of the festival had masked.

The words spoken that night played over in his mind—Dalmon's warning, Sir Tomas's encouragement, the townsfolk's praise, and the whispers of tension. And most of all, Ky'len's threat, seared into his memory like a scar. The way he had sneered, "Last time you were saved, this time we finish this," still echoed in his thoughts, heavy with intent.

A sudden movement caught Razma's attention. He glanced to the side, the hairs on the back of his neck prickling as he peered into the darkness between the trees. For a moment, he thought he saw a figure slip deeper into the woods, a shadow that could have been anything—or anyone.

He tightened his jaw, forcing himself to move on, even as the sense of being watched settled uncomfortably over him. The tension from the square hadn't been left behind; it followed him like a silent companion, lurking in the shadows.

Reaching the clearing where his home stood, Razma paused, casting a glance over his shoulder. The cottage's familiar silhouette, framed by the tall pines, should have felt like a haven. Tonight, it felt vulnerable, as though the dark secrets of the day had seeped into its very walls.

"Something's coming," he whispered to himself, the words tasting bitter in the cool night air. Today had been more than just a test of skill or a battle for pride—it had been the first move in a game much larger than he could see.

He stepped up to the door, the wood creaking as it opened. The warmth of the interior wrapped around him as he stepped inside, shutting out the chill of the night. But it didn't shut out the tension, the whispers of unease, or the shadows that seemed to cling just beyond the glow of the lantern.

He paused, glancing around. Shadows flickered on the edges of familiar surroundings, now cloaked in tension. The voices, still indistinct but rising, sent a chill down his spine. Though he couldn't understand the words, their tone was enough to make his pulse race.

He crept closer to the stable, each step feeling heavier, as if the ground itself sensed the impending storm. Then, cutting through the night, a sharp scream—a cry of fear—pierced the air. Razma broke into a run, fear urging him forward. He reached the stables and skidded to a halt, his eyes widening.

The stable doors hung askew, the wood splintered and blackened by unnatural flames. The fire seemed like a veil, casting eerie shadows over the figures within. His father stood in the center, sword drawn, fierce determination etched on his face. Razma's breath caught. He'd never known his father to wield a weapon—especially not one like the gleaming blade in his hand.

Beside Belazar stood a young girl with long, silver hair cascading around her pointed ears—Slivdhe. Her fear was evident, her gaze darting between Belazar and the dark figure facing them: an old woman cloaked in tattered red, her face obscured. Her voice cut through the air, a venomous hiss filled with malice.

"Lhúor en'thal! Ver'tir hin haenar, ara mara ni vrith'haenar!" the girl cried, her voice trembling with fear. *"We have to go! She's to strong!"*

Belazar's expression remained steely as he replied, his stance unyielding. "Mara ni vel, A'nara. Mara'thor hin vorn." *"I won't leave you, A'nara. Not to her."*

Razma's heart pounded, struggling to make sense of what he saw. This girl, A'nara, was clearly in danger, but who was she to his father? And why would Belazar risk everything for her? Questions buzzed in his mind, but all he could do was watch as the scene unfolded before him.

The old woman's mocking laugh cut through the tension like a knife, her voice dripping with contempt. "En vor veth hin. Ara vor eonar'tir, vel'tir hin—vorn'thal mara vor haenar." *"Return to the order, Belazar, and maybe, may they'll forgive you."*

Belazar's eyes flashed with anger. "Vor'tir ni en! Mara'tor vor ni mar." *"Never. You'll get to her over my dead body"*

The woman's voice twisted into a dangerous, taunting tone, dark energy gathering in her hands. "Dalmon mara ni or'tor haenar. Slivar Fang—vor ni en haenar, Half-blood." *"Dalmon can't save you now. Prepare to die, Half-blood."*

Razma could feel the air grow heavy, the very atmosphere pressing in on him. His chest tightened as if an invisible force was squeezing him, choking the life out of the air around him. His father's grip on the sword tightened, and he braced himself, preparing to defend A'nara at any cost.

The old woman's voice, dripping with contempt, taunted Belazar, her words sharp as blades. "Ther haenar'vor A'nara? Ver'tor ni ther en vorn vor'nir. Val'thor, en'thal, en ni." *"You think saving her will change anything? Seragora's fall is inevitable."*

Belazar's jaw clenched, but the woman continued, her words like poison. *"Aen'tor vor, en din eonar veth vor'tir men'tir haenar." "You will beg to return, Belazar, when you watch your friends die one by one."*

With a defiant growl, Belazar charged at her, his sword cutting through the air with deadly precision. The woman raised her hand, intercepting the blade with a wall of dark energy, and the clash sent shockwaves through the stable, forcing Razma back.

The woman sneered, her voice echoing in cruel amusement. "Din'thal veth Belazar? Din mara haenar ni'tir haenar vor'nir." *"Is this all the great Belazar has to offer? You were never worthy of your bloodline."*

With a flick of her wrist, she sent Belazar stumbling back, her dark energy coiling around him. He struggled against it, his sword glowing faintly as he fought to free himself. "Far'haenar vor ni en, Belazar. Din haenar faet mara haenar." *" You think this sword will save you? Fool, the Order will see to that."*

Razma's heart raced as he watched, a surge of fear and anger swelling within him. His father, bound by dark energy, looked up with fierce determination. With a roar, Belazar slashed through the magical bonds, shattering them like glass.

The woman's eyes darkened, her voice laced with cold fury. "Thor mara ni en haenar, Belazar. Fin'tor hin var vor." *"You are delaying the Inevitable. Your defiance means nothing."*

Her hands lifted, dark tendrils snapping toward Belazar with relentless fury. Belazar twisted, his sword cutting through the onslaught, each strike a blur of light against the darkness. But the tendrils kept coming, closing in around him, forcing him back.

"Din mara mara haenar, Belazar," she hissed, her voice filled with malevolence. "Ther haenar vor ser'han haenar—mara vor en din hanir." *"The Order will end you, Belazar. Your resistance is futile"*

Belazar gritted his teeth, his eyes blazing with determination. "Mara vor'tir haenar'tor. A'nara veth haenar." *"I will die before I let you take her!"*

The old woman laughed, sharp and cruel. "Ah, mara'voran, Belazar. Mara'thal, vor'ri halzor fin'thal mor'ael."*Ah, but you will, Belazar. But first, you will watch everything you hold dear burn to ash.* She raised her hand, sending a wave of darkness crashing toward him. Belazar's sword met the wave head-on, his blade flashing with a fierce, bright light that shattered the oncoming dark.

But she was relentless, summoning tendrils of shadows from all sides, each one snapping like a whip, closing in on him. Belazar met each one, his sword dancing in the air, but for every shadow he cut down, two more took its place. The darkness closed in on him, unyielding, inching him back step by step.

Razma watched, his heart hammering, desperate to help but held in place by some invisible force. The woman's voice echoed in the air, a cold and merciless tone. "Vor'ri sathen var. lenar'thal vor." *"Your time has come. I end this now."*

Just as the darkness seemed ready to consume him, a figure burst into the stable. A'nara raised her hands, her voice shaking as she shouted something Razma couldn't quite catch. A light began to shine around her, bright and warm, pushing back the darkness like the dawn.

The old woman's eyes widened, her face twisted in shock. "Ther or en haenar! Din Slivdhe en haenar mara haenar!" *"What is this? You Slivdhe and your paththic magic!"*

A'nara's voice quivered but held firm, her hands steady as the light expanded, forming a protective shield around her and Belazar. The woman snarled, her spell fizzling as it struck the barrier. In that moment, the tide seemed to shift, the oppressive darkness lifting, replaced by A'nara's light.

Belazar seized the opportunity, his sword burning with renewed energy. With a fierce cry, he charged forward, cutting through the last tendrils of darkness. His strikes landed with precision, each blow driving the woman further back.

The stable shook as light and dark clashed. The old woman hissed, retreating as Belazar advanced, his sword a blur of light. Her voice, sharp and venomous, filled the air, her anger turning to desperation. "Mor'tal! Vor'ri mara'sath en'thal vor'athar." *"Enough! Your struggle will end in ruin and death"*

Razma's chest tightened like a vice, his breath caught in his throat as he watched—helpless, frozen, drowning in the weight of the moment. His father fought with a ferocity he had never seen before, each strike an act of defiance, each movement laced with raw survival.

But the woman—the shadow-wreathed specter—did not falter. She did not tire.

She commanded the dark, and it obeyed.

Tendrils of blackness surged forward, coiling through the air like serpents, wrapping around Belazar's limbs and yanking him backward. He hit the ground hard, boots skidding against the dirt, his sword wrenched from his grasp as the shadows consumed him once more.

The woman stood over him, her silhouette merging with the swirling abyss at her feet, her presence a cold, suffocating weight.

Her voice dripped with triumph, thick with finality.

"En'tor vor haenar. Fin'tor en din!" *"Bound in thorns. There is no escape."*

The words slithered over Razma's skin like a curse. The shadows thickened, choking the very air, swallowing all light, closing in for the kill.

Then—

A sudden golden flare cut through the darkness, sharp and blinding.

A'nara.

Her shield burst with radiant energy, the impact sending a ripple of golden light outward. The tendrils recoiled violently, sizzling as if burned by the mere touch of her magic. The old woman snarled, momentarily blinded, her grip on the abyss faltering.

But she was not finished.

Not yet.

With a hiss of fury, she lifted her hands once more, her fingers curling like claws. The darkness snapped, convulsed, then rose again—stronger, wilder, spiraling around her in an uncontrollable storm.

The shadows did not just creep this time.

They devoured.

They rose like a tidal wave, thick and oppressive, curling inward, warping reality itself. The stable walls groaned beneath the weight of the unnatural force, wooden beams splitting, the air turning so thick it threatened to drown them all.

Razma gasped, feeling the pull of the void creeping toward him.

This was it.

She would consume them.

She would unmake them.

But then—

The earth rebelled.

A deep, guttural tremor rippled through the ground, not of human will, not of spellwork or control. Something older. Wilder. A force untouched by time.

The dirt split apart beneath them.

And from the gaping wound in the earth, the trees rose.

Not soft, not gentle. Towering. Rootless. Burning.

Massive blackened trunks erupted from the ground, twisting and gnarling, stretching toward the sky as if reaching for something unseen. Their branches cracked and split, birthing embers that drifted like dying stars. The wood groaned under some unseen force, as though alive—aware.

And then the fire took them.

The entire grove ignited.

The flames did not spread, did not consume anything beyond what had risen. The fire was the magic, a roaring, burning defiance that had no master, no allegiance. The inferno's glow bathed the battlefield in a sickly orange hue, its searing heat warring against the void's creeping chill.

The woman staggered, her dark magic flaring erratically as the unnatural trees closed in around her. Smoke curled through the air, thick and choking, swallowing all sound, all shape, all meaning.

The fire did not burn her.

It unmade her.

The shadows she had summoned screamed, a soundless wail that rattled Razma's very bones. The abyss convulsed, shrinking, retreating as the flames carved through it like a blade.

The trees shrank with it, their blackened limbs collapsing inward, twisting like dying creatures. The fire consumed everything, devouring all trace of what had just happened, leaving only cinders and ruin in its wake.

And then—

Silence.

The flames vanished in an instant, leaving behind nothing but ashen ghosts of what had been.

Not a single ember remained.

Not a single branch.

No proof.

Nothing.

Razma's body felt weightless, his vision swimming. The force of whatever had just happened crushed him under its enormity. The old woman was gone, her presence erased as if she had never been.

His father was alive, breathing, struggling to rise.

A'nara's shield had flickered, her golden light now dim, her body trembling.

But there was something else.

Something… watching.

Beyond the veil of lingering smoke, beyond the scorched earth where those trees had risen, something remained.

Not a presence.

Not a person.

But a force.

Unseen.

Waiting.

Razma's limbs felt heavy, his mind a blur as the last wisps of smoke coiled toward the sky.

Whatever had saved them…

Had done so for reasons unknown.

And as darkness took him, his last thought was not of victory—but of dread.

Who—or what—had answered?

Chapter 12: When The Gates Open

781, 17th Day Of The Eighth Moon

"My son returned just in time, for tomorrow, we ride to war. The marshfolk, once quiet and compliant, have risen in rebellion, brazenly questioning my right to rule. They claim I am unfit, that our authority should bow to theirs. But they shall be reminded who commands these lands. My son will ride at the head of our army, his strength a testament to our rule, and together, we will teach them to kneel. My wife and her kin urge caution, advising diplomacy. They warn against the path I've chosen, their voices laced with worry."

The narrow alleys of Seragora lay shrouded in shadow, a labyrinth of stone and whispered fears. Tala moved cautiously, keeping to the dark, her heavy cloak drawn tightly around her to conceal the telltale green of her skin. The towering walls on either side loomed cold and indifferent, amplifying the echo of each step and sharpening the edges of distant voices. Beside her, Yvonne walked with measured purpose, eyes sweeping their path. Though human and able to walk more freely, even she kept a guarded stance. The aftermath of the tournament had left the city simmering with unrest, with guards patrolling with an intensity that made every shadow feel like a threat. Their primary target: stirring up suspicion and finding a scapegoat in Bazel.

"Stay close, Tala," Yvonne whispered, her voice barely a breath. Tala's fingers tightened around the edges of her hood, pulling it lower to ensure no glimpse of green broke through. The muted conversations of townsfolk floated past, laced with anger and anxiety.

"The council does nothing!" The voice of an old man carried down from a cracked window, frustration ringing clear. "Refugees keep flooding in, and they sit there, talking instead of acting."

Tala clenched her jaw and met Yvonne's eyes. They exchanged a silent look before slipping down a narrower alley, where lantern light barely reached and darkness offered the cover Tala needed.

The damp air reeked of wet stone and rotting wood. Ahead, a small group of refugees huddled under a sagging awning, their blankets meager shields against the night's chill. Yvonne slowed, her posture softening as she approached. Tala held back, pressing herself deeper into the shadow, eyes watchful, every nerve taut. The homeless in Seragora were divided—some feared the Muckspawn, blaming them for the troubles from the marshes, while others, worn down by their own desperation, cared only for shelter and food.

"Good evening," Yvonne greeted, her voice calm and low. Hollow eyes lifted, wary and exhausted. An older man, thin and weathered, spoke first, voice rasping from deep in his chest.

"What do you want?" The words were brittle, born of fear and fatigue.

"Talk. We hear things, need to know," Tala said, her rough Common edged with her accent. She stayed within the shadows, barely a hint of her presence visible. Yvonne's eyes flickered toward her but returned to the refugees.

Recognition sparked in the old man's eyes before he shifted his gaze back to Yvonne. "We've seen enough. Guards from some noble come more often now, searching, finding reasons to drag people off. Some never come back." His eyes darkened with the mix of old and new fears.

Yvonne nodded, worry deepening the lines on her face. "We know. That's why we need to understand what's being whispered. What do you hear on the streets?"

A woman holding a child clutched him tighter, her voice thin and tense. "They talk of something from the marshes, something even the guards fear. They don't just search for Bazel spies anymore." Her eyes flicked to the alley's deeper shadows, as if expecting danger to spring from the dark.

Tala's heart hardened. *They fear us,* she thought. Her voice, carefully controlled, emerged from the dark. "Guards look for more. Not just men from Bazel. Yes?"

The old man's expression darkened. "Aye. They say the Muckspawn are stirring, seen slipping out of the marshes. Whispers of attacks, of things in the night. The council sits paralyzed, hands tied by fear."

Tala stayed silent, tension coiling tight in her chest. Before she could speak, a small voice, fragile and wavering, broke through. "Food?" A young girl, eyes wide and streaked with grime, peered out from behind the old man.

Tala's gaze softened. From the concealment of her cloak, she reached for a small bundle of bread taken from her rations and extended it into the dim light. The girl took it with reverent fingers, eyes glistening with gratitude. "Eat. Little strength needed," Tala whispered, her voice gentler than usual.

Yvonne's eyes warmed fleetingly, but she turned back to the old man. "What do you expect will happen next?"

His shoulders sagged, eyes drifting past them to the city's glow. "What always happens. When people are scared, they find someone to blame. Today it's spies; tomorrow, anyone different."

Tala's fingers flexed around the hidden dagger at her waist. "We leave now," she said, her voice low, shadow-wrapped. "Not safe here."

The echo of heavy footsteps cut through the night. Torchlight flared, slicing through the gloom and forcing Tala to shrink further into the dark as a group of guards emerged. Their faces were sharp, eyes cold and searching.

"Who's here?" one barked, his voice taut with authority.

"Just travelers, taking rest," Yvonne said, confidence steady in her tone.

The guard's gaze fell on Tala's shadowed form, suspicion glinting in the torchlight. "And that one?" he demanded, raising the torch higher.

Tala took a breath, careful to keep her voice steady. "Just... passing. No trouble."

The guard lingered, eyes narrowing, but with a grunt, he turned away. "See that it stays that way," he warned. His torch swept over the huddled refugees, casting fleeting warmth before the guards moved on, the alley falling back into shadow.

Yvonne exhaled, tension unwinding from her shoulders. "We need to move," she said, voice low.

Tala glanced at the refugees, their faces etched with worry. Some looked at her with fear, others with a hollow indifference born of desperation. "Hard for them," she murmured. "Too many fears."

Yvonne's gaze softened. "They're trapped in battles they'll never understand."

They moved deeper into Seragora's web of alleys, the night pressing close with its damp chill and the scent of rain in the air. Every corner felt like a watching eye, every sound an approaching threat. The voices of townsfolk, strained and accusatory, filtered through cracked shutters.

"Another attack last night—figures in cloaks, fleeing the guards."

"The Muckspawn will bring ruin. Should've pushed them back to the marshes when we had the chance."

Tala's jaw clenched, muscles coiling tight as Yvonne's hand found her arm—a silent reminder to stay calm. With a measured breath, Tala released the tension, though the anger still sat like a stone in her chest.

Suddenly, an old man's eyes lit with sudden recognition as he focused on Tala. His voice cracked as he shouted, "Guards! Guards, come quick!"

Panic surged through the group, a wave of movement and whispers. Tala's pulse quickened, and Yvonne's eyes scanned for an escape. They turned to run, the shouts growing louder, mingling with the distant thud of approaching boots.

"Here!" A small voice beckoned urgently from the shadows. A child, dirt-smudged and wide-eyed, gestured frantically from behind a broken crate. Without hesitation, Tala and Yvonne slipped into the narrow gap, pressing their bodies against the damp stone wall as the sounds of guards filled the alley.

Tala's breath came in shallow bursts, her heart pounding as the torchlight swept over the gathering. The guards' voices were harsh, demanding.

"Where are they?" one barked, eyes scanning the frightened refugees.

"They were here!" The old man's voice wavered now, uncertain as he glanced around the fire.

The child who had hidden them pressed a small finger to his lips, eyes bright with urgency. Tala nodded, gratitude swelling in her chest even as fear clutched at her. Yvonne's hand found Tala's, a silent reminder of their shared resolve.

The guards moved on after a tense moment, their footsteps echoing into the distance. The alley fell back into shadow, the fire's glow wavering as if exhaling a breath held too long.

Tala looked at the child, his thin face determined despite the fear. "Thank you," she whispered, her voice low and raw. The boy nodded, eyes wide as he darted back to his family.

Yvonne exhaled, the tension easing from her shoulders. "We need to move. Now."

Tala cast one last glance at the fire, at the uncertain faces that had almost given them away. But in the eyes of the child, she saw a glimmer of something that bolstered her—hope, fragile and fleeting. With a final nod, they slipped away into the night, the rain cloaking their escape in a shroud of whispered promises and renewed determination.

As they moved away from the flickering glow of the fire and deeper into the maze of alleys, the rain intensified, drumming against stone and cobblestone in an erratic rhythm. Water streamed down from the rooftops in steady rivulets, soaking their cloaks and making the ground slick beneath their boots. Each step felt uncertain, the city around them shivering under the night's relentless chill.

Tala's sharp eyes searched every corner, every dark doorway, her senses attuned to the smallest movement. The tension from their narrow escape coiled tight in her muscles, ready to spring. Yvonne walked beside her, eyes narrowed, brows knit with focused determination. They were alone for now, the shouts of guards lost in the distance, but that could change at any moment.

"We can't keep this up," Yvonne muttered, her voice barely audible over the rain. "We need a safe place to regroup and plan."

Tala nodded, breath misting in the cold air. "Where?" she whispered, her accent thickening with exhaustion. She knew the city's dangers, how quickly a hiding spot could turn into a trap if discovered. The rain was both a blessing and a curse—masking their presence but numbing their limbs.

Yvonne's eyes darted to the left, where a narrow passage led to the deeper, older parts of Seragora. "There," she said, gesturing. "An abandoned warehouse by the canal. No one goes there; it's too close to the water, and the stone is cracked and unstable. But it'll hide us for now."

They slipped into the narrow passage, the walls pressing in on either side, wet and slick with moss. The passageway opened into a wider lane, where the sound of water lapping against stone mingled with the rain. The canal glistened in the moonlight, its surface dappled with droplets, reflecting the pale glow of lanterns strung farther down the street.

Tala paused, ears pricking at a distant sound—voices, low and urgent. She motioned for Yvonne to stop, holding up a hand. The voices drew closer, accompanied by the clink of armor. Guards on patrol. The two women exchanged a quick glance, eyes full of silent understanding. Without a word, they pressed themselves against the rough stone wall, the chill seeping into their bones.

The guards' footsteps grew louder, echoing down the empty lane. Snatches of conversation reached them through the hiss of rain.

"Some say they're holed up with the refugees, hiding among them," one guard said, voice gruff. "Others think they've slipped back to the marshes."

"They won't get far," another replied, steel in his tone. "Orders from above are clear: stir up the hate. Let the city blame Bazel for its troubles."

The guards passed, their torches casting shifting, fleeting light that played across Yvonne's tense features and Tala's shadowed form. They stayed motionless until the glow faded into the rain-drenched dark.

Yvonne exhaled slowly, her shoulders dropping a fraction. "The council's watchtower," she whispered. "They're tightening their grip, feeding fear."

Tala's eyes narrowed, rain dripping from her hood. "Spies... Muckspawn... all the same to them," she muttered, anger simmering beneath the surface. "They will not stop until someone bleeds."

"We need to find allies," Yvonne said, her voice more determined. "People who see beyond fear, beyond the lines the council draws."

Tala's gaze turned toward the canal, where the water moved like ink under the moon's pale touch. "Yes. But trust is scarce here. We walk thin lines."

Yvonne nodded. "Then we start with those who have the most to lose—the ones already cast aside." Her eyes met Tala's, a flicker of resolve passing between them. "If they know there's hope, even a fragile one, they'll follow."

The warehouse loomed ahead—half-collapsed and long forgotten—its sagging stone walls leaning like old bones too tired to hold themselves upright. Tala and Yvonne slipped inside, ducking beneath the splintered frame. The space greeted them with the cold symphony of dripping water and the distant, lonesome cry of seabirds echoing off the docks.

It smelled of mildew and old wood, soaked in time and secrets, but it was dry enough. And for now, it was safe.

Tala exhaled slowly, her breath clouding faintly in the chill. Her bare feet moved soundlessly across the warped floor as she made her way to a broken window. Rain slid in lazy rivers down the cracked glass, distorting the outside world like a dream coming undone.

Lights flickered in distant towers. Lanterns swayed gently in the wind. The streets below were restless—people moving with hunched shoulders, glancing over them like shadows might leap from the corners. There was tension here, thick and waiting.

Tala tilted her head and whispered, voice soft and uncertain. "This city... she breathe heavy. But no sound. Like... waiting. Waiting for break."

Yvonne settled beside her, the weight of the night sinking into her limbs. She lowered herself with a soft sigh, resting her back against the wall.

"Then we'll be there when it does," she said, voice quiet but unyielding. "And we'll make sure it's not the innocent who pay the price."

Tala nodded, though her eyes remained fixed on the world outside. The rain continued its slow descent, tracing lines down the glass like tears. For a moment, everything was still.

Then—movement.

She tensed.

Below, down the nearest alley, lanterns began to bob more quickly. Guards. Their steady patrol broke rhythm as, one by one, they turned and withdrew—moving toward the main gate with sudden purpose. The clatter of armor, faint but distinct, echoed beneath the storm.

"What...?" Tala leaned forward. "Guards—they go. Why they go?"

The streets, once thick with tension, began to empty in rippling waves. Doors shut. Windows latched. Conversations died mid-sentence. Even the rain seemed quieter as the city shifted.

Then came the sound.

The creak and groan of the city gates opening cut through the air like a blade—sharp and wrong.

Tala's breath caught.

Shadowy figures began to emerge beyond the gates—armor glinting under fractured lamplight, boots splashing deliberately in the puddles. They moved in perfect synchrony, like parts of the same body, their presence swallowing the space around them.

"Yvonne," Tala whispered, her voice sharp. "Look. Something... wrong."

Yvonne was already at the window. Her eyes widened as the figures stepped further into the city, their armor dark and wet with rain, gleaming like the carapace of something unnatural. The guards at the gate said nothing. They simply stepped aside.

"They're not from the city guard," Yvonne muttered. "This… this is something else."

Tala's eyes narrowed. Her fear didn't fade—it shifted, turned inward and dense, sharpening into something colder.

"Something start," she said, voice low. "Something big."

Outside, Seragora exhaled. The stillness in the air was not peace—it was dread. And as the figures moved deeper into the city, the fragile calm they'd clung to began to unravel, thread by thread.

Whatever came next would change everything.

The rain picked up, drumming against the rooftops like a warning.

Tala and Yvonne moved quickly through the narrow alleys, keeping to the shadows. The city gates behind them remained wide open—unguarded, yawning like a silent threat. Ahead, Seragora crouched in eerie quiet. No guards. No crowds. No shouting merchants or laughing children.

They passed shuttered windows and bolted doors. The usual warmth of the city had vanished, replaced by a silence too heavy, too deliberate. Somewhere nearby, a child whimpered and was hushed. A window creaked shut. Even the dogs weren't barking.

Then—hurried footsteps splashing through the rain.

A boy burst from around the corner, soaked to the bone, maybe ten years old. He nearly barreled into them before skidding to a halt.

"You two shouldn't be out here!" he gasped, eyes wide. "Something ain't right—everyone's gone inside!"

Tala stepped back, startled. "What wrong?" she asked, voice quick and thick with accent.

The urchin looked back the way he'd come. "The gates are open, but no guard posted. No bells. Just... quiet. Sarah's pulling us all back—told everyone to stay off the street."

Yvonne leaned in. "Sarah's smart. Where are the others?"

"With her," the boy said. "She's sending runners to warn who she can. Said to tell anyone still out—get off the street now."

He looked between them once more, then vanished into the dark with a splash and the slap of bare feet.

Tala's brow furrowed. "He scared."

"Good," Yvonne said, already turning. "Means he'll live."

Tala caught up, matching her pace. "Where we go now?"

Yvonne didn't slow. "To Dalmon. A'nara's with him. If we don't move fast, we may not reach them before something worse comes through those gates."

Tala's jaw tightened. "We go. We run."

They turned east, heading deeper into the lower quarter—where stone gave way to crooked homes and narrow lanes. No guards. No voices. Only the steady fall of rain and the pressure of something unseen settling over the city like a storm held back by sheer will.

Whatever was happening in Seragora, it wasn't over.

And Tala could feel it in her bones:

Something had changed. And they were already late.

Chapter 13: Towns Unrest

765, 10th Day Of The Fifth Moon

"This union shall broker peace. With her beside me, I see the possibility of a world where old feuds are mended, where her kin and mine stand together at last. They call our bond a gamble, a risk that breaks tradition—but I know in my bones this is more than an alliance. It is the start of something lasting, something beyond blood and borders. If there is to be hope, it begins here, with us. And I will see it through, no matter the cost."

Ky'len sat on a wooden bench in one of the empty stalls near the arena, his grip tight around a half-empty flask of ale. The cheers and celebrations from the tournament echoed faintly in the distance, but they felt miles away. His gaze was fixed on the dirt floor, his mind swirling with frustration and regret. Around him, Iszell and the other Bazel squires sat in uneasy silence, unsure of how to approach him.

"I almost had him," Ky'len muttered, breaking the silence. His voice was low, the bitterness palpable. He took a swig from the flask, wiping his mouth with the back of his hand. "After Razma, I was sure I could win. But I lost… again."

Iszell, always the calm one, shifted in his seat, trying to offer some comfort. "Ky'len, you fought well. You nearly had him. Aelric's no easy opponent."

Ky'len shook his head, his jaw clenched. "It wasn't about skill, Iszell. I lost control. After my match with Razma… I let my anger get the best of me. If I hadn't hesitated, if I hadn't let it cloud my judgment, I could've beaten him. And Aelric? I wasn't giving it my all by the time we fought."

Iszell raised an eyebrow, his voice steady but with a hint of curiosity. "So, what stopped you?"

Ky'len sighed deeply, his hand trembling slightly as he took another swig of ale. "It was my anger, Iszell. I fought with everything I had, but it wasn't about the fight anymore. I wanted to win because I thought it would prove something to… him. My father. But I wasn't thinking clearly. I let my frustration take over. Alric beat me, fair and square, and I wasn't in the right mindset to fight back."

Iszell leaned forward, his gaze locked on Ky'len. "You know, acknowledging it is the first step to getting control. You fought with heart, but sometimes that's not enough if your mind isn't in the right place."

Ky'len nodded, rubbing his temples. "I know. I felt it. I could've beaten Aelric if I'd stayed focused. But the truth is… I didn't deserve to win. I wasn't fighting him. I was fighting the shadow of my father." He let out a bitter laugh. "If I had fought with all I had, it might've been different. But I didn't, and that's on me."

Iszell smiled slightly. "It's hard to keep your head in moments like that. But Alric's victory doesn't mean you're lesser. He was just the better man today."

Ky'len paused, reflecting on Iszell's words. "I didn't lose to Alric because he was better, not really. I lost because I didn't keep myself in check. My father always taught me control, and here I am, losing it when it matters most."

Iszell placed a hand on Ky'len's shoulder. "You're not your father, Ky'len. You're you. Don't let his shadow dictate your every move. You've got a path of your own to walk."

Ky'len gave a faint nod, the weight of his loss still pressing on him, but something in Iszell's words began to sink in. "You're right," Ky'len admitted quietly. "I don't want to become him. My anger got the best of me today, but I need to do better. Next time, I'll fight with clarity, not rage."

Iszell smiled, his tone lighter now. "That's the spirit, Ky'len. And hey, Alric may have won, but you gave him one hell of a fight. No shame in that."

Ky'len managed a small smile, the tension in his chest easing just a little. "It was a fair match. He earned his win. Next time… I'll be ready."

The squires around him relaxed, the tension lifting as Ky'len's anger gave way to acceptance. He wasn't defeated by the fight itself—only by the battle within. And next time, he vowed, he would be ready to face both.

The festival had long since settled into its rhythm of revelry, the sounds of laughter, music, and the occasional clink of mugs filling the air. Ky'len stood off to the side, lost in thought, his mind replaying the day's events. The sting of defeat was fresh, and though his outward expression was stoic, inside he wrestled with his frustration and anger. His loss to Aelric weighed heavily on him, and the fact that he'd nearly lost control in his earlier match with Razma gnawed at him even more.

Aelric approached, still riding the wave of victory, but there was no gloating in his eyes. He extended a hand to Ky'len, offering a nod of respect. "That was a good fight, Ky'len. You pushed me harder than anyone today."

Ky'len nodded absentmindedly, barely registering the words as he stared at the ground, lost in his thoughts. The frustration and anger boiled beneath the surface, but he wasn't angry at Aelric. No, his anger was directed inward—toward himself. He hadn't fought with clarity. His rage had clouded his judgment. If he hadn't hesitated in his fight against Razma, maybe things would've turned out differently. He felt like he had been battling more than just his opponents— he had been battling his own demons.

Aelric lingered for a moment, sensing that Ky'len wasn't fully present. He glanced toward the growing crowd, noticing the shift in atmosphere. The cheers were beginning to fade, replaced by low murmurs and drunken voices. He turned back to Ky'len and the other squires, his face more serious now. "You all should get out of here," Aelric said quietly. "The crowd's turning. I'll try to calm things down, but you need to go before it gets worse."

Iszell noticed it too. The once-festive crowd had grown restless, and the smiles were replaced by narrowed eyes and muttered curses. Seragorans, fueled by ale and resentment, were starting to gather in small groups, their gazes fixed on Ky'len and the other Bazel squires.

"We should move," Iszell muttered, nudging Ky'len. "He's right. This isn't going to end well."

Ky'len glanced around, his fists clenching involuntarily as he saw a few Seragoran men stumbling toward them, their expressions twisted with drunken malice. He felt his anger flare up again, but this time, Iszell's hand on his shoulder kept him grounded.

"Yeah," Ky'len agreed, his voice tight. "Let's get out of here."

As they turned to leave, a bottle shattered on the ground nearby, and one of the Seragoran men shouted, "Hey! Bazel scum!" His words slurred with drink, but the venom in his tone was unmistakable. "Think you can just show up here and act like you belong?"

Ky'len stiffened, the heat rising in his chest as the man stumbled closer. His earlier thoughts of anger and self-loathing threatened to boil over again. Iszell grabbed his arm, pulling him back. "Ignore them," Iszell said sharply, "Let's go."

But the Seragorans weren't backing down. Another man, his face flushed and his steps unsteady, joined in. "You think we forgot what your kind did during the war? Now you come here like you own the place?"

The crowd was swelling now, more voices joining the fray, their words laced with bitterness and old grudges. The tension snapped as one of the men lunged forward, shoving Ky'len hard in the chest.

Everything erupted at once. Ky'len reacted instinctively, his fist swinging up to block the next blow, but the crowd surged around them, fists flying. The mob was overwhelming, pushing them into a corner of the square.

"Run!" Iszell shouted, his voice barely cutting through the chaos. Ky'len swung back, blocking blows and trying to fend off attackers, but it was too much. They were outnumbered and outmaneuvered, forced into the narrow alleyways as the mob chased after them.

Aelric, standing at the edge of the crowd, called out to the Seragorans, trying to defuse the situation. "Enough! Let them go!" His voice carried authority, but the crowd was too far gone, fueled by drink and years of resentment.

Ky'len, breathless and bruised, ran through the darkened streets with Iszell and the other squires at his side. As they fled, the sounds of the mob grew fainter, but the weight of what had just happened settled heavy on Ky'len's shoulders. They had escaped for now, but he knew this wasn't the end.

His lungs burned with every breath, and his legs ached, but Ky'len pushed forward, his thoughts spinning. The mob's shouts still echoed in his ears, the hatred in their voices unmistakable. The clash between Seragora and Bazel hadn't ended in the arena—it had spilled into the streets, and now it felt like the entire town was ready to explode.

"This way," Iszell urged, guiding them down a side street away from the main square. The noise of the festival was a distant hum now, but it was clear the night had taken a turn for the worse. The Seragorans had been drinking too much, celebrating their victory, but Ky'len knew it wasn't just the tournament that fueled their anger. It was years of tension, of old wounds that hadn't healed, and tonight had brought it all to the surface.

Ky'len glanced over at Iszell, whose face was etched with worry. The other squires were silent, their breaths labored as they kept pace. None of them spoke, but the unspoken truth hung between them—they weren't safe here. Not anymore.

As they rounded a corner, Iszell slowed, his hand resting on Ky'len's arm to stop him. "We need to hide, just for a bit," Iszell said, glancing around the quiet street. "The mob's too riled up. We'll never make it back to the inn if they catch us again."

Ky'len nodded, his chest still heaving. "But where?"

Iszell scanned the area, then his eyes landed on a small bakery tucked between two larger buildings. "In there." He led the way to the door, pushing it open quietly. The smell of freshly baked bread greeted them, warm and comforting in contrast to the chaos outside.

The baker, a stout woman with flour dusting her apron, looked up in surprise. "What's this?" she asked, her voice a mix of concern and confusion as the boys stumbled inside, breathless and clearly on the run.

"Please," Iszell said quickly, "we need to hide. There's a mob out there—Seragorans. They're after us."

The baker hesitated, her eyes flicking to the door as if expecting the mob to burst in at any moment. Then, without another word, she nodded. "Behind the flour sacks in the back," she said, gesturing toward the rear of the bakery. "Hurry."

Ky'len and the others didn't need to be told twice. They darted into the back room, crouching behind large sacks of flour, trying to steady their breathing as the sounds of the mob grew closer. Ky'len's heart pounded in his chest, and for a moment, he feared they would be discovered.

Suddenly, the door to the bakery crashed open, and Ky'len held his breath, pressing himself against the wall. The mob leader stormed in, his eyes wild with fury. "Where are they?" he snarled. "We saw them come this way!"

The baker stood her ground, wiping her hands on her apron. "No one's come in here," she said firmly. "You're mistaken."

The leader's eyes narrowed. "You're lying."

Before things could escalate, the butcher from next door appeared in the doorway, his towering frame filling the entrance. "What's going on here?" he growled, his cleaver still in hand.

"They're hiding Bazel scum," the mob leader spat, his voice dripping with contempt.

The butcher's face hardened. "You're stirring up trouble where there is none," he said, stepping forward. "Leave before this gets out of hand."

The mob leader faltered, his gaze darting between the baker and the butcher. After a tense moment, he spat on the floor. "This isn't over," he muttered before turning and storming out, the mob trailing behind him.

The bakery fell silent, and Ky'len let out a long breath, his heart still racing. The baker poked her head into the back room. "You can come out now," she said softly.

Ky'len and the others emerged, their legs shaky with relief. "Thank you," Ky'len whispered, still trying to calm his breathing.

The butcher, leaning against the doorway, gave a sharp nod. "Don't thank us, boy. Just remember, not everyone in Seragora wants this fight."

Ky'len met the butcher's eyes, about to nod when something in the man's gaze made him freeze. "You know who I am, don't you?" he asked, a sinking feeling forming in his stomach.

The butcher's lips tightened. "I knew your father during the war," he said, his voice rough. "He gave me this." He gestured to the long scar running down his cheek. "Now go, before things get worse."

A scream suddenly pierced the night, sharp and desperate, coming from the direction of the arena. Ky'len's blood turned cold.

"We need to move," Iszell said urgently, tugging at Ky'len's arm, pulling him toward the door.

Ky'len followed, his mind reeling as they stepped back into the chaos of the streets. In the distance, amidst the shadows and flickering lanterns, he saw them—Bazel soldiers moving with purpose.

But something was off. As they turned a corner, Ky'len's eyes widened in horror. These weren't Bazel soldiers pursuing them. The attackers were smaller, hunched figures with green skin— Muckspawn, dressed in Bazel armor, wreaking havoc through the town.

"They're trying to frame us," Ky'len muttered, his voice filled with disbelief. But there was no time to process the realization. One of the Muckspawn spotted them, its beady eyes narrowing with malicious glee.

"Ky'len, move!" Iszell shouted as the Muckspawn lunged, brandishing a dagger. Ky'len drew his sword just in time, the force of the blow jolting through his arms as the battle erupted around them.

Ky'len's blade clashed repeatedly with the Muckspawn disguised in Bazel armor. His arms ached with every strike, the weight of the fight pressing down on him. His friends were equally overwhelmed, their movements growing frantic as the Muckspawn attacked with speed and ferocity.

"Stay together!" Iszell yelled, his voice strained as he parried a blow. "Don't let them split us up!"

Ky'len's heart raced as he caught sight of Ervin, desperately fending off two attackers. Time seemed to slow as Ky'len watched in horror—one of the Muckspawn's daggers slipped past Ervin's defenses, sinking into his side.

"Ervin!" Ky'len's voice cracked with desperation as he rushed toward his friend.

Before he could reach him, another Muckspawn struck, driving its blade deep into Ervin's chest. Ervin's eyes widened in shock before the life left them, and he crumpled to the ground.

"No!" Ky'len roared, grief and rage twisting inside him. He swung his sword wildly, cutting down the nearest Muckspawn, but it was too late—Ervin was gone.

Ky'len barely had time to grieve. The sound of footsteps and shouting reached them. The mob. The drunken citizens of Seragora, drawn by the chaos, were flooding the streets.

"They're attacking us!" someone screamed. "Bazel soldiers are attacking Seragora!"

Ky'len's stomach dropped. "No! It's not us!" he shouted, but his voice was lost in the growing fury. The mob only saw the Bazel armor—no one noticed the green-skinned Muckspawn hidden beneath it.

A hulking figure emerged from the shadows, larger than the others, clad in mismatched armor. The leader of the Muckspawn charged at Ky'len, striking with brutal force. Ky'len struggled to block the blows, each strike sending him stumbling back.

"We need to retreat!" Iszell's voice was full of urgency as he slashed at a nearby attacker.

Ky'len barely managed to parry another strike, but the impact knocked him off balance, and he fell to the ground. "I can't hold him!" he gasped, his arms shaking.

Iszell rushed to Ky'len's side, pulling him to his feet. "Come on!" he urged, dragging Ky'len away as the mob's angry roars grew louder.

They bolted through the narrow streets, dodging both the Muckspawn and the furious townspeople. As they rounded another corner, they came upon a shocking sight.

In the middle of the street, a lone figure fought off several Muckspawn with blinding speed. The man wielded a long staff, his movements fluid and precise. Each swing of his weapon sent attackers sprawling to the ground before they could react.

Ky'len's eyes widened in recognition. It was Dalmon—the quiet trainer who always kept to himself. But something about him was different now, something that made Ky'len's stomach twist with unease.

As Dalmon dodged a strike, his headband slipped, revealing pointed ears beneath his bloodied hair. Ky'len's heart skipped a beat.

"Slividhe," Ky'len whispered in shock, piecing it together. He had heard rumors about the Slividhe, their magic, their unmatched combat skills. But seeing it with his own eyes felt surreal.

Dalmon's eyes burned with fierce focus as he struck down the Muckspawn with deadly accuracy. His blond hair, now streaked with blood, whipped around as he delivered powerful blows, sending the remaining attackers crumpling to the ground.

"Run!" Dalmon shouted, his voice cutting through the chaos. He swung his staff in a wide arc, knocking back two more attackers. "Get out of town, now!"

Ky'len hesitated, his heart pounding. "But—"

Dalmon turned to face him, his pointed ears catching the moonlight. His expression was hard, determined. "I know Bazel didn't do this," he said firmly. "You need to warn them all. This is a setup! They want us to turn on each other!"

Iszell grabbed Ky'len's arm, pulling him away. "We need to go!" he urged, his voice filled with urgency. "He'll hold them off."

Ky'len's mind raced as he looked back at Dalmon, who continued to fight with blinding speed. He didn't want to leave him behind, but there was no time to argue.

"Run!" Dalmon shouted again, his voice commanding. "I'll hold them back. Go, warn everyone!"

With one last glance, Ky'len nodded, turning to flee with Iszell and the squires, Dalmon's warning echoing in his mind: This was all a setup.

Without another word, Ky'len turned and bolted, his heart heavy with both fear and confusion. Iszell followed close behind, their feet pounding the cobblestones as they weaved through the darkened streets. The sounds of battle and chaos faded into the distance, but the weight of what they'd seen pressed down on them. They ran until their legs burned, until they reached the outskirts of town. Yet Ky'len couldn't shake the image of Dalmon—fighting with inhuman speed, his pointed ears revealed, and his warning echoing in his mind.

The storm in Seragora was far from over, and Ky'len knew they had only just begun to understand the full extent of the danger.

Suddenly, Dalmon's voice pierced the night, filled with shock and anger. "MUTT? WHY?"

Ky'len's heart raced even faster as he glanced over his shoulder. Through the flickering light of a nearby lantern, he caught a glimpse of Dalmon locked in battle with a hulking figure—far larger than any Muckspawn Ky'len had ever seen. The creature loomed over Dalmon, striking with brutal force, but Dalmon held his ground, his movements precise as he deflected each blow with his staff.

Ky'len felt a surge of panic. Mutt? That was Mutt? He had heard the name whispered in fear, but seeing the monstrous leader in action made it all too real.

"We need to keep moving!" Iszell's voice was tight with fear, and Ky'len didn't need to be told twice. He pushed harder, forcing his legs to keep going despite the burning in his muscles. They ran through the twisting streets, dodging shadows and narrow alleyways, trying to put as much distance between themselves and the chaos as possible.

As they dashed through a wider street, they passed groups of refugees, wide-eyed and defenseless, some caught in the fray, crying out in terror as Muckspawn clashed with the desperate townsfolk. The realization hit Ky'len hard, twisting his gut. "Where are the guards?" he shouted to Iszell, barely catching his breath. "These people—they're being slaughtered!"

Iszell's expression darkened, a mix of horror and anger as he glanced around. "I don't know," he said, voice raw. "It's like they've vanished. Either they're dead, or someone wanted them out of the way."

Ky'len's thoughts raced. Who would stand to gain from such a betrayal? The missing guards, the open gates—it all pointed to a deeper treachery.

Then, out of the darkness, a small figure appeared, stepping out from the shadows. Ky'len's hand flew to his sword, but before he could draw it, the figure motioned frantically for them to follow.

As they reached the quieter edges of town, away from the chaos, the small figure guiding them stopped before a run-down building, nudging open a half-rotten door. "In," she whispered, her voice quick and broken but clear. "In now."

Without hesitation, Iszell grabbed Ky'len's arm, and they ducked inside, where the dim cellar light flickered against the old walls. Ky'len squinted, trying to make sense of the dusty shadows, when a low muttering caught his attention. A figure shifted, emerging with a grumble, "Lost half my herbs running in here… damn Muckspawn don't care a lick for a man's livelihood."

Ky'len squinted to make out the speaker, while Iszell raised an eyebrow, a trace of amusement in his expression. The man stepped forward, brushing dirt from his hands with a look of exasperation.

"Name's Jeff," he announced, catching their questioning looks. "Just a humble herb grower, if you must know—not looking to get caught up in whatever brought you down here."

Iszell sized him up, nodding. "Just passing through the trouble, then?"

Jeff rolled his eyes. "Passing through it, hiding from it—whatever keeps me in one piece. And if it means sharing a cramped cellar with a couple of strangers, so be it. But trust me, the last thing I need is more attention, so keep it down if you don't want any more trouble, yeah?"

Then the small figure who'd led them here stepped into the faint light. Ky'len's hand went to his sword, but she held her hands up, a nervous, earnest expression on her face.

Tala glanced at Ky'len, then Iszell, her gaze softening as she met Ky'len's confused eyes. "Why… help?" he asked, words stumbling out as his mind tried to catch up. "You're… a Muckspawn. Why risk yourself for us?"

Tala placed a hand over her heart. "Mutt want war. Me?" She shook her head. "I want peace. War bad… for all."

Jeff, still grumbling in the background, chuckled. "Sit down, kids. She's one of the good ones. Not many like her, but when you find one, you count yourself lucky."

Iszell, still slightly amused, offered a nod. "Well, Jeff, seems we're all stuck here for the time being."

Jeff shrugged, settling onto an overturned crate. "Guess so. But mark my words, if there's any storytime nonsense about to happen, better grab a seat, kids," he nodded at Ky'len, "or you'll be stuck hearing it from the back."

Tala gave the boys a reassuring look as she moved toward the stairs. In her broken Common, she spoke softly, "Stay here… I be back when… safe, yes?" She paused, glancing at Jeff as he settled onto his crate, muttering to himself about his lost herbs.

She smirked, a light laugh escaping her as she leaned in close to Ky'len and Iszell. "Him? He harmless," she whispered, a playful glint in her eyes, before straightening up. "Quiet now... keep low."

With a final nod, Tala turned, disappearing up the steps and leaving them alone in the dim, musty cellar with Jeff.

Chapter 14: Weight Of The Crown

772, 12th Day Of The Seventh Moon

Today marks five years for my twins, though it is a bittersweet celebration. My son could not be here; they tell me he's immersed in his training, though what that entails, I'm left to wonder. It saddens both myself and my little girl. She misses her brother fiercely, and yet, I can see she holds her own joy close today.

I had the gardener plant rows of red roses, her favorite, a gesture that brought a rare, softened smile from my wife. But the true marvel came from our former allies in the mountains—a gift beyond words. They brought forth a crystal rose, hewn from stone yet shining with a light that catches every color. My daughter clutched it tightly from the moment she held it, and tonight, she sleeps with it at her side, as though it holds the warmth of family that feels so distant now.

Today, at least, is about her and her joy.

King Tor'valis stood by the window of his private chambers, his gaze fixed on the distant horizon where the Bear Mountains met the sky. The sun was setting, casting long shadows across the rugged landscape that had served as both a fortress and a home to his family for generations. The golden light bathed the stone walls of the castle in a warm glow, but it did little to ease the tension that had settled deep within his chest.

The celebration of Seragora's 200th year of rule should have been a time of joy and unity. Seragora had always prided itself on being a land of peace and refuge—a place where those fleeing persecution, war, or poverty could find new opportunities and a fresh start. Over the centuries, the kingdom had welcomed countless refugees, offering them the chance to build new lives in a land that valued freedom and the dignity of every individual.

Yet beneath this proud heritage, there had always been a simmering tension. Despite their ideals, the people of Seragora harbored a deep-seated distrust toward Bazel, their ancient rival, and a lingering discontent toward the Muckspawn, whose chaotic nature and shifting allegiances made them unpredictable and dangerous neighbors.

This year was particularly significant—and tense—because it marked the first time since the end of the Thorin War that Bazel had been allowed to attend the celebration. The decision had been controversial, with many in Seragora questioning whether it was wise to invite their former enemies to such a significant event. The wounds of the war were still fresh in the minds of many, and the recent Muckspawn attacks had only heightened the sense of unease.

King Tor'valis sighed heavily, turning away from the window to face the small, intricately carved table where a decanter of wine and a single goblet waited. He poured himself a drink, his hand steady despite the turmoil in his mind, and took a slow sip, savoring the rich, earthy flavor. But even the wine, his usual solace, offered little comfort tonight.

The Thorin War. The mere mention of it was enough to silence a room, to send shivers down the spine of even the bravest soldier. To the people of Seragora, it was a war shrouded in both horror and heroism, a conflict that had defined a generation.

For many, the war was a story of betrayal and bloodshed, where the once peaceful lands were ravaged by Bazel's relentless aggression. They remembered the tales of Bazel's initial attack, swift and merciless, as they seized the Thorin Valley—an act that many in Seragora still viewed as a violation of their sovereignty.

The people spoke of King Tor'valis's leadership during those dark days, of how he had rallied his troops, leading them into battle after battle, never faltering, even when the odds seemed insurmountable. They remembered the rumors of Muckspawn, those twisted creatures who had allegedly fought for both sides, switching allegiances based on who could save their miserable hides. And they whispered of Silver Fang, the mysterious warrior whose presence on the battlefield had struck fear into the hearts of all who faced him.

Yet, amid the tales of heroism and sacrifice, there were also stories of loss and despair. Families torn apart, villages burned to the ground, and the lingering fear that the peace they now enjoyed was as fragile as glass, ready to shatter at any moment.

The recent Muckspawn attacks had only heightened these fears. Though smaller in scale than during the war, the attacks had been relentless, unsettling the countryside and spreading whispers of another conflict on the horizon. And then there was Bazel—always a shadow looming over Seragora, its people still wary of their old enemy despite the years of peace.

As Alric left the room, Tor'valis sighed, the weight of their secrets growing heavier by the day, threatening to crush them under their own silence. The window before him framed a scene of unrest—flickering flames and shifting shadows as the town below roiled with fear and uncertainty. The kingdom's survival rested squarely on his shoulders.

A creak at the door pulled him from his thoughts, and Raelle stepped in, her presence a calming force against the storm raging inside him. Her simple nightgown fluttered slightly as she moved, her hair cascading loosely, framing a face etched with deep concern.

"Tor'valis, the castle is in an uproar," she said softly, urgency lacing her words. "I can see the fire from here. What is happening?"

He turned to her, his face a mix of tension and relief at seeing her. "There have been more attacks, Raelle. Reports of Muckspawn near the outer walls, rumors of Bazel soldiers involved. It's chaos." His voice was tight, each word dragged down by the weight of the situation.

Raelle's eyes flicked to the glow of the distant fires, worry deepening their hue. "Attacks so close to the gates? And I've heard whispers that the guards were nowhere to be found. Were they killed, or… did they abandon their posts?"

Before Tor'valis could respond, the door swung open again, and Lord Alric returned, his eyes sharp and dark with urgency. "Your Majesty, I've questioned some of the captains. They claim the gates were opened without force—there are no signs of a struggle. It's as if they were left open on purpose."

A stunned silence followed his words. The crackle of flames from the town below seemed to echo the alarm that filled the room. Tor'valis's jaw clenched, a spark of anger and suspicion flaring in his eyes. "Left open… by whom? Who would dare betray the city at a time like this?"

Raelle stepped forward, her voice steady though her eyes were wide with disbelief. "This is not just a sign of negligence. It smells of sabotage. If the gates were opened willingly, someone within these walls is working against us."

Alric nodded, his expression hardening. "It could be an inside plot, Your Majesty. A means to stir up hate, to incite anger against Bazel or the Muckspawn. To fracture what fragile peace we have left."

Tor'valis turned from the window, his fists tightening at his sides. "This cannot stand. We will find the traitor, and we will root out this poison before it consumes Seragora. If the people see us falter now, the whole city will turn on itself."

Raelle placed a calming hand on his arm. "Be careful, my love. Fear is a weapon as much as any sword. We must wield it wisely, not let it control us."

The king met her gaze, the storm within him momentarily tempered by her words. "You're right. But tonight, we need answers, not just caution. Alric, get Dalmon here as soon as possible. We need his insight on who might have gained by opening those gates."

Alric bowed deeply, determination in his eyes. "I'll see to it, Your Majesty."

As he left, the room fell silent once more. Tor'valis turned back to the window, watching the flicker of firelight dance across the city like restless spirits. The peace they had fought for now hung by a fragile thread, threatened by forces within and without.

With a final, resolute breath, he whispered into the dark, "We will not fall to shadows. Not again."

Tor'valis turned decisively from the window, breaking away from his grim contemplation of the burning city below. His eyes hardened with determination as he strode toward the door, pulling it open sharply to address the guards waiting anxiously outside.

"Send scouts into the city immediately," he commanded, authority resonating in his voice. "I need reliable information—who is behind these attacks, what exactly has happened at our gates. Move swiftly but discreetly. Panic is already rising, and I won't add to the chaos."

The guards saluted promptly, their faces reflecting the gravity of the situation. They hurried down the stone corridor, footsteps echoing into silence. Tor'valis closed the heavy door slowly, the hollow sound underscoring the tension that hung between him and Raelle.

She watched him quietly, recognizing the turmoil he tried so hard to hide. Stepping gently toward him, she laid a comforting hand on his arm, pulling him softly toward the chairs beside the crackling hearth.

"Come, sit," she murmured, guiding him to sit with her. The firelight flickered gently, casting long shadows on the walls—reminders of darker times they both remembered all too well.

They sat quietly for a moment, the silence heavy with unspoken thoughts. Finally, Raelle spoke softly, her voice a gentle touch against the tension.

"Fifteen years," she said, her eyes fixed on the dancing flames. "It hardly seems possible, does it? Fifteen years you've carried your father's crown, yet at times like this, it still feels new."

Tor'valis sighed deeply, his gaze distant, burdened by memory. "Sometimes I still feel unprepared, Raelle. My father had a strength… a resolve. He carried us through the Thorrin War, even when the kingdom seemed ready to shatter. The decisions he had to make—"

He paused, haunted by the weight behind his words. "The decisions *we* had to make. I stood beside him, Raelle. I watched him sacrifice so much—our principles, our honor—in the name of protecting Seragora."

Raelle reached for his hand, gripping it firmly. "We did what we believed was necessary. Your father did. You did. Not every choice can be easy, and not every one is right in hindsight. We did the best we could with what we knew then."

His eyes met hers—vulnerable, full of remorse. "But the price we paid… the lines we crossed. The Muckspawn fought beside us. They trusted our promises, our visions of unity. Yet, when peace came, we denied them full citizenship. Reduced them to second-class lives. It seemed right then. Safer. But was it truly just?"

Raelle's expression softened, her own regret flickering in the firelight. "I remember those debates. We were young, driven by fear, shaped by years of suspicion. We told ourselves it was necessary—to preserve peace. But maybe it was fear guiding us, not wisdom."

He nodded slowly, her honesty grounding him. "And then the pact with the Vek'smed. The secret deals in shadowed chambers, trading for weapons and steel—knowing it would deepen mistrust if the people ever found out. Every choice seemed right in the moment, but now... they haunt me."

Raelle tightened her grip, eyes blazing with resolve. "Every ruler carries regrets. The past never lets go. But if you live there too long, you go blind to the present. Tonight, someone betrayed us. This unrest—it was planned. Our mistakes may still echo, but we can't let them weaken us now."

Tor'valis regarded her, admiration softening his burdened gaze. "You've always understood me better than anyone. You've always been my strength."

She smiled softly, brushing her thumb across his knuckles. "And you've always been mine. Do you remember those first days after the war? Before your father passed? We dreamed of peace. Of doing better. Of not repeating his mistakes."

He chuckled faintly, the edge of a smile breaking through. "He used to warn me—dreams are easy, ruling is hard. That even the brightest ideals become complicated once you're forced to protect something real. Now I understand what he meant."

Raelle leaned in, resting her head gently against his shoulder. "But our dreams weren't in vain. Look around. Yes, darkness stirs again, but Seragora has known years of peace. Refugees have found homes. Children grow up without war. That's because of you."

He sighed, the weight pressing against his chest. "And tonight could unravel all of it. One betrayal… one spark, and everything we've built burns."

Raelle lifted her head, meeting his gaze with quiet certainty. "Then we stop it. We find who did this. And we face it, openly. Fear might have guided us before—but not now. Not anymore."

Tor'valis held her gaze, the firelight flickering in her eyes. "I still remember the night I asked you to marry me," he said softly, the memory warming his voice. "It felt like the world had stopped. We had no idea how many storms were coming."

Raelle laughed, low and tender. "You were shaking so badly, I thought you might faint before you even got the words out. But I knew—even then—I knew we were strong enough to weather anything."

He reached up, gently brushing a damp strand of hair from her cheek. "Looking at everything we've faced… I see now how right you were. My father once said true strength isn't avoiding hard decisions—it's having the courage to face them. With you beside me, that courage never fades."

She smiled, warmth blooming in her eyes, casting aside the shadows that danced around them. "We've carried the past long enough, Tor'valis. Let it shape us, not chain us. Tonight, we lead wiser, stronger. Together."

He squeezed her hand, his voice steady, sure. "Together," he echoed. "Whatever comes, we'll face it side by side. This city—our people—they deserve nothing less."

Outside, the fires continued to burn, the future uncertain. But within their chambers, the weight of old regrets forged new strength, and two rulers met the coming storm—united.

The fire cracked, casting shadows like clawed fingers across the stone chamber. Raelle's face was half-lit, half-hidden—like the truth she and Tor'valis had carried for so long.

He stood at the window, unmoving, eyes fixed on the city below. Seragora stretched out in silence, the towers dark near the gates. Too dark. The north quarter, always restless, now seemed still in the wrong way. It wasn't peace. It was anticipation.

"Send a runner to Dalmon," he said finally, voice low. Heavy. "I want him here before the second bell. No delays."

Raelle moved to the desk without question, reaching for a fresh scrap of parchment and ink. Her quill scratched quietly across the paper. "If he's still alive out there," she muttered.

Tor'valis turned. "Don't say that."

She met his gaze, steady. "You're thinking it."

He didn't deny it.

The steward appeared at the door as if summoned by thought alone. Raelle sealed the message with a sharp press of her ring and handed it off. "To Dalmon," she said. "You deliver it yourself. No one else touches it."

The steward bowed and disappeared.

Tor'valis walked slowly back to the hearth. His hands rested on the back of the old chair—his father's chair. "If he knew what I've done with this kingdom," he said, "he'd spit on the stone I was crowned on."

Raelle didn't argue. "He ruled with fear. You've ruled with guilt. At least yours led to peace."

Tor'valis scoffed. "Did it?"

She said nothing.

He turned to face the fire. "Do you remember how many we had to silence in the early days? How many voices questioned the peace we were shaping—how many we buried for the sake of unity?"

Raelle's jaw tightened. "I remember. I remember the names. Every one of them."

"The muckspawn elders. The deserters. The Slivdhe emissary who refused the trade pact. The children on the border who saw too much."

His voice was hollow now.

"We swore we'd do better," he said. "And then we did exactly what we hated our fathers for doing."

Raelle stepped forward, her voice tight with restraint. "We did what had to be done. To end the war. To hold the kingdom together. We didn't want it—but we chose it."

Tor'valis looked at her. "We chose to shaft the muckspawn. Promised them place, honor, land— and then locked them out of the city walls with fear and silence. We used them, Raelle."

145

"I know," she said softly.

"And now they're back. Armored. Trained. Organized."

"And someone let them in."

He nodded grimly. "And they're not coming to talk."

She crossed the room slowly, her boots silent on the stone. "This is the reckoning. Maybe one we deserved."

Tor'valis looked into her eyes, tired and sharp. "But I won't let this city fall. Not after everything we've done to hold it together."

Raelle placed her hand over his. "Then we face it. All of it. No more lies between us. No more pretending we're clean."

The chamber door opened again. The steward returned, rain on his shoulders. "Lord Alric is on his way, my king. The others are gathering."

Tor'valis didn't move.

"Bring them into the chamber," he said. "If we're going to be judged for what we've done… then let it be now. But no one else dies in silence. Not again."

Raelle gave a sharp nod. "And if the council tries to hide behind old walls?"

"Then I'll tear them down myself." he whispred.

Chapter 15: Shadows of the Forge

759, 3rd Day of the First Moon

_ *"Today, we boarded the ship that will carry us far from home. Every crash of the waves sets my heart pounding, yet a fragile spark of excitement flickers in my chest. Father says the people across the sea are like us but live by stranger customs. I'm not sure what that means, only that our future lies in the unknown.*

*Below deck, wagons rattle with each swell, as if the sea itself warns us to turn back. But there's no turning back now. The wind tastes of salt and possibility, and despite the fear that twists my stomach, I refuse to let it root me in place. Our world is about to grow, and with it, perhaps so will we."_

In the lush underbrush of the Bear Mountains, Chief Zra'ka led his Webshroud tribe with a predatory stealth honed by the new, spider-like abilities granted by the elixir from Mutt and Thorn. These abilities allowed them to navigate the rugged, forest-covered terrain with unnerving silence and agility. Their mission was clear: track down Chief Arak and his tribe who had allied with the Vek'smed in their forge city deep beneath the mountains.

Grit'nar, Zra'ka's chief scout, signaled a halt. His sharp eyes, enhanced by the elixir, spotted a trap—a fine wire stretched between two saplings. It was a sign that their progress was still being monitored and hindered by the same lone Vek'smed warrior who had been a thorn in their side for days.

"Samme faen," Zra'ka muttered under his breath, frustration coloring his tone. *"This one again"*

This elusive Vek'smed was not confronting them directly but employing guerrilla tactics: traps, false trails, and sudden ambushes designed not to harm but to delay. His tactics were effective, keeping Zra'ka's warriors on edge and slowing their progress considerably.

With a fluid motion, Zra'ka directed his tribe to carefully disable the trap and move on. They pressed deeper into the mountain terrain, guided by the faintest traces left by their quarry. The natural geothermal warmth of the area grew as they neared the network of hot springs that signaled they were close to the Vek'smed territories.

As night fell, an arrow whistled through the dimming light, narrowly missing Zra'ka's head and embedding itself in a nearby tree. His warriors instinctively spread out, taking cover behind the thick trunks of ancient pines.

Zra'ka peered into the shadows, trying to spot their assailant. There, a brief movement—a shadow against shadows—betrayed the lone Vek'smed's position. With a series of hand signals, Zra'ka coordinated his tribe's approach, flanking the spot where the arrow had come from.

They closed in silently, but as they reached the position, they found nothing but a few disturbed leaves and a freshly notched arrow stuck in the ground—a message rather than a threat.

"Han leker," hissed Grit'nar, plucking the arrow from the soil. *"He's toying with us"*

"Gå," Zra'ka ordered, setting a relentless pace. *"Keep moving"*

The warrior's tactics were clear: delay them, frustrate them, but not engage directly. Zra'ka respected the strategy—it was smart, preserving the warrior's strength while depleting and demoralizing his foes.

The chase continued, each hour that passed without contact increasing the tension among the muckspawn warriors. They were deep in enemy territory now, the steam from the hot springs enveloping them in a warm, misty veil that obscured sight but not the sense of being watched and judged.

At a ridge overlooking a valley shrouded in steam and dotted with the glow of forges below, Zra'ka halted. The trail had gone cold. Below them lay the forge city of the Vek'smed—Arak's new sanctuary.

"Nok," Zra'ka decided. *"Enough"*

"Leir nå. Grytidlig inn—prat eller kamp." *"We set camp. At dawn, we move in—parley or battle."*

His warriors nodded, settling into the defensive perimeter they formed naturally. Zra'ka looked out over the forge city, pondering the elusive Vek'smed's intentions. Without direct confrontation, without even seeing his face, the Vek'smed had led them here, on his terms. It was a masterful manipulation of terrain and psychology, and Zra'ka could not help but feel a grudging respect for this unseen guardian of the Vek'smed city.

As the first light of dawn painted the rugged terrain of the Bear Mountains, Chief Zra'ka and his Webshroud tribe readied themselves for a critical push towards the Vek'smed city. The night's lingering chill was punctuated by distant forge echoes and the subtle disturbances of wildlife—a testament to the valley's deceptive tranquility.

Zra'ka's warriors, enhanced by the elixir given by Mutt, bore spider-like abilities that made them formidable adversaries. Their skin bore subtle, glistening traces of webs, and their movements were accentuated by an eerie grace and the ability to leap astonishing distances, adhering briefly to sheer surfaces.

Despite these enhancements, their progress was halted by a barrage of arrows that rained down from the cliffs at dawn. The lone Vek'smed warrior, exploiting his mastery of the terrain, had taken a high vantage point. His arrows found their marks with deadly precision, thinning the ranks of Zra'ka's tribe with every silent shot.

"Nett! Skjold!" Zra'ka commanded. *"Form webs! Shields!"*

Instantly, the air was filled with the sound of stretching silk as the warriors spun protective web barriers, weaving them between the trees and across their shielded ranks. This makeshift webbing caught several arrows, their deadly tips ensnared in the sticky strands.

Yet, the Vek'smed warrior adapted quickly. He shifted his position, his movements a whisper against the stone, barely perceptible even to the keen senses of the Webshroud tribe. He targeted the warriors scaling the cliffs, where the webs were less concentrated. Each fallen muckspawn was a testament to the warrior's tactical genius, leveraging his understanding of the terrain against the spider-enhanced invaders.

"Del! Flank!" Zra'ka barked. *"Split! Flank!"*

His command split the air, and his tribe obeyed, dividing their forces. Half attempted to ascend the cliff faces with their enhanced agility, leaping and clinging to the rocks as they moved to encircle their assailant. The others continued to press forward, using their webbing to create makeshift bridges and ladders over treacherous gaps.

The Vek'smed's response was a calculated retreat to a narrow pass within the valley, drawing Zra'ka's forces into a choke point. From hidden crevices and natural fortifications, he launched a devastating counter-assault. The confined space turned the tribal advantage of mobility into a liability, their numbers making them easy targets in the cramped terrain.

Despite their supernatural agility and the protective webs they spun defensively, Zra'ka's tribe suffered heavy casualties. The sticky webs, while useful, became as much of a hindrance as a help, catching wounded warriors and hindering rapid movement, making them easy targets for the Vek'smed's relentless arrows.

Faced with unsustainable losses, Zra'ka was forced to sound a retreat. His voice, hoarse with dust and defeat, carried the weight of the day's failures. As they retreated, the surviving members of his tribe supported each other, their withdrawal covered by volleys of webbing aimed at blocking the Vek'smed's line of sight and slowing any pursuit.

That evening, as they regrouped far from the valley of their defeat, the air was thick not just with the smell of damp earth and the iron tang of blood, but with the heavy silence of mourning. Zra'ka pondered their retreat under the shadow of the mountains that housed the Vek'smed city —a fortress never reached, defended by a solitary warrior whose prowess turned the mountain's natural defenses into an insurmountable barrier.

Sitting by the fire, Zra'ka's eyes reflected its flickering light, mirroring the flames that danced with the same ferocity as the Vek'smed's unseen presence. They had underestimated their foe, and the price was etched in the faces of every warrior who sat with him in that somber gathering. The webs they spun were now reminders of their entanglement in a battle they were ill-prepared to win, a battle dictated by the landscape they sought to conquer and the lone guardian who knew its secrets intimately.

As the fire crackled and the night deepened, Zra'ka's thoughts lingered on the lone Vek'smed, a shadowy protector whose single-handed defense had halted the advance of the Webshroud tribe. Their enhanced abilities, though formidable, were no match for the strategic mind and intimate terrain knowledge of their adversary. This defeat was a hard lesson in humility and strategy—one that Zra'ka would not soon forget.

Chief Zra'ka sat apart from his warriors, his form hunched over a small, flickering campfire. The light cast deep shadows across his face, reflecting the turmoil within as he pondered their recent defeat. Each arrow's whiz, each warrior's fall replayed in his mind, not just as a physical defeat but as a strategic blunder that questioned his leadership and the very essence of their mission to claim the Vek'smed forge.

His second in command, Gral'jin, approached with careful footsteps, arms tucked in a gesture of respect. He paused at the edge of the small fire circle, voice kept low so as not to disturb the other weary warriors sprawled around the camp.

"Høvding, mennene kaller Vek'smed et spøkelse. De skjelver." *"Chief, the men call the Vek'smed a ghost. They tremble."*

Zra'ka sat cross-legged by the flickering campfire, jaw set. He lifted a split log from a meager stack of wood and placed it on the flames, sparks dancing upward into the cold night air. He listened without looking up, his expression difficult to read in the play of light and shadow.

"La dem. Han er ingen ånd—bare fjellblod." *"Let them. He is no spirit—just mountain-blood."*

Gral'jin nodded, then lowered himself beside his chief. The firelight caught the faint sheen of web-like patterns on his forearms as he rested them on his knees, thoughtful. "Hva nå? Myrene?" *"What now? The marshes?"*

"No," Zra'ka replied swiftly, the determination in his eyes igniting like embers fanned by a sudden breeze. He prodded the fire with a stick, scattering glowing cinders into the darkness. "Vi lærer. Neste gang bestemmer vi slaget." *"We learn. Next time we decide the fight."*

Gral'jin lifted his head to meet his chief's gaze, tension evident in the set of his shoulders.

"Hvordan, Høvding? Mange borte, motet dødt." *"How, Chief? We lost many, and morale is low."*

Zra'ka exhaled, driving the tip of his stick deeper into the coals. Thin wisps of smoke curled upward as the wood crackled.

"Mutt ga styrke. Thorn ga list. Vi bruker begge. Feller, nett, skygger." *"Mutt gave strength. Thorn gave cunning. We use both. Traps, webs, shadows."*

A hush settled over them, broken only by the snap of the fire and the distant groans of wounded muckspawn. At length, Zra'ka spoke again, voice low but resolute.

"Speidere. Følg ham diskret. Lær stier, gjemmested." *"Scouts. Follow him discreetly. Learn paths, hideouts."*

Gral'jin pushed himself to his feet, the warrior's spark rekindled in his eyes. He nodded once, the corner of his mouth twitching in a faint show of renewed purpose.

"Nettene?" *"The webs?"*

"Til feller. Hans fjell skal bli bur." *"Make them traps. His mountain becomes a cage."*

As Gral'jin moved to relay the orders, the fire crackled, throwing off fresh heat into the growing chill. A biting wind slid between the trees, making Zra'ka tense his shoulders. He added another piece of wood to the blaze, watching sparks swirl up into the night. Beyond the ring of light, shadows shifted—reminders of an unseen enemy who knew these mountains far better than they did.

Yet Zra'ka allowed himself a measured breath. This time, at least, they would be the ones controlling the board.

For in the harsh laws of nature that governed their world, adaptability was not just a trait—it was the only way to survive.

As dawn broke over the rugged landscape of the mountains, the air hung heavy with the residue of the night's deliberations and the stench of blood. Chief Zra'ka stood at the forefront of his encampment, observing his warriors prepare for the day's harrowing challenges. Each face was etched with resolve, but beneath it lay a palpable tension; the memory of their fallen brothers weighed heavily on them all.

"Høvding, speiderne kom," Gral'jin announced, his voice bearing a note of urgency as he approached Zra'ka. *"Chief, the scouts arrived,"*

His expression was grim, the news clearly unfavorable.

Zra'ka turned, eyes narrowing. "Snakk." *"Speak."*

"They tracked the Vek'smed through the night," Gral'jin began. "He's cunning, leading small, lethal ambushes. We lost four more to traps in the forest—spikes hidden beneath leaves, snares that hoisted them into the air."

A muscle twitched in Zra'ka's jaw. "Vis meg." *"Show me."* he said his teeth grinding in his jaw.

Gral'jin led the way to a nearby ridge where they could overlook part of the forest. Below, the dense canopy was sporadically broken by innocuous clearings that could be death traps. Gral'jin pointed to several spots where the earth looked disturbed. "He moves like a shadow, leaving chaos in his wake. We're not just fighting a warrior; we're fighting a force of nature."

Zra'ka surveyed the rugged landscape, mind racing with tactics. Being outmaneuvered by a single Vek'smed—using guerrilla warfare no less—stung his pride like a lash. The mountain was no marsh, and the rules here were different. He needed a drastic shift in strategy.

"Ingen direkte kamp. Nett som snubletråd. Fjell blir bur," Zra'ka declared, voice resolute. *"No direct fight. Webs as tripwire. Mountain becomes cage."*

His warriors set to work, stringing dense, sticky webs across narrow passes and shadowed ridges. It was slow, deliberate work—an attempt to turn the terrain itself against their elusive prey.

Zra'ka watched from a high outcrop, tension never leaving his broad shoulders.

Days passed. Nerves frayed.

Every night, the Vek'smed danced just beyond reach—his movements nothing but faint echoes on the wind. He left no trail, only subtle signs of passage: a disturbed stone, a snapped twig, a whisper of breath before vanishing into the mountain's skin.

Then came another disaster.

A unit of Zra'ka's best fighters—tasked with guarding the northern perimeter—vanished without a trace. Only spatters of blood and shredded webbing marked where they had stood.

"Fant dette, Høvding," a scout reported, breath ragged as he handed Zra'ka a torn scrap of cloth. *"Found this, Chief."*

It was soaked in blood and embedded with thorns—foreign, sharp, precise. Vek'smed work.

Zra'ka's fingers curled around the cloth until it crumpled beneath his grip. Rage clawed at his chest, but so did something colder: doubt.

"Høvding... noen sier vi bør dra," another warrior said hesitantly. *"Chief, some say we should withdraw."*

He hesitated. "De tror fjellene sluker folk som myrene svelger fotspor." *"They believe these mountains swallow men as the marshes devour footsteps."*

Zra'ka scanned the weary faces around him—warriors hardened by swamps and battle, now looking as if they stood at the edge of something ancient and unknowable. His chest rose and fell with the weight of command.

Then, after a long silence, he drew a harsh breath and turned toward the gathered fighters.

"Vi drar." *"We leave."*

Gasps rippled through the camp—half relief, half disbelief.

"Tilbake til myra! Vi hente flere, flere krig'folk, mer blod—Vek'smed vinne kamp, men ikkje krig!" *Back to the marsh! We gather more, more warriors, more blood—the Vek'smed has won the battle, but not the war!*

There was no cheer. Only nods, solemn and slow. No one had to say it: the mountain had beaten them.

The journey back was silent save for the wind and the soft pull of web from rock. Each step away from the mountains felt like a bruise, but Zra'ka's mind churned, teeth grinding in thought. They would return. They would not forget.

The Forge's secrets would be theirs—no matter the cost.

As the Webshroud tribe vanished into the dense green of their homeland, the mountains loomed behind them in quiet judgment.

A reminder of the fierce battle fought… and the fiercer one still to come.

Chapter 16: Warden

781, 19th Day Of The Eighth Moon

"His fury—by the gods, what have I unleashed? Mira tells me it is the nature of my wife's bloodline, something ancient and powerful, but I never could have imagined it would manifest so... violently. He moved like a storm, swift and merciless, cutting through their ranks before they even knew he was upon them. By the time it was over, none were left to kneel—none were left to even draw breath. Her kin had warned me, and now I see the truth in their words. The mountain folk, once loyal, have withdrawn, leaving our halls empty, their whispers of fear growing louder. What have I brought upon us?"

✳✳✳

The hooded woman stirred from her thoughts, roused by the distant sounds of battle and the crackling flames that flickered ominously nearby. Rising to her feet, she dusted off her cloak, muttering a few arcane words that caused the flames to recoil, as if repelled by some invisible force. She turned just as Warden approached, his silhouette outlined against the burning horizon. His expression was hard, frustration simmering beneath his otherwise composed demeanor.

"Ah, Warden, you've caught up," she said, her tone casual despite the chaos surrounding them. "I take it your task is completed?"

Warden's voice was edged with tension. "I couldn't find the book," he replied. "Dalmon wasn't where I expected. I saw him fighting Mutt, but the town's in chaos. I had to pull back before I was recognized."

The woman's eyes narrowed at the mention of Mutt's name, but she listened without interruption.

"Belazar and A'nara also managed to slip through our grasp," Warden continued, his unease evident.

The hooded woman's lips curled in a faint smile, through her eyes remained cold. "No matter. Dalmon's clever, but his home lies in ruins, and Mutt is handling the secondary objective."

Warden's frown deepened. "I don't trust him. Mutt's volatile—he's out of control. He'll destroy everything without care for the larger plan."

The woman's voice sharpened. "Mutt may be unstable, but he gets results. Unlike others, he doesn't let doubt or hesitation get in the way." Her tone carried a quiet warning, her gaze unflinching. "We can't afford to be picky, Warden. You know that better than anyone."

Warden clenched his jaw but said nothing, the distant sounds of crumbling stone and muffled screams filling the silence between them.

Suddenly, a weak cry for help cut through the air. Razma, lying on the ground, tried to stand, but his injuries—deep burns and wounds that seared with every breath—kept him down. He groaned in agony, dragging himself weakly through the dirt, desperation clear in his voice. "Help me, please," he gasped, barely able to form the words.

Warden approached, his face unreadable. "Another one?" he said flatly, assessing Razma's condition. The young man's struggles were futile, his body wracked with pain, his movements sluggish.

The hooded woman stepped closer, peering down at Razma as if considering whether he was worth the trouble. After a moment's thought, she gave a dismissive wave. "Take him. He could be useful later. Inform Mutt to meet us at the waterfall once he's done. We'll regroup there."

Warden hoisted Razma effortlessly, the young man groaning in pain as he was carried away from the destruction. His body felt heavy, limp from shock and exhaustion, but his mind, though clouded, clung to the grim realization that he was at the mercy of these dangerous individuals.

The woman cast one last look at the burning town, her expression unreadable. "This is just the beginning," she whispered. "Seragora will burn, and from its ashes, a new order shall rise."

As they moved deeper into the woods, leaving the chaos of the burning village behind, Razma's thoughts swirled in confusion and terror. Each jarring step Warden took sent fresh waves of agony through his body, and Razma's mind struggled to make sense of the situation. The hooded woman's calm demeanor as she orchestrated the destruction unnerved him, and Warden's role in it all was equally perplexing. Why was he helping her? Why hadn't he left Razma to die?

"Keep quiet," Warden murmured as they trudged deeper into the forest. "You'll make it through this, but you need to be smart."

Razma's vision blurred with pain, but he managed to whisper, "Why… are you… doing this?"

Warden didn't answer immediately. Instead, he glanced over his shoulder at the hooded woman, who was walking several paces behind, seemingly lost in her own thoughts. When he finally spoke, his voice was low and filled with an unspoken burden. "Orders."

Razma's head throbbed, his body weak, but even through the haze of pain, he couldn't shake the feeling that Warden's answer was only part of the truth. Before he could ask more, they reached the waterfall.

Mutt was already there, his hulking form leaning casually against a boulder, his eyes gleaming in the dim light. He looked every bit the brute Razma feared him to be, but there was a sharpness in his gaze that hinted at something more dangerous than mere brute strength.

"Alt er som du befalte," Mutt grunted, his deep voice reverberating through the clearing. *"De*

sekundære målene er tatt hånd om. Beskjeden er sendt." "Everything is as you ordered. The secondary targets are dealt with. The message has been sent."

The hooded woman gave a curt nod, her gaze shifting briefly to the waterfall's rushing cascade before settling on Mutt. *"Bra,"* she said coldly. *"Nå samler vi styrkene våre. Seragora er sårbar, og vi slår til igjen før de får sjansen til å organisere seg."* "Good. Now we consolidate our forces. Seragora is vulnerable, and we'll strike again before they have a chance to organize."

Razma lay sprawled on the damp earth by the water's edge, body weighed down by exhaustion. Through half-closed eyes, he caught glimpses of them—the people responsible for the night's terror. Shadows of their conversation filtered into his awaren ess, every murmur filling him with unease. Helplessness gnawed at him as he tried to gather his scattered thoughts.

Then, the hooded woman turned, her sharp gaze slicing through him with unsettling intensity. She stepped closer, voice low and commanding. "You," she began coldly, "what do you know of Dalmon and Seragora's defenses?"

Fear shot through Razma, but defiance sparked too. "Nothing," he managed, voice cracking, his heart racing. "I don't know anything."

A mocking smile twisted her lips. "Oh, I think you know more than you believe," she murmured, a dark edge to her tone. "And you will tell me… when you're ready."

Razma forced himself upright, though pain screamed through his limbs. The burns across his skin flared with each breath, each beat of his heart. He had no answers, no idea who these people were, but the weight of her stare made him feel dangerously close to something he'd never imagined.

The woman crouched beside him, eyes narrowing. "Where did Dalmon and Belazar go?" she asked, voice smooth but threatening. "And where did they take A'nara?"

"A'nara?" he echoed, struggling to keep his voice steady. "The girl with my dad?"

Her disdain sharpened, and she spat, "Fool. She is no mere girl—A'nara is Slivdhe, beyond anything you could understand."

Razma felt a cold pit open inside him, the word "Slivdhe" foreign and strange. Who was A'nara, really? And what did his father have to do with her? He thought back to the fight, to the strange melody of the woman's words. The curiosity clawed its way out despite his fear. "What… what did you say back there? At the stable? It was… melodic, almost."

The woman's eyes flickered, and something shifted in her gaze—a dawning realization. "You don't speak Slivdhe," she muttered, her tone softening into something almost pleased. "Then Belazar's kept his secrets well."

Razma tensed as she leaned in, her voice dropping to a cold whisper. "Have you ever seen an old journal? A book hidden by Dalmon or your father?"

Confusion clouded Razma's mind, but he met her gaze, his own expression hardening with defiance. "I don't know about any book," he said, his voice barely above a whisper, but steady.

For a moment, the woman studied him in silence, the air between them taut. Then her lips curled into a chilling smile, and Razma understood with dreadful clarity—she believed he truly knew nothing, and that was exactly what she wanted.

The woman's gaze darkened, but she remained silent for a long moment, studying him as if weighing whether to believe him or not. Finally, she stood, her cold eyes shifting to Warden.

"Keep him alive," she ordered. "For now. He may know more than he realizes, and we'll need him if we are to find Dalmon."

Warden nodded, his expression unreadable as he glanced down at Razma. There was a flicker of something—pity, perhaps, or maybe regret—but it was gone as quickly as it appeared.

As the night deepened, Razma's thoughts grew hazier. The pain in his body dulled to a low, constant throb, and exhaustion threatened to pull him under. But one thing kept him anchored to the waking world: he had to escape. These people were dangerous, and if what they said was true, his father and the others were in more danger than he could have imagined.

He forced himself to stay awake, to listen, even as his body screamed for rest. Somewhere, deep in the back of his mind, a plan began to form. It wasn't much—a fleeting idea, born of desperation—but it was something. He would wait, bide his time, and when the moment came, he would act. He had to.

Warden remained nearby, his figure a looming presence in the shadows. Razma still couldn't quite figure him out. There was something about Warden that didn't fit with the rest of the group —the way he moved, the way he spoke, even the way he looked at Razma. His motives were unclear, but one thing was certain: Warden was not like the others.

As the hours dragged on, the waterfall's roar faded into the background, and the sounds of the night began to take over—the rustle of leaves, the distant call of an owl, the soft crackling of the dying fire. Razma lay still, conserving his strength, his mind racing with thoughts of escape.

He had to survive. He had to find his father and warn him of the danger. And most of all, he had to stop these people before they unleashed whatever dark plan they had in store for Seragora.

Razma, still reeling from the pain and shock of his injuries, watched as the hooded woman and Mutt hunched over a tattered map spread out on a rock. The flickering firelight cast eerie shadows against the dense foliage, making their movements look more like a sinister dance. Mutt's gruff grunts mingled with the woman's sharp, commanding voice, creating a tense atmosphere that hung heavy in the night air.

"Fokus, Mutt! Vi må slå her og her,"the hooded woman's voice cut sharply as she pointed to specific locations on the map. Her tone was cold, dismissive, as if Mutt was merely a clumsy tool, not a partner in this grim affair. She was all business, her presence chilling and domineering.

Mutt's massive frame seemed to grow even larger as his shoulders tensed. "Det e ikkje mitt navn. Eg samla stammene. Eg krev respekt" His voice, deep and booming, filled the clearing. His words were slow and deliberate, laced with a threat that hung in the air like a blade.

The hooded woman turned on him, her eyes gleaming with something far darker than annoyance. "Respekt må fortjenes, ikkje krevast," she spat, her words laced with venom. "Du e bare en mutt—uønsket og avvist av alle som ser deg. Husk plassen din."

Razma, lying half-obscured by the undergrowth, winced as he watched the tense exchange. His body throbbed from the beating he'd taken, but a deeper, primal fear clawed at him—a fear of what these two truly were. The hooded woman's voice was sharp and harsh, the words foreign to him, nothing like Slivdhe yet carrying a strange, guttural rhythm. Each syllable seemed to cut through the clearing with chilling intent, making her commands sound less like conversation and more like threats.

Beside her, Mutt's massive frame seemed to swell, his deep, growling voice booming in response. Though Razma couldn't understand the words, the defiance in Mutt's tone was unmistakable, echoing with the raw force of something wild. As Mutt shifted, Razma caught glimpses beneath his ragged cloak—a flash of something that seemed neither human nor beast. Scales? Claws? He couldn't tell in the dim light, but the fleeting sight of it sent a chill down his spine, layering his fear with a dark realization that whatever Mutt was, it was something he couldn't begin to comprehend.

Razma's pulse quickened, his mind racing as he tried to piece together the meaning behind their words. Though the language was lost to him, the tension and power struggle were painfully clear.

Mutt growled, a low, rumbling sound that seemed to vibrate through the ground. Yet despite the anger in his voice, he bowed his head slightly, submitting to the hooded woman's dominance "Som du vil" he muttered, his giant hands carefully navigating the edges of the map, as if afraid his strength would tear it apart.

From a distance, Razma caught Warden's gaze. The subtle nod was barely perceptible but spoke volumes. It was a warning, a plea for silence and vigilance. Razma gave the smallest of nods in return, his body tense with pain but his mind now fully aware of the critical nature of their situation.

The night deepened, and Razma's thoughts became consumed with escape. He ran through every scenario in his head, trying to find some way to slip away unnoticed. But with his injuries slowing him and the watchful eyes of the trio, escape seemed an impossible dream.

The silence was broken unexpectedly by Warden's quiet voice. "I know you're scared," he murmured as he knelt beside Razma, offering him a waterskin. "Drink. It'll help."

Razma hesitated for a moment before accepting the waterskin. His eyes locked onto Warden's, searching for some sign of what the man really intended. In that brief moment, there was an unspoken understanding—a shared recognition of their grim situation.

"Why are you doing this?" Razma croaked, his voice barely above a whisper as he took another sip of water, the coolness easing the raw dryness in his throat.

Warden paused, his face hardening, though not with cruelty—more with resignation. "We all have our orders, kid. Sometimes, the path isn't ours to choose."

Razma leaned forward, his desperation slipping through. "But you *can* choose. You could help me."

Warden's steps faltered. For a moment, he looked almost conflicted. His gaze flickered back to the hooded woman, busy sifting through ancient artifacts from her cloak. He muttered to himself, barely audible, "Not tonight. But I'm watching, listening. Be ready when the time comes."

Razma's heart pounded at the hint of promise, a fragile spark of hope. Warden turned back, but just as he moved to leave, he hesitated, then knelt down to meet Razma's eyes.

"One last thing," he said, his voice low. "She questioned you about the book. You weren't lying, were you? Because if she thinks you're holding back, she may make you pay for it." Warden's expression softened, something like concern crossing his face. "Listen, kid. In Slivdhe, you can't lie. The words themselves make it impossible. So, to put my mind at ease… tell me, in Slivdhe: do you know where the journal is?"

He held Razma's gaze, and then added, "Here. Yes is *Velin,* no is *Naroth.* Practice it. When she asks again, this could save you."

Razma swallowed, searching Warden's face before answering. He took a deep breath and, in a shaky voice, responded, "Naroth."

Warden nodded, a flicker of relief crossing his face. He didn't say more, just gave Razma a final, approving glance before returning to his post. Though cryptic, his message left Razma with a faint sense of reassurance. He might still survive, but he would need to stay sharp, ready for the moment when an opportunity presented itself.

The hours dragged on as Razma lay there, the symphony of the wilderness enveloping him— the rush of the waterfall in the distance, the soft rustle of leaves in the night breeze, and the occasional howl of distant creatures. Despite the pain, despite the fear, one thing became abundantly clear: survival wasn't just about making it through the night. It was about recognizing the exact moment when everything could change—and seizing it without hesitation.

Chapter 17: The Edge of Allegiance

771, 3rd Day Of The Fifth Moon

"The mountain people welcomed my wife and daughter with open arms, treating them as though they were kin long returned. With me, however, they were more reserved. Curious about their craft, I pressed Mira about their forges. She described them with a reverence that bordered on caution. When I asked if I might see them myself, my request was sidestepped, and more ale was brought instead. Mira, ever resourceful, later told me of an old tome hidden in the study, one that might contain the secrets of their techniques. She promised to teach me to read it, hinting that within its pages may lie the knowledge they guard so fiercely."

The council chamber was thick with tension as King Tor'valis and his advisors gathered for an emergency meeting. The grandeur of the room, with its high vaulted ceilings and stained-glass windows, did little to lighten the oppressive mood. King Tor'valis sat at the head of the table, his face etched with concern, while Lord Aric stood beside him, his loyalty to both king and people evident in his worried expression.

Lady Kira, her fingers adorned with jewels, was the first to speak, her voice sharp and filled with urgency. "Your Majesty, the riots in the streets and the fact Bazel attacked during the celebration have shaken Seragora to its core. The people are restless, and there are whispers of revolt. We must act swiftly before this unrest spreads further."

Lord Cedric, his voice low and calculated, leaned forward. "Lady Kira is right. The celebration drained our resources, and now, with the influx of refugees fleeing the Muckspawn attacks outside the city,our city faces turmoil. The people fear a long winter. If we don't address these concerns, we risk losing control. And with Bazel's delegation here, who knows what they might be plotting? They could easily use this unrest as an excuse for an attack."

King Tor'valis, his expression grim, leaned forward. "Bazel may not be our enemy in this. They face the same threat from the Muckspawn that we do. There's no proof they intend to move against us."

Lord Cedric scoffed. "No proof? Your Majesty, the people saw Bazel's armor in the streets, their knights in battle. If that doesn't concern you—"

Lord Cedric's voice dripped with disbelief as he leaned forward, eyes narrowing at King Tor'valis. "If that doesn't concern you, then what will? The people saw Bazel's colors in the streets, their armor, and their tactics. We can't ignore what's right in front of us."

The room fell into a tense silence, every noble present feeling the weight of Cedric's accusation. Lady Kira nodded in agreement, her jeweled fingers tapping the table as she added, "The people believe it was Bazel. Rumors are spreading like wildfire, Your Majesty. If we don't act swiftly, we'll have more than just riots on our hands. This unrest could lead to open revolt."

King Tor'valis rubbed his temples, the weight of the situation pressing down on him. "And what would you have me do, Cedric? Declare war on Bazel over what? A few sightings of their armor? Have you forgotten the Muckspawn's talent for sowing chaos? They've been using deception to turn foes against one another for years."

Lord Cedric shook his head in frustration. "It's not just the armor, Your Majesty. The reports mention a leader—a large general in Bazel armor, leading the charge. This was organized, coordinated. The Muckspawn are chaotic, disorganized. This had all the markings of a Bazel military operation."

Before King Tor'valis could respond, the grand doors of the council chamber swung open. Dalmon entered, flanked by two guards and a small group trailing behind him. At his side stood Yvonne, her gaze fixed and unwavering, and with them, a slender, hooded Muckspawn woman. The room fell silent as they made their way forward, all eyes shifting to the unexpected company.

Dalmon's face was lined with exhaustion, but his eyes held a steely determination. Bowing briefly, he addressed the king. "Your Majesty, I bring urgent news about the attacks tonight."

The king straightened, concern flashing across his face. "Speak, Dalmon."

Dalmon gestured to the cloaked figure, who hesitated before slowly lowering her hood. The chamber quieted as Tala, a small Muckspawn child, looked around nervously but with a determined fire in her gaze.

"This is Tala," Dalmon explained. "She witnessed the attack firsthand. And I can confirm our worst fear: the attackers were not Bazel soldiers but Muckspawn, disguised in Bazel armor."

The chamber erupted into shocked murmurs. Lord Cedric shot to his feet, eyes blazing with disdain. "A Muckspawn? And we're supposed to believe her? The people saw Bazel armor, not these creatures."

Before Dalmon could respond, Yvonne stepped forward, placing a steadying hand on Ky'len's shoulder. Meeting her gaze, Ky'len took a deep breath and stepped into the center of the room, his voice tight with controlled anger.

"Enough, Lord Cedric," he said sharply, silencing the murmurs. "I fought them myself. Tala was there and saved me and Iszell when no one else did. But where were the guards? The gates were left open, and we fought alone to protect the people. Yet, despite our efforts, innocent refugees were slaughtered."

The room fell silent, stunned by Ky'len's words. Lady Kira leaned forward, her expression composed but concerned. "Why were the gates unguarded? This points to more than mere negligence—it reeks of sabotage."

Lord Alric nodded, eyes narrowed. "If the gates were left open deliberately, someone within our own ranks is working against us."

Lady Seraphine's voice cut through the silence. "If guards were absent at such a critical time, we must consider this an inside plot to provoke chaos and pit us against Bazel."

King Tor'valis's expression darkened, his voice calm but unyielding. "We will find out who orchestrated this. If there is treachery among us, it will be exposed. Cedric, I will not tolerate baseless accusations clouded by bias. We need clarity, not division."

Cedric bristled, but under the king's authoritative gaze, he fell silent. Yvonne stepped forward, addressing the council. "Dalmon, Tala, Ky'len—you showed courage tonight. We must take their words seriously if we're to protect Seragora from further bloodshed."

The room stilled, the torchlight casting wavering shadows as the council absorbed the gravity of the situation. The question loomed heavy: who had left the gates open, and why were the guards absent when Seragora needed them most?

Dalmon took the opportunity to speak without interruption. "I fought them myself in the streets, Your Majesty," he said, turning to Tor'valis. "I fought Muckspawn wearing Bazel armor. They were small and quick, using the confusion of the night to attack while disguised. And I saw their leader. A large figure, bigger than any of the others—Mutt, the Muckspawn general. He was the one leading the charge. Not a Bazel knight."

The room grew still as Dalmon's words settled in. Lady Kira exchanged a look with Lord Alric, who frowned, his fingers tapping the edge of the table.

Tala, emboldened by Dalmon's support, added more, her words a blend of Muckspawn and broken Common. "Chieftain Mutt... han vil krig... make you humans fight hverandre. While he take land... mens dere begge svekket... weak."

Dalmon translated again. "She says Chieftain Mutt's plan was to force Seragora and Bazel into a war. With both of us fighting each other, the Muckspawn would seize power while our kingdoms were weakened."

Lady Seraphine turned to the others, her voice cautious but firm. "If there is any truth in this, it warrants our attention. Muckspawn wouldn't risk exposure unless they stood to gain significantly."

Lord Marten nodded. "A war based on assumptions is precisely what they want. Your Majesty, perhaps we should look beyond our grievances and give this warning due thought."

Ky'len, who had been watching the exchange, took a deep breath, his anger simmering just below the surface. "I'll lead a force to find these Muckspawn myself," he said, his voice steady despite the tension. "I'll prove that Bazel is innocent. We can find their camp, bring back proof, and stop this war before it starts."

King Tor'valis, who had been silently weighing the situation, finally spoke. His voice was calm but carried the weight of command. "We cannot make any decisions based on suspicion alone. We need proof. Ky'len, Dalmon—you will lead a small group to find these Muckspawn and confirm their involvement. If it is as you say, we will take action to prevent this war."

Ky'len nodded, his jaw tight with determination. "You'll have your proof, Your Majesty. I won't let this lie destroy us."

As the tension in the room began to settle, Tala's nervous voice broke through. "Der… mer," she stammered, her words halting as she struggled with Common. "En kvinne… name Thorn… Mrs. Thorn… works… med Høvding Mutt."

The name struck Dalmon and King Tor'valis like a blow. Both men stiffened, their expressions darkening as the weight of recognition set in. King Tor'valis's hand gripped the arm of his chair, his knuckles paling as he steadied himself, while Dalmon's usually calm face faltered, his eyes flashing with unease.

"Mrs. Thorn?" Dalmon asked, his voice barely more than a whisper. He leaned forward, his gaze locked on Tala, as if fearing he'd misheard. "Si det igjen… repeat that name."

Tala's gaze darted from Dalmon to the king, noticing their dread. She swallowed, hesitating before speaking. "Ja… Mrs. Thorn… she works with Høvding Mutt," she repeated, her own voice trembling.

King Tor'valis shared a glance with Dalmon, a flicker of shared fear passing between them. "Thorn," he muttered, the name slipping from his lips as though it carried a curse.

"Who is this Mrs. Thorn?" Cedric demanded again, though he kept his voice carefully restrained. "Why does her name make you both pale?"

Lady Kira leaned forward, her jeweled fingers drumming thoughtfully on the table. "Yes, explain! If this woman is working with the Muckspawn, the council has the right to know."

Dalmon and Tor'valis exchanged another glance, their expressions tight, refusing to reveal more than they had to.

"Who is she, Dalmon?" Lord Marten added, his voice rising with frustration. "Is she a threat we don't know about?"

"Enough!" King Tor'valis cut in, his voice booming, silencing the questions before they could spiral out of control. His eyes moved across the room, daring anyone to speak again. "In due time. Right now, urgency is needed more than answers."

Dalmon stood suddenly, his face set with grim determination. "I must go. I need to find Vil'elm and Belazar. If Thorn is involved, we don't have time to waste." Without waiting for further questions, he turned and strode toward the door.

"Dalmon!" Lord Cedric called out, but the man didn't stop. The door slammed shut behind him, leaving the council room buzzing with unrest.

As the echoes faded, King Tor'valis turned his attention back to Tala and Ky'len. "Tala, Ky'len," he said, his tone commanding but not unkind. "You must go to the Vek'smed. Warn them of this threat, and gather their support."

Ky'len nodded without hesitation, eager for action. "Yes, Your Majesty. But... may I take my friend Iszell with me? We can cover more ground together."

Tor'valis gave a curt nod. "Yes, yes, you may. Time is of the essence. Go at once."

Before Ky'len and Tala could leave, the lords erupted in protest, anger bubbling over as they demanded answers.

"You're sending them off without telling us what's really going on?" Lord Cedric rose, his voice brimming with indignation. "We need to know who this Thorn is! We cannot be kept in the dark!"

"Your Majesty, this is madness!" Lady Kira's voice was sharp, her tone bordering on insubordinate. "You expect us to act without understanding the full threat?"

Tor'valis's patience finally snapped. He slammed his fist onto the table, the echo silencing the room. His eyes blazed, anger radiating from him like a storm. "Yes, I do! For right now, I do not know who to trust. This council has questioned every one of my decisions while our kingdom sits on the brink of destruction!" His voice rose with righteous anger, each word striking the lords and ladies like a blow. "I do not want to hear grievances about rights or rumors. Many of you have never fought a day in your lives! You question me? Yvonne, Dalmon—they fought in that war. They know its horrors firsthand."

He turned his gaze toward Cedric, his voice cutting. "You speak of grievances, Cedric, but you did not fight. Your brother did, and he died with honor while you counted your coin."

Cedric's face flushed, but he did not dare interrupt.

"And you, Lady Kira," Tor'valis continued, his tone cold, "your family fled to the mountains when the war turned to fire and blood. While my people bled, your people took shelter in safety. Spare me your outrage about understanding the threat. You hid from it."

Lady Kira paled, her mouth tightening as she resisted the urge to retort.

"And you, Lord Marten, Lady Seraphina," Tor'valis said, his voice grim, "your fathers were my generals, fighting alongside me. They understood the meaning of loyalty, of honor, and sacrifice. They knew what it cost." His gaze swept over them, fierce and unyielding. "None of you know the horrors we faced, the lives that were lost, the shadows that nearly swallowed us.

None of you!"

The council sat in stunned silence, each of them cowed by the king's words.

Tor'valis's voice softened, though urgency remained in his tone. "Now, I send children to do the work of my lords and ladies. So, shut your mouths and do as your king commands. Your answers will come when I see fit to trust you."

The silence in the room was suffocating, none of the lords or ladies daring to speak. Tor'valis turned to Ky'len and Tala, his tone softening. "Go now. We are running out of time."

Ky'len gave a firm nod, then glanced at Tala, who was ready to lead him. Without another word, they left, leaving the room steeped in silence.

As the heavy doors shut, the murmurs of discontent began to rise once more among the lords and ladies, though none had the courage to speak aloud. Lord Cedric, however, his pride stung, could not help but voice one last concern. "Your Majesty, even if Bazel is not responsible, you cannot ignore what happened tonight. Hundreds were killed in the streets. How can we expect the people to accept this if they believe Bazel is involved?"

Tor'valis's expression darkened, his patience nearing its end. "You worry about the people now? Where were you and your guards when innocents were slaughtered? Do you think the people will care about your political maneuvering when blood stains the streets? You sit here questioning me when your inaction contributed to this chaos!"

A heavy silence filled the room as each council member looked away, unable to meet the king's gaze.

"I sent Ky'len and Tala because action is needed, not more questions. Dalmon seeks answers even now while you sit here in comfort. This is not the time for cowardice or hesitation." Tor'valis's words hung heavy in the air, laced with quiet fury. "I will do whatever it takes to protect this kingdom."

No one dared challenge him further, his words leaving a lasting mark on each member of the council. With a deep breath, he added, "Now, prepare for what is to come. Gather your guards, send them to clean the streets, and return here at sunrise. We have much to discuss."

The council members, shaken, rose in silence, filing out. Tor'valis remained, gripping the table as he stared into the flickering shadows, his expression weary.

A soft sound pulled him from his thoughts. He looked up to see Raelle standing in the doorway, her gaze solemn and steady. She moved closer, her eyes searching his face.

"I heard," she murmured, her voice trembling. "Is it true, Tor'valis? Is Thorn alive?"

Tor'valis nodded, his voice soft. "Yes, and I fear the shadows are growing again, love. I fear… what we must do to face them."

Raelle's hand found his, squeezing gently. "Then you must tell the council the truth. They need to understand the threat we're facing."

He sighed, the weight of the years pressing down. "The council questions me now, Raelle, questions every choice. But if they knew the full truth—what Dalmon and I did… what you had to do," he added, his eyes filled with regret. "I don't know if they'd trust me again."

Raelle brushed a hand across his face, her expression a mixture of love and sorrow. "We did what we had to. For Seragora. For those we swore to protect."

"I know," he whispered, his voice thick with emotion. "But sometimes I wonder if the price was too high. Thorn was supposed to be gone, her influence erased. Now she returns, and she's not alone."

Raelle's gaze sharpened. "If she is alive, then she's come back to finish what she started. And if you're right, if the council cannot be trusted with the truth… then perhaps it's time to face this storm alone."

Tor'valis leaned into her touch, finding strength in her warmth. "Perhaps. But I won't face this without you. We'll do what we must… together."

Raelle nodded, her voice steady though her eyes glistened with unshed tears. "Always, my love. Whatever shadows lie ahead, we'll face them side by side."

As Tor'valis and Raelle stood together, the silence in the room felt almost sacred—a fragile pause shared in a world teetering on the brink. Their gaze held the weight of scars and old sacrifices, a bond forged through trials that had taken too much and left them both changed. But this silence, too, would pass. Soon, they would face not only their enemies but their own people, their own fears.

Tor'valis finally broke the silence, his voice low. "Do you think they'll ever understand, Raelle? The price we paid to keep them safe? Sometimes I wonder if I ask too much, yet I know the cost of not asking."

Raelle's hand rested gently on his arm. "Perhaps they will one day, but remember, love… they weren't there. They didn't see what we did, and they don't carry the same scars." Her voice softened. "But they don't need to. That was the point, wasn't it? So they would never have to."

He nodded, her words a balm even as doubts lingered. "And yet, Thorn lives," he muttered, his expression hardening. "All our efforts, all the lives sacrificed… and still, she lives, spreading her poison in the shadows."

Raelle's expression darkened, her gaze drifting toward the chamber doors, where the council had filed out. "If Thorn has truly returned, vengeance will follow. And those lords—Cedric, Kira, Marten, Seraphina—she'll prey on them first. They're the easiest to manipulate. We've seen it before."

"Exactly." Tor'valis's tone turned steely, his resolve rekindling. "That's why we cannot reveal the

166

full extent of her reach. Each of them would wield this knowledge like a weapon, elevating themselves, settling old scores. They think they can fight this with politics."

Raelle's brow furrowed. "So what will you do?"

A glimmer of a plan began to take shape. "I'll start with those I can trust. I need warriors, not politicians. Ky'len, Tala… they're young, unseasoned, but they have heart. And Dalmon—he's already hunting for those who might help. He's wiser than any of those lords, and he's faced Thorn's wrath before."

Raelle nodded, understanding. "And what of the council? They're already suspicious. If you keep them in the dark too long, fear will turn them against you."

Tor'valis clenched his jaw. "Then we give them enough to pacify their doubts. No more. The last thing we need is Cedric whipping up the people with empty promises and half-truths."

Raelle's gaze softened as she watched him. "You've always carried this kingdom, Tor'valis. Even when they didn't deserve it."

A faint, sad smile touched his face. "And I'll continue to, as long as I have breath. But this time, we'll need more than our own strength to win."

She considered his words thoughtfully. "Perhaps it's time to reach beyond our borders—to those who remember the Thorrin War and what Thorn's return could mean."

Tor'valis's mind raced. "It's risky. Old alliances have faded, and peace has dulled memories."

"But some haven't forgotten," Raelle replied. "There are those who remember what we sacrificed. We'll need every ally we can gather."

His gaze sharpened. "Then we'll reach out, quietly. No proclamations, no fanfare—only the right words in the right ears. We have no time to waste."

As Tor'valis stood in Raelle's grip, his mind flitted back to that darkest day of the Thorrin War. The memory was as clear as if it were unfolding before him now.

✱✱✱

In the heart of the battlefield, King Aeldric had held the line against Thorn's twisted warriors, his blade moving with relentless purpose as he cut through enemies corrupted by her dark enchantments. Tor'valis, then a young prince, had fought beside Dalmon, his father's most loyal guard and right hand. Together, they had carved a path toward Aeldric, determined to reach him before Thorn herself did.

And then she appeared.

Thorn glided through the chaos like a specter, her gown flowing like a shadow given form, the scent of roses and decay trailing behind her. Her eyes burned with a deep, malevolent green, her magic wrapping around the battlefield like a living curse. In an instant, she was upon Aeldric, her powers binding him, forcing him to his knees.

"Father!" Tor'valis cried, rushing forward. But Raelle caught his arm, her grip ironclad.

"You can't go to him," she whispered, her voice tight with terror. "She'll kill you too."

Before Tor'valis could wrest himself free, the unthinkable unfolded before his eyes. Thorn raised her hand, and dark thorns erupted from Aeldric's limbs, twisting through his flesh and rooting him to the ground. His gasps turned to choking cries as vines burst from his mouth, his eyes, his hands—until he was nothing but a grotesque rose bush, blooming from the remains of the king.

Tor'valis was paralyzed by horror, his world fracturing as his father was consumed. He struggled against Raelle's hold, desperation clawing at his mind, but she held him back, whispering, "You're the only one left, Tor'valis. You have to survive."

In that moment, Dalmon, ever loyal, and his father's guard charged Thorn, their battle cries piercing the blood-soaked air. They slashed through the vines that spread across the earth, their blades striking with ferocity as they pushed her back step by step, forcing her to release her hold on the battlefield.

Out of the corner of his eye, Tor'valis saw something emerge from the shadows—a great silver werewolf, watching with intelligent, unblinking eyes. Its gaze locked onto him briefly, as if it recognized him, then flicked back to Thorn, who raised a hand to halt its approach. Bound to her will, it stopped, a silent sentinel of her power.

Dalmon shouted, his sword a blur as he cut down another wave of Thorn's warriors. "Get the prince out of here!" His voice was hoarse, every word strained as he blocked another one of Thorn's attacks, his blade glinting in the dark.

King Aldric, his strength fading, placed a trembling, blood-stained hand on Tor'valis's shoulder. His voice slipped into a dark, ancient verse, each line echoing with the weight of an old king's final plea.

"Fillidh an mørke, ciúin ach sterk,

Ag éirí fra bhfréamh, doimhne og dyp.

Nuair a dhúisíonn lost banríon, éist með kall,

Go dtitfidh fuil kong ársa—ekki bheidh hall.

Beidh an cloch quake, an t-áirse kald,

Cuirfear an treibh til daingean, mar leomhain sterkur.

Coinnigh an daingean, halda bac på doras,

Nó beidh gach ní gone, undir mørke fate.

Fan ar an wacht, áit a chuaileann rót og steinn,

Nó éilíonn an darkness ár ætt og lín."

With the last line, his hand slipped from Tor'valis's shoulder, his eyes dulling as he took his final breath. Tor'valis felt the weight of Aldric's warning settle into his soul—a last, solemn command. As Dalmon and the guard held the line, he and Raelle were drawn back, their gaze fixed on Aldric's fallen form as Thorn's shadow loomed and then withdrew—a dark promise of the chaos yet to come.

✶✶✶

In the dim light of the council chamber, Tor'valis recited his father's last words, his voice quiet but carrying a weight that echoed in the room. His gaze was distant, as if he could still see the battlefield where King Aldric had fallen, his words a binding spell cast in blood.

"Shadows return, in silent creep,

Rise from roots, from deep to deep.

When lost queen stirs, heed the call,

May old king's blood not let us fall.

The stone will quake, the forge go cold,

As tribes must gather, fierce and bold.

Hold fast the ward, and bar the gate,

Or all we've built succumbs to fate.

Where roots bind stone, we make our stand,

Or darkness claims both kin and land."

When he finished, silence settled over the room, broken only by the faint flicker of torchlight. Raelle, standing beside him, her brow creased with concern, turned to him and asked softly, "What does it mean?"

Tor'valis shook his head, a look of pained uncertainty in his eyes. "I don't know. Those were my father's last words to me. A warning, perhaps—a foretelling of what may come." He paused, searching Raelle's face as if hoping she might hold the answer. "But I fear we're seeing the shadows return, just as he said. And I've no choice now but to carry those words… and hope

169

my father's blood is enough."

Raelle's hand found his, steadying him as the meaning settled into the silence, a prophecy that felt closer with each breath.

Chapter 18: Price of the Forest

775, 12th Day Of The Seventh Moon

"After years of searching, we've uncovered it. The very thing Mira and I have toiled over, night after night, poring over dusty tomes and guarded whispers. My wife regards us with a wary eye, the shadow of suspicion clouding her gaze. She believes perhaps that Mira and I are entangled in some affair, a quiet betrayal of the heart. But if she knew the true depths of our findings, of what has been hidden in our own bloodline, her suspicions would shift to something far darker. I shall have to remedy that. No force, not even her kin, will keep my son from the legacy that runs in his blood."

The first light crept through the trees, casting long, ghostly shadows that wrapped around the camp like watchful sentinels. The forest was a dense, living maze of towering oaks and gnarled branches, their dark forms looming as if guarding secrets older than memory. The scent of damp moss mingled with the sharp tang of pine and earth, while the morning mist curled around the trunks, blurring the line between the waking world and dreams.

Amid this eerie stillness, the hooded woman turned sharply to Mutt, her movements fluid, almost serpentine. Her voice cut through the silence, cold and commanding, resonating with an authority that made the air around them seem colder.

"Dáleit, tóg an príosúnach eile… chuig an gcoimeád." *"Go, fetch the other prisoner… bring him to the keep."* Her Slivdhe words were sharp as the edge of a blade. "Ní féidir linn aon mhoill a fhulaingt." *"We cannot afford any hesitation."*

Mutt's expression flickered with doubt, a rare crack in his usually resolute demeanor. He muttered in a low, guttural tone, "Kvifor ikkje bruka vår eiga mål?" *"Why not use my own tongue?"*

Her eyes glinted beneath the hood, twin coals burning with disdain. "An bealach seo, ní féidir bréag a insint dom." *"This way, you can't lie to me."*

With a resigned nod, Mutt turned, the tension in his massive frame betraying his reluctance. He moved into the mist, his heavy form swallowed by the forest as if it were alive and intent on devouring him. The whispers of the trees seemed to follow, their branches swaying in a wind that did not touch the ground. Razma, lying bound and bruised, strained his ears to listen, heart thundering with each ghostly rustle.

The woman's gaze settled on Razma, a predator's stare that made his breath catch. Warden, standing a few paces behind, was a figure carved from shadow and intent. The woman's voice, as sharp as winter's bite, demanded, "Tell me, child… where is the book?"

Razma's jaw tightened, fear twisting in his gut, but he forced himself to reply in Slivdhe, a word steeped in defiance, "Naroth." *"No."*

Her eyes narrowed, and shadows gathered at her fingertips, swirling like ink in water. Pain lashed through Razma, searing and sudden, as though invisible talons were tearing at his very being. He screamed, the sound raw and uncontained. "Naroth! I can't lie! Naroth!"

Warden's voice sliced through the clearing, steady and cold. "Enough. You may wield power, but you won't break him—not while I stand here."

The woman's expression shifted, momentarily intrigued by his defiance. "Even for the child of your enemy?"

"Even then," Warden replied, his eyes dark, unwavering.

The forest seemed to hold its breath as the two figures stood locked in silent conflict. The branches overhead swayed, whispering secrets only the trees understood. At last, with a flick of her wrist, she released Razma from the spell, the pain dissolving as quickly as it had come. He collapsed, shivering against the cool, damp earth, each ragged breath a struggle. Without another word, the woman turned and melted into the mist, her cloak trailing behind like the tail of a storm cloud.

Warden dropped to one knee beside Razma, his usually cold eyes softened with worry. "Don't let them find your breaking point," he murmured, each word a fortress against despair. "They'll twist everything to reach it."

Razma's wide eyes met his, desperation clawing at him. "Help me escape," he gasped. "I need to find my father. Who is she, and why does she want the book?"

Warden's gaze shifted, scanning the dim light filtering through the forest canopy. "Her name is Miss Thorn. She is more shadow than woman, a whisper that became nightmare. The book holds power she craves—knowledge that could turn even the most noble into monsters. Your father and I have crossed paths with her kind before, but she's never been this strong, this relentless."

The mist swirled thicker, tendrils of it brushing past like cold hands, as if the forest itself were listening. Razma swallowed, fear growing roots in his chest. "We have to move, don't we?"

Warden's hand found Razma's shoulder, steadying him. "Yes. We need to disappear before she returns. Stay close and don't falter, not even for a moment."

The light of dawn bled through the trees in thin, golden rays, illuminating the undergrowth in fractured pieces. The ground was uneven, carpeted in fallen leaves that whispered underfoot. The towering trees seemed to press closer with each step, their branches intertwined, casting dark lacework shadows that played tricks on the eye. Warden's breathing was shallow, each spell taking its toll, but his resolve was iron.

As they moved deeper into the forest, its ancient silence became a companion, broken only by the creaking groan of trees and the rustle of unseen creatures. The air felt thick, almost sentient, as if the woods themselves were waiting, watching. Razma's small, fearful glances caught movement in the distance—flitting shapes that dissolved when he blinked. The scent of pine and decaying leaves filled his senses, mingled with the bitter tang of sweat and fear.

The trees, ancient and gnarled, stood as silent witnesses. Their bark was rough and cracked, etched with the passage of countless seasons, while twisted roots jutted from the ground like the fingers of buried giants. Shafts of pale light filtered through the canopy, catching on droplets of dew that clung to leaves—turning them into a thousand tiny mirrors. It was a place caught between beauty and menace, a realm that did not welcome them, but offered no choice but to press on.

Warden paused suddenly, eyes narrowing.

Two guards stood ahead, stationed at the edge of a clearing. Clad in dark armor, faces obscured by helmets, their weapons glinted dully in the half-light.

He dropped into a crouch.

An incantation slipped from his lips—soft, smooth, and sharp as wire. Magic surged through him, coiling tight around his senses until he could feel the forest's pulse like a second heartbeat.

The roots stirred.

They slid from the earth in silence, swift and sure—groping, twisting, alive with intent. The roots struck with practiced cruelty, wrapping around the guards' ankles like snakes. There was no time to scream. No time to react. One of the guards managed a muffled grunt before a thick vine surged upward and lashed across his face, yanking him down. Another root curled over his mouth, forcing silence where panic bloomed.

The second guard wasn't as lucky. He thrashed, slashing wildly at the roots with his blade, but the forest was faster. Thorns erupted from the soil, hooking into his arms and shoulders, anchoring him to the ground like prey in a web. His eyes widened beneath his helm, filled with a primal terror—then fury—then realization.

Warden stepped forward slowly, raising a hand.

The ground itself responded.

With a final, decisive pull, the roots coiled tight. Bone snapped. Armor buckled. The sounds were wet, final.

Then silence.

The earth shifted once more, swallowing the bodies whole. The soil sealed itself like skin, leaving no trace but a darkened patch of damp earth.

No graves.No names.Just silence.

Razma stood frozen, eyes fixed on the place where they had stood. His face was pale, lips parted like he meant to speak—but forgot how.

Finally, his voice cracked through the stillness. "Did you… have to kill them?"

Warden didn't flinch. "Yes, kid. It was us or them."

Razma took a step forward. "They didn't even draw their weapons."

"They didn't have time," Warden said, turning to face him. His voice was flat. "That was the point."

Razma's fists clenched. "They didn't even know we were here."

"No," Warden agreed. "And if I'd let them see us, they'd never stop coming."

He adjusted the pack on his shoulder, scanning the trees. His expression was unreadable, but something flickered beneath it—guilt or grim resolve, Razma couldn't tell.

"Thorn's watching," Warden continued. "Her hounds will be looking for blood, for bodies, for signs we're still out here. So we give them a message."

He gestured toward the soil. "We made it clean. Fast. Final."

He looked back at Razma, eyes hard and tired. "We want her to think we're in the wind."

The mist thickened as they pressed on, curling around their ankles like spectral hands. Warden's steps grew heavier. With each whispered incantation, the forest reshaped itself— branches bowed to create paths, roots shifted, vines recoiled. The way ahead opened for them… and then closed behind like a mouth sealing shut.

But magic was never free.

It gnawed at him—quietly, relentlessly. His breaths shortened. Sweat slicked his brow. His limbs trembled beneath the strain. Every step dragged more than the last.

Then—movement.

A flicker of red-brown fur in the canopy. A squirrel, round and sharp-eyed, perched on a branch. It watched them. Unmoving.

It didn't flee. It didn't blink.

Warden narrowed his eyes. Whispered three syllables, low and sharp, barely audible.

His fingers twitched.

The squirrel dropped.

It hit the earth with a dull, wet thud.

174

A heartbeat later, the cry came—a sharp, choking squeak that echoed faintly after the body had already stilled. The sound trailed like something disembodied. Delayed.

Razma turned toward it, brows drawn in confusion, but he said nothing.

Warden didn't break stride. He exhaled—slow, deliberate—and straightened. His steps grew smoother. His shoulders squared. The pallor in his face began to fade.

He said nothing.

But something had changed.

The forest, once whispering and watchful, seemed… sated.

Razma stumbled again. His legs shook beneath him.

He wiped sweat from his face, but it came faster than before. His breaths were shallow, irregular. His head spun.

Warden glanced back just in time to see him fall to one knee.

"Razma."

The boy didn't answer.

Warden cursed and dropped beside him. "Damn it…"

The forest had gone still. Waiting.

He shifted Razma onto his back. The boy's frame was light, almost too light—but the weight of him pressed like stone.

Razma's voice came weak against Warden's ear. "What's… happening to me?"

"You're tired," Warden said. His voice was too calm. Too practiced. "That's all. Grayleaf isn't far. Just hold on."

The branches overhead creaked in agreement. The path narrowed.

Still, Warden moved faster now. Steadier. The shake in his hands was gone. His gait smoother. The magic that had nearly broken him minutes ago no longer clung quite so tightly.

"Warden…" Razma whispered. "Why did you save me?"

The question struck harder than the boy's weight.

Warden didn't answer at first. He shifted the boy higher on his back, tightening his grip.

"Because some things are worth saving, kid," he muttered at last. "Even when the odds are against us."

They broke through the mist.

Grayleaf appeared like a painting—cottages leaning close, smoke curling from chimney tops, the smell of damp wood and baked bread still lingering in the air.

Warden staggered to the nearest door.

He knocked once. Hard.

The door opened.

Glendale stood there—worn, wary, weapon behind her back. Her eyes went from Warden to Razma, then back again.

"What have you done?" she asked, voice like flint.

"Saved him," Warden said. His voice had more strength than it should have.

Glendale stared a moment longer. Then stepped aside.

Warden crossed the threshold, laying Razma gently on the cot by the hearth. The boy was pale. Quiet. Breathing—barely.

Warden sank to the floor beside him, every joint screaming in protest.

Glendale worked quickly, gathering herbs and tools with practiced hands. She glanced down at Warden only once, her eyes narrowed.

"Rest while you can," she said. "We have much to discuss."

Warden leaned back against the wall, eyelids heavy.

The last thing he heard before sleep took him was the wind brushing past the door.

And something behind it still listening.

Still waiting.

Still hungry.

Warden didn't sleep.

He sat with his back to the wall, the fire throwing long shadows across the floor. The wood popped softly, and the warmth barely touched him. His eyes stayed fixed on the cot across the room.

Razma lay still, wrapped in a blanket too big for him. One arm had slipped free during sleep, hand curled like he'd been holding onto something before the dream took it.

Warden exhaled slowly, the breath rattling just a little on the way out.

He looked too young.

Too much like someone else.

And that was dangerous.

His hand drifted to the faint scar on his wrist. A whisper of the past, still pulsing beneath the skin.

The memories rose uninvited.

The Thorrin War.

He'd been no older than Razma. Just another scared boy standing in mud that soaked up blood too fast to dry. He hadn't fought for glory. Not for kings. Just fought because the people beside him were bleeding, and no one else knew the right words to speak into the dirt to keep them breathing.

He remembered the night the mercenaries burned the outer camps. Remembered the screaming. The thunder. The firelight in the trees. And a boy—quiet, younger, always holding Warden's sleeve when the sky cracked too loud.

Warden had taken him. Carried him through ash and swamp when others said he wouldn't make it. He hadn't asked if the boy wanted to be saved.

He'd just done it.

Because someone had to.

Because survival didn't always wait for permission.

Now Razma lay there, too still. Pale. Touched by magic that wasn't his.

Warden dragged a hand across his face, fingertips pressing against his temple as if the ache behind his eyes could be pushed back inside.

"I didn't want to draw," he muttered under his breath. "Didn't mean to."

The fire crackled. The shadows shifted.

"But the forest takes what it needs. Sometimes… that means blood."

He rose slowly, knees tight, and moved to the cot. Crouched beside Razma. Watched the small twitches in the boy's face—like even his dreams couldn't quite settle.

"You don't get to know the cost yet," Warden whispered. "That's the thing about being young. The world takes from you and pretends it's doing you a favor."

He adjusted the blanket at Razma's shoulder, smoothing it down like the gesture could erase everything that had come before.

"She would've done worse. You don't know what she's capable of. I do."

Silence followed. Long and hollow.

Then, more to himself than the boy:"Remember this part, kid. When you hate me later."

He stood. His voice softer now, like it wasn't meant for the room at all.

"It was me who got you away."

He crossed to the window, resting one hand against the frame. The trees stood beyond the fog, silent, watching. They always did.

And somewhere deep inside him, the question stirred again—quiet and cruel:

How many times can you carry someone away before you become the thing they need to run from?

Warden didn't have the answer.

But he stayed at the window anyway.

Waiting.

Chapter 19: Rising Past

770, 17th Day Of The Ninth Moon

"Today, my son gripped his first blade—a small one, dulled at the edge, yet he held it with fierce determination, eyes alight with a hunger that I know all too well. The elders looked on with cautious eyes, muttering of his 'thirst' and calling it a fire that must be tempered. They speak as though his spirit is a threat, something to be controlled, fearing it will blaze beyond their comfort. I assure them it is only natural; my forefathers were shaped by the same fire, by the same unyielding will to forge their own path."

Belazar and A'nara awoke amidst the wreckage in the forest, the horses panicking wildly. They swiftly secured the animals as the flames engulfed the barn. "We have to go after them, we can't let them escape," A'nara urged. Belazar looked sorrowfully at his home of the past fifteen years, now in ruins, his gaze lingering on Razma's room in what remained of the house. "Yes... they went east, I can smell them," he murmured, pained by the loss of his home and the danger at hand. Quickly gathering essentials, Belazar and A'nara secured Cleo and the other horses they could catch, setting off eastward into the dense, aromatic embrace of Wolf Creek Woods. The crisp scent of pine and the rich, damp earth filled their lungs as they ventured further into the wilderness. The rustling leaves and distant calls of birds formed a symphony that enveloped them, the shadows of nightfall dancing upon the forest floor.

As Belazar saddled Cleo, a prickling unease crept over his skin, prompting him to voice his concern. "Fágáil gan Razma—dainséarach é." *"Leaving without Razma—it's risky."*

A'nara's voice cut through the tension, steady and sharp as a blade. "Beidh Dalmon ag breathnú air; níl duine níos fearr lena chosaint." *"Dalmon will look after him; there's no one better to keep him safe."*

"Is é mo mhac é," Belazar muttered, anguish woven into his tone. *"He is my son."*

"In am beidh sé ag tuiscint. Beidh Dalmon air a chaomhnú," A'nara replied, her voice holding the weight of conviction. *"He will understand in time. Dalmon will watch out for him."*

Belazar's anger ignited, erupting with a fury that echoed through the trees, causing Cleo to rear up. The clash of metal and the beat of his own heart seemed to merge. "Mura raibh tusa tagtha ar ais, ní bheadh sé i dteideal cosaint!" *"If you had stayed away, he wouldn't need protection!"*

Sparks of anger flashed in A'nara's gaze, like embers set to burst into flame. "Tá an talamh seo chomh liomsa agus atá sé leat, Belazar Silverfang. Tá fiacha ort." *"This land belongs to me as much as to you, Belazar Silverfang. You owe me."*

Belazar spat, resentment seething through his voice. "Nar vor'thal ienar!" *"Nothing do I owe*

179

you!"

"Slivar Fang vor'ri mara en'thor falir, vel'tir hin ni'thal or'hira. Ienar vor hin'thar valen sarith fin tel'thal Dalmon mara ienar fin'tir." *"Silverfang shall remain a scar of the past, sealed never to be reopened. I can still taste the metallic tang of the veins Dalmon and I breached."* His brow furrowed, the weight of remorse and days long past mirrored in his eyes.

"Belazar, tuigim…" *"Belazar, I understand..."*

"An mara'vor?" *"Do you?"* he shouted, his voice tearing through the forest.

Nar vor'tor hin'tar mara ienar sarith. Ienar vor mara'thal. Ienar vor atheran mara elorin." *"You have no idea what I've endured. I left that life. I made a family and friends."*

Tears glistened in A'nara's eyes, catching the moonlight filtering through the trees. "Tuigim. Mharaigh siad mo shráidbhaile, ag spáráil mise agus Dalmon amháin." *"I do. They massacred my village, sparing only Dalmon and me."*

A wave of regret washed over Belazar, as tangible as the cool breeze through the forest. "Tá brón orm. Ba bhotún é a bheith páirteach leo, a scrios muid araon. Guím go bhfaighidh Dalmon Razma agus go mbeidh muid in ann bualadh le chéile." *"I'm sorry. Joining them was a mistake that destroyed us both. Let's hope Dalmon can find Razma and meet us."*

They stood in silence, the scent of pine and the whispers of the wind their only witnesses.

A'nara's question broke the stillness. "Cé a shábháil muid ansin, Belazar?" *"Who saved us back there, Belazar?"*

"Ní fhios agam," he admitted, a weight settling on him. *(I don't know.)* "Ach buíochas leis na flaithis gur rinne siad. Ní dóigh liom go bhféadfainn an bhean sin a mharú." *"But thank the heavens they did. I don't think I could have killed that woman."*

A'nara quickened her stride, evading his touch as his memories tormented him. They rode in silence for hours, the only sounds being the whisper of the forest leaves rustling in the breeze and the rhythmic clopping of the horses' hooves on the soft, mossy ground. Finally, they arrived at a serene moonlit clearing, ancient oak trees standing sentinel around a waterfall that cascaded gracefully into a mist-covered pool, the sound of the water splashing onto rocks creating a soothing melody.

"Campaeir or'har fin vel'eth," *"We'll camp here for the night,"* said Belazar, breaking the cold silence that hung in the dewy air.

"Velin, fin'thar capell vor sarith. Enar vor'ath thir'vell," *"Aye, the horses are exhausted. I'll take the first watch,"* A'nara replied, the grass sinking beneath her boots as she slowly led her horse around the camp.

Belazar sighed deeply as he dismounted, the leather of his saddle creaking in protest, the smell of wet earth and pine filling his senses. He began setting up camp in a secluded grove of oaks, the rough bark scraping against his fingers. His eyes followed A'nara's every step, reading the simmering tension in her movements. He considered apologizing, even taking a step towards her, but then thought better of it. Instead, he allowed her to walk off her emotions, their shared history weighing heavily like a thick blanket in the cool night air, punctuated by the distant calls of nocturnal creatures.

Belazar got a small fire going just as A'nara returned from her walk, the crackle of kindling adding to the natural symphony around them.

"Vor mara'thal? Hin mara vor'thal'nar," *"Is that wise? We could be seen,"* she asked quietly, her voice barely rising above the low noise.

"Is ea, tá sé riosca. Rinne mé cinnte gur roghnaigh mé áit shábháilte." he said, feeling the heat from the fire on his face as he began to skin a rabbit, the scent of fresh meat mixing with the smoke. *"Aye, it is a risk. I made sure to choose a secure location."*

A'nara, looking at the meat, sighed deeply. "Vor mara?" *"Must you?"* she asked, her voice tinged with reproach.

"Velin'thor. Mara'thor ienor," *"Sorry, I forgot"* he admitted, the knife pausing in his hand.

"Nar vel'thal. Ienar vor hin val'tir. Beir'thal mara," *"It's okay. I know you need the protein. Just be gentle"* she said, turning away, the soft rustle of her cloak slipping into her bag.

They ate in silence as the moon cast elongated shadows, each lost in their own thoughts.

As darkness fell, Belazar broke the silence. "Lig dúinn codladh. Tá go leor eile le taisteal amárach," a dúirt sé go brónach *"Let us sleep. We have much farther to travel tomorrow"*.

A'nara sighed heavily as she unrolled her sleeping mat, her head sinking into the folds of her worn, travel-stained cloak. The weight of her weariness pressed down on her like a heavy, unyielding yoke. Belazar, standing nearby, shook his head in silent grief, a silent storm brewing within him, before leaning his tired back against the rough bark of an ancient oak tree, which stood like a stoic guardian of time. He sought the solace of sleep but found himself stuck in a turbulent sea of restless stirrings, as the encroaching shadows of the night cast a tapestry of long-lost memories, each thread rewoven with the somber colors of sorrow and pain anew. As the smoke of the fire rose, he was cast back, lost in the echo of lives past.

Young Belazar charged forward, his heart a thunderous beat of desperation, his sword gripped so tightly his knuckles turned white. His teacher's arm lashed out in a ruthless sweep, sending him crashing to the ground. Pain erupted along his side as he landed on a gnarled root that dug into his ribs. "Éirigh, buachaill! Cruinneas, ní fearg! *"Get up, boy! Precision, not fury!"* his teacher's voice snapped, as cold and sharp as steel. Belazar staggered to his feet, his face smeared with cold mud, his breath catching from the shock of the blow.

A taunting voice cut through the air, dripping with mockery. "B'fhéidir go caithfidh mo dheirfiúr a thaispeáint duit conas smidiú a dhéanamh. *"Maybe my sister should teach you how to do makeup."* Belazar's eyes locked onto his rival, Dalmon, the sneer on the boy's face igniting a blaze of fury within him.

"Dún é, Dalmon! *"Shut it, Dalmon!"* he spat, tasting the bitter tang of leaves and dirt as he pushed himself upright. Dalmon's laughter grated against his pride, the sound a cruel reminder of his failures.

But the teacher's icy tone sliced through the mockery. "Sea, dún é—mura dteastaíonn uait mo chlaíomh a bhaint amach *"Yes, shut it—unless you want to meet my sword."* Dalmon's mirth vanished, his posture snapping to attention, fear widening his eyes.

"Tá brón orm, Máistir. Fanfaidh mé ciúin. *"Sorry, Master. I shall keep quiet,"* Dalmon muttered, the bravado gone.

With a swift, brutal hiss, the teacher's blade flicked across Dalmon's cheek, and a mist of blood filled the air before spattering to the earth. "Tarraing do chlaíomh, mo dhalta. *"Draw your sword, my pupil,"* he commanded, his gaze shifting back to Belazar. Dalmon staggered, clutching his bloodied cheek, his eyes dark with rage and humiliation.

Belazar's heart pounded with a mix of fear and determination as he lifted his sword, barely steadying it with his trembling grip. He blocked the first two strikes—one coming from his left, another aiming toward his middle—but the third cleaved into his thigh, a devastating blow that sank deep into muscle and bone. He fell to the ground with a scream wrenched from his lungs, his vision dimming as the agony seared through him.

The teacher sheathed his blade with a disgusted sigh. "A'nara, tabhair leat do dheartháir agus an náire seo go dtí an leighis. *"A'nara, take your brother and this disgrace to the healer."*

Through blurred vision, Belazar caught sight of A'nara stepping forward, her golden hair catching the faint light, casting her in a cold, ethereal glow. She moved with careful grace, assisting her brother as he clutched his bloodied cheek. Dalmon glared down at Belazar, hatred glinting in his eyes, his fingers red with his own blood. "Tarraing, A'nara. Níl mórán ama againn; tá Athair ag fanacht. *"Come, A'nara. We must not keep Father waiting."*

Belazar tried to push himself up, his body failing him, his strength evaporating as he gasped for air. Using his sword as a crutch, he managed to lift himself halfway, only to collapse again as white-hot pain seared through his leg.

A'nara hesitated, her gaze flickering toward him with a glimmer of empathy, of regret. She took a step forward, her hand slightly extended. But Dalmon's harsh voice halted her. "A'nara, tarraing. Lig don dirt-dweller titim; tá Athair ag fanacht. *"A'nara, come. Let the dirt-dweller fall; Father is waiting"*

Ignoring her brother's command, A'nara returned to Belazar, kneeling beside him. Her hands hovered over his leg, her eyes meeting his in silent understanding. "Tost," she whispered, her voice low and firm. "Ní dhéanfaidh sé mórán ama. Fan socair "*Quiet now. It won't take long. Stay still.*"

Belazar's pain was sharp and relentless, but he held his breath as A'nara's hands glowed faintly with a soft, silver light. Her touch was gentle yet powerful, the warmth seeping into his skin and dulling the ache. The bleeding slowed, then stopped altogether, the wound knitting itself closed in seconds.

"Cén fáth? "*Why?*" he managed to whisper, confusion and awe mixing in his gaze as he looked up at her.

A'nara's lips formed a sad smile as she stood, brushing the dirt from her hands. "Ní fhágann muid ár ndreama, fiú amháin más rud é nach dtuigeann tú é fós. "*We don't leave our own behind, even if you don't understand it yet.*"

With a final look, she turned back to join her brother, who watched her with a frown, his face still twisted with scorn. Belazar lay there, the lingering warmth of her healing touch spreading through him, filling him with a sense of gratitude and confusion. In that moment, he knew this small act of kindness, defying both her brother and the bitter rivalry that hung between them, would stay with him forever.

Pain shot through Belazar's knee as he glanced down, instinctively swatting at a small snake coiled near his leg. The sudden motion disturbed A'nara from her light sleep, her eyes fluttering open as the snake slithered off through the leaves. "Níl aon rud ann, téigh ar ais a chodladh," he murmured, his voice laced with fatigue. "i*t's nothing, go back to sleep.*" A'nara nodded slightly, rolling over as her breathing slowed, allowing Belazar's own exhaustion to finally pull him into a fitful slumber.

Belazar awoke to the gentle crackle of the fire and the faint scent of damp earth. Shafts of sunlight filtered through the trees, casting a warm glow on A'nara's golden hair. The savory smell of mushrooms sizzling in a pan filled the air. He touched his knee gingerly, seeing the two scabbed-over wounds dark with dried blood. A'nara's gaze met his as he rose. "Ith. Rachaidh mé ar aghaidh ag breathnú," she said, her tone firm but tinged with concern. *Eat. I'll scout ahead.* With a practiced grace, she mounted her horse and rode off with an easy, fluid pace.

Belazar watched her vanish down the trail, rolling up his bedding slowly. A heavy sigh escaped him, his thoughts drifting to distant memories. "Tá súil agam go dtuigeann tú lá éigin, a mhic. Dalmon, cosain é," he whispered to the morning air. *I hope you understand someday, son. Dalmon, protect him.* He packed up the camp and saddled his horse, eventually catching up with A'nara further along the path.

She cast a sideways glance at him, a spark of mischief in her eye. "Tá tú mall go leor," she teased. *About time you caught up.*

"B'éigean dom do praiseach a ghlanadh," he retorted, an amused glint in his voice. *I had to clean up your mess.*

"Cosúil leis na seanlaethanta," she grinned. *Just like old times.*

"Sea, cosúil leis na seanlaethanta," he echoed, rubbing his knee with a touch of nostalgia. *Yes, like old times.* "Rachaidh muid ar aghaidh. Déan iarracht coinneáil suas," he challenged with a grin, urging his horse into a gallop. *Let's ride. Try to keep up.* A'nara laughed, a familiar sound that warmed the air as she spurred her horse past him, her laughter mingling with the rush of wind as they raced. For a moment, joy replaced their weariness, threading through the trees with them. Eventually, they slowed, and silence fell between them once more, broken only by the occasional stolen glance, each careful to keep it hidden.

Suddenly, A'nara's voice shattered the peace. "Féach, Belazar—rianta. Rinne duine éigin a mbealach tríd anseo le déanaí." *Belazar, look—tracks. Someone came through here recently.*

Belazar's gaze dropped to the ground, eyes narrowing. "Fanaig i ngar; b'fhéidir go mbeidh orainn troid," he murmured, hand instinctively moving toward his weapon. *Stay close; we might need to fight.*

A gravelly voice cut through the night in harsh Common. "Is that how you treat old friends?"

Belazar stiffened, his gaze darting to a short, muscular figure cloaked in crimson. The scent of incense mixed with pine, curling through the cool air.

"Surprised?" The man stepped forward, his green, scaly skin glinting in the dim light, a mocking smile twisting his lips. Spiked ridges lined his back, adding a sinister edge to his appearance.

Belazar's voice was tight, a blend of anger and shock. "How did you find us, Iaggardo?"

A sly smirk danced across Iaggardo's face, the malice in his eyes catching the faint moonlight. "I have my ways."

Belazar's face hardened as he forced himself to stay composed, even as a flicker of fear tightened his chest. "You had help," he deduced, the accusation hanging heavy in the air. "Someone from the village?"

Iaggardo's laughter was sharp, reverberating against the stone with a chilling echo. "Yes, indeed. But you'll never guess who."

Belazar's heartbeat hammered against his ribs. "Who?"

Iaggardo savored the moment, letting the tension stretch before finally replying, "Our old friend, Vil'elm."

Disbelief rippled across Belazar's face, his voice breaking. "Vil'elm would never betray us!"

"Oh, but he did." Iaggardo's smile widened, reveling in Belazar's shock.

"Liar!" Belazar's voice rose, a fierce growl, as rage boiled within him. "What lies did you feed him?" His eyes blazed, casting wild shadows in the flickering torchlight.

"Only the truth," Iaggardo replied calmly, his voice as cold as steel. With a cruel smirk, he snapped his fingers. "Bring him out, boys."

From the shadows, hunched Muckspawns appeared, dragging a battered and broken Vil'elm between them. His face was bloodied, his gaze pleading. A faint, whispered apology escaped his lips, weighed down with regret.

A'nara's anguished scream tore through the silence, only for Belazar to clamp a hand over her mouth, holding her back with steely resolve. Answers mattered now more than vengeance.

"Why, Vil'elm? Why betray us?" Belazar's question rang out, raw and choked, against the muted forest sounds.

"They left me no choice," Vil'elm rasped, his voice thin and ghostly. But before he could say more, Iaggardo's clawed hand clamped over his shoulder, the sickening crack of bone silencing him.

"You'll answer my questions," Iaggardo sneered, pressing his claws against Vil'elm's throat, a thin line of blood tracing down his neck. "Or he dies."

Vil'elm's gaze turned to Belazar, a faint plea in his eyes. "Don't… tell him… anything."

In a flash, Belazar drew his sword, the blade gleaming in the faint moonlight. "Let him go!"

"Or what?" Iaggardo taunted, tightening his grip, blood dripping to the ground below.

"You need him too," Belazar countered, stepping closer, his tone unwavering.

"Perceptive." Iaggardo's grin twisted as he reached out, snatching A'nara, holding her dagger to her own throat. "But she…" He grinned darkly. "She's expendable."

"Let her go," Belazar growled, the mix of fear and fury clear in his eyes.

"Only if you cooperate," Iaggardo sneered, pressing the dagger until a thin line of blood appeared on A'nara's neck, the metallic scent heavy in the air.

Belazar's scream of anguish tore through the forest as A'nara slumped to the ground, her blood mingling with the damp earth. His rage consumed him, his voice raw as he stared at Iaggardo, who looked on with mock amusement.

"You loved her, didn't you?" Iaggardo's voice was a twisted delight.

"Shut up!" Belazar's voice trembled, all control slipping in the face of his pain.

Iaggardo's chuckle was dark, almost gleeful. "Just like I killed your precious lover!"

"I'll kill you," Belazar charged, eyes blazing, but Vil'elm's faint voice halted him.

"Don't… make my mistake," Vil'elm gasped, his breath labored, eyes pleading with him.

"What mistake?" Belazar demanded, his steps faltering as confusion crept in.

Even Iaggardo tilted his head, curiosity piqued. "Yes, what mistake?"

Voice heavy with regret, Vil'elm whispered, "Forty years… it's haunted me…" His words hung in the air like a curse.

A'nara's weak voice broke through, a touch of desperation clinging to it. "Vil'elm, don't…"

"They deserve to know," he replied, his tone thick with sorrow.

"A'nara… you're alive!" Belazar's voice filled with hope, stepping toward her, but Iaggardo blocked him, his presence an unyielding wall.

"Back off," Iaggardo threatened, his eyes glinting with malice. "Or I'll finish her."

Belazar held his ground, sword steady, his gaze cold. "No, you won't."

Iaggardo sneered, gesturing to the other Muckspawns, their eyes glinting like predators. "You're outnumbered."

"Not for long," came a voice from the forest. Dalmon stepped out, his movements smooth and dangerous, drawing his sword in one practiced motion.

"I see mutt did not finsh you, no matter your outnumbred" Iaggardo, undeterred, decalred.

"Not for long," Dalmon whistled sharply. Arrows flew from the darkness, the sharp twang of bowstrings followed by the thudding of Muckspawns falling.

"Who's there?" Iaggardo demanded, panic edging into his voice like cold fingers.

A woman, her dark hair tied back, stepped forward, the moonlight casting a silver glow. "Me."

"Krevst!,Yvonne, so nice to see you" Iaggardo sneered, retreating cautiously, his eyes shifting nervously like a trapped animal.

"Ære vær meg, firfisle." *Honor's all mine, lizard.* Yvonne responded coldly, her green eyes unwavering, as sharp and unyielding as emerald blades.

Belazar's heart pounded in his chest as the situation grew more dire. Iaggardo was cornered, but he was far from defeated. The twisted grin on his face never wavered as he glanced at A'nara's prone form and the thin line of her blood mingling with his own. There was something unsettling in the way he looked at her—something darker than mere malice. As the group closed in, surrounding Iaggardo, he snarled and drew a crude dagger from his belt, the blade already stained with old, darkened blood. With a swift motion, he dragged the blade across his palm, letting his life force mingle with A'nara's on the forest floor. The ground beneath them seemed to tremble as the blood soaked into the earth, and the air thickened with a palpable sense of ancient power awakening.

"What is he doing?" Yvonne's voice was tense, her grip on her bow tightening as she stepped closer, her green eyes narrowed in suspicion.

Dalmon, his sword at the ready, took a cautious step back. "He's tapping into something primal —something that goes beyond our understanding."

Before their eyes, Iaggardo began to change. His body contorted, muscles bulging as the power he had drawn from the blood bond twisted his form into something monstrous. His eyes glowed with an unnatural light, and his teeth elongated into sharp, jagged points. His nails grew into claws, and his skin took on a rough, almost scaled texture.

"Stop him!" Belazar shouted, but it was too late. Iaggardo let out a guttural roar that reverberated through the trees, sending flocks of birds scattering into the night sky. The group lunged forward, weapons at the ready, but Iaggardo was faster. He moved with a speed and ferocity that defied logic, slashing at them with his claws and fending off their attacks with ease.

Dalmon, Yvonne, and the others fought valiantly, but it became clear that they were outmatched. Iaggardo's newfound strength was overwhelming, and the group found themselves slowly being pushed back, struggling to keep him at bay.

Belazar's mind raced. He could see the desperation in his friends' eyes, the fear that they might not survive this encounter. He had sworn never to become Silver Fang again, to leave that cursed part of his life behind. But now, as he watched Iaggardo tear through his comrades, he realized that he had no choice.

"I'm sorry," he whispered to himself, feeling the familiar pull of the transformation deep within him.

As the battle raged around him, Belazar closed his eyes and let go of the restraint he had fought so hard to maintain. His body began to shift, his bones cracking and muscles bulging as he took on the form of Silver Fang. Fur sprouted from his skin, and his hands became deadly claws. His senses heightened, and the world around him became sharper, more vivid. When he opened his eyes, they were no longer those of a man, but of a beast—piercing, glowing with an inner fire that mirrored the rage building within him.

With a feral growl, Silver Fang leaped into the fray, his claws slashing through the air with deadly precision. Iaggardo, caught off guard by the sudden appearance of another monster, staggered back, momentarily losing his advantage.The battle was brutal and chaotic, a whirlwind of claws, teeth, and blades. Silver Fang fought with the ferocity of a cornered animal, his mind teetering on the edge of madness as he tore through the Muckspawns and engaged Iaggardo in a deadly dance of power and rage.

Just as Silver Fang was about to land the killing blow, bringing his claws down toward

Iaggardo's exposed throat, Iaggardo's voice rang out, sharp and desperate.

"Stop!" Iaggardo cried, his voice cutting through the chaos. "Dalmon lost Razma! He didn't protect him like he was supposed to!"

Belazar's rage, already teetering on the brink of uncontrollable, flared even hotter at the mention of his son. His claws hovered inches from Iaggardo's throat, trembling with the intensity of his fury. "What do you mean, he lost Razma?" Belazar snarled, his voice barely human, dripping with both anger and desperation.

Dalmon, standing a short distance away, looked stricken, guilt etched deep into his features. "I —Belazar, I—" he stammered, but before he could find the words, Yvonne stepped between them, her voice firm and commanding.

"Belazar, focus!" Yvonne ordered, her gaze steady as she placed a calming hand on his arm. "This is exactly what Iaggardo wants. Don't let him manipulate you. We need to stay united, or we'll lose more than just Razma."

A'nara, still shaken from her ordeal, flinched at the sight of Belazar in his Silver Fang form. The once-controlled, measured man she knew was gone, replaced by this feral creature driven by nothing but rage and pain. She stepped back, her hand instinctively reaching for Yvonne, who gave her a reassuring nod.

In the confusion, a weakened but cunning Iaggardo took his chance. With a swift, desperate motion, he broke free from the group, his form a blur as he dashed toward the shadows of the forest. But he couldn't resist one final taunt. Turning back briefly, his eyes gleamed with malicious satisfaction.

"Since we're old pals, Silver," Iaggardo sneered, the nickname dripping with mockery, "I'll tell you where your precious boy is. Thorn took him, and warden is with her. Good luck finding him… if you can!" His laughter echoed through the trees as he disappeared into the darkness.

Belazar's rage was incandescent, his body trembling with the need to chase Iaggardo down and tear him apart, but Yvonne's grip tightened on his arm, anchoring him to the present.

"We need a plan," Yvonne said, her voice calm amidst the chaos of emotions. "If Iaggardo's telling the truth, we have to act fast. But we can't let our anger cloud our judgment. Razma needs us."Belazar, still breathing heavily, looked around at the faces of his companions— Dalmon's guilt, Yvonne's resolve, A'nara's fear. Slowly, painfully, he reined in the beast within, his claws retracting as he forced himself back into his human form.

With a final, deep breath, he nodded. "We go to Halzor's Keep," he said, his voice rough but determined. "But Dalmon," he added, turning to his old friend with a look that held both anger and hurt, "you'd better have a damn good explanation for what happened to my son."

Dalmon opened his mouth to respond, but before he could, Yvonne interrupted. "Save it for later," she said, her tone brooking no argument. "We need to move—now."

As the group began to gather their belongings, a heavy silence settled over them. Each member moved with deliberate care, their eyes flickering to Belazar with a mixture of concern and fear. The air was thick with the unspoken acknowledgment of what had just occurred—that the man they followed had been forced to become the monster once again.

Belazar's shoulders drooped as he bent to retrieve his sword from where it lay on the ground, its weight foreign in his grip. He had not once lifted it in the fray, yet the savage force of Silver Fang had still surfaced, leaving him hollow. A'nara, who had always seen him as an unshakable pillar, looked upon him now with both fear and pity. Dalmon lingered at a distance, guilt heavy upon him, while Yvonne—usually sharp-eyed and resolute—regarded her leader with a sorrow that cut deeper than any blade.

The journey ahead felt like a burden, not just for the mission at hand, but for the fragile bonds that had been stretched nearly to breaking.

As they set off into the forest, the sound of Iaggardo's laughter still echoing faintly in the distance, Belazar was left alone with his thoughts, the shadows of his past pressing in on him. The cost of becoming Silver Fang again was evident in the wary glances from those he once called friends.

And as they walked, each step forward felt like it was pulling him deeper into a darkness he feared he would never escape from. The path to Halzor's Keep was ahead, but the path to redemption, to peace within himself, seemed further away than ever.

The cold night air stung with the bitter taste of remorse, and though they traveled together, Belazar had never felt more alone.

As the group moved through the forest, the silence between them was heavy with unspoken words and unresolved tension. The night was cold, the air crisp, and every step seemed to echo louder in the stillness around them. Dalmon lingered at the back of the group, watching Belazar's hunched shoulders, the way his friend seemed to carry the weight of the world on his back. He could see the torment etched into every line of Belazar's posture, the way his footsteps dragged as though the ground itself was pulling him down.

Finally, unable to bear it any longer, Dalmon quickened his pace and moved to walk beside Belazar. For a moment, he said nothing, simply matching his friend's pace, letting the silence speak for them both.

Then, in a voice low enough that only Belazar could hear, Dalmon spoke. "I know you hate it, Belazar. I know how much it tears you apart inside to become him. But you had to do it tonight. There was no other choice."Belazar kept his gaze fixed on the path ahead, his jaw clenched tightly. "I never wanted to be Silver Fang again, Dalmon. I swore I'd leave that part of me behind." His voice was rough, laced with the pain he was trying so hard to suppress.

Dalmon nodded, understanding the depth of his friend's struggle. "I know, my friend. I know. But sometimes we don't get to choose. Sometimes the world forces our hand, and we have to do things we swore we'd never do again. That's the curse of being who we are."

Belazar's steps faltered for a moment, the truth of Dalmon's words hitting him hard. "They call me a hero, you know," he said bitterly, his voice barely above a whisper. "But they don't know what it did to me, what it cost me."

Dalmon placed a hand on Belazar's shoulder, offering what little comfort he could. "No, they don't. They see the legend, the stories, the victories. They don't see the man behind the myth. But I do. I've seen what it did to you, and what it's still doing to you. And so has she, even if she can't fully understand it yet. "Belazar glanced sideways at Dalmon, seeing the sincerity in his old friend's eyes. "A'nara… she speaks of it, but you're right. She never really saw it for what it was, for what it did to me. And now… now she's afraid."

"She'll come around," Dalmon reassured him. "Give her time. She's strong, but this… this is a lot for anyone to take in. Especially when it's someone they care about."

Belazar sighed deeply, his breath visible in the cold night air. "I just don't want to lose her. I don't want her to see me the way everyone else does—as some kind of monster."

"You're not a monster, Belazar," Dalmon said firmly. "You're a man who's done what he had to do to survive and protect those he loves. And anyone who truly knows you will see that too. She'll see it."

They walked in silence for a few more moments, the night growing darker around them. The others in the group had moved ahead, giving the two friends space.

Belazar's anger flared up once more as he whipped around to face Dalmon. "He's with Warden now, in Halzor's Keep! How could you let this happen?"

Dalmon's face tightened with guilt, but his voice remained steady. "I never got the chance to reach Razma. The riots in Seragora broke out so suddenly after Vil'elm's story spread, and the king called for me immediately. It was chaos, Belazar. I thought Warden would never get close to him, but I was wrong."

Belazar's fists clenched at his sides, frustration and fear spilling over. "And now my son is in the hands of that… that monster!"

Dalmon nodded grimly, fully understanding the gravity of the situation. "I should have seen it coming, Belazar. I should have sent him to Raelle, where he would have been safe. But I didn't, and for that, I'm sorry. But we know where he is now, and that means we have a chance to get him back."

Belazar paused, his anger momentarily giving way to a deeper concern. "No, it's good we didn't involve Raelle. We don't need to bring attention to her. Is she... is she okay?"

Dalmon softened at the mention of Raelle. "Yes, she's as good as can be, given everything. Tor'valis is keeping his word; she's safe."

Belazar's shoulders slumped slightly, the fight momentarily draining out of him. "Why is Warden helping Thorn after all she did?"

Dalmon shook his head. "I don't know, but whatever the reason, we have to act fast. Warden is dangerous, and if he's taken Razma, it's for a reason. We need to figure out what that reason is and stop it before it's too late."

Belazar took a deep breath, trying to steady himself. "We can't waste anymore time, Dalmon. We have to get to get my son back."

Dalmon nodded in agreement. "We will, Belazar. We'll gather our strength and go after him. We'll bring him home, no matter what it takes."

Dalmon gave Belazar a hearty slap on the back, trying to pull his friend out of the dark thoughts that seemed to weigh him down. Belazar offered a weak smile before lowering his gaze, the burden of their situation pressing heavily on his shoulders. Sensing the heaviness in the air, Dalmon walked ahead to where A'nara was, ruffling her hair in a brotherly gesture. "Stop it, Dal!" A'nara playfully protested, dodging his hand with a light laugh, though her eyes betrayed the tension she was still feeling.

The two siblings fell into their familiar rhythm of banter, their voices lightening the atmosphere as they walked. But behind them, Belazar remained quiet, his steps slow and heavy. Noticing Belazar's struggle, Yvonne fell back to walk alongside him. Her expression was stern, as it often was, but there was a softness in her eyes that only those who truly knew her could see.

"She cares about you, you know," Yvonne began, her tone sharp but laced with concern. "A'nara. She's scared, but not of you—of what she doesn't understand. She was young during the war, Belazar. She only knows the stories, the legends of Silver Fang. She doesn't know the man behind them, not like we do."

Belazar nodded slowly, the truth of Yvonne's words sinking in. "Caring for Razma has been the only thing keeping me in check, Yvonne. He gave me a reason to keep the beast at bay. But if I lose him... if something happens to him like it did to Raelle... I don't know if I can hold back the beast this time." Yvonne's gaze softened slightly, though her voice remained firm. "You're stronger than you give yourself credit for, Belazar. But you don't have to do this alone. We've been with you through the worst of it. We know what the beast is, but we also know it doesn't define who you are."

Belazar sighed deeply, the weight of his fears pressing down on him. "I've pushed everyone away, thinking I could protect them by keeping them at a distance. But all it's done is isolate me further." Yvonne smirked, her usual sharp edge returning. "You're a fool if you think pushing us away will keep us from caring. Dalmon, A'nara, me—we've all got your back, even if you're too stubborn to admit you need it. And just so you know, if you ever do lose control, I'll fill you with arrows and put you down myself. I mean it."

Belazar chuckled, the sound rough but genuine. "Thanks, Yvonne. You've always been there, even when I didn't want you to be."

Yvonne shrugged, a mischievous glint in her eye. "That's because I know what you need, even when you don't. And by the way, don't think I haven't noticed Dalmon pining after me. He's sweet, but we both know he's too chicken to ever do anything about it."

Belazar's smile grew wider, a blend of amusement and sympathy shining in his eyes. "He cares about you, Yvonne. But I suppose he knows his place." Yvonne rolled her eyes, though her expression softened slightly. "He's a good man, but we both know he's better off admiring from afar. Besides, someone needs to keep him in line—and you, for that matter."

Belazar nodded, feeling a sense of camaraderie and relief in their conversation. "You're a good friend, Yvonne. Even if you are a bit of a pain."

Yvonne grinned, giving him a playful nudge. "And you're a stubborn fool. But that's why we get along."

Belazar's thoughts drifted back to A'nara and Razma, his heart heavy with worry. "I just don't want to lose them, Yvonne. If I lose them… I don't know what I'll become."

Yvonne's voice softened, though it stayed firm. "You won't lose them. We won't let that happen. But you have to trust us, Belazar. Trust that we'll be there when you need us, just like we've always been." Belazar nodded, feeling a small measure of comfort in her words. "Thanks, Yvonne. For everything."

Yvonne smirked, giving him a sideways glance. "Just remember, Belazar, we're in this together. And if you start to lose control, I'll be there with my bow. But until then, let's keep moving forward. We've got a lot of work ahead of us."

Belazar chuckled softly, the tension in his shoulders easing just a bit as they continued walking side by side, the darkness of the night no longer lonely.

As Belazar and Yvonne walked in silence, a sudden movement caught their attention. From the corner of their eyes, they saw Vil'elm—who had been silent and seemingly recovering—slipping away into the shadows.

Belazar's brows furrowed in frustration. "Vil'elm!" he called, his voice echoing in the night. But it was too late. While they had been catching up, he had managed to slip away, disappearing into the forest before anyone could stop him.

Yvonne let out a sharp breath, shaking her head. "That slippery bastard."

Belazar sighed, the brief moment of peace shattered."I should've seen it coming. Thorn's got her claws in him, deep."

Dalmon, having noticed the commotion, jogged over, a look of frustration spreading across his face as he realized what had happened. "Did he run?" he asked, though the answer was clear.

Belazar nodded grimly. "He's gone."

Dalmon clenched his fists, but then relaxed. "We'll deal with him later. Right now, we focus on Razma."

Yvonne nodded, her gaze hardening once again. "We've got enough to handle without chasing after Vil'elm. Let him run—he'll face his own consequences soon enough. For now, we focus on what's ahead."

Belazar took a deep breath, steadying himself. "You're right. Razma's the priority. We'll deal with the rest when the time comes."

With Vil'elm's escape behind them, the group pressed on, their mission clear: they would gather their strength, face whatever dangers lay ahead, and do whatever it took to bring Razma home.

Chapter 20: Tale Of Remorse

788, 21st Day Of The Tenth Moon

I have done it... and now, what have I wrought?

My wife turns from me, my children's eyes harden with scorn, their love hollowed into distrust. I didn't know—how could I? Her kin never spoke of the "Sanguine," only whispers and warnings left to fade like smoke. And now, I see the devastation it has brought upon us, lurking in every shadow, filling the corners of our lives with silence and fear.

They all look at me as if I knew. As if I welcomed this curse, wrapped in secrets and deceit. But what was I to believe when they hid so much? Their warnings, spoken like riddles, too veiled for any man to understand until it was too late.

Now, I carry the weight of my choices, a weight that grows heavier each time I meet my family's cold eyes. I would undo it if I could—but some things, once unleashed, cannot be taken back.

May the gods forgive me, for I am unsure if they ever will.

In the dimly lit room, the fire crackled and hissed softly, casting fleeting shadows across Glendale's face as she stared at Warden, her gaze sharp with disapproval. The tension was almost tangible, weaving through the thick air, while the muffled sounds of the wind against the shutters played a quiet, uneasy tune.

"So, you come here because you had nowhere else to go?" Her voice was controlled, clipped, every word deliberate. "Thorn is back, gathering an army. But let's not pretend you're innocent, Warden. You're no stranger to shadows. I should have left you there."

In the background, the faint rustling and occasional murmurs from Razma's room interrupted the stillness. The boy tossed and turned, as though even in his sleep he felt the weight of the tension between them.

Warden's shoulders sagged, laden with years of regret. "I know, Lilah," he said quietly. "I'm not asking for trust. But I had nowhere else to turn."

A quiet sigh escaped her as she glanced toward the small room where Razma lay unconscious, her expression softening just a little. "The boy… he doesn't know the whole story, does he?" she asked, her voice barely above a whisper.

Warden's jaw tightened. "Not entirely," he admitted. "Thorn tried to turn him against me, hinting that Belazar is my enemy. But Razma… he saw through it. I may not have always been an ally to his father, but I won't leave him to Thorn's schemes."

The fire crackled again, sparks floating upward as Glendale studied him. Her sharp gaze softened, though suspicion lingered. "You're here to protect the boy, then?" she asked. "If that's true, Warden, you'll tell me everything. You know what's at stake. You always have."

Warden nodded, his resolve hardening. "I'll tell you what I can, Lilah. I'm here to stop her, no matter what it means, even if it drags up the past."

She held his gaze, searching for any sign of deceit. "So, what do you know, Warden?"

He took a steadying breath. "Not much," he said. "Thorn's after a book, but I don't know why. A'nara's in town, too. She and Belazar fought Thorn at his barn before she escaped and torched the place. And… Mutt, he's leading the Muckspawn now."

Glendale's face contorted in disbelief. "Mutt? That brute?" She took a sharp breath, as the realization settled in. "I've heard rumors—Muckspawn dressed in Bazel's armor attacking Seragora. Thorn's trying to start another war."

She shook her head, frustration darkening her tone. "After everything—after the Thorrin War, the bloodshed, the promises made to keep the peace. Fifteen years, and she seeks to unravel it all."

Warden's gaze darkened, bitterness seeping into his voice. "Yes, she wants to reopen those wounds. And don't misunderstand me, Lilah—I wouldn't care if Seragora and Tor'valis burned, after what he—"

"Stop right there, Warden!" Glendale's voice cut through his bitterness like a blade. "That man is my king. He may not be a saint, but he held this kingdom together through blood and ashes. He brokered peace when no one believed it possible! And you? You're no saint yourself. You know the devastation you wrought—you know what you did."

As she spoke, Warden's hand clenched, his fury stirring. A faint, eerie rustling came from the floor, as thorny vines began to emerge, writhing and twisting in response to his rising anger. The fire seemed to dim as his magic thickened the air, coiling around them, threatening to consume the room.

But Glendale didn't so much as flinch. She raised her hands, a word of power leaving her lips, and a silence fell over the room, smothering the wild energy. The vines stilled, his magic dissipating as quickly as it had come.

"Not in my house, Warden," she said icily. "Your quarrel is not with me. Let your anger go, or leave."

Warden exhaled shakily, his rage ebbing as her words settled into him like cooling rain. He looked away, guilt shadowing his face. "Fine, Lilah. But… this isn't over."

Glendale studied him for a moment, her gaze softening ever so slightly. "I know it's not," she murmured. "But we have more pressing matters now."

The crackling of the fire punctuated the silence as Warden lowered his head, the weight of it all bearing down on him. "I miss her, Lilah," he whispered, his voice cracking under the burden. "I miss Rae… my sister."

Glendale's expression softened as she took a step closer, placing a hand on his shoulder. "I know, Warden. But what's done is done. We have to look forward now."

A distant look passed over her face before she spoke again. "You may carry your resentment for Tor'valis, but know this—he's done right by Raelle. She's found her place as queen, and she's happy. It wasn't easy for her. Earning the people's trust was no small feat, especially with so many still ignorant of her true role in the war."

Warden's gaze grew distant as he listened, taking in her words. "I just… I wish things had been different. I wish she could forgive me."

Glendale gave his shoulder a gentle squeeze, the soft light of the fire catching the hint of sadness in her eyes. The quiet returned, punctuated only by the fire's soft murmurs and the low hum of night sounds outside, casting a fragile peace over them in the quiet of the night.

The room was quiet, save for the occasional snap of the burning wood, with an ember popping now and then, scattering brief sparks that flickered before fading. Glendale's gaze remained fixed on Warden, her expression softened by a rare hint of compassion.

"Maybe she will, in time," Glendale said softly, as if answering a question Warden hadn't dared to voice. "Maybe she already has. But you need to forgive yourself first, Warden. You can't carry this burden forever."

Her eyes traveled downward, noticing the faint trails of blood staining the floor and edge of the cot. "And for the gods' sake, you're bleeding everywhere. Get cleaned up. I don't want my home looking like a battlefield. You'll have plenty to explain to Razma when he wakes."

A weak chuckle escaped Warden's lips, easing a bit of the tension that had weighed on him all evening. "He seems like a good kid," he murmured, rubbing a weary hand over his face.

Glendale's face softened, a small smile breaking through her stern expression. "He is," she said, glancing back toward Razma's room. "A shame his father's all bark…"

Warden's grin widened, despite himself, and he gingerly touched an old scar on his arm. "Oh, he's got bite too. Trust me."

Groaning, he rose, wincing as he stretched his stiff limbs. "Fine, I'll clean up. But I'm exhausted. Too much magic today."

Glendale's expression shifted to a mix of exasperation and acceptance as she watched him limp to the washbasin she'd set out. "Then rest," she ordered, her tone soft but firm. "Tomorrow will bring enough challenges without you passing out on my floor."

Warden splashed the cold water over his face and hands, the chill seeping into his bones, clearing his mind as the blood and grime washed away. The low crackling of burning wood was steady in the background, and for a fleeting moment, the shadows seemed to retreat, leaving him in a rare moment of peace. Glendale stood nearby, her presence a quiet reminder of the strength he still had to find.

After a pause, she spoke gently, "Rest tonight, Warden. Tomorrow, we'll start fresh. There's work yet to be done, and we'll need every bit of strength we can muster."

Warden lifted his head, meeting her gaze, his voice barely a whisper. "Lilah… do you think Rae will ever forgive me? For what I did?"

Glendale's gaze hardened, though her voice remained steady. "Warden, I can't say if she'll ever truly forgive you. What happened back then hurt her deeply. She's carried that pain for a long time." Her tone softened as she continued, a mix of regret and resolve coloring her words. "But Rae's stronger than any of us gave her credit for. Maybe, with time, she'll see that you're trying to make things right. That has to count for something."

The weight of Glendale's words settled over Warden like a heavy cloak. He stared into the flames, their embers sparking occasionally as they danced. "I'll try, Lilah. Even if it takes a lifetime… I'll try."

Glendale's expression softened further, and she offered him a rare look of encouragement. "Get some sleep, Warden. Tomorrow may bring as many scars as it does answers, but we'll face it together."

With a faint smile, Warden let himself sink into the cot, exhaustion pulling him under like a dark tide. The wood snapped softly beside him, and at last, he let himself drift into a deep, much-needed sleep.

But his slumber was haunted, shallow, as memories flickered behind his closed eyes like embers—fires that had torn through homes and lives alike. He saw Thorn, her face twisted in sinister delight as she wielded magic that bent the world to her will. And then, there was Raelle, standing alone on a battlefield, her gaze full of sorrow he could no longer reach. The memories tugged him deeper into a shadowy realm, his mind swirling with old missteps and failures.

In the midst of his dreams, the sounds of wood splintering and hissing filled the room, mingling with the faint rustle of Glendale moving about, casting a watchful glance his way as he tossed in his sleep. When his eyes opened, bleary and unfocused, Glendale was there, studying him with a calm intensity.

"You didn't sleep long," she noted, her voice gentler now, perhaps softened by whatever she'd seen on his face while he slept.

Warden let out a groan, rubbing his face as he pushed himself upright. "Didn't expect to. Can't seem to shake the past..."

Glendale sighed, her gaze shifting back to the embers that glowed faintly in the dim light. "We all carry the past with us, Warden. The difference is what we choose to do with it."

A quiet hung between them, punctuated only by the occasional pop of the fire's embers. "I need to find Thorn," Warden murmured, almost to himself. "She's too far gone now. If we don't stop her, everything burns. She won't stop at Seragora; she'll tear down kingdoms just to watch them fall."

Glendale's eyes turned sharp. "And you think you can stop her?"

He hesitated, his hands clenching into fists. "I don't know," he admitted, his voice low. "But I have to try. For Rae, for everything I've done wrong... I have to at least try."

"Rae doesn't need you to be her savior," Glendale said, her voice equal parts softness and steel. "She's strong enough on her own. She always was."

He looked down at his hands, absorbing her words. "I know," he murmured. "But I can't just stand by and let her face this alone."

With quiet deliberation, Glendale moved closer, her gaze cutting through his resolve. "Trying to redeem yourself is fine, but redemption doesn't come from more bloodshed, Warden. You're no good to anyone if you let her drag you back into the shadows."

Warden's jaw tightened, a flicker of defiance in his eyes. "I know I'm not a saint. But if I don't stop Thorn, no one will. She's become something even she doesn't understand."

After a moment, Glendale looked away, sighing. "Just don't lose yourself again, Warden. We need you... for this, and for what comes next."

His gaze returned to the glowing embers, their warmth seeping into him as he took in her words. Thorn wasn't just a threat to Seragora or to the kingdom—she was a threat to everything he had left behind. To Raelle, to his family, and to the peace they had all fought so hard to secure.

"I should have killed her when I had the chance," he whispered.

"You couldn't have," Glendale replied, her back still to him. "Back then, you were too blinded by your own anger and grief. None of us saw what she was becoming."

Warden leaned back, his exhaustion settling in again. "And now it's too late."

Glendale's voice softened. "It's never too late. But you need to be smart about this. Thorn has her army, and she's more dangerous than she's ever been. You won't be able to stop her alone."

A bitter chuckle escaped Warden. "Who said I was alone?"

Glendale raised an eyebrow, casting a doubtful glance at the room where Razma lay unconscious. "You're putting a lot of faith in a boy who barely knows the stakes."

"Sometimes, the ones who don't know the weight of the world carry it best," Warden said with a faint smile, though doubt flickered in his gaze.

Glendale shook her head, retrieving a thin blanket and laying it over his lap. "You're going to need more than hope and a kid with spirit," she replied, her tone serious. "Thorn has grown beyond what we ever expected. You need allies, Warden. And you need a plan."

He nodded, grim determination tightening his expression. "I know. But first, we need to regroup. Figure out her next move. That book… it's tied to all of this."

Glendale's sigh seemed to fill the room as she sat across from him. "And you still don't know why she wants it?"

"No," he admitted, frustration tightening his voice. "But whatever it is, it's powerful. And she'll stop at nothing to get it."

They sat in heavy silence, the fire's glow casting flickering shadows across their faces. Finally, Glendale broke the stillness. "Rest now, Warden. You're no good to anyone if you fall apart before the real fight begins."

Warden nodded, leaning back against the wall, the weight of exhaustion pulling him under once more. "Thanks, Lilah."

She watched him a moment longer, then quietly left the room. Warden's breathing slowed, the quiet warmth of the embers lulling him deeper into sleep. But even as he rested, his mind churned, haunted by plans, fears, and regrets, all weaving together in the darkness.

In the adjoining room, the low, rhythmic crackle of the fire cast dancing shadows against the walls, warming the dim space with an amber glow. Razma stirred, his body wracked with pain and confusion. He groaned softly, his eyes fluttering open, trying to make sense of the unfamiliar surroundings. The memories of the attack flooded back, sharp and overwhelming, filling him with a fresh surge of fear.

From across the room came the occasional muffled murmur, Warden's voice heavy with fragments of dreams, his words incomprehensible yet laced with tension. Every now and then, he tossed and turned, the bed creaking beneath him, mirroring the turmoil that seemed to haunt him even in sleep.

As Razma shifted, he heard a soft voice from the doorway. "You're awake."

His head snapped toward the sound, alarm tightening his muscles. Glendale stood there, her expression calm but watchful, framed by the gentle firelight flickering behind her.

"Where am I?" Razma croaked, his throat dry and voice rough.

"You're safe, for now," Glendale replied, stepping into the room with a steady gaze. "You've been through a lot. Rest is what you need most."

His mind raced, fragments of the attack returning in disjointed flashes. The hooded woman, Mutt, the fire... "The woman," he muttered, his voice shaky. "And Mutt... they attacked my home. They're—"

Glendale nodded, her expression darkening. "Yes, they're responsible. But for now, focus on recovering, not on what happened. There will be time to face it soon enough."

Razma swallowed, the weight of fear thick in his throat. "Warden... where is he?"

"He's here," Glendale assured him, her voice softer now. "He's resting, too. You both need your strength for what's coming."

"What's coming?" he asked, his voice barely above a whisper, dread tightening his chest.

Glendale's gaze softened with something akin to compassion. "More than you're ready for, I'm afraid. But you'll learn soon enough. Rest now, Razma. You'll need it."

Razma closed his eyes, though his mind remained stormy with uncertainty. The soft crackle of the fire mixed with the quiet, restless murmurs from Warden's sleep in the next room, grounding him in this strange, fragile sanctuary. He had no idea what lay ahead, but he sensed he was caught in the heart of something far bigger than himself, something dark and dangerous.

As the night deepened, the outside world fell silent, leaving only the warmth of the fire and the sounds of breathing, steady and fragile. The battle for Seragora was only just beginning, and soon, they would all be forced to choose their sides.

Interlude: 2

Queen Raelle paused just inside Sergora's newly opened gates, taking in the soot and rubble left by the recent attacks. Loose stones crunched under her slippers, and the acrid smell of charred wood clung to the still air. On either side of her, two guards stood at attention—armor polished but dented from the fighting—while her handmaiden, Rowanna, hovered close by, eyes darting left and right as though expecting another wave of danger at any moment.

A murmuring crowd gathered, curiosity and relief in their faces. Raelle raised a hand in gentle acknowledgment, stepping forward with a calm grace that betrayed none of her inner worries.

"Your Majesty!" A voice cut through the hush. A baker's apron, smudged with ash, fluttered around a young woman who pressed her palms together in a bow. "Thank you for coming out here. We feared..." She trailed off, glancing at the scorched buildings.

Raelle offered a reassuring smile. "I had to see how my people fared with my own eyes. How are you holding up?"

The baker's eyes filled with tears. "My shop… half of it burned when those… beasts came." She shook her head fiercely. "But if you're here, it must mean we can still fight back."

"We can," Raelle said with quiet certainty, resting a hand on the baker's shoulder. "We are. Together."

Rowanna watched the exchange with evident concern. Her gaze flicked from the baker's trembling hands to the dark streaks staining the cobblestones. "Your Majesty," she said in a low voice, "perhaps we should move on. More of the city needs to see you."

Before Raelle could reply, a wobbly cart rattled up behind them. An older man, breathing heavily, struggled to keep his goods—a heap of salvaged produce—balanced atop the listing wheels. Raelle stepped aside, but the man's eyes widened when he recognized her. He nearly toppled his cart, hastening into a bow.

"My Queen, I—I'm sorry—didn't expect…" He trailed off, clearly flustered.

"No need for apologies," Raelle said gently. She moved closer, helping stabilize the cart with steady hands. Softly, she added, "Thank you for braving the streets. People here need food and hope in equal measure."

His cheeks burned with gratitude as he nodded. "Long as we've got you watchin' over us, we'll manage."

Nearby, a child lingered by a fragment of collapsed wall. Dirt smudged her cheeks, and she clutched a ragged cloth doll. Raelle stooped to eye level. "Hello," she greeted softly, noticing the little one's trembling lip. "Where's your family?"

"She lost them in the attacks," Rowanna whispered, having overheard from a cluster of townsfolk.

Raelle's breath caught. She reached out, brushing tangled hair from the child's face. "You're safe with us now, little one," she promised, glancing around until she spotted a pair of community healers sorting supplies. "Over there—see those men and women in white aprons? They'll help you."

The girl gave a hesitant nod. Raelle rose, guiding her gently toward the healers. As they approached, one of them—a stocky man with kind eyes—knelt and opened his arms for the child. The queen exchanged a silent look of thanks with him, an unspoken agreement passing between them.

Rowanna cleared her throat softly, reminding Raelle of her own guard detail waiting at a respectable distance. A moment later, the queen resumed walking through the debris-littered street. Some buildings stood half-collapsed; others, scorched from roof to foundation. Voices of distressed merchants rose here and there, though they often hushed when Raelle drew near— unsure if they should trouble her, hopeful she might carry answers.

A bearded tailor stepped forward, wringing his hands. "They took everything from my shop," he said, voice raw. "All my cloth, my thread… gone."

Raelle clasped his hands gently, meeting his gaze. "I'm sorry. I know it's not easy to start over, but we will rebuild." She turned to her guards. "Let's see to it that we gather what resources we can spare to help him—and others like him."

They bowed in acknowledgment, already making notes on what could be arranged. The tailor blinked back tears. "Thank you," he whispered. "I'll do my best to make clothes for anyone who needs them, once I can gather supplies."

A flame of pride flickered in Raelle's eyes. "Sergora stands because of people like you," she said. "Don't lose heart."

Each new corner they turned revealed fresh signs of damage: shattered windows, scorched beams, and torn banners. Soldiers patrolled in small groups, saluting the queen with solemn respect. Now and then, Raelle paused to exchange words with them—asking about their injuries, their spirits, whether they needed anything urgent. She listened deeply before moving on, Rowanna trailing at her elbow, ever watchful.

A hush fell over the group when they came upon a makeshift memorial: a line of simple wooden markers arranged outside the charred remains of a small chapel. Fresh flowers and ribbons adorned them, a quiet testament to lives lost. Without a word, Raelle stepped forward, bowing her head. Her guards did the same. Rowanna hovered protectively, tears shining in her eyes.

The townspeople observing from a distance saw the queen's gesture and some joined her. An older woman placed a trembling hand on Raelle's shoulder, whispering, "We'll never forget them. Thank you for standing with us."

Raelle exhaled slowly, steeling herself. "No one will be forgotten," she murmured, letting her eyes roam over the markers. "We fight so others won't share this fate."

After a moment, she straightened, squared her shoulders, and turned to the crowd that had gathered. Many gazed at her with anticipation or weary hope. In a gentle, steady voice, Raelle spoke:

"We have endured the first of many battles, but I promise you—Sergora will not break under these attacks. Each of you has shown courage beyond measure, and I am humbled by it." She paused, glancing at a guard whose bandaged arm spoke of a recent wound. "We will hold our walls. We will mend our streets. And we will not let fear take root in our hearts."

A hushed ripple of agreement passed through the onlookers. Some lowered their heads, tears glistening, while others nodded grimly, fists clenched in resolve.

Rowanna touched Raelle's elbow, gently encouraging her onward. The queen offered the crowd one last solemn look of empathy before following her handmaiden through the battered streets. Though the setting sun cast elongated shadows across the rubble, there was a renewed spark among the people who watched their monarch depart.

Halfway down the next lane, where dust still swirled in the golden evening light, Rowanna turned to Raelle with a half-smile that held both relief and sadness. "You've given them hope, Your Majesty," she said softly.

Raelle's eyes flicked over the ruined buildings, the shape of her city bruised but not beaten. "They give me hope," she returned, voice hushed yet resolute.

Stepping through the debris, the queen and her small entourage continued, weaving past piles of shattered stone and splintered beams, each footstep a quiet vow that neither she nor Sergora would yield.

Lord Cedric's private hall glowed with the subdued light of crystal sconces and half-burned candles. Despite the opulence, a chill hung in the air—one that neither the crackle of embers in the ornate fireplace nor the soft murmurs of passing servants could entirely dispel. Through tall windows, the skies bore the faint smudge of smoke, the last reminder of muckspawn raids harrying Sergora's outskirts. Yet here, in Cedric's domain, the conversation turned on delicate alliances and personal gain.

Across from him, Lady Kira sat perched on a velvet-backed chair, posture ramrod straight, her lips curved in a thin line of disapproval. They had endured **King Tor'valis**'s condemnation that morning—an impassioned rebuke aimed at any noble who placed their fortunes above the city's well-being. Neither Cedric nor Kira found the king's sermon particularly moving. To them, Sergora needed only to remain stable enough to protect trade routes and keep profit flowing.

"Imagine," Cedric said with a quiet scoff, swirling a dark red wine in his goblet, "Tor'valis expecting us to squander a small fortune on reinforcing gates and paying soldiers. All for a few muckspawn skulking about with stolen armor." His gaze flicked over Kira, gauging her reaction. "We both know where our priorities lie."

Kira let out a short, bitter laugh. "He's so intent on feeding the masses, shoring up defenses— noble ideals, certainly. But if the city falls apart, who truly loses? We do. And if it's just a question of coin, I'll invest only as much as is strictly necessary to keep markets open."

A thin smile touched Cedric's lips. "Precisely. A thriving Sergora is good for business. Yet I refuse to throw away my fortune on doomed heroics." He paused a moment, swirling his drink. "Of course, if the worst did happen, I do like to keep… contingency plans. There's more than one way to maintain power and influence. After all, not every realm is run like ours."

Kira cocked her head, narrowing her eyes. "And what realm did you have in mind?" she asked, her voice terse. "Don't tell me you're entertaining any illusions of running off to some backwater."

Cedric's reply was deliberately nonchalant. "Not illusions, just an understanding of how business can flourish elsewhere. You've heard whispers about Bazel, no? Rumor claims merchants practically run the place—few kings, if any, to meddle. A realm governed by coin, not crowns." He let the statement hang, as though it were merely an idle observation.

Kira tapped her manicured fingertips against the chair's arm, a pensive crease forming between her brows. "I've heard rumors. If half of them are true, it means no figurehead to answer to—just a council of wealthy traders dictating the law. Though I can't see why that concerns us here and now. Unless…" She trailed off, suspicion glinting in her eyes. "Unless you've had dealings in Bazel you haven't mentioned?"

Cedric took a measured sip of his wine, his face betraying neither agreement nor denial. "I don't rush into alliances blindly, my dear Kira. But I do like to be prepared for the winds of change. Sergora's profits mean everything to us, but if, hypothetically, such profits were threatened, I'd look for opportunities elsewhere."

The corners of Kira's mouth drew tighter. "You had best tread carefully. If Tor'valis even suspects you're flirting with foreign arrangements—especially amid these muckspawn troubles—he'll have your head on a pike, or at least your reputation in tatters."

A quick spark of annoyance flared in Cedric's eyes. "King or no king, I'm not sabotaging my own estate. I want Sergora to flourish… or at least survive. If the city collapses, you and I both lose our most profitable ties." He paused, letting out a carefully neutral sigh. "But should that collapse ever become inevitable, I won't be left empty-handed."

Kira's expression flickered between relief and concern—her suspicion soothed by Cedric's insistence that he wasn't suicidal enough to invite the muckspawn in, yet unsettled by the breadth of his ambition. "Of course," she murmured, a touch of sarcasm lacing her words. "We do our part—barely—to keep Sergora on its feet, all while hedging our bets that it might stumble. That's a risky game, Cedric."

He shrugged, setting aside his goblet. "Every profit turns on a gamble. Besides, this city needs us—our investments, our influence. As long as King Tor'valis sees we're not openly betraying him, we'll remain above reproach."

Kira folded her hands in her lap, leaning back against the chair's velvet cushion. "You speak of these so-called options you have if things go awry. Are you sure you aren't courting a disaster of your own making?" Her words were pointed, but underlying them was a cautious curiosity, as though she wasn't entirely opposed to hearing about Cedric's plans—provided they proved advantageous for her as well.

A hint of a grin tugged at Cedric's lips, though he kept his response vague. "Let's just say I won't be caught off guard, my lady. The city thrives, we benefit. If it falters, I have alternate routes for trade—perhaps some discreet dealings with… certain contacts in merchant-run territories. Nothing more needs saying."

An uneasy silence followed, with Kira's eyes drifting to the flickering candles. When she glanced back, her brow had smoothed, but her stare remained unwavering. "You're an ambitious man, Cedric."

He dipped his head in a shallow nod, neither confirming nor denying her appraisal. "Ambition is the lifeblood of nobles like us, is it not? We just ensure it doesn't feed the wrong cause."

Kira's lips curled into a slightly forced smile, torn between intrigue and wariness. "I only hope your ambition doesn't drag us both into ruin," she said softly, rising to stand by the window. In the reflection of the glass, the distant glow of watchfires danced across Sergora's skyline, still marred by faint smoke. "Because if it does, no wealth in the world will save us from Tor'valis's wrath—or the muckspawn."

Cedric also stood, retrieving his goblet for one last sip before setting it down with a decisive clink. "Have faith, my dear Kira. We both want Sergora on its feet—and we both want to prosper from it. As long as our goals align, I see no cause for alarm."

She glanced back at him, a silent tension lingering. "Very well," she finally said, voice low. "For now, I'll trust you know exactly how far to push. I'm… intrigued by your approach, but remember: one misstep, and this entire house of cards collapses."

He gave a smooth half-bow, gesturing for her to pass. "Your caution is noted. Let's keep the city afloat, keep our coffers full, and keep the king none the wiser about any discussions we might have outside these walls."

They parted with measured nods, Lady Kira's skirt whispering against polished floors as she moved away. In that hush of the lavishly lit hall, Cedric lingered for a moment, eyes flicking to the window and the faint glow of a troubled city beyond. He was determined to keep Sergora thriving—for his own interests above all. Yet the possibility of an alternate, merchant-ruled horizon in Bazel seemed an enticing backup plan—one he refused to deny or confirm. If Kira was uneasy about his ambition, so be it. He had long since learned that success often demanded a careful balance of secrecy and confidence… and he intended to maintain it.

Lord Cedric stood by the arched window in his private hall, idly tapping his fingers on the cold stone sill. From here, he could see the torchlit courtyard below, where horse-hooves clopped and servants bustled about in near silence. Moments earlier, Lady Kira had swept out in a swirl of perfume, her pointed farewell still echoing in the corridors. Now, all was quiet save for the faint footfalls of distant attendants.

A discreet cough drew his attention. A young servant bowed low. "My lord, your guests have arrived. They used the rear entrance, as you requested."

Cedric turned from the window, smoothing his expression into guarded politeness. "Good. Show them in."

The servant vanished, and in his place strode two knights dressed in well-worn armor bearing the crimson fang of Lord Darth. Sir Alywan and Sir Garrick carried themselves with the unhurried arrogance of men who believed they answered to no one—certainly not to kings. Bazel had no crown, but Darth's reach was considerable, and these two exemplified his might.

Alywan spared only a cursory glance for the chamber's finery. "Not bad, Lord Cedric," he remarked. "Though I have to say, that lady we passed looked more impressive than your décor." He shot Garrick a conspiratorial grin. "She had… quite the assets."

Cedric's expression chilled at the crude mention of Lady Kira. "She is no subject for your jest," he said, voice tight. Regaining his composure, he added, "I assume you're here to discuss business, not my associate."

Garrick shrugged off the rebuke with casual indifference, removing his helmet and setting it on a nearby bench. "Naturally. Business is what we do best. Word is your caravans are getting hit by muckspawn raids. You want protection, we want coin. Straightforward enough."

Cedric clasped his hands behind his back and stepped away from the window. "Precisely. King Tor'valis won't secure every road, and my trade routes suffer. I want my shipments safe. You're here to make sure they remain untouched."

Alywan wandered deeper into the hall, pausing to admire a tapestry depicting a heroic Sergoran triumph. "We can handle muckspawn. We cut down a few on our way here—nasty brutes, but manageable," he said, meeting Cedric's gaze with a faint smirk.

Cedric waved away the topic. "Muckspawn are a nuisance, but I have another concern. Word has reached me of a certain swordsman from Bazel—Ky'len, Lord Darth's son. I hear he's been roaming Sergora, stirring up trouble."

Garrick snorted. "Ky'len may be the old man's heir, but that doesn't mean we follow his orders. We traveled from Bazel with him, sure, but there's no love lost. Our loyalty goes to Darth, not his idealistic pup."

Cedric inclined his head. "Then I trust, should the boy interfere with my affairs, you'll do what is necessary?"

Alywan lifted a shoulder in a dismissive shrug. "If Ky'len stands in our way, we won't spare him. Simple enough—particularly if he thinks he's going to protect peasants who owe you coin."

Cedric steepled his fingers, his gaze turning calculating. "Good. Now, about those peasants and my caravans: I need the roads clear. Do this, and you'll be compensated handsomely. But I understand you've been pushing for higher fees?"

Alywan and Garrick exchanged a knowing look before Alywan answered. "You're asking us to handle bigger muckspawn nests—and potentially a meddling heir. That kind of risk costs extra."

Cedric arched an eyebrow, recalling some intelligence he'd received. "I also hear Ky'len gave a few of your men quite a thrashing at a local tavern. Are you certain you're up to dealing with him —or anything else that lurks in Sergora?"

Garrick's jaw flexed at the slight. "We've never lost to that whelp. If he crosses our path, he'll learn what knights of Bazel are made of."

Alywan let out a short, mirthless laugh. "That sums it up. Pay us what we're worth, and we'll handle muckspawn, insolent lordlings—whatever you need."

Cedric permitted himself a thin smile. "Very well. Keep my roads open, handle any… complications, and your coin purses will stay heavy. Do we have an agreement?"

Alywan nodded. "Agreed. And if you decide Ky'len needs to be dealt with more permanently, we can discuss an additional fee."

Cedric's eyes flickered with satisfaction. "Then let's hope he keeps his distance. Otherwise…" He let the implication trail off. "We'll adjust the terms accordingly, so long as I see results. The next caravan departs in three days. Keep it safe and avoid drawing attention from King Tor'valis's men. Understood?"

Alywan swiped a cup of wine from a sideboard, raising it in a half-mocking salute. "Discretion is our strong suit, my lord. And if young Ky'len wants to play hero, well…" He smirked but left the threat unfinished.

Cedric's attention strayed briefly to the door through which Lady Kira had exited. "In that case, we're done here—for the moment. My steward will show you to your quarters. Rest while you can. Tomorrow, you'll receive the caravan schedule and details of our most vulnerable routes."

Garrick performed a careless bow as Alywan drained his wine and set the cup aside. "Pleasure doing business, Lord Cedric," Garrick said. "We'll secure your roads—and if we see that brat, we might find a use for him." He chuckled to himself.

Cedric's mouth tightened. "Just make certain your promises hold. Sergora's prosperity depends on it—and so does our mutual profit."

Armor clanking softly, the knights turned to leave. At the threshold, Alywan cast a last roving glance over the chamber, a sly grin tugging at his lips. "A shame we couldn't spend more time with Lady Kira," he remarked. "She looked like she'd be more fun than chasing muckspawn."

Cedric's posture stiffened, but his voice remained carefully level. "Mind your words. She's worth more than any tapestry in this hall—and infinitely more than your loose tongues."

Their mocking laughter echoed off the vaulted ceilings as they strode into the corridor. Silence reclaimed the space, punctuated only by the fading clang of armor. Cedric stood there, inhaling slowly, then returned to the window. He surveyed the rows of lanterns illuminating Sergora's streets, each light a symbol of the delicate order he strove to maintain.

Between muckspawn attacks, an ambitious heir from Bazel, and mercenaries who knew no tact, the city's stability felt precarious. But Cedric intended to keep everything in balance—just long enough to ensure a steady influx of gold, and perhaps remove any threat to that flow, whether rampaging creatures or a meddling lord's son. As for Lady Kira… he could only hope her ambitions remained fixed elsewhere, safely away from the shadows he was spinning around Sergora. One misstep, and everything—Kira, the knights, even Tor'valis's fragile peace —could collapse like a tapestry set ablaze.

***

Lyra, a slight but nimble young woman with smudges of city grime across her cheeks, crouched behind a stack of warped barrels. The alley she'd taken refuge in was cramped, the walls damp from the day's drizzle, and the air carried the faint tang of decaying refuse. Yet her heart pounded with excitement rather than fear. Just around the corner, two Bazel knights strode by, the crimson-fang emblazoned on their armor catching the flicker of a nearby torch. Their stride was purposeful, boots clacking on the worn cobblestones as they made their way toward Lord Cedric's sprawling estate.

She knew enough about knights to recognize their top-tier armor and the confident set of their shoulders—features that spoke of skill and, more importantly, an agenda. Trouble, Lyra thought, pulling her hood further over her forehead. Where knights roamed, so did conflict. And in Sergora's shadowy corners, conflict often brought opportunities for those clever enough to stay unnoticed.

The moment they vanished around a bend, Lyra slipped from her hiding spot. She navigated the winding backstreets as though born to them—vaulting a broken fence, sliding along a mossy wall to avoid a patrolling guard, and finally ducking into the charred shell of an abandoned blacksmith's shop. At first glance, it appeared derelict, but Lyra knew better. Concealed behind a stack of rusting equipment was a hatch that led into a cellar lit by a single, sputtering lantern.

Inside waited Harlek, a quick-witted thief-lord despite being only in his twenties. His reputation for cunning had spread through Sergora's underbelly almost as quickly as rumors of Cedric's latest schemes. Leaning against a decaying beam, he studied a map of local trade routes and scrawled notes. Across from him, perched on a rickety stool, was Sarah—hair so white it gleamed in the lamplight, her seventysomething frame still sturdy despite the passage of years. She was absorbed in mending a tattered blanket, thick fingers deftly working needle and thread. Around her, baskets overflowed with scraps of fabric and jugs of the special ale she brewed to trade for healing herbs.

Lyra took a breath to steady herself. "Master Harlek," she said, bowing her head with a mix of respect and excitement. "Bazel knights—two of them. They're heading straight for Lord Cedric's. They didn't seem like they were out for a casual stroll."

Harlek's eyes lit up with keen interest, and he set aside his map. "So Cedric's hired muscle from Bazel, has he? Could be big news. Might mean a bigger score for us." He tapped a fingertip on the dagger at his hip, clearly relishing the possibilities.

Sarah peered at Lyra over the rim of her spectacles. "Knights rarely bring good tidings for the likes of us," she said, her voice gentle but laced with concern. "Have you any sense of what Cedric's planning?"

Lyra shook her head. "No, Grandmother Sarah. All I caught was that they were marching with a clear purpose. Their faces... they looked ready for a fight."

208

Sarah tsked softly and returned to her sewing. "This city hardly needs more conflict. The folk in the lower quarters suffer most whenever Cedric stirs the pot. You be careful."

Harlek smirked, confidence shining in his eyes. "We'll do more than be careful—we'll be profitable." He stood straighter, brushing stray dust from his cloak. "Cedric's dealings often leave cracks we can slip through. If these knights cause chaos, we'll fish out whatever coin we can before the dust settles."

Sarah frowned, glancing up again. "Remember, lad, there's a difference between making ends meet and adding to the city's troubles." Though older than both by decades, she spoke with the authority of someone who'd nursed half the district through winter fevers.

Harlek inclined his head respectfully. "I know, Sarah. But we don't thrive on chaos alone. Your ale and healing keep these streets alive, and my little maneuvers pay for it all—like it or not."

Turning back to Lyra, Harlek continued, "Follow them for a few days. Track where they go, who they meet. Keep the littles—our youngest watchers—posted near Cedric's estate. If an opportunity presents itself, we'll be ready."

Lyra felt a rush of adrenaline. "Yes, Master," she said, already imagining the labyrinth of alleys she'd slip through to tail the knights unseen.

Harlek grabbed a small pouch from the table, the clink of coins inside faintly audible. "I'll be leaving shortly to replenish my herbs. A clear head is an asset in our line of work."

Sarah paused her needle, worry evident in her features. "Be safe out there, Harlek. We all need you back in one piece."

He chuckled softly. "Don't worry, Grandmother. Trouble might lurk in every alley, but I know these streets as well as any knight knows the battlefield."

With that, he climbed the creaking ladder, disappearing above. Sarah exhaled, the lantern's glow accentuating the lines of weariness on her face. "Go on, Lyra," she said, offering a small smile of encouragement. "And do try not to stir up more trouble than necessary."

Lyra inclined her head. "I'll be careful."

As she ascended the ladder into the dim evening light, her thoughts swirled. Knights on Cedric's doorstep, Harlek poised for new schemes, and Sarah's gentle warning lingering in her ears—Sergora was on the cusp of upheaval. Whatever Cedric intended, Lyra was determined to stay two steps ahead of the storm. After all, in this city of secrets, a quick mind and a sharper eye could be the difference between survival and ruin—and she intended to choose survival every time.

Chapter 21:The Edge Of Honor

782, 18th Day Of The Ninth Moon

Liora called for me tonight, asking for tales of the mountains and what waits beyond them. Her illness weakens her, but her curiosity remains unyielding. She clutched her stone rose as I spoke, the same as when she was a child. The rose, she told me once, makes her feel brave. And now, as I watch her fight each day, I understand she has always been braver than.

Lord Aric stood resolutely at the gates, his silhouette framed by the first light of dawn as it spilled across the world, casting elongated shadows at his feet. The air was thick with anticipation as he looked upon the trio before him—, Iszell, Ky'len and Tala. His face, a careful mask of approval intermingled with a solemn caution, mirrored the gravity of their undertaking. This was no simple errand; it was a moment stitched into the very fabric of Seragora's destiny. Stepping closer, Aric's hands rested deliberately on the pommel of his sword, his voice resonating with purpose.

"Strange times we find ourselves in," he began, his tone grave yet compelling. "Two squires of Bazel and a Muckspawn girl, now tasked with bearing the weight of our future. But it is often those we least expect who ignite the flames of change." He nodded thoughtfully at each of them. "Go forth. The gods speed you on your way."

As Ky'len took a step toward the widening path, Lord Aric halted him with an outstretched hand, presenting a bundle of gray Seragoran robes. "These will aid you. The people may well be more amiable if they do not see you as outsiders, but as one of their own."

Ky'len hesitated, his eyes studying the fabric for a moment that felt stretched by uncertainty. Finally, he shook his head, resolve painting his features. "Thank you, Lord Aric, but I must decline. If we are to carve our place among your people, we shall do so under Bazel's banner. This path may burden us, but our honor must lead the way."

A flicker of admiration softened Aric's gaze, a subtle glimmer overshadowing his previous caution. He placed a steady hand on Ky'len's shoulder, grounding the young man. "You are not your father, Ky'len. Control your anger—it's a flame to be nurtured, not a wildfire to be unleashed."

Ky'len returned the look, his conviction unyielding. "I understand, my lord. I will hold your words close."

With a final, somber nod, Lord Aric stepped back. "Then go, with haste and purpose."

The guards drew near, handing the group packs laden with provisions for their journey—dried meat, hard bread, and waterskins, essentials for the path ahead. A senior guard, his eyes cautious yet respectful, spoke with a low urgency. "Stay vigilant. There are unsettling whispers from the mountains—shadows shifting where they should not."

A younger guard, a fresh scar marking his brow, cast a supportive glance toward Tala. "Guide them well, lass. Your knowledge of these lands is unmatched."

Iszell nodded confidently, though the weight of their mission pressed down on him, muting his characteristic smile. "We'll bring honor to you all," he said earnestly. "Rest assured, we'll tread carefully."

As they passed through the towering gates, another guard called after them, "May your path be safe, and may you return stronger than you left." The immense wooden doors groaned closed behind them, the city slipping away into the distance. Each step became a testament to their skill, their courage, and their unwavering trust in one another. Aric's words lingered in Ky'len's mind, a steadfast reminder of the balance he would need to maintain—a blend of restraint and resilience on the road ahead.

Just as they moved to take their leave, a familiar voice called out, breaking the formal air. "Hold on, hold on!" Jeff emerged, weaving his way through the guards, clutching a bundle of fresh herbs and dried plants in his arms. His tunic was covered in dirt, and his usual grin was as wide as ever.

"For the road!" Jeff declared, extending the bundle toward them. "Can't have you lot going off without a bit of good ol' Seragoran spice." He winked at Tala and added in a conspiratorial whisper, "Stuff to keep you lively out there, you know?"

Tala took the herbs with a grateful nod, sniffing them appreciatively. "Thank you, Jeff," she replied, managing a small smile amidst her usual solemnity.

Jeff then turned to the guards standing stoically by the gates, a mischievous glint in his eyes. "You lot look like you could use some of these, too. Might make those 'stuffy lord expressions' a bit easier to manage, eh?" He nudged one of the guards with his elbow, who tried to keep a straight face but failed, letting out a reluctant chuckle.

One guard, an older man with a wiry mustache, gave a smirk. "Stick to your herbs, Jeff. We've no need for your ideas on 'livening up.'"

"Ah, that's what they all say!" Jeff laughed, flipping a mock salute to the guards. "Stay safe, you pack of stone-faced statues."

Turning back to the group, he gave a final nod. "You all take care, yeah? The road's a tricky friend. Listen to it, and maybe it'll lead you back here. And Tala," he added with a grin, "you keep 'em out of trouble."

With the herbs stowed away, Ky'len, Tala, and Iszell exchanged a last look with Jeff before stepping onto the path ahead. Jeff waved them off with a cheerful shout, his laughter trailing after them as they walked through the gates and into the awaiting wilderness, his parting words of humor and care settling in the quiet resolve of their journey.

As they continued along the narrow path, the scenery shifted subtly but unmistakably. Trees lined the edges of the trail, their once lush branches now bent and sparsely covered, as though even they were retreating from an invisible threat. The ground, usually alive with the bustling energy of wildlife, was eerily quiet; the occasional rustle from underbrush revealed small animals dashing towards the distant lights of Seragora. Birds scattered from the trees, their wings slicing through the heavy air, disappearing toward the safety of lower lands.

Villages they passed along the way looked bare, houses shut tight with their windows dark and empty. What few people they spotted wore tense expressions as they worked in silence, casting wary glances towards the group. Some held bundles of food and belongings, as if prepared to leave at a moment's notice.

Ahead, Tala took in the landscape with a quiet vigilance, her gaze tracking the trails of disturbed earth and broken branches. Every few moments, she glanced over her shoulder to check on Ky'len and Iszell, her expression a mix of encouragement and warning. She seemed to sense their unease as keenly as she sensed the foreboding stillness that had settled over the mountains.

Iszell, visibly unnerved by the empty villages and fleeing animals, leaned towards Ky'len, his voice barely louder than the soft breeze that stirred the mountain air. "How did we even get roped into this?" he murmured, casting a glance at the silent homes. "We're just barely of age… and we've never even faced a real battle. Do you think it's really going to come to war?"

Ky'len's eyes darkened as he took in the same sights. His voice, though steady, held a note of reluctance. "I wish I could give you a clearer answer, Iszell. But it feels like we're standing on the edge of something—something we can't fully see or understand, waiting to spill over."

Tala caught their hushed exchange and looked back, a flicker of understanding brightening her eyes. Switching briefly to the common tongue, she smiled softly, though her tone was tinged with gentle rebuke. "You worry… too much."

The brief respite brought Ky'len to another thought, and he hesitated before clearing his throat. "Tala… do you happen to know the Vek'smed tongue?" The question felt awkward, his cheeks heating with the realization of his own ignorance. Tala's amused glance told him she noticed, but her voice was warm when she replied.

"Yes," she chuckled lightly, a playful glint in her eyes, "their language comes more easily to me."

The lightness of the moment emboldened Iszell, who leaned forward, his grin broad as he attempted a clumsy greeting in the Vek'smed language. "Halló, unga fröken," *Hello, young miss,* he said, his accent rough but earnest.

Both Ky'len and Tala exchanged a surprised look, though Tala's eyes sparkled with amusement. Encouraged, Iszell ventured further, attempting what he thought was a compliment in the Muckspawn tongue. "Augu þín… víð og fegurð," *Your eyes… wide and beautiful,* he said, with a bit too much focus.

Tala's brows knitted in confusion as his mispronunciation twisted the words. "Bak þitt... við og jörð?"*Your... backside smells of the earth?*, she repeated, torn between surprise and amusement.

Ky'len's laughter echoed through the quiet mountains, reverberating off the stone walls. He clutched his stomach, tears gathering in his eyes. "Oh, Iszell, charming women in every language!" he teased, his voice barely steady between bursts of laughter.

Red-faced, Iszell shook his head, sputtering, "I was trying to say something nice!"

Tala, grinning, corrected him with the proper phrasing, her voice soft and fluid, carrying the cadence of Muckspawn with ease. She demonstrated, saying, "Augu falleg og við,"*This way is 'eyes beautiful'*, her tone lilting gracefully. Then, with a mischievous glint, she imitated his mistake with exaggerated seriousness, repeating, "Bak þitt... við og jörð," and even Ky'len laughed harder, their voices mixing with the occasional snap of twigs underfoot as they pressed onward.

As they climbed higher, the laughter faded, replaced by a growing sense of urgency. The landscape remained strangely still, nature itself seeming to recoil from some unseen force.

Iszell, hands thrown up in mock defeat, chuckled despite himself. "Languages are trickier than they look," he remarked, a sheepish grin breaking through his embarrassment.

Ky'len continued to tease, shaking his head in disbelief. "You're hopeless!"

Feigning offense, Iszell shot him a playful glance, raising an eyebrow. "Enjoy your laughter, Ky'len! Do you need me to remind you of Lady Anwen?"

The laughter faded from Ky'len's face, replaced by a look of sheer horror. "You wouldn't..."

"Oh, but I would!" Iszell exclaimed, turning to Tala, mischief glimmering in his eyes. "Picture this, Tala—our esteemed Ky'len, bold as a lion, attempting to woo Lady Anwen at court. All gallant and noble, he leans in and declares she 'moves with the grace of a... noble warhorse.'"

Ky'len groaned, his cheeks ablaze. "I meant it as a compliment! Grace and strength combined!"

"Grace and strength, sure," Iszell retorted, grinning widely, "but a warhorse? You should have seen her expression!"

Tala erupted in laughter, covering her mouth as she passed glances back and forth between the two. "So, both of you possess a... unique charm."

Rolling his eyes, Ky'len finally joined in on the laughter, his spirits lifted by the warm camaraderie. "Alright, alright, perhaps we both have a bit of room for improvement."

With a friendly nudge, Iszell grinned at him. "That's one way to keep things interesting."

As they trudged along the winding, rocky trail, Ky'len glanced at Tala, curiosity flickering in his gaze. Noticing his friend's interest, Iszell ventured the question they both had been wondering. "Tala… what is your world like?" he asked. "I mean, all we've really seen of your people is… well, fighting and raids."

Tala paused, choosing her words with care, her tone carrying a quiet pride. "Not all fight," she said slowly. "Muckspawn… we live different from humans. More… simple, maybe. We don't build walls like you." She gestured to the mountains around them. "Mountains, rivers—our walls are here," she explained with a soft reverence, as though the land itself was sacred to her people.

Ky'len nodded, listening closely. "But what about honor? I mean… for us, honor is everything."

"Honor important, yes," Tala replied, a small smile touching her lips, "but… different." She paused, her gaze distant. "Not like Vek'smed—die for honor. Or Slivdhe, where honor is in words… like shining blade." She mimicked a blade cutting through air with her hand. "For Muckspawn… honor is strength, survival." She tapped her chest with a clenched fist. "If someone… how you say… 'slight' us?" She hesitated, searching for the word, then grinned. "We call it 'bogsmal'—a challenge to settle."

"Bogsmal?" Iszell repeated, the word strange in his mouth. "And then you fight?"

"Ja," Tala nodded firmly. "Fight with rules, though. For honor—only to settle." She thought for a moment, then shrugged. "Winner is… respected. Loser, too. Respect for fighting, even if lose." Her eyes brightened as she explained. "If you walk away, no fight… no respect. Weak." She spat the word with disdain, her face hardening.

Ky'len tilted his head, intrigued. "But… that's not all, right? You must have tribes, families?"

"Ja, ja," Tala agreed, her voice filling with warmth. "Tribes, like Crowfeather, Venomfang… my own, Wolffang. Family close. Each tribe has elders, guides. They speak for us, tell stories, teach us. Not all are warriors. Some are… makers, healers, storytellers." Her gaze softened, memories lighting her eyes. "But when we fight, we fight together. For all, not just self."

Iszell, sensing the depth of her words, nodded. "It sounds… like your tribes are strong, but not just with swords."

Tala chuckled. "Strength not always sword, no. It is… spirit, maybe. Family. And we live with land, not on it, understand? Trees, water—they are… like kin. They give us what we need. Humans see Muckspawn and think 'raiders.' But we fight only when we must." She looked back at him, her gaze steady. "Even if you only see fight, that is not all of us."

Then, after a pause, Tala leaned in, her tone intense. "Bogsmal… it is not like human duel. It is… settle."

Iszell leaned forward, brow furrowing. "Final? Like to settle it once and for all?"

Tala's eyes darkened as she nodded. "Ja, to settle… but… loser… gone."

Ky'len's eyes widened as the meaning dawned on him. "Gone?"

With an unflinching gaze, Tala nodded. "Ja. Honor is… like blade. Only sharp if strong. Weak one cannot bring honor to tribe. Weak one… gone." She mimed the snapping of a thread between her fingers, her meaning unmistakable.

Iszell and Ky'len exchanged a glance, each realizing the weight of her words. In their world, honor was earned in battle but rarely at such a final cost. Tala's people, however, saw strength and survival not as ideals, but as unbreakable laws.

"Your people are… fierce," Ky'len said softly. "That kind of honor…"

"Ja," Tala affirmed, pride gleaming in her eyes. "It is our way."

The mountain path narrowed, shadows thickening around them like a closing shroud. Tala halted suddenly, her arm snapping up to signal Ky'len and Iszell to stop. They pressed against the nearest trees, hearts pounding with an instinctual fear as if hiding from a predator. The forest held its breath; even the birds had fallen silent. Tala's fierce gaze fixed on a distant figure emerging from the misted gloom of the trail.

Advancing up the rocky path was a cadre of Muckspawn warriors, their movements synchronized, deliberate, with an unsettling rhythm as if they were a single, breathing entity. Tala's voice, barely more than a whisper, held a tremor of reverence mixed with dread. "Urshak… Chief of the Crowfeather Tribe."

Her words hung in the air, the name heavy with an unspoken threat. Ky'len and Iszell exchanged wide-eyed glances of understanding. The Crowfeathers, once known for their intricate feather markings and fierce loyalty, were now twisted beyond recognition. Their green skin, once adorned with symbols of honor, had grotesque, feathered masses embedded within the flesh. Hunched and bestial, they moved with jerking, unnatural steps.

These were no longer the warriors Tala had once known—they were monstrous relics of a once-noble tribe, their honor twisted and forgotten.

The haunting murmur of their voices floated through the trees, each word tinged with an eerie melody that sent chills down Tala's spine. Straining to listen, she caught the gravelly growl of Urshak, his words cutting through the stillness. "Skynd deg! Vi må nå Høvding Zra'ka før marsjen starter. Allierte venter ikke på nøling." *Hurry! We must reach Chief Zra'ka before the march starts. Allies don't wait for hesitation.*

As the Crowfeathers passed by, their footfalls grew muffled, swallowed by the dense mist clinging to the forest floor. A shiver crawled over Tala's skin as the realization took hold—they were marching toward something dangerous, a gathering that could change everything.

Tala turned to her companions, the severity in her gaze unyielding. "We must follow them," she breathed, her voice as steady as it was urgent. "If the Crowfeathers and the Webshroud tribe are gathering, it's worse than we anticipated."

Ky'len tightened his grip on his sword, nodding with grim determination. "If the chiefs are uniting, they're plotting something bigger than we can imagine. We need to find out why."

Iszell swallowed, a fierce resolve lighting in his eyes as he glanced between Tala and Ky'len. "Then we move, but we keep to the shadows. If they spot us…" His voice trailed off, the unspoken danger hanging heavily between them.

With practiced silence, they slipped from the brush and began to trail the Crowfeathers, each step calculated, each breath measured. The path took them deeper into the woods, where the air grew colder and thick with a sense of foreboding. Their only company was the rhythmic crunch of distant footsteps and the occasional rustle of unseen creatures fleeing toward the safety of the city, sensing something amiss.

As they pushed onward, the woods grew denser, darker, as though the trees themselves leaned inward, conspiring to hide the secrets unfolding on the trail. At last, the Crowfeathers veered off the path and into a secluded glade encircled by towering pines. Tala motioned for them to crouch low, barely daring to breathe as they crept to the edge of the clearing.

In the misted center of the glade, an imposing figure awaited—the unmistakable form of Chief Zra'ka of the Webshroud tribe. His armor shimmered like spun webs under the dim light, woven from glistening leaves and silken threads that seemed alive. He stood unmoving, as though woven into the very fabric of the glade, a shadowed sentinel awaiting his ally.

Tala glanced at Ky'len and Iszell, a steely resolve in her eyes. "Now, we watch," she murmured, as they hunkered down, hearts hammering in anticipation, hoping to uncover the twisted alliance forming in the shadows.

Urshak approached, his and Zra'ka's solemn nods carrying the weight of an unspoken pact. The chiefs' voices barely rose above the whisper of leaves, yet each word cut through the air with ominous intent. Tala, Ky'len, and Iszell crept closer, breaths shallow, ears straining to capture their exchange.

"Tida es kommen," Urshak intoned, his voice dark and steady. "Grenzene har svekket seg, og landene som var våre er nå åpne og sårbare."

Tala leaned in, her voice barely a breath, translating for Ky'len and Iszell. "He says... the time has come. Our lands, once ours, now lie open. Weak."

Zra'ka replied, his words winding through the silence like a hiss. "Da skal vi handle ved neste måne. Myra vil våkne igjen."

Tala's voice tightened as she whispered, "Under the next moon... the marsh wakes. They plan to move soon."

The weight of her words settled like a boulder in Ky'len and Iszell's stomachs, fear flashing between them as they grasped the threat looming over their world.

Just as they began to pull back into the shadows, a sudden, overpowering presence descended upon them. Out of nowhere, a Muckspawn warrior emerged, a glimmering, shadow-draped figure, moving with the stealth of a predator. Before they could react, tendrils of sticky web shot toward them, coiling around their arms and legs, binding them tightly in place.

"Inntrengere i Webshroud-domene..." the warrior sneered, his voice laced with mocking disdain *Trespassers in the domain of the Webshroud....* "Hva skal vi gjøre med de små spionene? *"What shall we do with the little spies?*

Ky'len struggled against the restraints, panic gripping his voice. "Release us! We mean you no harm!"

The warrior's chuckle echoed off the trees, each note tightening the web. "Vi får se om det," he taunted, pulling them toward the glades' center where Urshak and Zra'ka awaited, their unreadable gazes revealing nothing but hinting at a storm about to break. *Oh, we shall see about that.*

As they were brought forward, the two chiefs cast menacing shadows in the dim light, their eyes narrowed with sinister amusement. Urshak's dark gaze settled on Tala, his lips curling into a sly, cruel smile. "Ah, lille Tala, så langt borte fra Araks favn... en fornøyelse," he sneered, his voice dripping with venom *Ah, little Tala, so far from the safety of Arak's embrace... how splendidly amusing.*

Tala gritted her teeth, her body taut as she fought the urge to recoil. "He... he mocks us," she whispered through clenched teeth.

Urshak's eyes swept toward his warriors. "Fang henne. Og guttene... la dem møte sin ende." *Seize her. As for the boys... let them meet their end.*

The surrounding Muckspawn stirred, their hands inching toward weapons, eyes glinting with a bloodlust that sent a chill down Ky'len and Iszell's spines. Struggling frantically against the restraints, their gazes darted to Tala, terror written across their faces as they began to realize the deadly predicament.

Ky'len, his voice cracking with desperation, whispered urgently, "Tala... what are they saying?"

Iszell, fumbling with fear, stuttered as he managed, "T-they... they're going to kill us, Ky'len. That's what they plan...

Ky'len's mind surged with a memory—a powerful, solitary word he'd heard from Tala, one uttered only in the gravest of situations. Summoning every ounce of courage, he took a deep breath and shouted, "BOGSMAL!"

An eerie silence swept over the clearing, chilling the air. The Muckspawn warriors froze, their fierce gazes snapping to him. A shared look of confusion flickered between them as they turned their attention to their leaders, searching for guidance.

An uneasy stillness blanketed the clearing, as if the word Ky'len had shouted carried with it some ancient, unspoken weight. Urshak's triumphant sneer flickered with the faintest hint of doubt, and his companion stilled, assessing the sudden tension among their warriors. In that suspended moment, Tala locked eyes with Ky'len, a silent surge of resolve passing between them.

Then, with a slow, deliberate step, Urshak advanced. His cruel smile returned, and his voice rumbled through the hush like distant thunder. "Bogsmal? Hah! Dreg'uk fal ormeyngel! Tala, si dem hva de har gjort. Jeg aksepterer deres patetiske rop om ære."

Tala swallowed hard, forcing herself to speak in a steady tone so Ky'len and Iszell would understand "He says, 'Bogsmal? Ha! You dare speak it, you worms! Tala, tell them what they have done. He accepts… our desperate cry for honor.'"

The Muckspawn hesitated, weapons half-drawn, glancing nervously at the two chiefs. Shadows shifted beneath the faint, flickering light, and the air seemed to grow colder with every breath. Tala felt her pulse hammering in her ears as she fought against her restraints. Despite her fear, that single word had ignited something in her—hope, or perhaps desperation—enough to stand against the looming threat.

Urshak's gaze swept over them, his eyes glinting with a newfound interest. He bared his teeth in a mocking grin. "Er dere så sultne på døden? La oss se om 'Bogsmal' virkelig beskytter dere."

"He says, 'If you're so eager to die, then by all means—let us see if "Bogsmal" truly protects you.'"

A chill wind seemed to stir through the clearing, and even Urshak's warriors glanced at each other in uncertainty. The breathless hush weighed on them all, bearing down on Tala, Ky'len, and Iszell just as surely as the rope that bound them. And yet, in the midst of terror, a small spark of defiance took hold.

Whatever dread or salvation the word *Bogsmal* might bring, there would be no turning back now.

Chapter 22: Ashes Of Seragora

765, 17th Day Of The Ninth Moon

Honor. My wife's people carry it like a quiet flame, woven into every word and deed. I once thought it mere pride, stubbornness—how wrong I was. For them, honor is not a show but a core; it's in their sacrifices, their unspoken vows, their silent courage before battle. They see dishonor not in failure, but in the refusal to rise again. It humbles and haunts me, this devotion.

Curious, I asked Mira what honor is to her. She huffed, barely glancing my way. "Honor?" she said, "Honor is a lie we tell ourselves to feel good." Yet I wonder if she believes that, or if it's simply easier to tell herself so.

The forest path was thick with the acrid scent of smoke, mingling with the damp earth and pine. Each step forward pressed the weight of dread deeper into their chests. The familiar skyline of Seragora began to take form ahead, though veiled in a sinister haze as black smoke billowed into the dawn sky. An unnatural quiet cloaked them; even the birds were silent, their usual song stifled by the suffocating smoke.

As they neared the stables, once a place of bustling life, A'nara's gaze sharpened, her eyes narrowing as she took in the charred remains. "This was no accident…" she murmured, her voice strained and tight. "Someone torched this place." Her words lingered heavily in the thick air as she surveyed the ashes, now only faintly glowing embers.

Belazar's expression darkened, his face contorted with fury as he slammed a fist into the crumbling structure. "My home… my livelihood!" he roared, sending a cascade of debris falling around him, dust and ash twisting through the air. The smoky haze settled over them, carrying the scent of burnt wood and scorched earth, filling their lungs with bitter heat.

Trying to pierce the tension, Yvonne attempted a wry smile. "Well, now all of it is destroyed." But even her voice fell flat, lost amid the devastation.

Dalmon crouched beside the scorched remains, running his fingers along the brittle, blackened wood. His jaw tightened as he spoke, his voice grim. "No, this was deliberate… not just a fire, an attack." His words cut through the smoky silence like a blade, leaving an unsettling stillness in their wake.

As Yvonne scanned the area, the growing thickness of smoke drifted upward, carrying an ominous stillness. Her voice wavered with disbelief and anger. "Who would do this?" she demanded, her eyes darting over the destruction. "This wasn't only for destruction… someone wanted to send a message."

Belazar's hand clenched tightly around the hilt of his sword, his entire frame shaking with a mixture of fury and fear. "It was Thorn," he spat, his voice thick with bitterness. "She has my son, Razma…" His voice cracked, his anger giving way to a rare glimmer of desperation. "We need to find him! We need to get him back."

Dalmon placed a steadying hand on Belazar's shoulder, his voice a soft reassurance. "It will be alright, Belazar. We'll get him back."

Ever the pragmatist, Yvonne's eyes flicked toward the spreading fires. "I know… but look around." She gestured toward the smoldering ruins of the town. "We must help save the town first, or there won't be anything left."

Dalmon's gaze traveled to the smoke-choked streets, the faint sound of swords clashing drifting through the air as fires rose. "The council will be in the heart of this chaos." Drawing his weapon, he turned, his voice low and steady. "If we're to stop Thorn and save Seragora, we need to reach them."

The group exchanged tense glances before making their way down the hill toward the city. As they descended, the full extent of the destruction became clear. Seragora was burning. Flames climbed from rooftops, casting an eerie orange glow across the horizon. The streets were choked with smoke, and the faint cries of the wounded and dying carried through the air.

Dalmon, Belazar, A'nara, and Yvonne pushed their way toward Seragora's gates, their surroundings thick with smoke and the flicker of flames casting grim shadows. As they approached, they were met by desperate refugees pressing against the gates, pleading for sanctuary. Clothes torn, faces streaked with soot, the crowd surged forward, panic mounting as guards tried to hold them back.

"You can't come in!" a guard barked, his voice strained as he struggled against the tide of bodies. "There's fighting in the streets! We're at capacity!"

"My child is in there!" a woman wailed, clutching a tattered shawl around her shoulders, her plea echoing through the chaos.

The group spotted Clive, one of Aleric's men, through the haze. "Clive?" Dalmon called, cutting through the throng.

Relief washed over Clive's weary face as he recognized them. "Dalmon! You've no idea what a mess this is—people in a frenzy, guards overwhelmed," he explained, catching his breath. "We could use all the help we can get."

Dalmon turned to the crowd, his voice steady and commanding. "Everyone, listen! Pushing the gates will not help. I promise, we're working to keep you safe, but we need your cooperation."

Belazar added, his own voice firm, "We'll get you through this, but only if we all stay calm. Order is key."

Yvonne stepped up, her gaze sharp and unyielding as she spoke. "If you want to save your families, listen to us! We'll get you to safety."

The crowd hesitated, and the urgency in their voices seemed to take hold, the desperation easing. The guards lowered their shields, a few exchanging relieved glances as Clive nodded to Dalmon. "You heading to see Lord Cedric?" Clive asked. "Convincing him might be a challenge."

Dalmon's eyes narrowed. "Tell Cedric he has no choice. If he denies these people refuge, he'll find his precious wine supply cut off."

Clive chuckled, nodding as he signaled the guards to guide the refugees inside. Just then, a familiar grumble rose above the crowd.

"Stuffy lords, locking out their own folk!" Jeff's voice cut through, loud as ever. Covered in ash and clutching a handful of charred herbs, he stomped toward them. "And my best batch of herbs, all burnt! If anyone's paying for that, it's those high-and-mighty pricks, not the townsfolk."

A'nara and Yvonne exchanged a grin, chorusing, "Hi, Jeff." Dalmon and Belazar both sighed, shaking their heads with amused resignation.

Jeff's eyes narrowed on Dalmon. "Going to see Cedric, are you?" he asked, his voice rising. "Good! Tell him he owes me! That fancy wine budget of his could surely cover a man's herbs!" He jabbed a finger at Dalmon, his tone defiant. "And you tell him double for the trouble!"

Belazar chuckled. "We'll pass it along, Jeff. But maybe get to shelter?"

"Shelter? Leave my herbs to the wind?" Jeff scoffed, waving him off before muttering, "Fancy lords and their stuffy city walls…" His complaints followed him as he wove through the crowd.

Yvonne laughed. "Jeff might be a thorn to the lords, but he's loyal to the rest of us."

Dalmon smirked, glancing back at the retreating figure. "He's tenacious. Let's hope Cedric's ready for his… requests."

The group entered the town slowly, stepping over the splintered remains of the city gate. Smoke hung thick in the air, clinging to their clothes and stinging their eyes. The buildings on either side loomed in shadows, their once-familiar forms twisted by fire and neglect. Broken carts and scattered belongings lay in the streets, remnants of lives upturned.

A'nara's gaze darted between the charred remnants, her fingers grazing the edges of a burnt sign. "Thar ir… níath ta heiren,"*It's all… fallen to ash"* she murmured, her voice carrying a trace of sorrow.

Yvonne's expression was grim as they moved forward, stepping over debris and sidestepping shattered stones. "Thar fir vel vor vélnar,"*It is as if the very heart of the city has been stolen.*

With silent agreement, they pressed on, the eerie quiet broken only by the distant crackling of fires and the faint, uneasy whispers of those who still hid in the shadows.

A'nara glanced around, her wild eyes scanning the destruction. "Ceorán fir vin'en...?"*How do they live like this...?* she muttered, her voice barely above a whisper for the others. "Tán allníor fir... de'or hiran... ní talir se atho." *So confined, stacked on top of each other... There's no room to breathe, no space to move.*

Yvonne, walking beside her, nodded. "Lán fir vél mara'tor ar, iorin vel'thar or hian'ce."*We've spent so long moving from place to place, living under the sky.* She paused, her gaze hardening as she observed the looters moving through the wreckage. "Thar ir'vel vor... ni orádh vor harma rinon'ce. "*Though I'll never understand how people can turn on each other so quickly when things go wrong.*

Dalmon overheard their conversation and slowed his pace, turning to his sister. "A'nara, remember—speak only in common here. You and Yvonne may be used to the wilds, but this city is nothing like that." He reached over, pulling her hooded cloak lower to conceal her Slividhe ears. Adjusting his own bandana, he cast a glance at the suspicious eyes around them. "We're not among friends here, not with tensions running this high."

A'nara nodded, tightening her hood further. "I haven't forgotten, brother," she whispered. "But something is wrong here. These people move like caged animals, ready to attack the moment they see an opening."

The group pushed forward through Seragora's shattered streets, the air thick with smoke that stung their eyes and coated their throats. Embers drifted down like sinister fireflies, catching in hair and clothes. As they stepped over fallen beams and scorched belongings, the weight of the city's suffering hung around them like a shroud. The deeper they moved into the city, the more refugees crowded the alleys, their faces gaunt and hollow, some clutching meager bags of what little they'd managed to salvage. Families huddled by crumbling walls, sheltering small children from the violence and destruction surrounding them.

They passed charred remnants of shops and homes, once vibrant with life, now reduced to smoldering husks. The acrid smell of burning wood and flesh lingered in the air, mingling with the despair of those who had lost everything. The butcher's shop, now a heap of blackened beams, stood beside the baker's; the latter still faintly emitting the pungent scent of burnt bread. A few people scoured the ruins, eyes desperate, hoping to find anything salvageable amid the devastation.

In the middle of the crowded street, a quick-footed thief darted by, fingers reaching for Belazar's coin pouch. But Belazar's hand shot out, capturing the thief's wrist in an iron grip. With a swift twist, he forced the thief to the ground, a pained gasp escaping the man's lips. "Consider that a warning," Belazar growled, voice low and edged with threat. "Next time, you won't have a hand to steal with." The thief scrambled away, clutching his injured wrist, casting fearful glances over his shoulder as he melted back into the crowd.

"We don't have time for this," Yvonne muttered sharply, pulling Belazar's attention back to the grim scene around them. "Dalmon's shop is close. If we don't get there soon, the looters will strip it bare."

Dalmon nodded, glancing warily at the growing chaos. "We'll see what we can salvage." They pushed forward, passing more families huddled in alleyways, clutching their belongings tightly as thieves slinked in the shadows, ready to pounce on any sign of weakness.

As they neared the remains of Dalmon's shop, the baker—a soot-streaked woman with hollow eyes—was outside, attempting to gather anything that hadn't been reduced to ash. She looked up as Dalmon approached, her gaze desperate. "Have you seen Razma?" he asked urgently. "We're looking for Belazar's son."

The baker shook her head, her voice laced with sadness. "No, I'm sorry, Dalmon. I haven't seen him. But… I heard the boy Ky'len and his friend Iszell were here. They mentioned something about bringing back the Vek'smed if they could." Her gaze flitted nervously to Belazar, her voice dropping to a hushed tone. "People are saying Bazel did this… but I'm not so sure."

Dalmon grimaced, his eyes hard. "It wasn't Bazel." He cast a quick look around and leaned in closer. "This was Thorn's doing, manipulating the muckspawn against us. But we can't let people know—if word spreads, they'll turn on both Bazel and the muckspawn, and Seragora won't survive the aftermath."

The baker nodded, though confusion clouded her features. "Nothing makes sense anymore," she murmured.

"Trust us," Dalmon replied firmly. "We'll make sure the truth comes out. But for now, stay safe."

The group moved on, threading their way through narrow streets where the smoke grew thicker, filling their lungs with every breath. The din of chaos surrounded them—shouts, clanging swords, the cries of the injured and displaced. Each turn revealed more bodies strewn across the cobblestones, their blood staining the city in stark, crimson reminders of the violence that had unfolded here. Belazar's hand tightened on his sword, his expression grim as he scanned the streets.

"This is what Thorn wants," he spat, his voice trembling with restrained rage. "She wants Seragora to burn, and she'll keep pushing until there's nothing left."

As they rounded the final corner toward the shop, A'nara, her instincts honed by years of survival, leaned closer to Yvonne, whispering, "The air feels wrong… like everything's on the edge of breaking."

Yvonne nodded, her gaze scanning the crowd of desperate faces and looters lurking in the shadows. "It's already broken, A'nara," she murmured, her tone heavy with determination. "We just need to stop it from shattering completely."

Just as Yvonne's words left her lips, her gaze fell upon a heart-wrenching scene near the edge of the square. Among the crumbling ruins and scattered debris lay the still form of an older woman, her brown hair streaked with ash, green eyes now lifeless and fixed on the smoky sky above. Beside her, a young child clung desperately to her body, small hands trembling as they tried in vain to rouse her. The child's soft cries cut through the noise around them, raw and full of confusion, a grief too vast for such a young heart to bear.

Yvonne's face tightened, her expression caught between anguish and fury. Her own memories flickered to life, haunted by a similar loss, and for a moment, the destruction around her seemed to quiet, as if time itself was holding its breath. The firelight cast a warm, terrible glow over the scene, illuminating the unspoken devastation in the eyes of the child as they whispered to their fallen mother.

As the smoke and chaos of Seragora's streets swirled around her, Yvonne's mind slipped back to another fire, another night when she was just a child, back in her own village. She could still feel the bite of the wind on her face, smell the crisp autumn air as she wandered the fields, carefree and laughing, ignoring her chores as she often did. The last thing she remembered thinking was how she'd explain herself when she finally returned to her mother.

Then, a scream shattered the quiet, piercing through the field like a blade. Her mother's scream.

Yvonne's heart jolted, freezing her in place, her body tense with instinctual terror. The desperate, anguished cry echoed through the air, and in that instant, she was running, her small legs carrying her over fields and through trees. Voices followed—the shouts of men, the clash of steel. Each beat of her pounding heart matched her frantic footsteps, the terror swelling with each stride as the distant crackle of fire filled her ears.

Smoke twisted up into the sky above the village, dark and menacing. Her chest tightened as she neared her mother's workplace: the lord's house. She'd promised to help with the washing, but she'd slipped away for one last hour of freedom. Now, thick black smoke spiraled into the air from the manor grounds, twisting her stomach with a dread she didn't yet know how to name. Stumbling over roots and rocks, she forced herself forward, barely able to process the panic tearing through her mind.

She broke through the edge of the trees, and chaos hit her like a wave. The manor was aflame, its once grand structure now wreathed in fire. Shadows flickered across the walls as bandits swarmed through, their laughter cold and callous as they looted and tore through everything in their path. Villagers fled in every direction, and the air pulsed with the sounds of chaos, heat, and horror.

And there, by the side door, she saw her mother.

Yvonne stumbled, the world spinning around her as she took in the scene. Her mother lay crumpled against the stone wall, her clothes torn, her hands bloodied from the struggle. She seemed so small, so fragile against the unyielding stone. Yvonne fell to her knees, her hands trembling as she crawled toward her, desperate and terrified.

"Mama…" she choked out, barely able to breathe. She reached out, her fingers brushing against her mother's cold skin. "Please… please wake up. I'm here—I'm sorry… I should have been here…"

But her mother's green eyes, once so full of warmth and laughter, stared lifelessly into the smoke-filled sky. The familiar life in her gaze was gone, replaced by a hollow emptiness. Yvonne's throat burned, her heart breaking as tears spilled down her face, each tear as sharp as glass.

She clutched her mother's body, her small hands clinging to her torn sleeve, desperate to hold on, unwilling to believe the truth. Around her, flames crackled and the world continued to crumble, but Yvonne heard nothing. She was locked in her own grief, a raw, unbearable ache.

Then she saw it—her father's bow, lying just feet away, dropped by the men who had taken everything from her. Her small fingers reached for it, trembling as they wrapped around the familiar wood. The weight of it, the feel of it, was grounding, powerful. Rage surged alongside her grief, filling the hollow left by her mother's death, a fierce, unyielding flame burning in her chest.

In that moment, the innocent child she had once been was gone. Only her mother's memory and her vow remained: she would never be weak again. She would protect, she would fight. She would never allow anyone to suffer as her mother had.

As A'nara's hand settled on Yvonne's arm, grounding her, Yvonne blinked, the weight of her childhood vow bearing down as heavily as ever. But now, it was a source of strength. She wiped away a single tear, straightening, her voice fierce and unyielding. "They'll pay for this," she whispered.

The group pressed forward through Seragora's ravaged streets. The sounds of children crying blended with desperate pleas for help, echoing from the alleys and doorways where refugees huddled together, clutching the few remnants of their former lives. Smoke drifted down like an oppressive shroud, thickening the air, while the acrid smell of charred wood and flesh turned their stomachs and tightened their throats.

When they arrived at Dalmon's shop, they found it gutted—windows shattered, the door barely hanging from its hinges. Inside, shelves were overturned, belongings scattered across the floor, stripped bare.

"Bastards," Dalmon muttered, stepping carefully over broken glass and debris. "They took what they could and trashed the rest."

Belazar kicked a broken chair aside, frustration simmering in his posture. "We don't have time to waste here. What can we salvage?"

Dalmon sifted through the wreckage, finding a few intact vials and scrolls. "Not much," he said, lifting a small chest from beneath a fallen cabinet. "But this is what we came for."

Footsteps sounded outside, and the group instinctively reached for their weapons, tensing until they saw a familiar face. Alric entered, his expression grim but relieved, followed by King Tor'valis, whose regal bearing was marred by soot and exhaustion.

"Dalmon, Belazar," Alric greeted them, his voice edged with weariness. "We need your help—things are spiraling out of control."

Tor'valis surveyed the group, his gaze lingering on Dalmon. "The people are turning on each other," he said, voice heavy with urgency. "They're attacking the Bazel emissaries at the inn. I've managed to prevent an all-out war for now, but it's barely holding."

A'nara's expression darkened. "What's being done to stop this? Thorn's behind it all, but the people don't know."

Tor'valis nodded. "We know. Thorn has spread the rumor that Bazel is responsible. It's fueling panic, and our soldiers are barely containing the crowds. Fear has turned people into a mob."

Yvonne crossed her arms, her gaze steely. "What do you need from us?"

Alric gestured toward the city's heart. "The worst of it is at the inn. We need to protect the emissaries and calm the mobs before this spirals out of control."

Belazar's grip tightened on his sword, jaw set with determination. "Let's go. We need to act now, or there'll be no city left to save."

As they prepared to leave, Dalmon turned to Alric. "What about the council?"

Alric shook his head. "They're trying to secure a refuge for the displaced, but resources are thin. The king's preparing to address the people at high sun, but that won't stop what's happening in the streets right now."

Dalmon exchanged a glance with his companions, resolve hardening. "Let's move quickly."

As they pushed through the winding streets, the devastation of Seragora grew more apparent. Smoke hung heavy, and the once-lively city was reduced to a desolate expanse of ruins and scattered rubble. Parents clutched their children, their faces etched with fear, while others searched desperately for food among the debris. Grief and despair radiated from every corner, their silent weight pressing down on the group.

Yvonne's gaze swept over the suffering, fists clenched. "This isn't just war," she murmured. "It's annihilation."

When they reached the inn, they found chaos waiting. A furious mob surged against the soldiers, shouting at the Bazel emissaries barricaded inside. Rocks pelted the inn's walls, windows shattered, and doors splintered under the assault.

Belazar moved forward, his expression dark. "If this turns bloody, we lose the city."

A soldier was struck by a rock, staggering as the crowd pushed forward, anger building.

Yvonne's voice cut through the noise, sharp and commanding. "Enough!" She stepped in front of the crowd, her tone unyielding. "These people are not your enemies!" Her presence stilled the crowd, their rage momentarily held in check.

"They came here for peace, not war!" she continued. A man in the crowd sneered, "They're Bazel! They're why this city's burning!"

Dalmon raised his hands, his voice firm. "No. This isn't Bazel. This is Mutt's doing, under the orders of Mrs. Thorn."

Murmurs rippled through the crowd, some nodding, others confused.

Dalmon pressed on. "Thorn is disguising her muckspawn as Bazel soldiers to turn us against each other. She wants Seragora to tear itself apart."

A'nara stepped forward, voice clear. "She's manipulating you—don't give her the satisfaction."

The mob hesitated, anger giving way to doubt. The soldiers exchanged relieved glances, while Alric nodded in gratitude. "We'll handle it here," he assured Dalmon.

Yvonne turned to Dalmon. "What's next?"

Dalmon glanced over the ruins, his expression grim. "To the council. We stabilize the city first, then we deal with Thorn."

A'nara looked over the smoke-laden city, her jaw set. "Let's hope we're not too late."

Chapter 23: Webs and Flames

764, 17th Day Of The Eleventh Moon

The Bog People have emerged again, swarming from the marshes like shadows cast by the muck that spawns them. They move with the stealth of creatures born in mire, slipping in and out of our lands, harrying our caravans and taking what they can before vanishing back into the bog.

They come swift and silent, leaving no trace but the cries of our people and the emptiness of our stores. We've attempted to post guards along the trade routes, yet somehow, they elude even our best soldiers, as if the marsh itself aids in their flight. The council whispers that the Bog People carry magic in their bones, a dark inheritance from the swamps they call home.

This is no isolated raid but a pattern, a warning perhaps, or an invitation to war. Their ways are foreign, their motives obscured by the mist. Some urge we respond with force, to drive them back and make an example of any who dare to return. Yet, part of me wonders if there is more to these raids, a message lost in their silence.

As Urshak's eyes locked onto Ky'len, his mocking smile faded, replaced by a dark interest that rippled through the crowd. His voice rumbled in the thick, guttural tones of Muckspawn, "Så vi har en Bogsmal, da. En utfordring." *Ah, we have a Bogsmal, then. A challenge.* The anticipation in his voice made the warriors around him shift with edgy excitement, their bloodlust momentarily held at bay.

With a slow, deliberate motion, Urshak raised a clawed hand, gesturing toward the clearing as a wicked grin returned to his face. "Så slåss, hvis du tør" he taunted, his chilling glee echoing ominously in the air.

Tala turned to Ky'len, her face pale. "He… he says we have a Bogsmal—your challenge. And then, 'Fight, if you dare,'" she whispered, her voice filled with dread.

Tala's expression shifted from disbelief to sheer dread, her body instinctively recoiling as she turned to Ky'len, her voice a trembling whisper. "You… have done something terrible here," she warned, "He never loses."

Ky'len felt the weight of his decision settle heavily upon him, jaw clenched and throat tight. Leaning closer, he spoke low and urgent, "When it begins, run. I'll hold them off as long as I can."

Iszell's eyes darted between them, panic etched on his face. "Ky'len, are you out of your mind?

This is Urshak—he's… he's a legend!"

Ky'len nodded grimly, resolve shimmering in his gaze. "I know what I'm up against. But if this is our only chance to escape, I'll take it." He tightened his grip around his weapon, fortifying his spirit as he searched Tala's worried eyes. "You two must survive. That's an order."

The air in the clearing vibrated with tension as Urshak stepped forward, a twisted grin spreading across his face. With a flourish, he raised his arms, inciting the warriors around him. They erupted into wild jeers and cheers, a cacophony of voices eager for the impending bloodshed. Some called out Ky'len's name mockingly, others chanted Urshak's, their voices growing louder, feeding the frenzy of anticipation.

"Modige ord, gutt," Urshak sneered, his voice thick with mockery. "Vi får se om bladet ditt kan leve opp til dem."

Tala leaned close to Ky'len, translating urgently under her breath, "He says your words are brave, but… he doubts your blade can live up to them."

Before Ky'len could respond, Urshak lunged forward, moving with unnatural speed. His cloak of feathers swirled around him, making it appear as though he were gliding through the air. The crowd roared, some cheering him on, others taunting Ky'len, while a few voices jeered, hoping he'd crumble.

Ky'len barely managed to raise his sword in time, the blade catching against Urshak's feathers, which clung to it like living tendrils, slowing him down. The jeers turned into boos from one side of the crowd, and shouts of encouragement erupted from another.

"Slå ham i bakken!" a warrior shouted, and others took up the cry, urging Urshak on.

Ky'len gritted his teeth and pushed back, trying to dislodge his blade. Urshak's claws struck like lightning, slashing through the air, forcing Ky'len into a defensive stance. He could feel the weight of every eye on him, the relentless energy of the warriors fueling Urshak's attacks.

"Bogsmal ære? Du er bare et bytte," Urshak hissed, disdain dripping from his words.

Tala's voice reached Ky'len's ears, her tone tight. "He… he says you're just prey. Not worthy of Bogsmal honor."

Ky'len clenched his jaw, his grip tightening on the hilt of his sword. He swung with all his strength, but the feathers tangled around his arm, pulling him off balance. The crowd erupted, half of them cheering wildly as Urshak took advantage, spinning around him like a dark whirlwind, his claws slicing dangerously close to Ky'len's face.

The warriors cheered louder, their voices a mixture of thrill and bloodlust. "Drep ham, Urshak!" came the call from several warriors, their fists raised, while others booed, displeased with Ky'len's struggle.

"Stille!" Chief Zra'ka's voice boomed over the crowd, his cold gaze silencing the chaos. The warriors fell into a tense hush, though their eyes remained fixed on the fight, eager for the next move.

Urshak's cloak tightened around Ky'len, the feathers like iron chains, squeezing the air from his lungs. Ky'len struggled, his breath coming in shallow gasps as Urshak grinned, his eyes gleaming with cruel delight. Every movement was met with resistance, his sword arm bound tighter with each desperate twist.

Just then, Ky'len's eyes caught sight of something—a web spun between two trees, shimmering faintly. The Webshroud's mark. With a final surge of strength, he yanked Urshak toward it. The sticky threads latched onto the cloak, dragging Urshak back.

Urshak's eyes flared with rage and surprise as he fought against the web, his movements turning wild and frantic. His once-graceful strikes faltered, his feathers twisting and tangling as he struggled.

The crowd fell silent, watching Urshak's furious attempts to free himself, but a few voices broke through with mocking laughter and disdainful boos. Some warriors shouted, "Hva skjedde, Urshak?" while others muttered darkly, questioning his honor as he thrashed.

Seizing the chance, Ky'len knocked Urshak to the ground, holding his sword over the fallen chief. The crowd surged forward, cheers and boos mixing, waiting to see if he would strike.

Ky'len hesitated, his breath coming in heavy gasps. "I won't kill you," he said, voice hoarse. "I'm not like you." He looked to Tala, nodding. "Tell them."

Tala stepped forward, her voice steady but tense as she translated his words to the assembled warriors: "Eg vil ikkje drepe deg. Eg er ikkje som deg."

Urshak's eyes burned with fury, his body still ensnared in the web, his voice a guttural growl. But before he could speak, another voice rang out from the crowd:

"Den som taper dør i Bogsmal ære."

Tala leaned toward Ky'len, her face drained of color. "Ky'len… in Bogsmal… it means to the end."

Iszell's face paled, understanding dawning. "She means… to the death."

Ky'len shook his head, defiance sparking in his eyes. "I won't kill him," he repeated firmly, looking at Tala. "Tell them."

But before Tala could speak, Chief Zra'ka stepped into the clearing. He moved forward, his expression unreadable, his warriors at his side. With a slow, deliberate motion, he raised a hand, releasing a sickly green mist that drifted toward Urshak, coiling around him.

Ky'len watched, horror-stricken, as the mist wrapped around Urshak, his flesh beginning to disintegrate. A tortured scream tore from Urshak's throat, echoing across the clearing as his body collapsed into a dark, viscous pool. Webshroud warriors moved in, spinning webs over the remains, sealing what was left.

The crowd was deathly silent, the mocking and cheering forgotten. Zra'ka turned his gaze to Ky'len, a sneer spreading across his face.

"Du er svak," he spat.

Tala's voice shook as she translated, "He… he says you are weak."

Iszell stared in horror. "They… cooked him alive."

Zra'ka's cold smile twisted. "Du kjempet godt," he said, his tone mocking, "Men din nytte er over. Drep dem."

Tala's voice quivered as she translated, "He… he's ordering them to kill us."

Iszell swallowed hard, managing a faint, grim laugh. "Yeah, I think we understand that part."

"Run!" Ky'len shouted, bolting toward the trees. Tala and Iszell followed close behind, the Webshroud warriors giving chase, their hissing webs filling the air, their voices rising once more in a bloodthirsty cry. The forest closed in around them, each shadow a reminder that they were not yet free.

Tala and Iszell pushed themselves to the brink, each pounding step sending shockwaves of pain through their legs, as they pursued Ky'len toward the faint glimmer of light ahead. The uneven ground was scattered with sharp stones and twisted roots, threatening to trip them at every turn. Behind them, the hissing of the Webshroud warriors spurred them on—low snarls and the crack of webs slicing the air punctuating their flight.

Tala gasped as a sticky strand zipped past her shoulder, latching onto a nearby branch. She staggered, nearly losing her balance, until Iszell seized her arm and hauled her upright.

"Faster!" Ky'len's voice strained above the thunder of footsteps. Tala and Iszell exchanged a desperate look, but they didn't dare slow. They forced their legs to move, driving themselves up the hillside where a flickering light—like a wavering beacon—beckoned them onward.

Their lungs burned, each ragged breath of cold night air doing little to quell the ache in their limbs. The incline steepened, demanding more from muscles already on the edge. The Webshroud warriors' hissing grew louder behind them. Another sticky web whistled through the darkness, wrapping around Tala's wrist. She stumbled, pulse hammering, but Iszell yanked her free, and the two lurched onward.

Only when the elusive light brightened—revealing a rocky wall with a narrow shadow of an opening—did Tala feel a glimmer of relief. She and Iszell were spent, gasping for air, yet somehow they reached it, close on Ky'len's heels. As soon as they slipped inside, they all collapsed against the cool stone. The damp smell of earth enfolded them, dulling the lingering adrenaline.

Outside, the hissing continued, the warriors' voices weaving through the forest. Tala pressed a trembling finger to her lips, silently urging Iszell and Ky'len to keep quiet. Slowly, their frantic breathing eased, though the dread of being cornered remained.

A faint glow in the recess drew their attention: a small fire pit near the back wall, its embers still warm. Tala inched toward the coals, extending a tentative hand.

"It's warm," she whispered, voice taut with suspicion and relief. "Whoever was here… didn't leave long ago."

Ky'len eased down next to her, exhaustion palpable in his every movement. "I don't care who it was," he said, voice ragged. "I just need to breathe. We'll rest—a minute or two."

Iszell sank to the ground, struggling to steady his inhalations. "We've been running all night," he rasped. "I… I can't feel my legs anymore."

The three of them huddled around the dying embers, letting the fire's lingering heat seep into their strained limbs. Gradually, the hissing outside retreated, as if the Webshroud warriors had turned elsewhere or simply lost the trail. Though relief began to settle in, none of them fully relaxed.

Ky'len let his head loll against the stone, his breath growing a bit steadier. He caught Tala's eye, hope kindling faintly in his gaze. "We… we made it," he murmured, though fatigue clung to every word.

"For now," Tala agreed, voice hushed, gaze flickering to the shadows dancing beyond the firelight. She knew they'd bought only a fragile, precious reprieve—and that soon enough, they'd have to plunge back into danger.

Silence enveloped them, broken only by their slowing breaths and the soft crackle of embers. Eventually, Tala tore her gaze from the alcove's entrance, edging closer to the fire. Tension still radiated from her stiff shoulders, but the warmth was a necessary comfort she couldn't ignore.

Ky'len noticed her trembling hands, and his voice gentled. "We're safe for the moment," he told her, though a flicker of doubt clouded his eyes. "Let's catch our breath, then figure out what to do next."

But Tala's hands flew to her head, her words tumbling out in a panicked rush as she lapsed into her native tongue: "Eg veit ikkje… Eg forstår ikkje korleis eg skal stoppe det! Dette er ikkje naturleg—ikkje for oss. Alt er feil, alt." Her voice quivered with fear, nails digging into her scalp.

Iszell swiftly shifted closer, grasping her by the shoulders to calm her. "Tala, quiet!" he hissed. "They're out there—if we're loud, we're done."

Tala's panic, however, only deepened. "Eg må finne ein måte å stoppe det på… men eg veit ikkje korleis…" Her frantic words trailed off into breathless sobs, eyes flicking from Iszell to Ky'len like a cornered animal.

In a desperate bid to silence her before she gave them away, Iszell leaned in, pressing his lips against hers—an impulsive, clumsy kiss.

Tala froze, eyes wide, shock overriding terror. For a moment, everything—her babbling, her shaking, even the crackle of the embers—ceased. They pulled apart, both flushed, neither sure what to say.

Ky'len, having averted his gaze, cleared his throat awkwardly. "Guess that's… one way to settle things," he muttered.

Iszell stammered, face reddening. "I—didn't—sorry, I…" The rest of his apology died on his tongue.

Still flustered, Tala exhaled shakily, looking at the fire as if it might offer answers. Silence unfurled once more, only broken by the distant whisper of wind outside.

Eventually, Ky'len's gaze shifted to the glowing coals, and a question formed on his lips. "If none of us made this fire," he said slowly, "then who did?"

Their eyes took in the alcove more carefully. Against one wall lay a battered bedroll, scattered tools, and a neat pile of ore that shimmered with a silvery-blue sheen.

Tala knelt, her fingers running over the metallic surface. "Vek'smed ore…" she whispered, a tremor in her voice. "We've found them."

At her words, a new unease rippled through the group, tension rising once again. They were still alive, still hidden, but they were far from free of danger—and with the dawn soon to break, there would be no denying the confrontation looming just ahead.

A low, rumbling voice filled the cave. "Ek taldi ekki að þú myndir koma með gesti, Tala. Eitthvað fórst þú lengra en venjulega, ekki satt?" *"Didn't expect you to bring company, Tala. You've gone farther than usual, haven't you?"*

Ky'len and Iszell exchanged a wary look, hands still gripping their weapons as Tala blinked, taking in Flak'tin's sudden presence. She managed to stammer out, "Flak'tin… hvað ertu að gera hérna?" *"Flak'tin… what are you doing here?"*

Flak'tin smirked, dropping his pack with a heavy thud that echoed in the cave. "Ég veiddi mat fyrir fólk þitt, og nú sit ég hér fastur með ykkur," *"I was out gathering food for your tribesmen, and now I'm stuck here with all of you,"* he said, his tone half-amused. He looked at Ky'len and Iszell's tense hands on their swords, raising a brow before switching to a rough, slang-laden Common. "Oi, you blokes can ease up. Not look-in' for a row, eh?"

Tala glanced at the boys, relaying, "He's… saying we're safe. Just happened on us while out hunting for the tribe."

Flak'tin chuckled, brushing off her cautious tone. "And your faðir'll be right pleased to see ye, though I'd say we've got bigger messes than these lil' embers here." He gestured to the faint glow around the fire, his expression turning serious. "Thorn's got her lot stirrin' up a fair bit of stríð. If we don't keep an eye out, they'll find us here faster than a roo on a hot track."

Iszell leaned into Tala's translation, "Stríð… war?"

"War, chaos—she's givin' 'em powers they can't even bloody control," Flak'tin added in Common, meeting Ky'len's gaze with a knowing nod. "Now, we've got enough daylight and a bit of a head start, but any plan means movin' fast as, got it? Reckon you lot are up for that?"

Ky'len and Iszell nodded, their nerves softened by the unexpected relief of this ally. Iszell, still shaken, whispered, "So… they're not doing this on purpose? Thorn's… she's done this to them?"

"Exactly," Flak'tin replied, his eyes hardened. "Not by choice. Thorn's twisted your people, Tala, filled 'em with powers they've no way to rein in. They're not just dangerous to us—they're dangerous to themselves."

Ky'len and Iszell nodded, the tension in their shoulders easing slightly, softened by the unexpected relief of finding an ally in Flak'tin. Iszell, still visibly shaken, leaned closer, his voice barely more than a whisper. "So… they're not doing this on purpose? Thorn… she's done this to them?"

"Exactly," Flak'tin replied, his gaze darkening. "Not by choice. Thorn's twisted your people, Tala," he said, his voice filled with sympathy and frustration. "She's filled 'em with powers they've no way to rein in. They're not just dangerous to us—they're dangerous to themselves."

Tala's face fell, her fingers tightening around the edge of her cloak. "My kin... they've always been close to nature, not tried to control it. This… it's not right," she murmured, sorrow roughening her voice. "My faðir fights to keep our people safe, but with Thorn twisting everything, he may be outnumbered."

Ky'len clenched his fists, anger flickering in his eyes. "So Thorn is using them as weapons," he muttered. "Twisting them into something they're not, just to get what she wants. She's trying to tear Seragora apart, and now she's dragging the Vek'smed down with her."

Flak'tin nodded solemnly, his expression dark. "Aye. That's why we need to act fast. Every day she's got her claws in 'em, they're led further down a dark path. Rest tonight while ye can; tomorrow, we head for the fjöll, the mountains. We'll seek out the ones still true to their kin, and with luck, yer faðir's held 'em safe."

As Flak'tin's words sank in, the fire crackled softly, casting shadows on the walls. The silence was heavy, each of them bearing the burden of what lay ahead. Ky'len finally gave a determined nod. "Then we stop her—together. For Seragora and your people."

Quiet settled over the cave, broken only by the crackling of the fire. Tala was the first to succumb to exhaustion, curling up close to the embers, while Ky'len and Iszell, still wide awake, let curiosity tug at their thoughts.

"So… what's it like living up in the fjöll?" Ky'len asked, watching as Flak'tin expertly turned the rabbit over the fire.

Flak'tin chuckled, settling back against his pack. "It's quiet, mostly," he replied, his voice warm with his mountain drawl. "We Vek'smed folk, we keep to ourselves. Forge a few blaðs, trade for supplies, and let the world turn without us." He patted the hilt of a Claymore strapped across his back, his eyes glinting with pride.

Ky'len's eyes widened, clearly impressed. "What about that sword?" he asked, nodding toward the Claymore. "Where'd you get a blade like that?"

Flak'tin grinned, patting the Claymore's hilt. "Family heirloom, lad. Been handed down for generations. Seen more battles than I've had hot meals," he said with a smirk. "Not just any málmur, metal, either."

"What's it made of?" Iszell asked, eyes bright with fascination.

Flak'tin shook his head, laughing. "Ah, that'd be tellin', wouldn't it? Let's just say it's got secrets of its own—like any góð weapon should." He winked, turning the blade slightly so the firelight caught its edge. The boys exchanged glances, intrigued and slightly frustrated by his cryptic answer.

As their conversation turned to the turmoil in Seragora, Ky'len and Iszell recounted the fires, the chaos, and the conflict between Bazel and Seragora. Flak'tin listened intently, his face growing more somber as they shared their stories.

"It's a mess down there," Ky'len said finally, leaning against the cave wall, his expression grim. "Most people think it's Bazel's fault, but it's Thorn and her Muckspawn stirring everything up."

Iszell nodded, brow furrowed. "Everyone's scared. If we don't stop her, Seragora won't survive."

Flak'tin nodded, lost in thought as he poked the fire. After a while, he noticed the boys' eyes drooping, exhaustion finally catching up to them. He smirked. "Get some rest while ye can," he murmured. "Tomorrow we've got a fjöll to climb and kin to convince."

As they settled in, Flak'tin cast a sly glance at Iszell, his grin returning. "So, lad," he drawled, "that kiss earlier… planning to tell her faðir about it?"

Iszell's eyes shot open, his face flushing. "What?! No—I mean, it wasn't like that!" he stammered, pulling his blanket over his face to hide.

Ky'len burst into laughter, clutching his sides as it echoed around the cave. "Oh, you should've seen your face!"

Iszell groaned, sinking deeper into his blankets as if he could disappear. Even Flak'tin chuckled, shaking his head. "Ah, relax, lad," he said with a wink. "It'll be our little leyndarmál… secret… for now. But ye might want to think on it, eh? Some things don't stay hidden long."

With that, the cave fell quiet once again, the fire casting warm, flickering shadows on the walls. The weight of the day still hung over them, but as they finally drifted into sleep, the warmth of companionship—and a faint glimmer of hope—kept the darkness at bay.

Chapter 24: Betrayal and Brothers

773, 9th Day Of The Third Moon

Today, Mira and I managed to smuggle out three volumes from my wife's kin's archive. Ancient texts, dense and brittle with age, yet filled with knowledge almost lost to time. Mira's eyes gleamed with excitement, whispering that these books hold secrets even the elders might not know. I find myself equally captivated, though a trace of guilt nags at me. But this knowledge, hidden from us, must be ours to understand.

Mrs. Thorn jolted awake, instincts prickling with a sudden awareness that something was very wrong. The crackling of the fire was absent, replaced by an unnatural silence echoing through the cave. Her eyes snapped open, immediately locking onto the entrance, where eerie shadows danced from the waterfall's faint light.

Fresh, disturbed soil lay where her guards had been.

Fury ignited within her like wildfire. "Warden..." she spat, voice trembling with rage as she stalked toward the mound, fists clenched so tightly her nails bit into her palms. "Thou filthy atharracht!" "*You filthy traitor!* Her voice echoed in the emptiness.

Her mind spun, anger blinding her thoughts. "Why do they always betray me? Again, every time I give someone power, they twist it against me." First her old allies, and now Warden. He had stolen Razma, killed her guards, and vanished into the night without a trace.

Her breaths came in sharp, furious gasps as her fury climbed, her gaze locked onto the soil. "Go deimhin, tá an feall ag éirí searbh liom," "*Indeed, betrayal is becoming all too familiar*" she growled under her breath, each word seeped in venom.

"Mutt!" she roared, her voice cutting through the silence like a blade.

From the cave's shadowed edges, the hulking figure of Mutt, her brute of a lieutenant, lumbered forward, his scarred face curled in a sneer as he approached. He took in the mound of dirt, sensing the rage pulsing off Thorn.

"Sea, Bhean Uasal?" "*Yes, Mistress?*" he rumbled, his tone low and expectant.

"Tá Warden imithe! Tá Razma imithe! Féach ort!" she shouted, jabbing a trembling finger toward the soil mound. "Uaigh, amhail is go raibh siad ina ndríodar! An fealltóir chuir sé adhlactha orthu!" "*Warden's gone! Razma's gone! Look at this! Buried like filth! The traitor buried them!*"

Mutt knelt by the mound, sifting the dirt through his fingers. His lips twisted into a grim grin.

"Bronntanas beag dúinn, nach ea? An bastún... chuaigh sé domhain le healú." *"Left us a little gift, didn't he? The bastard... buried 'em deep."*

"Nílim ag déanamh imní faoi na gardaí!" [I don't care about the guards!] Thorn's voice oozed venom, her eyes flaring dangerously as she stepped closer to Mutt, her presence crackling with violent threat. "Faigh Warden! Faigh Razma! Tabhair ar ais iad chugam." *"Find Warden! Find Razma! Bring them back to me."*

Mutt straightened, towering over her, his usual sneer returning. "Cuirfidh mé na Muckspawn ina ndiaidh, a Bhean Uasal. Ní bheidh Warden i bhfad." *"I'll send the Muckspawn after 'em, Mistress. Warden won't get far."*

Thorn's face darkened further, a sinister smile spreading across her lips. "Ní hea," *"No"* she hissed coldly. "Tiocfaidh tú féin. Ní chuirim muinín iontu seo chun an obair seo a dhéanamh i gceart. Ba mhaith liom go dtabharfá bás mall air." *"You will go personally. I don't trust those little minions to get this right. I want Warden to pay, slowly."*

Mutt's eyes flickered with discomfort, but Thorn's unyielding gaze left no room for argument.

"An dtuigeann tú?" *"Do you understand?"* she added, her tone sharp with finality.

Mutt gulped and nodded slowly. "Gheobhaidh mé é, a Bhean Uasal. Pearsanta." *"I'll find him, Mistress. Personally."*

Thorn took another step toward him, her voice dropping to a venomous whisper. "Agus má éiríonn leat, faigh do dhearthair amadán Iggy freisin. Tá mé ag iarraidh déileáil leo beirt." *"And while you're at it, find your idiot brother, Iggy. I want them both dealt with."*

Mutt tensed, visibly uneasy. "Iggy? Tá sé... dochreidte." *"Iggy? Mistress, he's... unpredictable."*

Her eyes narrowed, glinting with a dangerous frost. "Ní miste liom cé chomh dochreidte is atá sé. Faigh é. Úsáid é. Agus, Mutt..." *"I don't care how unpredictable he is. Find him. Use him. And Mutt..."* She sneered darkly. "Má chasann tú liom riamh, bainfidh mé an fhuil asat de réir bláthanna." *"If you ever cross me, I will bleed you, thorn by thorn."*

At her feet, red roses burst from the earth, blooming briefly before withering to blackened thorns. Mutt stiffened, the blood draining from his face as he took in her display.

"Gheobhaidh mé iad," *"I'll find them,"* he muttered, backing away. "Tógfaidh mé Warden, Iggy, gach duine acu." *"I'll get Warden, Iggy, all of them."*

"Déan cinnte go bhfaighidh tú,"*See that you do"* Thorn replied, her voice chilling as the last of the roses crumbled into dust. "Agus Mutt... ná teip orm arís." *"And Mutt... don't fail me again."* Without another word, Mutt hurried out of the cave, her threat heavy on his shoulders as he disappeared into the night.

As the silence settled once more, Thorn's expression shifted, a furious whisper escaping her lips. "Warden... is measa thú ná an tréas féin. Cad atá i gceist agat anois?" *"Warden... you filthy traitor. What do you have planned?"*

The cave grew darker, as if the flames themselves feared her wrath. Summoning vines from the ground, she watched red roses bloom and then wither, unable to match the depth of her anger.

Standing over the dirt mound, Thorn conjured a final rose from the earth, the deep red petals lush with life only to crumble into dust in her fingers. Her eyes glistened with unshed tears as she watched them fade away.

"Fiú mo rósanna, imíonn siad uaim" *"Even my roses leave me"* she whispered, voice frail. The tears that had pooled finally broke free, yet quickly transformed to a blazing anger.

Steeling herself, she wiped her face with a trembling hand and turned to a crystal-clear puddle in the cave. The reflection showed only calm, though her heart was pounding as she prepared to face the one within.

A shadowed figure emerged in the water's surface, a silky, venomous voice rippling from the reflection.

"Thorn," it hissed, cold and relentless. "Mo gníomhairí a insint dom go bhfuil tú ag teip orm. Níl aon leabhar. Tá Sliverfang beo. An A'nara éalaíonn. Agus Warden tá an leanbh aige. Tá a fhios agat cé chomh míshásta a chuireann teip orm." *My agents tell me you've failed me. No book. Sliverfang lives. A'nara escapes. And Warden has the child. You know how I feel about failure.*

Thorn's heart tightened, but she squared her shoulders, her voice defiant. "D'fholaigh Dalmon an leabhar. Ní raibh muid in ann é a fháil. Agus is ea, thóg Warden an buachaill, ach tá mo fhear ag iarraidh…" *Dalmon hid the book. We couldn't find it. And yes, Warden took the boy, but my men are searching—*

"IS FÍOR-LÁIDRE," *YOUR MEN ARE FILTH,* the voice bellowed, filling the cave with its roar. "DHÚIRT MÉ LEAT GAN MUINÍN IAD A DHÉANAMH." *I WARNED YOU NOT TO RELY ON THEM.*

Thorn winced, but her anger flared. "Déanaim an méid is gá dom!" *I do what I must!* she spat. "Tá do chumhacht lag, agus úsáidim an méid atá ar fáil. Caithfidh mé torthaí a fháil!" *Your power is weak, and I use what's at hand. I get results!*

A deadly silence filled the cave. The shadow in the water shimmered, tone softening but no less menacing.

"Tabhair aire do do theanga, Thorn," *Watch your tongue, Thorn,* the voice warned. "Géillim don mímhuinín sin… ar feadh tamaill. Ach ná tóg mo foighne mar maithiúnas." *I will allow your insolence... for now. But do not mistake my patience for forgiveness.*

Thorn's jaw tightened. "Gheobhaidh mé Warden. Gheobhaidh mé an leanbh. Agus ní theipfidh orm arís." *I will find Warden. I will find the boy. And I will not fail you again.*

The shadow wavered, the voice fading as it hissed, "Bíodh sin, ar do mhaith féin." *See that you don't, for your sake.*

As the reflection faded, Thorn's pale, wide-eyed face stared back at her from the puddle, her body trembling with simmering rage and a hollow ache.

Turning sharply, she stalked deeper into the cave, mind racing with plans for revenge. Warden had betrayed her, but he wouldn't escape. She'd find him, tear him apart piece by piece. And the boy? He'd pay too.

Just as she moved away, the voice from the pool chanted softly, filling the cave with red roses that bloomed along the walls, their scent thick in the air. Thorn stopped, watching the cave bloom around her, a rare, twisted smile flickering on her lips.

But as quickly as they appeared, the roses withered and burned to ash.

Thorn muttered under her breath, a bitter smirk tugging at her lips. "Fælan" *asshole.*

The voice responded with a chilling, echoing laugh that lingered in the cave, fading slowly into the silence. "Ne en'failor mara, Thorn" *"Don't fail me, Thorn"* it warned one last time before vanishing completely

✶✶✶

The forest was unnaturally quiet as Mutt trudged through it, his large frame moving with surprising stealth. His eyes scanned the ground, picking up broken branches and faint trails of blood. The air was thick with decay, a clear sign that death had passed through recently.

As he pushed through a dense thicket, his eyes narrowed at the sight ahead. Three muckspawn lay sprawled on the forest floor, arrows protruding from their bodies—human arrows. Mutt growled low in his throat, muscles tensing. Whoever did this wasn't far.

He crouched to inspect the bodies, noticing the precision of the shots. Clean, efficient. They hadn't stood a chance. Mutt's jaw clenched, irritation flaring. It was one thing for humans to kill muckspawn, but these were Thorn's own men. Whoever had done this was either bold or very, very foolish.

Wiping the sweat from his brow, Mutt continued. He wasn't here to mourn the dead. He was here for Iggy.

After another half mile, he found Iggy slumped against a tree, bleeding from a wound in his side. Iggy's usual mischievous grin was present, though his face was pale with pain.

Mutt approached, his voice a mix of annoyance and concern. "Alltid finn trøbbel, ikkje sant, Iggy?" *Always finding trouble, aren't you, Iggy?*

Iggy smirked up at him, wiping blood from his lip. "Trøbbel fin meg, bror! Har betre dagar sett." *Trouble finds me, brother! Seen better days, though.*

Mutt crouched, examining the wound. "Blør ille," *Bleeding bad,* he muttered, pressing a strip of cloth to staunch the blood. But as he worked, he felt Iggy's hand suddenly shove against his head, pushing him back.

"Raskare enn deg, då," *Still quicker than you,* Iggy teased, his grin widening as he darted up, stumbling back onto his feet.

Mutt's eyes narrowed, frustration flickering in his gaze. "Raskare, men svakare," *Quicker, but weaker,* he growled, lunging to grab Iggy's shoulder, but Iggy sidestepped with surprising agility despite the wound.

They squared off, each brother trying to gauge the other. Iggy, with his quick, light steps, barely standing but dodging just out of Mutt's reach; Mutt, slower but powerful, his muscles tensed like a coiled spring.

Iggy threw a smirk, taunting, "Kunne ikkje treffa meg om du prøvde heile dagen." *Couldn't hit me if you tried all day.*

Mutt grunted, rolling his shoulders. "Ein gong, Iggy. Éin gong er alt eg treng." *One time, Iggy. One time's all I need.*

Iggy darted forward, aiming a quick jab at Mutt's side. Mutt, sensing the move, sidestepped just as Iggy's fist whistled through the air, grabbing his wrist in one swift, practiced motion. Mutt yanked Iggy down, but Iggy twisted hard, breaking free. He stumbled a few steps, gritting his teeth as fresh blood seeped through his bandage.

"You're like a blasted fly," Mutt growled, lunging forward with an open hand. But Iggy, light on his feet, ducked just in time. His fingers jabbed Mutt's ribs before he scrambled away, his laughter ringing through the trees.

"Ow! You little pest," Mutt snarled, his patience thinning. His arm shot out, fingers snagging the back of Iggy's tunic as he heaved him down, throwing Iggy hard into the dirt. Leaves and soil scattered as Iggy hit the ground, kicking up a cloud of dust around them. Mutt planted a heavy hand on Iggy's chest, pinning him with a smirk.

"Ferdig?" *Done?* Mutt asked, his grip solid even as Iggy wriggled and pushed back, desperate to break free.

Iggy's grin was fierce, his eyes glinting with defiance. "Å, ferdig? Aldri, bror." *Oh, done? Never, brother.* With a quick movement, he lifted his leg, hooking it around Mutt's neck and yanking him sideways. Mutt growled as they tumbled together, rolling through the dirt as small creatures darted out of their way, and the underbrush shuddered from their struggle.

Mutt's moves were heavy and calculated, each motion aimed to pin Iggy for good, but Iggy was relentless. He ducked, twisted, and rolled beneath Mutt's arms, slipping out of grasp just as Mutt's hands closed around empty air. They rolled again, each trying to gain the upper hand, twigs snapping and leaves crunching beneath them. Birds burst from the trees above, startled into flight by the brothers' wrestling.

"Hold deg stille, då," *Hold still, then,* Mutt grumbled, a flash of frustration coloring his voice as he reached out, finally managing to snag Iggy's ankle. He held on tight, feeling Iggy's leg tense as he tried to shake free.

With a swift kick, Iggy nearly caught Mutt in the face, but Mutt was ready, jerking his head back just in time. A low snort escaped Mutt as he finally got the younger muckspawn pinned, his knee pressing Iggy's back into the ground.

"Prøv å gjera noko rett for ein gong skyld, idiot." *Try doing something right for once, idiot.* Mutt's voice was dark, irritation spilling through as he looked down at his scrappy younger brother.

Despite the pain and effort, Iggy's grin stayed, though it was weaker now, a bit more desperate as he panted, "Kva? Er ikkje mi skuld Yvonne er for rask for deg." *What? It's not my fault Yvonne's too fast for you.*

Mutt's face went cold, the lighthearted wrestling vanishing in an instant. His grip tightened, fingers pressing into Iggy's shoulders. "Så du mista Vil'elm òg?" *So you lost Vil'elm too?* His voice was sharp, edged with an anger that bit deep.

Iggy's grin faded, and he muttered, barely audible, "Ho… ho hadde hjelp, Mutt. Dalmon og hans gjeng, dei var med henne." *She… she had help, Mutt. Dalmon and his gang, they were with her.*

Mutt's hand clenched into a fist, and he brought it down, barely restraining himself as he gave Iggy a solid smack on the back of the head. "Kan du ikkje gjera noko rett?" *Can't you do anything right?* he growled, the anger seething beneath his voice like a barely contained flame.

Iggy winced, rubbing his head where Mutt's hand had connected. "Ja vel… såg ikkje deg her ute og stoppa dei heller." *Yeah, well… didn't see you out here stopping them either.*

Mutt's patience snapped as he hauled Iggy roughly to his feet, dirt still clinging to their clothes. "Torn kjem til å drepe oss begge om vi ikkje fiksar dette rotet." *Thorn's gonna kill us both if we don't fix this mess.* His hands clenched on Iggy's shoulders, his glare drilling into him. "Vi må få Vil'elm tilbake. Fort." *We need Vil'elm back. Fast.*

Iggy gave a half-hearted squirm, too exhausted to resist much longer. "Ja, ja, eg veit. Berre… ikkje slå meg igjen, ok?" *Yeah, yeah, I know. Just… don't hit me again, okay?*

With an irritated sigh, Mutt pulled Iggy's arm over his shoulder to support him. "Heldige du ikkje er død endå, veslebror. Berre ikkje rot meir til." *Lucky you're not dead yet, little brother. Just don't mess it up more.*

As they trudged through the dark forest, Iggy let out a faint chuckle, breaking the tension. "Så… Torn kjem ikkje til å vere blid, ikkje sant?" *So… Thorn's not gonna be happy, right?*

Mutt shot him a glare. "Torn likar ingenting bra. Men ho verdset resultat. Om vi får Vil'elm tilbake, kanskje slepp vi unna." *Thorn likes nothing well. But she values results. If we get Vil'elm back, maybe we survive.*

Iggy, not fully reassured but still smiling, gave a lopsided nod. "Og Warden? Trur du han vil vere like lett?" *And Warden? Think he'll be as easy?*

Mutt scowled, his voice lowering. "Warden… alltid joker. Smart, farleg… aldri trudd han ville snu." *Warden… always a wildcard. Smart, dangerous… never thought he'd turn.* He kept his eyes on the trail, deep in thought. "Men om vi ikkje stoppar han, ingen ende godt." *But if we don't stop him, nothing ends well.*

They paused to rest near a large rock, Mutt leaning Iggy against it as he wiped sweat from his brow. Iggy, breathing heavily, managed a weak grin. "Så kva er planen, storbror? Først Warden eller Vil'elm?" *So what's the plan, big brother? Warden or Vil'elm?*

Mutt's eyes were cold but resolute. "Begge. Warden er nær. Fangar han, finn vi Vil'elm. Torn vil ha hovudet hans." *Both. Warden's close. Catch him, we find Vil'elm. Thorn wants his head.* He glanced down at Iggy, smirking darkly. "Leverer begge, og kanskje overleve vi dette." *Deliver both, and maybe we survive this.*

Iggy, still grinning but looking a bit queasy, chuckled. "Og Torn… ho verdset resultat, sant?" *And Thorn… she values results, right?*

Mutt finally allowed himself a small, exasperated smile. "Ja, berre ikkje rot meir til, Iggy." *Yeah, just don't mess it up more, Iggy.*

With a last shared look, Mutt lifted his brother to his feet, and they moved deeper into the silent forest, hoping their path would lead to redemption—before Thorn decided otherwise.

Chapter 25: Speeches and Boars

767, 5th Day Of The Tenth Moon

Mother arrived today, her face etched with sorrow, the weight of Father's passing still heavy upon her heart. She mourns him deeply, speaking of the man he was, of the times he was kind. I listen and offer what comfort I can, though I know she clings to memories that ease the pain.

But in truth, a quiet relief settles within me. He can no longer harm us, no longer cast his shadow over her life, or mine. Seeing her here now, free from his influence, I find myself silently grateful. She deserves peace, and perhaps, at last, she will find it.

The midday sun hung high in the cloudless sky, casting harsh light over the still-burning ruins of Seragora. The city's central square was packed with people—refugees, citizens, soldiers—everyone gathered for the king's address. Anxiety buzzed in the air, whispers of fear and suspicion darting from one person to the next like ripples in a pond.

King Tor'valis stood atop a hastily constructed platform, his expression grim. His crown, once a symbol of unity and strength, now felt like a weight of failure. The suffering of his people was etched into their faces—faces drawn with fear, exhaustion, and the growing realization that they were losing control. The city was fraying at the edges, and Tor'valis knew this speech was his last chance to hold it together.

Alric stood by his side, his hand resting on the hilt of his sword, eyes sweeping the crowd for any sign of trouble. Soldiers flanked the square, shields raised, their posture tense and ready for the inevitable.

Tor'valis raised a hand, and the crowd's murmur died down. The square fell into a heavy silence, all eyes on him. He felt the weight of their expectations—this speech had to give them hope.

"My people," he began, his voice carrying over the crowd. "I stand before you today not just as your king, but as one of you. Seragora is wounded, yes—but we are not broken. We are still here. And we will rise from this."

The crowd stirred, uncertainty flickering in their eyes. Their city was in ruins, their lives uprooted—how could they rise from this?

Tor'valis continued, his tone steady but heavy with the weight of truth. "Many of you have lost homes. Some of you have lost loved ones. All of us have lost something. But we cannot let our grief turn into rage. That is what our enemies want."

He paused, letting the words sink in, his eyes scanning the crowd. "The enemy we face is not Bazel," he declared, his voice rising in defiance. "There are forces at play here darker than a kingdom's rivalry. Forces that seek to tear us apart, to make us turn on each other."

Whispers rippled through the crowd. They had heard rumors, but many still clung to the belief that Bazel was behind the chaos.

"The woman called Mrs. Thorn," Tor'valis said, his voice bitter with regret, "has sent her minions to destroy our city from within. She manipulates the muckspawn, and with them, she seeks to deceive us, to make us believe that our neighbors are the ones attacking us."

A wave of murmurs swept through the crowd. Some shook their heads in disbelief, while others exchanged nervous glances. Thorn was a name a few had heard in hushed conversations, but most only knew the name Mutt, the infamous brute whose name struck fear along the borders of Seragora.

"That can't be right," one man muttered, turning to his neighbor. "I've seen Bazel soldiers myself."

"Bazel wouldn't hesitate to take us down," another voice shouted, and a ripple of angry agreement passed through the crowd. "They're the ones who let these muckspawn in, just like they always wanted!"

At that moment, a gruff voice called out, breaking through the crowd's growing fury. "You idiots!" Jeff's voice rang out, and heads turned as he shouldered his way forward, his face flushed with frustration. "Bazel didn't do this. It was Thorn and her damn muckspawn!"

Some people stared at him, bewildered, but others muttered angrily, "Who are you to say?" and "Who even let him in here?"

Tor'valis raised a hand, directing his attention toward Jeff. "Thank you, Jeff, but I can take it from here." He gave a small nod of acknowledgment, even as Jeff muttered and reluctantly stepped back, still fuming.

The king pressed on, "Thorn is not alone," he continued, his expression darkening. "She has sent her lieutenant, Mutt—yes, you've all heard of him—to lead these attacks. But it's not just them."

He hesitated, his eyes flicking to Alric, then back to the crowd, pain lacing his voice. "I must also share something... something that wounds me deeply." His voice faltered for a moment, but he pressed on, knowing his people deserved the truth.

"Someone we trusted... someone close to us... opened the gates that let Thorn's forces into our city."

A collective gasp echoed through the square. The crowd struggled to process this revelation. Many looked at one another in shock, unable to fathom that such a betrayal could come from within.

"That's not possible!" a woman cried out from the back. "Why would anyone do such a thing?"

Tor'valis raised his hand, calling for calm, but the crowd's shock had turned into confusion and suspicion. "I do not know why it happened," the king said, his voice laced with sorrow. "But this is the truth we must face. Thorn's forces gained entry because of a betrayal within our own ranks."

"We cannot change what has happened," Tor'valis continued, his voice taking on a commanding tone as he stepped back to the edge of the platform. "But we can decide what happens next. Thorn may have turned one of our own against us, but we will not fall to her tricks. We will stand united."

The crowd's confusion began to turn to quiet resolve, the shock slowly fading as the king's words sank in. The betrayal was a deep wound, but it was also a reminder of how fragile their unity was—and how vital it was to protect it.

The whispers in the crowd gradually died down. The people of Seragora were wounded, yes, but there was something in the king's words that sparked a glimmer of hope—a fragile hope, but one that could hold them together.

But just as the tension seemed to ease, a new sound broke through the air—a deep, rumbling vibration that sent tremors through the ground.

"What now?" someone shouted.

"Now we rebuild and we prepare," King Tor'valis proclaimed, his voice strong and unwavering. Dalmon stood beside him, nodding in agreement. "Alric is already gathering his men, and Dalmon and Belazar will fight for us again. Together, we will stand against this threat."

The crowd, though shaken by the king's earlier revelations, listened with rapt attention. Their emotions were conflicted—fear, anger, and exhaustion mingling in their hearts—but the resolve in the king's voice held them steady.

"I have also sent a boy you all know—Ky'len. A brave soul, a squire of Bazel," Tor'valis continued, his tone shifting to one of urgency. "I know some of you harbor hate for Bazel, but that hate must end here. The fighting among ourselves ends today."

The crowd murmured, uncertainty rippling through them. Whispers of Ky'len's name passed between them, the familiar figure now cast in a different light.

"And not only Ky'len," the king added, his voice rising above the murmurs. "But a muckspawn girl. She fights for us. They go together to the Vek'smed—we need allies now more than ever. If we are to survive this, the prejudice, the hate, the division... it must stop here, with us."

His words were met with stunned silence. A muckspawn girl? Fighting for Seragora? The crowd shifted uneasily, old prejudices surfacing. A few faces twisted with disgust, but others, seeing the truth in the king's words, nodded reluctantly. They had seen what division had already cost them.

"I know how you all feel," Tor'valis said, softening his tone. "I have felt it too. But this racism, this hatred—if we continue to divide ourselves, we will fall. The races must unite if we are to stand any chance against Thorn and her forces."

Dalmon stepped forward, his voice calm but firm. "We have fought this enemy before, and we will fight them again. But we cannot fight them alone."

Belazar's deep voice joined Dalmon's. "We fought Mutt, and we saw the destruction they can bring. If we remain divided, Thorn will tear us apart. We need every ally we can find."

A'nara stepped forward and looked at the king. "Tell them," she urged.

"Fifteen years ago," King Tor'valis began, his voice steady but laced with regret, "you were all led to believe that my men and I, along with Silverfang, fought Bazel and won. But that... that is not the whole truth." He paused, letting the weight of his words settle over the crowd. "Mrs. Thorn was our true enemy. She led a coalition against us—Bazel, the Vek'smed, the Slivdhe, and even, at one time, some within our own, including Silverfang. But worse than her army was the dark, forbidden magic she wielded, twisting everything we thought we knew."

The crowd stirred uneasily, whispers of disbelief echoing through the square, but the king pressed on. "And now, I must admit something you've long been told was impossible. Magic is real. Thorn used it to tear apart our ranks. We had no choice but to fight back... with the same kind of magic. Dark magic."

He hesitated, the next part clearly weighing heavily on him. "Mutt... Iggy... they are not just creatures of Thorn. We created them. Using Slivdhe magic, human blood, a muckspawn child, and Vek'smed runes, we forged these beings. They were meant to be weapons, tools to destroy Thorn and her forces. We thought we could control them. But we were wrong."

The crowd gasped, horror spreading through them as they began to realize the true depth of what had been done.

"Your queen, Raelle, wielded her own magic to subdue Thorn's powers," Tor'valis continued, his voice heavy with solemnity. "We believed Thorn was vanquished after that battle. We thought we had purged the world of her malevolence... But we were wrong." He paused, drawing in a deep breath to steady himself. "Mutt and Iggy—those abominations—are the living proof of our failure. They have turned against us, serving the very woman we believed we had defeated."

The crowd was stunned into silence, the revelation striking them like a thunderclap. Then, the murmurs began, swelling into a cacophony of outrage and disbelief.

"Why reveal this now?" a man shouted, his voice hoarse with indignation. "Why were we kept in the dark?"

"She must be cast out and purged by fire!" another cried, eyes wide with a blend of fear and fury. "Magic like hers brings only corruption and death!"

"Magic is a blight—a scourge upon us all!" a woman near the front roared, fists clenched and trembling with dread.

The hall reverberated with the chaotic uproar, the collective voices echoing off the stone walls in a rising storm of panic and mistrust. Faces twisted in shock, fear, and betrayal as the truth sank in, revealing that not only had Thorn survived but that their own queen, Raelle, had wielded hidden powers—powers concealed from them all.

Tor'valis raised his hands, his voice cutting through the din like the sharp edge of a blade. "Enough! I understand that this truth wounds you deeply. The decisions made in the shadows have brought us to this perilous moment. But now is not the time to turn on each other. Raelle's magic once shielded us from greater darkness, and it can do so again. We must stand together if we are to face Thorn and her creations."

The crowd's shouts fell to a tense, simmering silence, eyes still alight with mistrust and uncertainty. The unease in the air was palpable, as if the entire hall held its breath, wavering between allegiance and rebellion.

Suddenly, Dalmon stepped forward, his expression fierce, defiant. "Then burn me!" he shouted, his voice echoing with a challenge that silenced the crowd. A whisper of magic rippled through the air as he lifted his hands, and a sudden gust of wind swept through the hall, rustling cloaks and extinguishing nearby torches. His eyes glowed with a faint, unearthly light, the power thrumming around him like a storm on the verge of breaking.

The people stared, their initial shock shifting to awe and apprehension. The wind whirled around Dalmon, a visible testament to the power he held. "If magic is a blight, then see me as I am!" he declared, his voice resonating with authority. "But know this—it is only with power united that we can hope to survive the darkness that comes."

Tor'valis watched the scene unfold, his jaw set, eyes locked on Dalmon as the hall remained caught between fear and revelation.

The tension in the hall was electric, the charged air prickling skin and quickening hearts. Whispers hissed among the crowd like snakes in the underbrush, but none dared raise their voice in defiance. Dalmon's figure stood at the center, illuminated by the eerie glow of his eyes, the wind swirling around him as if nature itself obeyed his command.

Tor'valis stepped forward, his expression steady and resolute. He nodded, signaling unity with Dalmon. "Listen to him," the king said, his voice deep with authority. "Many of you here did not witness the true terrors of that war—the horrors that unfolded in tents under the cover of night, the desperate acts behind battle lines. You saw the battles, but you did not see the sacrifices that kept those battles from becoming worse."

Dalmon's eyes swept the hall, the glow in them softening but holding steadfast conviction. "I stood among the dying, watched as magic was wielded not as a weapon of power, but as a last bastion of hope. Raelle's magic was not born of deceit; it was a shield against a darkness most of you have never known. She protected us when others would have fled."

The crowd, who held deep respect and even love for Dalmon, felt their initial shock begin to fade. His words carried the weight of trust, forged through years of unwavering leadership and sacrifice. Their eyes shifted from one another, the edges of fear and anger dulling as they recalled stories whispered by veterans—stories of battles that ended only because of unseen hands working in secret.

The wind calmed, settling into a quiet hum as Dalmon lowered his arms. The torches flickered back to life, casting long, wavering shadows that seemed to breathe with the crowd's collective realization.

An elder, with lines etched deep from a life of hardship, stepped forward, his voice trembling with age but clear. "But what of those choices? What of the cost, hidden from us?"

Tor'valis's gaze swept over the crowd, a somber understanding in his eyes. "Yes, choices were made in shadow, and burdens were carried that you were spared. But those burdens were not carried lightly. We are here now, not to condemn those who protected us, but to stand with them and face what comes."

Dalmon took a step forward, his expression softening as he spoke. "If you trust me, trust that I know what must be done. Thorn will not wait for hesitation, and the horrors we once faced pale compared to what will come if we falter now. We must stand together, as we did before—united, not divided by fear."

The murmurs shifted again, softer now, as the crowd grappled with the memories of stories passed down, tales of wounds and miracles unseen. They trusted Dalmon; he had led them through battles, bled for them, and stood before them now with the same unwavering courage.

A young man, barely old enough to have seen a skirmish, stepped forward, voice steady though his hands shook. "I stand with Raelle. I stand with you, Dalmon."

Others nodded, some with lingering hesitation, others with expressions of fierce determination. The atmosphere in the hall shifted—a collective breath taken, a silent understanding shared. They would not let the past shackle them, nor would they abandon those who had fought for them in the unseen shadows.

Tor'valis straightened, meeting Dalmon's gaze with a nod of respect. "Then we prepare. We fight not as a fractured people, but as one. For Raelle. For each other. And for the dawn that must follow the dark."

The hall erupted into a roar—not of outrage, but of unity. The echoes of their voices surged beyond the stone walls, spreading into the night where unseen eyes watched and calculated. The wind whispered through the trees, carrying the message that the realm had chosen to stand together, bracing for the storm that approached.

A deep, low rumble suddenly reverberated through the ground, beginning as a distant tremor but rapidly building until it seemed the very earth beneath Seragora was groaning in protest. The crowd stiffened, fear rippling through them like the shockwave of an earthquake. Gasps and panicked cries shattered the tense silence as eyes turned instinctively toward the southern gate.

At first, there was nothing but shadow beyond the crumbling stone arch. Then, monstrous figures emerged, stepping into the light with slow, deliberate menace. The crowd recoiled in unified horror.

Mutt, towering and grotesque, lumbered forward with a twisted grin that stretched across his scarred, misshapen face. His green skin glistened under the harsh sunlight, and his eyes gleamed with a sadistic delight. At his side hung a massive, blood-stained club.

Beside him, Iggy moved with wiry agility, his gaze sharp and cruel as it swept over the gathering. A smirk played on his lips, cold and calculating, as though he had already determined how the chaos would unfold.

But worse still, hulking figures from the Boar Tusk Tribe appeared behind them, more fearsome than ever. Their bodies rippled with unnatural strength, transformed into something even more savage, more beast-like. Once known for their brutal, tusk-led combat and relentless ferocity, they now seemed possessed by an even darker force.

King Tor'valis's face paled slightly as his eyes locked onto the advancing creatures. "Oh no," he muttered under his breath. "Thorn has changed them. They're more beast-like now… feral."

The crowd erupted in chaos as the Boar Tusk muckspawn emerged, their massive frames towering over the soldiers. Tusks gleamed menacingly in the sunlight, and guttural, primal snarls escaped their twisted mouths. These were no longer the warriors from the legends—these were monsters, corrupted beyond recognition.

Panic surged through the people, shouts and screams blending into a cacophony. Parents clutched their children, guards shouted orders that were lost in the noise, and some pushed toward the exits in a desperate attempt to flee. Fear spread like wildfire.

Tor'valis raised his hand, trying to regain control. "Calm yourselves!" he shouted, his voice strained but authoritative. Members of the council stepped forward, attempting to restore order. Lady Seraphine's voice wavered as she called for calm, while Lord Marten's face tightened with barely contained fear. Cedric's eyes darted around before he turned and bolted, abandoning his post in a rush. Dalmon's eyes narrowed as he watched Cedric flee. He had known Cedric was a coward, but seeing it confirmed in this moment twisted his stomach.

Mutt's deep, mocking voice boomed across the square, cutting through the chaos. "Look at him run," he said with a cruel smirk, his eyes following Cedric's retreating form. "Your brave council, scattering like rats."

The crowd stilled, stunned by Mutt's observation, their fear magnified by the sight of a council member fleeing. "We come with an offer," Mutt continued, his tone cold and deliberate. "Hand over Dalmon, Belazar, and the Slivdhe girl, and we may spare your lives."

He paused, letting the threat sink in before his grin widened. "Refuse," he said, eyes narrowing, "and we will kill everyone here."

The weight of his words suffocated the crowd, and whispers of doubt and fear began to spread. "Maybe we should do it," someone muttered, eyes shifting nervously. "If it spares the city..."

"Yes," another voice trembled. "Better to give them what they want than see us all slaughtered."

Iggy stepped forward, his wiry frame taut with cruel energy. His gaze settled on Yvonne, and a sly smirk crossed his face. "And her," he said, pointing directly at her. "I want to see her kneel before me. Make her beg."

The murmurs grew louder, torn between yielding to fear and clinging to their resolve. Tor'valis's eyes swept over his people, his expression hardening. He raised his hand once more, his voice cutting through the panic. "No! We do not yield to threats. We do not surrender our own."

The crowd hesitated, caught between terror and the king's fierce determination. Mutt's grin faltered for a moment before twisting back into a grim smile.

"Ah, Father," Mutt said, his voice resonant with both bitterness and a strange sadness. "You forget, don't you? You made me. How can you kill your own creation?"

A stunned silence followed as the meaning of his words settled over them. All eyes turned to King Tor'valis, who stiffened, pain and regret flickering across his face as he met the eyes of the creature he had helped create.

"You used Slivdhe magic, muckspawn blood, forbidden runes," Mutt continued, his tone lowering, almost pleading. "I am your creation, Father. Can you really destroy me?"

The crowd shifted, shock and disbelief rippling through their ranks. Tor'valis's grip on his sword tightened, the regret in his eyes deepening. "You were a mistake," he said, his voice thick with the weight of past choices. "And I will not let you destroy what's left of this kingdom."

Mutt's eyes narrowed as his grin returned, colder and sharper than before. "Then we end it here."

With a roar, Mutt raised his blood-stained club, and Iggy moved with swift, predatory anticipation. The Boar Tusk muckspawn bellowed, tusks gleaming as they charged, a force of raw, feral power.

The battle for Seragora had begun.

Chapter 26: Unsung Hero's

780, 12th Day Of The Sixth Moon

My daughters' cough has worsened. She keeps her stone rose close, fingers brushing over its surface as if it might hold some cure. I cannot bear to watch her suffer, her spirit dimming with each day. She was always the fire, the vibrant heart. Now, that fire flickers, and I fear it may soon fade. Her mother watches over her with a sorrow I can barely withstand.

✱✱✱

The cave remained dark and still, save for the occasional crackle from the fire. Exhaustion claimed them quickly, but sleep offered little comfort. Ky'len found himself tossing and turning, his dreams filled with shadowy figures and distant screams. Faces flashed through his mind—his father's stern gaze, the mocking grin of Alric after the tournament, and the twisted expression of Mutt, looming over him.

Tala, too, was restless, murmuring in her sleep, her brow furrowed with the weight of everything that had happened. Her tribe, her father, the dark magic that had corrupted her people—it haunted her even now. Every time she closed her eyes, she saw Thorn's wicked grin and her father's desperate face.

As the hours crept by, a low wind began to howl outside the cave, whistling through the cracks in the stone. Iszell was the first to stir, blinking into the dim light of the fire. His body was sore from the day's run, but it was the sound of the wind that roused him. He sat up, glancing at Ky'len and Tala, both still lost in uneasy sleep.

Flak'tin, however, was already awake, his sharp eyes fixed on the cave entrance. He had barely slept, and when he spoke, his voice was low, almost a growl. "Wind's pickin' up. We'll need ta' move come first light. No choice in that, lads."

Iszell frowned, rubbing his hands together to fight off the cold creeping in from outside. "What time is it?"

"Just 'fore dawn," Flak'tin replied, standing and moving to the cave entrance. He peered outside, his expression hardening as he scanned the horizon. "Storm's brewin', a real kraka-storm."

Iszell stood beside him, shivering slightly as the cold wind whipped against his face. "A storm? Now?"

Flak'tin nodded grimly. "Aye, and it'll be a right bugger slowin' us down. We'll have ta' hoof it quick if we want ta reach my kin 'fore it hits."

Behind them, Ky'len stirred, his dreams disrupted by the sound of the wind and low murmurs of conversation. He sat up, blinking groggily. "What's going on?"

Flak'tin glanced over his shoulder. "Bad weather on the way, mate. We leave soon."

Ky'len groaned as he rubbed the sleep from his eyes, casting a glance at Tala, who was still sleeping fitfully. "And what about Tala? She needs rest."

Flak'tin gave him a knowing look. "Rest'd be good for us all, but ain't no kraka gonna wait. Sit here too long, and we'll be buried right along with this cave."

With a sigh, Ky'len nodded. "Alright. Let's get ready."

As the group began to prepare for their journey, packing up what little supplies they had, Iszell stole a glance at Tala. The memory of the kiss weighed heavily on his mind, and the awkwardness lingered like a heavy fog. He hesitated for a moment before approaching her, rubbing the back of his neck as he mustered the courage.

"Tala," Iszell began, his voice uncertain as he spoke quietly. "About… before—back in the cave. I didn't mean to—"

Tala's face flushed red as soon as she realized what he was trying to talk about. Her eyes widened, and before Iszell could say another word, she quickly stood, brushing herself off and tightening the straps on her pack. "We should get moving," she interrupted, her voice hurried. "The storm's gettin' worse."

Iszell's face fell, and Ky'len, overhearing the exchange, couldn't help but chuckle. "Sorry, bud," Ky'len said, grinning as he clapped Iszell on the shoulder. "Looks like that one's gonna take some time."

Iszell's cheeks flushed with embarrassment, and he glared at Ky'len, though there was no real anger behind it. "Shut up."

Ky'len just laughed again, shaking his head as they all gathered their things and prepared to leave. The moment of levity was short-lived, however, as the wind outside grew fiercer, and the looming storm pressed them onward.

As they stepped out of the cave, the chill of the wind biting at their skin, Ky'len felt the weight of the task before them settle on his shoulders. The path ahead was long and treacherous, and the storm looming overhead was only the beginning.

Together, they set off into the wilderness, their footsteps swallowed by the growing roar of the wind, leaving the safety of the cave behind them.

The wind howled as they descended into the valley, the sharp chill cutting through their clothes as the jagged rocks of the mountains gave way to the sparse and rugged terrain below. Flak'tin led the way, his pace quick but cautious, while the rest of the group followed close behind, their eyes scanning the horizon for any signs of movement. The forest behind them still felt dangerous, as though the muckspawn might emerge at any moment.

As they neared the camp, Tala's breath caught. Dark tents dotted the valley, their silhouettes stark against the twilight sky. Smoke curled from several small fires, and figures moved about, casting long shadows across the ground.

Flak'tin raised a hand to halt them just before they approached the camp's edge. "Stick close, aye?" he warned, his voice low. "Tala, you'll be recognized, but yer mates here might cause a fair bit of unease."

Tala nodded, her heart pounding in her chest. She hadn't seen her people in what felt like an eternity, and now she was returning with strangers—Bazel squires, no less—at her side. "I'll handle it," she whispered back.

As they stepped into the camp, several muckspawn turned to greet them. Their eyes lit up when they saw Tala, and she was immediately swarmed by a few familiar faces. A middle-aged muckspawn with leathery green skin and tired eyes grinned as he embraced her, while others nodded, their expressions filled with relief.

"Tala! Vi tenkte du var tapt," the elder muckspawn exclaimed, his voice thick with emotion. *"We thought you were lost."*

Tala hugged him tightly, her eyes shimmering with the weight of everything she had been through. "Eg er her, Telvar. Eg kom tilbake." *"I'm here, Telvar. I made it back."*

However, the moment was brief. As the rest of the muckspawn in the camp noticed Iszell and Ky'len, the warmth shifted. The welcoming gestures faded, replaced by wary glances and murmurs of suspicion. A few muckspawn stood back, their eyes narrowing as they watched the two outsiders approach. The tension in the air was palpable, and the camp's easy camaraderie quickly dissolved into silence.

Ky'len and Iszell exchanged uneasy glances, their hands instinctively hovering near their weapons as they felt the weight of the muckspawn's distrust. They knew this reaction was coming, but the hostility still stung.

Flak'tin, sensing the tension, moved to speak, but Tala stepped forward first, raising her hand to address the crowd. "Dei er med meg," she said firmly, her voice cutting through the whispers. *"They're with me."* "Dette er mine venner, Iszell og Ky'len. Dei har kjempa med meg, og dei er her for å hjelpe oss." *"These are my friends, Iszell and Ky'len. They've fought alongside me, and they're here to help us."*

There was a pause, the murmurings quieting as the muckspawn processed her words. While a few seemed to soften at her assurance, many still looked uncertain, their eyes flicking between Tala and the two humans. Trust wasn't something easily given.

Telvar, the elder muckspawn who had greeted Tala, looked Ky'len and Iszell over with a critical eye, his expression cautious. "Bazel og Seragora-folk, ja?" he muttered, though there wasn't outright hostility in his tone. *"Bazel and Seragoran folk, eh?"* "Merkelege dagar når vi slepp inn fremmede." *"Strange days indeed if we're welcoming outsiders."*

Tala's gaze swept across her kin, fierce and unyielding as she faced their wary glances. With a steadying breath, she stepped closer to Ky'len and Iszell, placing her hands gently on their shoulders, a grounding touch meant as much for her people as for the two squires beside her.

"Vi har ikkje val," Tala said, her voice a steady anchor amid the murmurs. *"We don't have a choice. Thorn is coming for all of us. My father knows that."* Her grip on Ky'len and Iszell's shoulders tightened briefly, a sign of trust and reassurance.

"Desse to," she continued, gesturing to Ky'len and Iszell, "har møtt hennar styrker, slik som oss. Vi treng kvar ein alliert vi kan få." *"These two have faced her forces, just like us. We need every ally we can get."*

An elder named Telvar stepped forward, his stern, wary gaze sweeping over the two squires before finally softening. "Desse to… dei har mot?" he asked, lifting an eyebrow in skepticism. *"These two… they have courage?"*

Tala nodded firmly. "Ja, Telvar. Dei har kjempa ved sida av meg." *"Yes, Telvar. They have fought by my side."* Her voice softened, a hint of pleading entering her tone. "Ingen fiendskap trengs her." *"No hostility is needed here."*

Flak'tin, noticing the shift in the crowd, leaned in with a sly grin, his voice loud enough to reach Telvar and beyond. "Og ikkje berre mot, men styrke òg! Ky'len her vann Bogsmal, sjølv mot Ursak." *"And not just courage, but strength too! Ky'len here won the Bogsmal, even against Ursak."*

The name "Bogsmal" sent a ripple through the crowd, sparking murmurs and a few skeptical laughs. One young muckspawn, barely up to Ky'len's waist, stared up at him in wide-eyed awe. "Bogsmal?" he repeated, his voice barely a whisper, the word carrying a sense of wonder. Soon, several children crowded closer, their curious eyes fixed on Ky'len.

Flak'tin leaned toward Ky'len, chuckling. "Ja, Bogsmal," he said with a smirk. *"Yes, the Bogsmal."* "Ursak var ein bølle, men Ky'len her… han sette Ursak på plass." *"Ursak was a bully, but Ky'len here… he put Ursak in his place."*

Seeing the admiration from the crowd, Tala gave Ky'len a reassuring nod. Ky'len, guessing the exchange was about him, looked at Tala, unsure, and whispered, "What did he say?"

"He's tellin' 'em you beat Ursak in a fight," Iszell muttered, catching some of the words with a grin. "Apparently, you're famous now."

Ky'len nodded, laughing a bit as he tried to match the enthusiasm he saw in the muckspawn's faces.

At that moment, one brave child dashed forward, poking Ky'len in the side before skittering back with a high-pitched giggle. More children joined in, emboldened, each taking turns to poke or tug at Ky'len's arm before darting away, squealing with laughter. Though Ky'len couldn't understand their chatter, he laughed, pretending to fend off the young attackers, moving awkwardly as he tried to dodge their quick hands.

He glanced over at Iszell, clearly in over his head. "What are they saying?"

Iszell grinned, catching some words as he listened. "They're calling you their 'giant enemy,'" he said with a chuckle. "And, uh, they seem to think you're easy to defeat!"

Ky'len raised his hands in mock surrender, laughing. "Alright, alright, you win!" he said, though the children couldn't understand, they shrieked in delight, taking his reaction as a challenge. One child, emboldened, grabbed a stick from the ground and began poking at Ky'len, prompting others to follow suit, waving sticks like tiny swords.

Ky'len looked down at the makeshift "weapons" in amusement, then bent to pick up a sturdy stick of his own, holding it out in a mock guard position. "If you're going to have a sword, you'll need to learn how to use it," he said, motioning for them to come closer. He glanced at Iszell, hoping for some help with the translation.

Iszell shrugged with a grin. "Not sure how to say it all, but…" He turned to the kids and gestured toward Ky'len, pointing to his stance. "Lære… å bruke," he said haltingly, gesturing with his stick to show learning the moves. *"Learn… how to use."*

The children hesitated but soon came closer, giggling, their sticks held aloft. Ky'len held up his own stick, then slowly swung it in a wide, careful arc, keeping it slow so they could follow along. Some of the older children mimicked his moves, trying to copy his stance and balance.

Not to be left out, Iszell grabbed a stick of his own and joined in. "Watch this!" he said with a wink at Tala, demonstrating an exaggerated parry, dodging dramatically to the side. "Dodge like this—" he showed them a sidestep, then pretended to be struck, clutching his chest. "And if that fails, you fall!" he cried, collapsing to the ground with a loud groan. "Nei! Eg er slått!" he added for effect. *"No! I am defeated!"* The children shrieked with laughter, piling onto him victoriously, patting his arms as they declared themselves the victors.

Ky'len laughed, holding his stick out like a shield as more children took turns tapping it with theirs, enjoying the impromptu sparring. "Careful with those swings," he coached gently, gesturing to keep their feet planted. "Strong stance, like this." He bent his knees, demonstrating, while Iszell leaned over to the kids and added, "Sterk… slik." *"Strong… like this."* The children wobbled as they tried to stay balanced, copying his stance.

One young girl, small but fierce, tapped Ky'len's leg with her stick and gave him a triumphant grin. He exaggerated his reaction, stumbling backward and pretending to stagger. "A powerful warrior!" he exclaimed with a grin, looking to Iszell.

Iszell laughed and turned to the girl. "Stor krigar!" he said with a smirk, repeating Ky'len's praise in simple Muckspawn. *"Big warrior!"* The girl's delighted giggle needed no further translation.

Tala watched the scene unfold, her usually serious expression softening at the sight of laughter and smiles surrounding her. Even the elders exchanged approving glances, entertained by the rare moment of lightness in the camp. Flak'tin, watching from the sidelines, gave a small grin, nodding as Ky'len and Iszell continued to humor the children.

Finally, with mock solemnity, Ky'len and Iszell held up their sticks in surrender. "Alright, alright, warriors—you've bested us," Ky'len said, bowing as he lowered his "sword." The children cheered in triumph, dropping their sticks to dance around their "vanquished foes."

Tala chuckled, shaking her head at the two squires. She caught Ky'len's eye, giving him a nod of approval before murmuring to Flak'tin, "Ingen betre måte å vinna deira tillit." *"No better way to earn their trust."*

The elders watched on, some chuckling quietly, their approval clear as they witnessed the bond between the muckspawn children and the newcomers grow stronger through shared laughter and play.

Amid the laughter, Flak'tin stepped forward, calling the camp to attention. "Eg vil at de møter nokon," he announced, gesturing proudly to a boy at his side. *"I want you to meet someone."* "Flin'thor, Tala… kjenner du denne ungen igjen?" *"Flin'thor, Tala… do you remember this young one?"*

Tala's gaze fell on the boy, his wide, curious eyes meeting hers as he stepped forward. Recognition sparked in her expression. "Flin'thor?" she murmured, surprised at how much he'd grown.

"Aye," Flak'tin chuckled, resting a hand on his son's shoulder. "Han har vakse mykje sidan sist. No trur han seg stor nok til å vere med på vegen vår til Smia." *"He's grown a lot since then. Now he thinks he's big enough to join us on the road to the Forge."*

Flin'thor stepped forward with quiet pride, holding out a small bundle of herbs wrapped carefully in cloth. "For deg, Tala. Dei seier det held deg trygg," he said softly. *"For you, Tala. They say it'll keep you safe."*

Tala accepted the bundle, her expression softening. "Takk, Flin'thor," she replied, the warmth in her voice unmistakable. *"Thank you, Flin'thor."* She placed a gentle hand on his shoulder, his proud smile lingering as he returned to his father's side, standing a bit taller.

Noticing Ky'len and Iszell's curious glances, Tala shifted to Common, her tone firm. "This is Flin'thor, Flak'tin's son," she explained with a nod. "He has grown much since last you saw him."

The moment of quiet passed, and Tala's face grew serious once more. She turned to her kin, her voice steady. "Og Zra'ka? Han er der ute, jaktar på oss." *"And Zra'ka? He's out there, hunting us."*

The elders exchanged somber glances, their voices low but filled with anger and purpose. Nyrra, a fierce woman with graying hair, spat into the dust, her face twisted with scorn. "Zra'ka og dei som sveik oss—ormar, alle saman." *"Zra'ka and those who betrayed us—snakes, all of them."* Beside her, Thorl, his fingers curled tightly around the hilt of his dagger, muttered a curse under his breath. "Blodet deira er ingenting for oss no," he hissed. *"Their blood means nothing to us now."*

Elda, gripping her staff, narrowed her eyes with determination. "Då må vi vera klare," she murmured, her voice edged with resolve. *"Then we must be ready."*

Hakon, a tall elder with a long scar down his cheek, lifted his head thoughtfully, glancing toward the mountains. "Kanskje fetterane våre bak fjella vil sjå det på same måte," he said, voice low. *"Perhaps our cousins past the mountains will see it the same way."*

The other elders murmured in agreement, nodding as they considered this idea. "Fleire allierte vil aldri skade oss," muttered Brynd, a sharp-eyed woman who'd remained quiet until now, giving Tala an approving look. *"More allies will never hurt us."*

Iszell noticed Ky'len's confused expression and leaned in to translate softly. "They're talking about Zra'ka, cursing him for betraying the tribes," he explained. "They might reach out to their cousins past the mountains for help."

Ky'len nodded, piecing it together, and finally spoke up in Common, his voice uncertain but clear. "I can't go to the Forge," he said, looking to Tala for her reaction. "I need to return to Bazel and warn them. Iszell, go with Tala and Flak'tin to the Forge. I'll gather support... and face my father."

The camp fell silent as Tala translated his words, a flicker of concern crossing her face as she turned back to him. "Ky'len, det er farleg å gå åleine," she cautioned, switching to Muckspawn before adding in Common for his understanding, *"Ky'len, it's dangerous to go alone. Thorn's forces could be anywhere."*

Flak'tin crossed his arms, watching Ky'len with a wary gaze before nodding slowly, a thoughtful expression on his face as he considered the young squire's plan. Then, in Vek'smed, he muttered, "Det er klokt, Tala. Han treng å dra attende til Bazel for å advare dei." *"It's wise, Tala. He needs to return to Bazel to warn them."*

Tala's eyes narrowed, her jaw set in defiance. "Nei, Flak! Å splitte oss no er farleg for alle. Han burde vere med oss til Smia." *"No, Flak! Splitting up now is dangerous for everyone. He should come with us to the Forge."*

Their voices rose as they argued, each stubbornly holding their ground. Flak'tin gestured emphatically toward the mountains, speaking quickly, "Vi har ikkje tid til å vere samla heile vegen. Kvifor risikere alt når han kan gi oss tid ved å dra til Bazel?" *"We don't have time to stay together the entire way. Why risk everything when he could buy us time by going to Bazel?"*

Iszell, struggling to keep up, leaned toward Ky'len. "Uh... they're saying... it's about time... or, buying time if you go to Bazel..." he whispered, clearly trying to translate the rush of words as best he could.

Ky'len frowned, his gaze shifting between Tala and Flak'tin, who spoke with increasing urgency.

Tala's voice was resolute. "Ingen tryggleik der. Han er ein av oss no. Vi vernar han ved å halde oss samla." *"There's no safety there. He's one of us now. We protect him by staying together."*

Iszell translated what he could. "She's saying… safety… staying together." He looked a bit lost as their argument grew faster, and his translations trailed off as they spoke over each other.

Flin'thor, watching the exchange intently, stepped forward, his young face determined. He took a deep breath and spoke up, his voice clear amid the back-and-forth. "Eg kan dra med han. Eg kan vere vegen hans," he offered, his tone resolute. *"I can go with him. I can be his guide."*

Flak'tin looked sharply at his son, shaking his head. "Nei, Flin'thor, du er for ung for denne reisa. Vi veit ikkje kva farar som lurer." *"No, Flin'thor, you're too young for this journey. We don't know what dangers lie ahead."*

Tala put a hand on Flak'tin's arm, her voice calm but firm. "Og kva er forskjellen, Flak? Ky'len er ikkje mykje eldre." *"And what's the difference, Flak? Ky'len is not much older."* She gestured between the two boys, her gaze steady. "Flin'thor kjenner landet, veit korleis han kan leia Ky'len. Det er ikkje noko vi kan nekta han." *"Flin'thor knows the land, knows how to guide Ky'len. It's not something we can deny him."*

Flak'tin looked between Tala and his son, uncertainty shadowing his face. Before he could respond, Flin'thor stepped closer, meeting his father's gaze. "Far, eg kan gjere dette. Eg er sonen din. Du veit at eg er klar." *"Father, I can do this. I am your son. You know I am ready."*

Flak'tin hesitated, pride and worry battling in his expression. Finally, he let out a heavy sigh, his eyes softening as he looked at his son. "Du er bestemt som din far, det ser eg," he muttered with a reluctant smile. *"You are as determined as your father, I see that."*

Turning to Ky'len, Flak'tin placed a firm hand on his shoulder, nodding. "Då er det bestemt," he said, his tone full of reluctant acceptance. *"Then it's settled."* Switching to Common, he added, "We stick saman, no matter where the spor takes us." *"We stick together, no matter where the path takes us."*

With renewed resolve, the camp prepared for the journey ahead, bound by trust and strengthened by Tala's leadership, as Flin'thor, ready and determined, stood poised to guide Ky'len on his dangerous path.

Chapter 27: Battle In The Streets

761, 29th Day of the Fourth Moon

"The mountain folk—small in stature, yet they wield a strength that belies their size. I'd always believed that strength came with size, yet these people defy every expectation. Their bodies, hardened by the unforgiving terrain they call home, are resilient and powerful. And their weapons—stronger than anything we've forged in Tantora—carry an edge our smiths cannot seem to replicate.

It is a curious thing, this strength born from hardship. Perhaps there is wisdom in their ways, wisdom in the materials and methods they guard so fiercely. There is more to them than meets the eye."

The arena, once a proud symbol of Sergora's strength, now lay as a monument to ruin. Stone walls were shattered, massive chunks of marble and twisted metal littered the ground, and banners that had once flown with honor now hung in tatters, stained with blood and ash. The acrid stench of smoke and burning wood choked the air, mixing with the thick metallic tang of blood that coated the arena floor, now a chaotic graveyard of rubble and bodies. The deafening clash of weapons and feral snarls were punctuated by the screams of civilians scrambling to escape the carnage.

At the center of it all, Mutt towered like a monstrous giant, a living embodiment of destruction. His spiked club, stained red and dripping, swung with reckless fury, reducing everything in its path to debris. Each brutal swing sent tremors through the ground, turning stone and steel into rubble beneath his unstoppable force. His wild eyes searched the battlefield, settling with deadly intent on anyone who dared stand in his way, his booming roar drowning out all other sounds.

Around him, the remnants of the Boartusk muckspawn tribe surged through the crowd like beasts unleashed from a nightmare. Hulking, grotesque figures with elongated tusks and twisted bodies tore into the fleeing masses with brutal abandon. Their jagged tusks gored through soldiers and civilians alike, tearing armor and flesh as agonized screams filled the air. Blood pooled across the arena floor, slicking the stone in a gruesome carpet as bodies piled under the onslaught.

Tor'valis, battered and bloodied, held his ground, slashing his way through the Boartusk warriors with grim determination. His sword flashed as he parried and countered, driving his blade into the neck of one muckspawn only to face two more in its place. He gritted his teeth, exhaustion bearing down with every strike, but his resolve remained as fierce as ever.

"We need to get the civilians out of here!" he shouted, his voice barely carrying over the chaos.

His gaze darted across the wreckage, searching for any path to safety, but there was only more death and destruction.

Amid the carnage, A'nara, hands glowing with the soft light of healing magic, moved swiftly through the crowd, her heart racing as she urged people toward the exits. "This way! Quickly!" she called, her voice steady despite the terror seizing her. But every step forward brought another Boartusk warrior in their path, cutting down anyone too slow to escape. She knelt beside a fallen man, pressing her glowing hand to his chest to stop the bleeding, but for each life she saved, three more fell. The Boartusk muckspawn moved through the crowd like a relentless tide, tusks tearing through armor and flesh, every scream piercing A'nara's heart.

Sweat ran down her brow as she fought back tears, the weight of helplessness pressing down on her as bodies piled around her. Her breaths grew shallow, her vision blurred, but she forced herself onward, even as she realized she couldn't save them all.

Seeing A'nara's desperation, Yvonne's expression hardened with resolve. Slinging her bow over her shoulder, she climbed to a high vantage point in the crumbling stands. She drew an arrow, eyes sharp, and focused on the Boartusk muckspawn tearing through the crowd. "Stay back!" she shouted, her voice cutting through the din as she unleashed a hail of arrows. Each one struck with deadly precision, slowing the Boartusk muckspawn just enough for A'nara to lead more civilians toward safety. Yvonne gritted her teeth, her fingers moving in steady rhythm, determined to thin their numbers, if only by a few.

In the thick of the battle, Belazar felt the primal call clawing its way to the surface. Watching Mutt's rampage, he clenched his fists, his breathing ragged as he released control, letting the Silver Fang take over. With a final, guttural snarl, he transformed, his body twisting and bulging with powerful muscles, fur bristling along his limbs. A fierce, feral howl tore from his throat as he locked his blazing eyes onto Mutt.

Dalmon, catching sight of Belazar's transformation, nodded grimly, knowing what it meant. They both understood that ending Mutt was the only way to end this madness.

Without hesitation, Belazar surged forward, claws digging into the earth as he charged at Mutt with terrifying speed. He collided with him, claws raking deep into Mutt's flesh, leaving bloody trails across the monstrous form. Mutt roared, stumbling but swinging his massive club with brutal force. Belazar twisted and dodged, moving with animalistic reflexes as he and Mutt clashed in a chaotic blur of teeth and claws.

Dalmon darted through the debris, flanking Mutt with his sword raised. "We end this now!" he shouted, his voice steely as he joined Belazar in the relentless assault. They struck in tandem, each blow precise, wearing Mutt down little by little.

High above, Yvonne's arrows flew, each one finding its mark in Mutt's back, though the brute only seemed to grow stronger, his fury keeping him on his feet. The Boartusk muckspawn, sensing their leader's rage, fought with renewed savagery, tearing through anyone in their path with reckless abandon.

In the heart of the arena, Alric's gaze sharpened as he faced Iggy. The muckspawn moved with shadowy grace, his mocking grin taunting Alric as they clashed in a fury of steel. Alric noticed the faint scar on Iggy's side—a wound that still slowed him just slightly. Seeing the weakness, Alric pressed forward, aiming each strike at Iggy's tender side until his blade sank deep. Blood poured from Iggy's wound as he staggered, a look of shock crossing his face as he collapsed, lifeless.

A furious roar shattered the air as Mutt turned, his eyes blazing with raw fury as he bellowed, "Du drepte Iggy!" *"You killed Iggy!"*

Tor'valis charged toward Mutt, his sword raised. "Mutt! This ends here!" he shouted, but Mutt moved faster than expected. His massive club swung with brutal force, knocking Tor'valis back. Alric barely had time to react as Belazar leapt from the shadows, claws sinking into Mutt's back. Yet even with blood pouring from his wounds, Mutt remained unyielding. With a powerful throw, he slammed Belazar to the ground.

Above, Yvonne continued her assault, her arrows finding their mark. "I'll kill you all!" Mutt roared, his voice thick with fury as he swung his club wildly, sending shards of stone flying.

A'nara, still frantically guiding civilians to safety, glanced back at the chaos unfolding. Her heart clenched as she saw Mutt tearing through anything in his path. "We need to stop him!" she cried out, panic lacing her words.

Tor'valis, wiping blood from his brow, pushed himself to his feet. "I'm trying!" he shouted back, charging back into the fray.

Belazar, shaking off the impact, growled deeply before leaping forward again. His claws slashed at Mutt's legs, trying to slow him down, while Dalmon struck at his exposed flanks. But Mutt's monstrous strength and fury were unyielding, every strike only seeming to drive him into a deeper rage.

Despite Mutt's ferocity, the tide of battle began to shift. Alric, Yvonne, Tor'valis, Dalmon, and Belazar pressed in, each strike chipping away at his strength. Mutt's hulking form began to falter, his body riddled with arrows and bleeding from countless wounds.

Breathing heavily, Mutt's gaze flickered to Iggy's lifeless body, and his face twisted with a snarl of grief and rage. "You killed my brother," he growled, his voice thick with venom. "But this isn't over."

With a final, deafening roar, Mutt slammed his club into the ground, sending a shockwave through the arena. Dust and debris flew up, blinding everyone for a brief, chaotic moment. As the dust settled, Mutt turned and fled, his massive form vanishing into the wreckage.

His voice echoed through the ruins, a chilling promise. "We finish this later!"

Belazar, still in his Silver Fang form, let out a low, menacing growl, ready to give chase. But the battle was over, for now.

The arena lay in ruins. Blood soaked the stones, and the cries of the wounded filled the air. Sergora had survived, but the cost had been great, and the war was far from over.

As the dust settled and Mutt's massive form vanished into the haze of ruin, Belazar, still consumed by the Sliverfang's primal fury, growled low and menacingly. His yellow eyes fixed on the retreating Boartusk muckspawn, and an unquenchable hunger surged through him—a call for blood, for vengeance. The beast inside him had tasted the rush of battle, and it craved more.

The once-mighty arena lay in ruins: pillars toppled, debris scattered across blood-streaked stones. Survivors clung to one another in small clusters, some tending to the wounded, others too stunned by the horror to move. Healers darted among the fallen, doing what they could for the dying as the stench of sweat, dust, and blood swirled in the hot air.

Amid the swirling dust and frantic cries, Sliverfang prowled through the ruins like a nightmare given flesh. Torchlight and scattered lanterns flashed across his muscled frame, revealing every ripple of sinew beneath the blood-matted fur. A muffled whimper rose from two villagers huddled behind a toppled column, their wide eyes tracking his every motion. One clutched a ragged scrap of cloth over her mouth, stifling a scream each time his claws scraped the broken stone. Yet on the far side of the arena, a ragged knot of survivors lifted trembling fists and called out in desperate cheers. Their voices, raw with smoke and fear, carried the faint hope that this half-legendary beast might turn the tide against the tusked Boartusk warriors. In that charged moment—awash in firelight, sweat, and the copper tang of spilled blood—Sliverfang loomed as both savior and specter, the final barrier between a broken city and the snarling horde closing in.

A massive Boartusk, its tusks slick with gore, tried to flee. Sliverfang lunged with unnatural speed, razor-sharp claws slicing through the beast's torso in a single, lethal swipe. The muckspawn collapsed, letting out one final choking squeal. The crowd gasped; many shrank back, while a few roared approval at Sliverfang's brutal efficiency.

"Fòrstad, nach eil!" came a desperate shout. Dalmon stood a short distance away, his face taut with worry. Though he dared not speak the name *Belazar* in front of the gathering masses, his plea was clear. "*Stop—no more!*"

Sliverfang gave no sign of hearing. Another Boartusk thundered across the broken arena, tusks poised to gore. Sliverfang whirled and caught it by the throat, crushing its windpipe with a sickening crunch. Blood sprayed across the stones, and a feral snarl escaped his lips. He wanted more. More carnage. More death.

Dalmon grit his teeth. He knew too well that once this monstrous form took hold, the man he cared about was locked away, unreachable by reason alone.

Amid the shrieks of the dying, A'nara forced herself closer to the rampage. She had known the darkness lurking beneath a certain man's calm exterior, but witnessing it unleashed in full churned her stomach with dread. Still, she refused to abandon hope that somewhere within this beast, he still existed.

Clambering over debris, she shouted, voice breaking with raw urgency: "Stad! Tha thu nas motha na seo!" *"Stop! You are more than this!"* But the arena's clamor swallowed her words.

Sliverfang's claws raked yet another Boartusk warrior. The creature's final squeal ended in a gruesome sputter before it collapsed, lifeless. A'nara's heart clenched, but she pressed forward, tears burning her eyes. She would not lose him—no matter how hopeless it appeared.

"Gràdhaich mi, stad seo!" she cried in Gaelic, a confession she had never dared speak so openly."*For the love of me, end this!"* Her voice trembled, yet she prayed he could hear the truth beneath her desperation.

For an instant, Sliverfang's blazing yellow gaze snapped to hers. Something flickered there—a fleeting spark of recognition. Then, with a guttural roar, he flung himself at the next target, the beast's lust for blood too strong to break.

Dalmon arrived at her side, panting, swords in hand. He kept his voice low, anxious not to reveal the beast's identity. "He won't stop unless we force him," he murmured, gaze darting between A'nara and the frenzied creature. "If he loses all restraint, we could lose him forever."

A'nara steeled herself, recalling all the words left unspoken. If anything could reach the man beneath the monster, it would be the truth of her heart. Summoning the last of her courage— and a faint shimmer of magic around her trembling palms—she stepped forward.

"I… I love you," she whispered, letting the tears fall. Though her voice was low, she poured every ounce of devotion into those words, hoping they might pierce Sliverfang's fury.

For a singular moment, the din of the battlefield faded in her ears. Sliverfang's blood-soaked form twitched as if caught between two minds. Yellow eyes glinted, bestial fury warring with a deeper humanity hidden beneath.

"Thig air ais thugam, a ghràidh… Tha thu nas làidire na seo," A'nara pleaded, her slividhe hushed yet unwavering."*Come back to me, my love… You are stronger than this."*

Belazar stumbled through the haze of battle, every heartbeat pounding like a war drum. He fought to silence the snarling presence coiling at the edges of his mind, but it loomed closer with each breath. For years, he had drowned Sliverfang's voice beneath ale, numbing the beast when it stirred. Yet now, with his city in ruins, Razma taken, and Thorn's power rising, oblivion was no longer an option.

A thin rivulet of blood—his or someone else's—slid down his forearm. At the corners of his vision, an oily darkness whispered, full of predatory promise. Belazar pressed a trembling hand to his temple, trying to hold onto clarity. Still, the voice seeped into him like hot iron.

They are weak, Belazar. Let me show them how true strength tastes…

He clenched his eyes shut, forcing ragged breaths. *This isn't me,* he told himself, fighting the beast. *I won't lose control—not again.* He summoned the image of A'nara—her comforting gaze, her gentle steadiness whenever he wavered.

Sliverfang snarled in mocking contempt. *Comfort? They need power, Belazar—power you can only wield by letting me in.*

Belazar's pulse hammered, heat surging through his veins. *No,* he spat. *I have to protect them, not tear them apart.*

A cruel laugh rasped in his skull. *Protect? Is this pathetic struggle what you call protection? You fear me because you crave the violence I offer. You know the thrill of claws and blood.*

A memory seized him: a Boartusk warrior's final terror before his claws—Sliverfang's claws—ripped it open. Blood. Sinew. The choking stench of death. Belazar almost collapsed, nausea gripping him. *No,* he breathed, teeth clenched. *I refuse to become a monster.*

Sliverfang's presence coiled tighter, suffocating his thoughts. *You lie to yourself. Without me, you're just a weary man, easy to break. Let go and taste what it means to be unstoppable.*

Belazar's nails dug into his palms, warm blood welling. *I'm not like you,* he vowed, *even if you're part of me.* He forced himself to picture A'nara's face—the hope shining there. *I have a reason to stay in control.*

For one heart-stopping moment, the rage ebbed, leaving only desperation. Sliverfang hissed at the edges of Belazar's mind. *Keep resisting, Belazar, and the day will come when I am all that's left.*

Belazar inhaled shakily, the battlefield swimming into grim focus. *Then I'll fight you that day, too,* he promised, gripping the last thread of his resolve. *Every day until you're nothing but a memory.*

A searing wave of wrath coursed through him, making him tremble. Then, with a final snarl, Sliverfang receded—like embers waiting for the slightest spark. Belazar sank to one knee, gasping as he regained a tenuous hold on himself.

Corpses littered the field—friends, enemies, and bystanders caught in the chaos. The bitter taste of bile rose in his throat. *But I'm still here,* he told himself, *which means I can still choose to be better.*

Sliverfang's voice wormed its way back, quieter yet no less haunting. *Better? You forget we are not alone, Belazar. The Faolicara waits in the shadows you flee. One day, you must return to lead them. And that means letting me guide you.*

A chill crept up Belazar's spine. He exhaled slowly, pushing the beast's words aside. *I'm not a beast; I'm a man,* he told Sliverfang. *I will keep you at bay—no matter how often you rise.*

A dark chuckle reverberated in his mind. *Keep pretending, Belazar. We both know you need me if you hope to save them. You always have.*

Gritting his teeth, Belazar stood amid the carnage. Each shaky breath reminded him just how narrow the line was between man and monster. Though Sliverfang taunted him with talk of the Faolicara—a destiny he wanted no part of—he clung to the fragile victory of this moment. He would do it all again tomorrow, and every tomorrow to come, until Sliverfang's promise of unstoppable might faded into nothing but an unheeded echo.

Yet even as relief washed over him, Belazar sensed Sliverfang prowling at the edges of his consciousness, ready to pounce the moment his resolve wavered. The war for his soul was far from over. But for now, at least, he had reclaimed himself—and he would cling to that fragile victory, however brief it might be.

Slowly—agonizingly—his ragged breathing began to steady. Coarse fur sloughed away, fangs receded, and bones cracked in a sickening reversal of nature. With one final, anguished groan, Sliverfang collapsed onto his hands and knees, morphing into a battered man drenched in sweat and blood. His eyes, wide with horror, flicked over the gore-strewn arena.

Dalmon, hovering protectively, caught sight of onlookers craning their necks for a glimpse of the legendary beast. A few pointed at the empty space where Sliverfang had stood, confusion etched on their faces. Others noticed the wounded stranger in tattered clothes, but failed to connect the two. Alarmed whispers rose, speculation swirling about whether Sliverfang had fled or vanished like a ghost. To keep his friend's secret, Dalmon motioned A'nara to block the gawkers' line of sight.

But the man—fighting shame, lingering rage, and the beast's presence gnawing at his mind—wrenched free of A'nara's gentle hold and staggered toward a broken archway. A'nara and Dalmon hurried after him, weaving between dazed survivors and rubble. High above, the king tried to reassure the gathering crowd, commending the mysterious creature that had saved them from the Boartusk horde. Yet no real explanation was offered for Sliverfang's sudden disappearance.

By the time A'nara reached the edge of the rubble-strewn field, the man—her Sliverfang—had slipped into the city's dark corridors. A hush settled over those left behind, wavering between relief and dread. They had witnessed raw legend unleashed—and never suspected that, among them, an ordinary soul bore the monstrous curse.

A short while later, hidden from prying eyes in the shelter of a partially collapsed wall, the man knelt beside scattered Boartusk carcasses. Only A'nara, Dalmon, and a handful of others knew him as Belazar. His features twisted with shock and guilt as he stared at his bloodstained hands. "I… I heard you," he rasped, voice hoarse with exhaustion.

A'nara dropped to her knees, tears slipping free. "You came back," she whispered, pressing her forehead against his. "That's all that matters. You are not a beast."

Belazar winced, shame clenching his voice. "No," he managed. "I'm not. But Sliverfang is… and he's inside me." He glanced at the congealing gore smeared across his arms. "Every time he appears, he's stronger—harder to force aside. I can feel him, even now."

Gently wrapping her arms around him, A'nara's voice trembled with empathy. "You held him off once. You'll do it again."

He let out a harsh, humorless laugh that turned into a cough. "I don't know how long I can keep him caged," he admitted. "He's always there, scratching at my mind—like he's waiting for me to slip." Then he paused, his gaze searching hers. "A'nara… you said you love me?"

Tears still clung to her lashes, but her nod was certain. "I do. More than anything."

Belazar's throat tightened; the edges of his self-loathing softened at her confession. "Then…maybe I stand a chance," he whispered, letting his hand close around hers. Though he shook with exhaustion, relief flickered in his eyes. "If you believe in me, I'll try to believe in myself."

They knelt there, blood and dust caked in every crease of their clothes, while Dalmon kept watch—ensuring no curious onlooker realized that the wounded figure in the shadows was the very monster they feared. Sliverfang might hunger still, but in that moment, Belazar found a fragile hope that he could fight him back—and perhaps, one day, conquer him entirely.

All around them, Sergora lay in ruins. Fires sputtered in the debris, illuminating the fearful faces of men, women, and children who had barely survived the onslaught. Choking smoke hung in the hot air, stinging eyes and throats. King Tor'valis, perched atop a fractured pillar, did his best to restore some semblance of calm, though raw panic lingered in every whisper.

When the surviving fighters gathered, Tor'valis wiped grime from his brow and addressed the crowd. "This was a targeted strike," he said, voice echoing off the fallen stones. "Mutt and Iggy didn't come here simply to cause chaos. They carried a message: *none of us are safe anymore*."

Nearby, Alric sheathed his sword, still breathing heavily from the battle. "They've thrown in with Thorn," he said, grim-faced. "Whatever's brewing, it's more dangerous than any of us thought."

A bow slung across her shoulder, Yvonne shook her head. "We witnessed it ourselves—Thorn's magic has twisted the Boartusk, turned them into something worse."

Stepping among the wounded, A'nara nodded, her healing magic flickering around her fingertips. "These people can't withstand another assault like this. War is one thing, but this corruption is… it's spreading."

Tor'valis surveyed the damaged arena with weary eyes. "Mutt will strike again soon. We need to move fast, find allies. Sergora can't hold if they return with an even larger force."

Dalmon stood beside Belazar, a supportive hand near his shoulder. He shot Belazar a worried look but remained silent, clearly unwilling to leave his friend's side.

Just then, Belazar stepped forward, tension visible in his stance. His voice emerged low and strained. "Mutt won't stop until everything is destroyed. He's fueled by rage and empowered by Thorn. Killing Iggy will only make him more dangerous. And now Warden has Razma."

A'nara's eyes widened in alarm. "But… that means your son is—"

Belazar swallowed hard, guilt etched in his face. "We only know Warden took him. Why or where, we haven't a clue. But I can't leave Razma in his hands."

Tor'valis gave a firm nod, sympathy and resolve mixed in his expression. "We'll do everything in our power to find him," he said. "But first, we must keep the rest of Sergora safe. This city is too exposed."

Alric caught the king's meaning and inclined his head. "I'll dispatch scouts immediately. We need to know where Warden is taking Razma—and track Mutt and Thorn's next move. Dalmon," he added, glancing at Belazar's staunch companion, "stay here and look after our friend."

Dalmon simply nodded. "Understood."

Belazar exhaled slowly, wiping sweat and grime from his brow. "But finding Razma isn't enough to stop Thorn. We have to do more. We need to go to Halzor's Keep—where Sliverfang first arose. That's where this curse began."

A'nara frowned, concern flickering across her face. "What secrets lie there that can help us?"

Shadows darkened Belazar's eyes. "I'm not certain, but I know it's tied to Thorn's power. If we're to stand any chance of ending all this, Halzor's Keep holds the key."

Tor'valis ran a hand through his sweat-damp hair. "We'll muster what strength we can," he said. "Send word to Bazel, the Vek'smed, even the Slivdhe—any who will stand against Thorn. Meanwhile, Belazar, you and your companions make for Halzor's Keep. Alric's scouts can search for Razma and track Warden's whereabouts."

Belazar forced a tired smile, though tension still lined his face. "We'll save Razma, and we'll stop Thorn. Otherwise, we lose everything." He paused, a flicker of doubt crossing his features. "But I… Sliverfang… might be a liability."

Dalmon clapped his friend's shoulder gently. "We won't let that happen," he promised quietly. "You won't face this alone."

A'nara placed a comforting hand on Belazar's forearm. "We'll stand together," she said softly, her voice firm despite the devastation around them.

Moonlight spilled across the rubble-strewn arena, revealing the battered city and its frightened survivors. Though the air still crackled with the remnants of battle, a new urgency gripped the group: the need to find Razma, end Thorn's corruption, and unravel the dark secrets buried within Halzor's Keep. Sliverfang lingered beneath Belazar's skin, but for the moment, he clung to hope—hope that they could unite in time to save not only Razma, but all of Sergora from the shadows gathering at its doorstep.

Chapter 28: To Return and To Remember

775, 3rd Day Of The Seventh Moon

Today, I caught her in the garden, her laughter light as she tended to the roses she loves so dearly. She has a way of bringing life to every corner of this place, a quiet strength that settles even the most restless heart. I find myself drawn to her still, as much as when we first wed, grateful for the patience she brings to my endless hours of work and the lightness she adds to this home.

When she looks up and smiles, I remember why I can face all else.

As the first light of dawn crept over the jagged peaks, Ky'len stood at the mouth of their tent nestled in the valley, looking out over the mountain range that stretched endlessly before him. The crisp air bit at his skin, a stark reminder of the journey that lay ahead. Beside him stood Flin'thor, a young Vek'smed with sharp eyes and an even sharper awareness of the mountains surrounding them. The boy adjusted the straps on his small pack, his youthful face set with determination that seemed to age him beyond his years.

Behind them, the others gathered around the fire, now reduced to smoldering embers. Flak'tin approached, his heavy boots crunching over the rocky ground.

"The lad knows these mountains like the back of his hand," Flak'tin said with a rough edge in his voice, clapping a firm hand on Flin'thor's shoulder. "He'll get ya back to Bazel safe. No worries—ya can count on him."

Flin'thor straightened, meeting Ky'len's gaze with a quiet but determined glint. "I can take ya, sir," he said, his words a blend of broken Common and his native tongue. "Know these here spor… uh, tracks… like me own hand." He gave a quick nod, his face radiating confidence as he added in Vek'smed, "Eg vil verna deg." *I'll protect you.*

Ky'len studied Flin'thor for a moment, then nodded with a smile. "Alright, Flin'thor. Looks like we're in this together."

Flin'thor returned the nod, his eyes bright with purpose.

Iszell, still reluctant, cast a wary glance between Ky'len and the boy. "I don't like this. You're better off staying, Ky'len. I can handle the Vek'smed. You should be here, not running off to Bazel."

Ky'len clapped Iszell on the shoulder, a grin breaking through the tension. "I'll be fine. Besides, you've got your work cut out here, convincing the Vek'smed to join the fight."

He turned to Tala, who had been unusually quiet through the exchange. "And don't worry, Tala. I'll be back soon enough. Just make sure you two don't practice kissing until I'm back."

Tala's face flushed instantly, her eyes narrowing as she shot Ky'len a withering look. "You're hilarious, Ky'len," she muttered, but a small, reluctant smile tugged at her lips.

Iszell groaned, rubbing the back of his neck in embarrassment. "I swear, Ky'len..."

Flak'tin chuckled, folding his arms across his chest. "You two better be careful, or Ky'len'll have a whole new reason to give you grief when he returns."

Amused, Flin'thor leaned close to his father and whispered in Vek'smed Icelandic, "Tala og Iszell... saman?" *Tala and Iszell... together?*

Flak'tin shook his head with a chuckle, whispering back, "Enno ikkje, gut, men det kjem." *Not yet, boy, but it's coming.* He clapped his son on the shoulder, pride gleaming in his eyes.

The banter did little to lighten the weight of the tasks ahead, but Ky'len's grin lingered as he adjusted his pack. Leaving with a bit of humor felt like a shield against the uncertainty that lay before him.

The fire crackled softly, settling into the quiet of the early night as the group prepared to rest. Tomorrow, Ky'len would begin his journey back to Bazel with Flin'thor as his guide, while Tala, Iszell, and Flak'tin made their way to the Vek'smed Forge. Their paths would split, but their goals remained the same—gathering allies and standing together against the looming threats of Thorn, Warden, Mutt, and Vil'elm.

As they settled down, Ky'len exchanged one last look with Tala and Iszell. "Tomorrow, we forge alliances not seen since the war," he said, his voice filled with hope.

Flak'tin huffed, shaking his head. "Alliances? Those were no alliances, mate; more like opportunities."

Iszell looked at Flak'tin with curiosity. "What do you mean?" he asked.

Flak'tin waved him off. "Nothing. Get some sleep." Flin'thor and Tala shared a glance with Iszell and shook their heads, signaling him to leave it be.

As dawn began to break over the jagged peaks, Tala, Iszell, and Flak'tin prepared to set off, joined by Ky'len and Flin'thor at the camp's edge. The entire camp had gathered, a quiet show of support and solidarity. Elders watched from a distance, their eyes somber yet resolute, while the younger muckspawn crowded closer, faces alight with curiosity and admiration for the departing group.

One of the elders, Elda, nodded solemnly at Flak'tin. "Hold fjellet i hjarta ditt, Flak," she murmured, placing a gnarled hand on his arm. *Keep the mountain in your heart.* Thorl, gripping his walking staff, added, "Kom attende til oss med gode nyhende." *Come back to us with good news.*

Flak'tin nodded, glancing toward the path ahead, and then turned to Ky'len and Flin'thor. "Listen up, both of ya," he said with a rough but caring tone. "Keep yer heads down, watch each other's backs, and don't go wanderin' off any side paths—these mountains'll chew ya up if ya don't respect 'em."

Ky'len nodded earnestly, feeling the weight of Flak'tin's words as he adjusted his pack.

Flin'thor gave his father a firm nod, determination flickering in his eyes. "Eg vil gjere deg stolt, far," he murmured. *I will make you proud, Father.*

Flak'tin's face softened, and he ruffled his son's hair in a rare show of affection. "I know ya will, lad. Just keep steady, and remember—stick together. You're in this side by side."

Nearby, a few muckspawn children lingered, watching the departing group with wide eyes. One of the bolder kids stepped forward and handed Ky'len a roughly carved stone, muttering, "For hell, ja? Til å beskytte." *For luck, yes? For protection.* Ky'len accepted it with a warm smile, tucking it into his pack.

Iszell chuckled, reaching over to pat Ky'len on the back. "See? The kids believe in you, too."

With a final nod to the elders and the gathered crowd, Tala, Iszell, and Flak'tin set off on the narrow, winding path deeper into the Vek'smed mountains. The rocky ledges and steep cliffs framed their journey as the crisp air pressed around them, matching the weight of their purpose. Behind them, Ky'len and Flin'thor stood side by side, watching their friends disappear into the distance.

As the elders and children returned to their duties, Flin'thor touched Ky'len's arm and spoke softly. "Ready, Ky'len? Spor waits," he said, switching seamlessly between his broken Common and Vek'smed.

Ky'len glanced back at the camp, then faced the distant path, steeling himself. "Ready, Flin'thor. Let's get to Bazel."

The quiet resolve shared between them was clear. Together, they set out, their steps echoing along the mountainside as they embarked on the separate journey that lay before them, each bound by a mission that would, with hope, see them reunited on the other side.

As dawn light crept over the jagged peaks, Flak'tin led the way with the easy stride of someone who knew every rock and shadow of these mountains. Tala followed closely, her gaze drifting to the towering cliffs as doubts crept into her thoughts. Behind her, Iszell trailed with an uneasy expression, his fingers flexing and clenching as he took in the rugged landscape.

"Vi burde ha gått saman," Iszell muttered, his voice tense as he glanced over the terrain. *"We should have gone together."* After a pause, he added, "Uh... that means, uh, 'stick together,' right?"

Flak'tin chuckled, glancing back. "Vi burde ha gått saman," he repeated slowly. "It's 'we should've gone together.' But close enough, lad."

Iszell rolled his eyes, catching Tala's amused smile. "Fine, fine. Close enough."

Tala's laughter faded as she remembered the brutal force of Mutt, and her doubt spilled into words. "Iszell... du såg dei. Folket mitt... eller kva dei no er. Kan nokon stoppe dei? Mutt slo to høvdingar som ingenting. Ky'len overlevde berre på grunn av Zra'ka sitt vev," she said, her voice full of uncertainty. *"Iszell... you saw them. My people... or whatever they are. Can anyone stop them? Mutt took down two chiefs like they were nothing. Ky'len only survived because of Zra'ka's webbing."*

Iszell caught only bits, his brows furrowing. "Uh, something about Ky'len and webbing...?"

Tala sighed, translating softly, "I'm asking if we can stop them."

Iszell nodded, his gaze softening. "Look, Ky'len got lucky, I won't deny that. But it proves something—they think we're weak. And Mutt? Let the older warriors handle him," he assured, taking her hand. "Eg vernar deg, Tala." *"I'll protect you, Tala."*

Tala smiled, some tension easing as she embraced him. "Eg fryktar for folket mitt... og for mine nye vener," she murmured, her voice quiet. *"I fear for my people... and for my new friends."*

Flak'tin's voice cut in, gruff but reassuring. "Ja, det er farleg, men nødvendig. Vi treng allierte, og Vek'smed vil kanskje kjempe viss vi får dei med oss," he said, looking back with a nod. *"Aye, dangerous—but necessary. We need allies, and the Vek'smed might fight if we can convince them."*

Iszell blinked, lost in the flow of words. "Alright, so... something about it being dangerous but, uh... necessary?"

Tala chuckled, nodding. "Not bad, Iszell. You're getting there."

As they climbed higher, Flak'tin glanced back with a glint of humor in his eye. "Det er ein spøk frå landsbyen min," he started, smirking, "Kva skjer når ein muckspawn, ein Slivdhe, ein menneske og ein Vek'smed blir fanga i eit steinsprang?" *"There's a joke from my village: What happens when a muckspawn, a Slivdhe, a human, and a Vek'smed get caught in a rockslide?"*

Tala grinned. "Kva?" *"What?"*

Flak'tin's smirk widened. "Muckspawnen graver eit hol og gjøymer seg, Slivdhe'en forvandlar seg til tåke og forsvinn, mennesket skuldar på alle andre, og Vek'smeden? Han er allereie halvvegs ned fjellet med ein sekk edelsteinar og ein ny plan." *"The muckspawn digs a hole and hides, the Slivdhe turns to mist and floats away, the human blames everyone else, and the Vek'smed? He's already halfway down the mountain with a bag of gems and a new plan."*

Tala laughed, Iszell scratching his head. "Alright, that… sounded like… a joke?" he guessed, looking at Tala for confirmation.

"Aye," Tala grinned. "Flak says the Vek'smed always seem to get out of trouble with a little extra in their pocket."

"Would've appreciated the punchline," Iszell muttered, but a smile tugged at his lips as he caught on.

They continued onward until Flak'tin grew serious, his eyes scanning the towering peaks. "Men spøk til side, kva veit de om folket mitt?" he asked, his tone shifting. *"But jokes aside, what do you really know about my people?"*

Iszell perked up, catching the question this time. "Something about the Vek'smed?" he guessed, glancing at Tala for help.

Flak'tin nodded, repeating in Common. "My people, the Vek'smed. If you're gonna convince 'em, you've got to know 'em."

Iszell thought a moment. "I've read they value their isolation, their mountains, and craftsmanship," he said, piecing his words carefully.

Flak'tin nodded. "Aye, det er sant. Vi verdsett styrke og uavhengigheit," he said. *"Aye, that's true. We value strength and independence."* "Men Thorn's rekkevidd går djupt, og Vek'smed kan ikkje ignorere det lenge." *"But Thorn's reach goes deep, and the Vek'smed can't ignore it for long."*

Tala and Iszell exchanged a determined look. "Då må vi vise dei," Tala replied, her tone resolute. *"Then we'll show them."*

As they trudged up the final stretch, the imposing stone gates of the Hidden Forge loomed above them like ancient, silent giants, casting shadows that seemed to chill the air. Flak'tin's confident stride slowed, his steps tentative as memories flickered across his face, his gaze drawn to the massive walls.

"Det har gått ei stund sidan eg var heime," he muttered, more to himself than anyone else, his voice tinged with an unfamiliar vulnerability. *"It's been a while since I was home."*

Two guards stepped from the shadows, their armor gleaming dully under the low light, faces hard as granite. Recognizing Flak'tin, their eyes narrowed, and one's hand instinctively tightened around his weapon. "Flak," one of them growled, his tone thick with scorn, "du er ikkje velkommen her. Det er ille nok at du sendte Arak hit!" *"Flak, you're not welcome here. It's bad enough you sent Arak here!"* His voice echoed off the stone, each word heavy with accusation.

Tala's eyes widened as her father's name hung in the air. "Far min? Han er her?" she burst out, barely able to contain her shock. *"My father? He's here?"*

Iszell, though he only understood fragments, could see Tala's reaction and sensed the tension in the guards' tone. "Your father's here?" he echoed, concern flashing in his eyes as he studied Tala.

Flak'tin lifted a hand toward Iszell, signaling him to hold back, his face hardening as he squared his shoulders to address the guards. "La meg ordne dette," he said, his voice low but firm. *"Let me handle this."* He took a step closer to the guards, meeting their hostile glares. "Lat oss komme inn. Du har høyrt kva som kjem. Eg må snakke med far min," he demanded. *"Let us in. You know what's coming. I need to speak to my father."*

One of the guards sneered, his disdain practically dripping from his words. "Far din vil ikkje ha noko med deg å gjere, Dhor'vakir," he spat. *"Your father doesn't want anything to do with you, Dhor'vakir."* His tone turned bitter as he uttered the word, eyes cold as he looked Flak'tin up and down like something unworthy of notice.

Iszell, catching the strange word, leaned close to Tala, his voice barely a whisper. "What's a… Dhor'vakir?"

Tala's expression turned grim as she glanced at Iszell. "It means… exile," she murmured, her voice soft yet filled with the weight of the word.

The word lingered in the cold air, and before anyone could speak further, heavy footsteps echoed from beyond the gates. A massive figure emerged, his silhouette imposing as he strode forward, armor glinting with faint, worn symbols. He wore a look that was equal parts authority and menace. His voice, deep and unyielding, rumbled out, "Lat den gamle Vorrak'ten inn," he commanded, his tone edged with cold amusement. ("Let the old Vorrak'ten in.") His gaze pinned Flak'tin, unyielding. "La han endeleg møte syndene sine.""*Let him finally face his sins."*

Iszell looked to Tala again, uncertain. "Vorrak'ten?" he asked, struggling to piece it together.

Tala's voice dropped to a near-whisper. "It means… prince."

The captain strode up to Flak'tin and, without warning, delivered a harsh punch to his jaw. Flak'tin's head snapped back, but he didn't flinch. Instead, he held the captain's gaze, his face expressionless even as the pain registered. Then, before Tala or Iszell could react, the captain pulled Flak'tin into a rough embrace, patting his back with a mixture of camaraderie and disdain.

"Velkommen heim, gamle tosk" the captain chuckled, his tone wry, though there was a flicker of warmth beneath the gruff words.*"Welcome home, old fool."*

Iszell, still trying to make sense of what he'd witnessed, blinked, glancing between Tala and Flak'tin, the implications slowly dawning on him. "Wait… does this mean you're… royalty?" he asked, looking at Flak'tin with wide eyes.

Flak'tin rubbed his bruised cheek, offering Iszell a weary smile tinged with irony. "Yes, lad," he replied quietly. "Once, I was."

Chapter 29: Forgeing Allinces

770, 14th Day Of The First Moon

Today, the chief of the Bog People came to me, standing no taller than my waist, yet commanding as much respect as any noble in my court. Though small in stature, his presence was anything but; his eyes held a fierce determination, a reminder of a life spent on harsh marshlands where survival itself is a battle.

He came with a request that's sparked debate in my council: land—a piece of soil his people could defend and call their own. The Bog People are not known for alliances but for their resilience, enduring the swamps and shunning the aid of kingdoms. He spoke of their struggles, of the isolation they have endured for generations, not asking for pity but recognition.

Some among my advisors worry that granting them land might bring complications, fearing the old magics the Bog People wield and their deeply rooted distrust of outsiders. Yet, others see the potential for alliance, a chance to welcome a people who understand endurance better than any.

In that small frame, the chief carried a strength I'd rarely seen. He wasn't here to plead but to bargain for his kin's future, and for that alone, he's earned my consideration.

As they made their way down from the high mountain pass, Ky'len's nerves began to gnaw at him. The looming responsibility felt like a weight around his neck, each step toward Bazel filled with the pressure of rallying his people. The idea of inspiring them to stand against Thorn's forces seemed daunting, and as his mind raced with doubts, he glanced over at his guide, hoping for some reassurance.

Flin'thor moved with quiet, effortless grace through the dense brush, blending into the landscape like a shadow. Though young, he had the alertness and agility of someone far older, his sharp gaze sweeping their surroundings for any signs of danger. Yet there was also a spark of curiosity in the boy—a lightheartedness that seemed at odds with his focused demeanor.

"Thraak'tel," Flin'thor muttered, squinting up at the sky. The unfamiliar Vek'smed word made Ky'len hesitate, and he wondered if it was something important about the path ahead or the weather.

"Uh… sure," Ky'len replied awkwardly, trying not to sound clueless and hoping he hadn't just agreed to something risky.

Flin'thor glanced over, his serious expression breaking into a grin. "Your Vek'smed… not great, huh?" he teased, his broken Common carrying an unexpected lightness.

Ky'len chuckled, feeling a bit sheepish. "I could say the same about your Common, Flin'thor," he countered, though his own tone was friendly.

Flin'thor shrugged, unconcerned. "I speak… better Vek'smed. Like father," he replied, clearly proud of his native language.

Their journey continued, the initial tension easing as Flin'thor's humor lightened Ky'len's mood. Every now and then, Flin'thor would mutter something in Vek'smed—"Rakh'tor" or "Kel'meth"— and Ky'len would nod along, pretending to understand. Despite the language barrier, Ky'len felt comforted by Flin'thor's presence; the boy was capable and knew the mountains as well as anyone.

At one point, Flin'thor stopped and pointed toward a distant ridge, speaking rapidly in Vek'smed before catching himself. Switching to Common, he gestured toward the forested valley below. "That… is where… big deer run," he said, his Common slow and careful. "Good hunting."

Ky'len smiled, appreciating Flin'thor's effort. "You hunt often?"

Flin'thor nodded eagerly. "Yes. Father teach… much."

Ky'len noted the quiet admiration in Flin'thor's voice and couldn't help but feel a pang of envy. It was clear Flak'tin had taught his son a lot, not just about survival but also about respect for the mountains and the creatures within them. Ky'len thought of his own father, their relationship more about duty and expectations than shared wisdom or understanding.

The trail became steeper, and as they navigated a particularly tricky descent, Ky'len glanced over at Flin'thor, who was muttering directions to himself in Vek'smed. "Hey, teach me some of that," Ky'len suggested, nodding to encourage him. "You know, so I can follow along if I need to."

Flin'thor's face brightened, and he stopped to think. "Alright… Rakh'tor," he said slowly, pointing to the path. "Means… uh, dangerous rock?"

Ky'len nodded, testing the word. "Rakh'tor. Got it."

Flin'thor continued with another word, tapping the ground. "Kel'meth. That means… step slow. Careful."

"Kel'meth… careful," Ky'len repeated, trying to absorb it, though his pronunciation made Flin'thor chuckle.

"You… not so good, but close enough," Flin'thor said with a teasing grin. Then, with a mock-serious expression, he added, "I teach. You learn. Soon, speak like real Vek'smed."

"Guess I'll have to rely on you until then," Ky'len laughed. He wasn't entirely sure how much he'd retain, but Flin'thor's quiet confidence was reassuring.

As they moved forward, trading bits of language back and forth, Ky'len found his earlier anxiety easing.

The path was rough, jagged rocks underfoot and a biting wind pressing against them as Ky'len trudged forward, thoughts heavy with what lay ahead. The responsibility of rallying Bazel's people to face Thorn's forces weighed on him, and doubt gnawed at his resolve. Beside him, Flin'thor moved with ease, weaving through the brush like a shadow, his sharp eyes scanning the surroundings.

At one point, Flin'thor stopped, raising a hand for Ky'len to halt. "Rak'tin, noko nært," he murmured in Vek'smed, his tone low and cautious. *"Hold. Something nearby."*

Ky'len froze, his hand instinctively resting on his sword. He followed Flin'thor's gaze, waiting in tense silence as the boy crouched, motioning for him to do the same. They listened, the quiet broken only by the rustle of leaves and the distant sigh of the wind. After a few tense moments, Flin'thor relaxed, shaking his head. "False alarm… small creature only," he said, switching to broken Common with a faint grin.

Ky'len released a breath, managing a relieved chuckle. "You're good at this," he remarked, impressed by Flin'thor's instincts.

Flin'thor's face lit up with pride. "Father say… always ready. Never know… what hides in forest." He paused, thinking, then added in Vek'smed, "Gode krigare er aldri uforberedt." *"Good warriors are never unprepared."*

As they continued on, the terrain became steeper, shadows deepening in the fading light. They arrived at a clearing, and Ky'len slowed, a shiver running down his spine as he recognized it. "This is where it happened," he said softly. "We fought the Webshroud and Crowfeathers here… barely made it out. Pure luck."

Flin'thor glanced back at him, his eyes narrowing slightly as he muttered in Vek'smed, "Lukke er ein svak strategi."*"Luck is a weak strategy."* Then, switching back to Common, he added, "Should finish enemies. No enemy better than… enemy later."

Ky'len chuckled, though the words lingered. "I'll keep that in mind."

As they descended from the rugged mountain path, Ky'len's nerves tightened. Every step toward Bazel only amplified his doubts about the monumental task that lay ahead: convincing the people of Bazel of Thorn's threat, rallying allies, and somehow finding a way to face the monstrous forces that lurked just beyond the horizon.

Flin'thor, moving with an easy, practiced grace, was a reassuring presence beside him. Barely more than a boy, he moved with the confidence of someone who had lived in these mountains all his life. His sharp eyes scanned the trees, always alert, always aware. Despite his youth, Flin'thor seemed to carry a wisdom beyond his years—a seriousness mingled with a curiosity that Ky'len found both comforting and humbling.

"Rak'tin," Flin'thor muttered suddenly, holding up a hand. *"Hold. Stop."*

Ky'len, catching the meaning from the words he'd managed to pick up, froze immediately, his senses on high alert. He reached for his sword, his eyes following Flin'thor's intense gaze into the dense brush.

"Uh... noe her?" he attempted, his pronunciation awkward. *"Something here?"*

Flin'thor flashed a small, approving smile at Ky'len's efforts. "Ja," he whispered, nodding. "Yes. Something." His tone dropped to a murmur as he glanced around, "Hald deg stille... kanskje byttedyr." *"Stay still... maybe prey."*

Ky'len held his breath, hoping that Flin'thor's instincts would prove right. They waited, listening to the forest's rustling and whispers. Just as Ky'len started to relax, a figure lunged out of the shadows—a Webshroud muckspawn, shrouded in sticky webs and screeching as it leapt toward them.

Ky'len barely managed to draw his sword in time, meeting the creature's claws with a powerful block. His muscles strained against its weight as he held his ground. Beside him, Flin'thor darted in, his movements swift as he slashed at the muckspawn's exposed sides.

"Slå sida, Ky'len!" Flin'thor barked, gesturing sharply to the creature's flank. *"Hit the side, Ky'len!"*

Ky'len, following the gesture rather than fully understanding the words, dodged the muckspawn's next swing and struck at its side, his sword slicing through the thick, webbed hide. The creature screeched and stumbled but continued its frenzied assault, spraying webbing in all directions as it thrashed.

Flin'thor weaved through the sticky strands, cutting away any that tried to ensnare him. "Ikkje... stå still...!" he urged, fumbling for the right words in Common. *"No... stand... still!"*

Ky'len caught the gist, dodging aside as the muckspawn lunged at him again. The two fought in tandem, wearing it down with every strike. Finally, with one decisive swing, Ky'len drove his blade deep into the creature's side. It gave a final, tortured cry before collapsing in a tangled heap of webs, its body shuddering in its last moments.

Breathing hard, Ky'len wiped sweat from his brow and looked over at Flin'thor with a weary grin. "Good... good fight," he managed between breaths.

Flin'thor, equally winded, nodded, giving him a quick thumbs-up. "Bra slåstkamp," he replied with a grin. *"Good fight."*

But before they could rest, a dark shadow passed overhead, and both looked up to see a Crowfeather muckspawn gliding above, its feathered cloak fluttering as it swooped down. It screeched out in Muckspawn, "Zra'ka thrak va'ten korak'dir a'toh vekar no'ra!" its voice echoing with venom. *"Zra'ka will claim your heads and feast on your blood!"*

The creature vanished into the trees, but its mocking words lingered, chilling the air.

Ky'len's pulse quickened. He glanced at Flin'thor, understanding only fragments of the muckspawn's speech but knowing enough to recognize the threat. "We've been found," he said, his voice tight with urgency.

Flin'thor gave a quick, tense nod. "Ja... ikkje god." He paused, then added in halting Common, "Not... good."

Ky'len managed a weak laugh, though the gravity of the situation weighed on him. "You're saying... Zra'ka doesn't like us?"

Flin'thor's expression turned grim as he replied, "Zra'ka... ikkje ven." *"Zra'ka... no friend."*

They pushed forward at a quickened pace, weaving through the dense underbrush. The darkening sky and thickening forest added to the weight pressing down on them as they fled. Dusk was falling when they finally emerged onto a high ridge. From their vantage point, they could see a plume of dark smoke rising in the distance—Sergora, ablaze, its walls glowing with the sinister red-orange of fire and destruction.

"Gudar..." Ky'len murmured, the disbelief heavy in his voice. *"Gods..."*

Flin'thor, though too young to understand Sergora's full significance, sensed the gravity of what he was seeing. He glanced at Ky'len, his usual lively expression now subdued, filled with silent acknowledgment.

Together, they stood on the ridge, the crackling flames of Sergora below a reminder that their path ahead was only growing darker.

They skirted the edge of the city, staying clear of the crowds of people pouring out of Sergora. As they pushed forward, Ky'len's eyes caught sight of a familiar group up ahead. Through the smoke and fleeing civilians, he recognized them—King Tor'valis, Dalmon, A'nara, Yvonne, and Belazar, moving purposefully away from the burning city.

"We need to find the king," Ky'len muttered, quickening his pace.

Flin'thor nodded, his gaze sweeping over the destruction. He said something in Vek'smed, a phrase Ky'len couldn't fully understand, but the sorrow in the boy's voice was unmistakable. "So much loss," Flin'thor added in broken Common.

As they continued forward, Flin'thor spotted a blacksmith frantically sifting through his remaining stock, trying to decide what to take and what to leave behind. Without hesitation, Flin'thor walked over, pulling out a small piece of Vek'smed ore from his pack. The blacksmith's eyes widened in disbelief as Flin'thor handed it to him.

"Thank you," the blacksmith said, lifting the boy off the ground in a gesture of gratitude. Flin'thor simply smiled, nodding shyly.

Ky'len watched the scene unfold with a faint smile. "That was a good step, my friend."

Moments later, Ky'len's eyes locked onto the royal soldiers ahead. "There they are," he said, quickening his pace.

Dalmon was the first to spot them, his expression shifting from surprise to urgency. "Ky'len? What in the gods' names are you doing here?"

Ky'len, still breathless from the sight of Sergora's devastation, shook his head. "It's... a long story," he said hoarsely, glancing back toward the ruined city. "We were heading for Bazel, but... what happened here?"

King Tor'valis stepped forward, exhaustion lining his face. "Sergora's fallen. Thorn's forces hit us hard while we were still reeling from Mutt's attack. We've lost the city." He paused, searching Ky'len's face. "Where are Tala and Iszell? Are they—?"

Ky'len quickly reassured him, "They're safe. They're with Flin'thor's father, Flak'tin, heading to the Vek'smed Forge."

As he introduced Flin'thor with a respectful nod, A'nara and Dalmon exchanged a few warm words in Vek'smed, welcoming the boy. Flin'thor gave a shy nod, sticking close to Ky'len, his eyes darting between the elders with curiosity and caution.

Dalmon's face brightened as he turned to Ky'len. "Flak'tin, er det sant? God Vek'smed den mannen. Skam korleis folket hans behandler han." *"Flak'tin, is it true? A good Vek'smed, that man. A shame how his people treat him."*

Ky'len's brows shot up in surprise. "Wait—Flak'tin's... a prince?"

Flin'thor straightened, pride evident in his tone. "Ja. Han er dhor'vakir, prinsen av Vek'smed," he replied. *"Yes. He is dhor'vakir, prince of the Vek'smed."*

A'nara gave a solemn nod, sharing a knowing glance with Dalmon. "A hard path, but Flak'tin is a strong man. He can lead his people, if they're willing to listen."

Ky'len shook his head, trying to process the revelation. "I had no idea..."

Dalmon noted his surprise and added gently, "It's true, Ky'len. His lineage runs deep in Vek'smed. But his status has become... complicated."

The weight of their task began to settle over Ky'len. He looked from Dalmon to Flin'thor, urgency clear in his voice. "We need allies—Bazel, the Vek'smed, anyone who will fight. We can't do this alone."

A'nara met his gaze, her face resolute. "Then we must gather those who stand strong, regardless of the past. Flak'tin may be the key if his people can forgive."

Dalmon's gaze softened with nostalgia as he murmured, "Flak'tin, prince of the Vek'smed...

haven't seen him since he was a young one."

A'nara's voice softened as she looked to Dalmon. "Flak'tin, a prince, and now a man on a long path."

Turning to Ky'len, Dalmon's tone grew warm and reflective. "Yes, prince… once held him as a babe," he said quietly. "A good man, Flak'tin. Shame his people… struggle to see it."

Taking a deep breath, Ky'len looked at Flin'thor with a new understanding. "Your father's reputation… it could help us, couldn't it?"

Flin'thor nodded, though a flicker of uncertainty crossed his face. "If the people will listen. But they need someone to follow," he said with quiet reluctance.

A'nara turned to Ky'len, her gaze steady. "And it might be you, or Flak'tin, or someone else… but the alliance must be forged."

King Tor'valis nodded slowly, absorbing their words. "That's where we're heading now. But we have enemies on all sides—Warden, Vil'elm, Mutt, Thorn. And we can't rely on the Vek'smed alone. They keep their cities strong, but whether they'll fight with us is uncertain."

Flin'thor stepped forward with a note of defiance. "My father will get them to fight. He is dhor'vakir," he added firmly, repeating the word "prince" with pride.

Ky'len smiled, encouraged by the boy's confidence. "We have to rally whatever forces we can," he said, turning back to the king. "Bazel has to help… I will make them understand."

Belazar, who had been silent until now, finally spoke up. "Has anyone heard anything about Razma?"

Ky'len shook his head. "Not since the tournament. I'm sorry… And I'm sorry for the trouble I caused there."

Belazar waved off the apology. "That was just two headstrong kids throwing punches—no reason to dwell on it."

Dalmon folded his arms, brow knitted. "There's one place we can't ignore: Halzor's Keep. We may have to go back there."

Ky'len's stomach clenched at the name. "Halzor's Keep?"

Tor'valis gave a grave nod. "If we aim to stop Thorn, that may be the only place left to face her."

A somber quiet settled over them, until Belazar cleared his throat. "We should head to Lilah Glendale first. She might have some insight—perhaps even news of Razma."

Dalmon quirked a faint grin. "And I suppose you want me to do all the talking again?"

Belazar's own smile was brief but genuine. "You've always been better at it than me."

Yvonne, who had been standing off to one side, chimed in. "Tor'valis, take Alric and the others to reinforce the castle. Gather up whoever can still fight. We'll go to Glendale and see what we can learn."

Tor'valis arched an eyebrow, a wry smile tugging at his lips. "You do realize I'm the king, right, Yvonne? I'm no longer some soldier under your command." His tone was more playful than reprimanding, and his eyes sparkled with amusement.

Yvonne gave a light shrug, half-smiling in return. "A habit, I suppose. Old ways die hard."

With a faint chuckle, Tor'valis nodded. "Well, I admit it's a good plan, so I'll allow it—this time."

Then he turned to Ky'len. "You should go with them. An extra sword is always useful, and you've seen firsthand the threat we're facing."

Ky'len inclined his head, carefully avoiding Yvonne's gaze. With deliberate steps, he moved to stand beside Dalmon and Belazar, making his intention clear. Yvonne noticed and seemed ready to speak, but Ky'len shifted ever so slightly, directing his attention to Dalmon instead. A subtle tension rippled between them.

Tor'valis caught the exchange and offered a nod of understanding. "Then it's settled. We'll meet again soon."

As the paths diverged, Yvonne lingered for a moment, her eyes tracking Ky'len's back. He did not look her way, instead drawing closer to Dalmon and Belazar with a steeled resolve. Together, they made for Lilah Glendale's home—each step carrying them nearer to answers, and perhaps a reckoning, none of them could avoid.

Tor'valis turned to Flin'thor, his expression softening as he spoke in Vek'smed, his tone respectful. "Flin'thor, son av Flak, eg ber deg bli med meg. Eg vil gjerne snakke om folket ditt og korleis vi kan bygge bru mellom Vek'smed og Bazel." *"Flin'thor, son of Flak, I ask that you accompany me. I'd like to discuss your people and how we can bridge the gap between the Vek'smed and Bazel."*

Flin'thor blinked in surprise at the request, his young face shifting from surprise to determination. "Ja, Kong Tor'valis. Eg skal tale for far min og folket mitt," he replied, his voice steady. *"Yes, King Tor'valis. I will speak for my father and my people."*

Ky'len watched the exchange with pride, recognizing the weight on Flin'thor's shoulders. Despite the turmoil around them, Flin'thor was stepping up, ready to take on a role that would influence the future of his people.

Turning to Ky'len, Belazar spoke, his tone steady. "I appreciate your willingness to join us. You may not fully realize how critical this journey to Lilah Glendale is, but it could change everything. We'll need all the support we can muster."

Ky'len nodded, the gravity of the situation sinking deeper. "I'm with you, Belazar. Whatever it takes."

Dalmon clapped Ky'len on the back. "Good to have you with us, lad. Let's not waste any more time."

Tor'valis stepped forward, his eyes sweeping over the group. "We're all walking separate paths for now, but our goal remains the same—stopping Thorn and uniting whoever we can. Stay safe, and when we meet again, we'll be ready."

With that, the group split, each team setting off in their own direction. Ky'len watched as Tor'valis led Flin'thor away, the young Vek'smed walking beside the king with newfound purpose. Ky'len, Dalmon, Belazar, Yvonne and A'nara began their trek toward Lilah Glendale's home, the weight of the task ahead pressing down on them.

Chapter 30: Confessions

785, 16th Day of the Eighth Moon

After all these years... why say it now?

Mira confessed her love for me today.

I have valued her deeply, not for her beauty, but for her mind and the way she's aided me in my research. She has been more than a mere confidant; her knowledge and counsel have often illuminated paths I might have overlooked. Yet never would I cross that line with her. My love for my wife is steadfast, unwavering as stone, and my family—my wife and children —comes before all else.

It was at my wife's urging that Mira returned to her kin. She left quietly, without a word of farewell, and though her absence is felt in the household, I know it is for the best. Perhaps this distance will bring peace for her heart and steadiness for mine. We have taken on a new handmaiden now, and, with time, I trust that this unsettling moment will pass into memory, leaving no ripple behind.

✱✱✱

The low crackle of the hearth did little to dispel the shroud of tension clinging to the room. Razma lay on a simple cot, every muscle aflame with exhaustion, his thoughts clouded by fragments of violence and sorcery. Sitting across from him was Liliah Glendale—his mentor— her features drawn with both concern and sorrow. The weight in her eyes told him that no mere explanation could mend the fractures in his world.

Teeth gritted, Razma tried to stand, but his legs wobbled beneath him and threatened to send him sprawling. Glendale lunged to catch him, tears glistening in her eyes as she guided him gently back onto the cot.

"Razma," she whispered, voice vibrating with emotion. "You've survived so much. Rest—just for a moment."

He forced his breathing to steady, and memory slowly threaded its way through his mind: his father battling a blonde-haired woman… Thorn, swathed in malevolent magic… then Warden's firm grasp as he tore Razma from Thorn's clutches. Razma swallowed, his voice raw with confusion. "My father… I never knew he could fight like that. And Thorn—she was so powerful. Warden rescued me, but… why?"

His gaze darted anxiously to Glendale, who exchanged a tense look with Warden, pacing near a window as though trying to escape his own thoughts. Razma's hand gripped the edge of Glendale's sleeve, desperation cutting through his words. "Who is this Warden? And why would my father fight someone so… monstrous?"

Warden halted, agitation stark in every line of his body. Glendale exhaled, then turned to Razma, her eyes filled with a gravity he had never seen before. "Your father kept terrible secrets from you. Warden's told me part of it, but I need you to tell me everything you remember."

Razma recounted his hazy memories: Thorn's vicious magic, his father's blinding speed in battle, the deafening flare that knocked him unconscious. Then waking in a cave, unable to decipher the words Thorn and Warden exchanged, until the final moment when Warden turned on her. After a narrow escape through the forest, everything went dark again. When he finished, Glendale's expression tightened with both compassion and grim resignation.

"You've stumbled into a war older than you could guess," she murmured. "Thorn unleashed forbidden magic once before, nearly destroying Seragora and Bazel. Your father fought to stop her, but he wasn't simply another soldier. He was Sliverfang."

Razma's stomach knotted. Tales of Sliverfang were folklore at best, horror stories at worst. "That—no. My father… he's just a stable master."

Warden's voice emerged low and taut. "Your father was transformed. Faster, stronger… lethal beyond belief. He became Sliverfang, and when the darkness took hold, no one was truly safe."

Glendale's face darkened, a tremor running through her words. "My husband, Marros, tried to stop him once. He stood in Sliverfang's way—your father's way—and was killed." She paused, anguish flickering in her gaze. "I don't hate your father, Razma. But I can't forgive him, either. He was changed, yes, but it doesn't undo what happened."

Razma felt ice congealing in his veins. The father who had taught him kindness and care had slain Glendale's husband? He cast a desperate look at her. "Why… why wouldn't he tell me?"

Glendale's grip on his arm tightened. "He believed you'd be safer not knowing. He buried the war and its horrors—along with the power he once wielded. To keep that power at bay, he drinks —trying to numb the old darkness inside him. But Thorn's return has dragged everything back into the light."

Warden lifted his shirt, revealing a brutal scar across his side. "I earned this trying to stop Sliverfang after the shadows consumed him," he said grimly. "We were allies once, but war can turn brothers into enemies."

Razma's world swam. His father, hiding a bloody past and wrestling with an inner beast he drowned in bottles. Thorn looming over them all, bent on reigniting a nightmare. "So… what do we do now?" he whispered, fear squeezing his chest.

Glendale's tone was resolute, if tinged with sadness. "We don't let Thorn finish what she started. We protect you, and we figure out how to stop her for good."

Warden resumed his pacing, tension radiating off him like sparks. Razma, numb from shock, managed a shaky nod. As he fought to reconcile the gentle father he knew with the monstrous legend he'd just discovered, a flicker of determination mingled with his dread.

"Whatever it takes," he said softly, eyes brimming with tears he refused to let fall.

Glendale squeezed his shoulder, sharing a small, solemn nod. The firelight danced on the walls as they huddled there, bound by old wounds, hidden truths, and the looming threat of Thorn—a threat that would not rest until it consumed them all.

Warden, who had been pacing once again, stopped at the far end of the room. He glanced at Glendale, then looked toward the door. "Now… we prepare," he said, his voice low and tired. "Thorn's coming"

The fire crackled softly, casting long shadows across the room. Razma sat in stunned silence, the weight of what he'd just learned pressing heavily on his chest. His father, Sliverfang, the legendary warrior of the Thorrin War—his father had kept all of this hidden. It was almost too much to process.

Liliah Glendale stood abruptly, her sharp movements breaking the tense silence. "Wait," she said, her voice decisive, "I may have something that can help." She crossed the room swiftly, heading toward an old chest tucked into the corner, its surface covered in dust and age-worn scratches.

Warden's pacing came to a sudden halt, his eyes narrowing with curiosity as he watched Glendale. "Hmm," he muttered under his breath, eyeing the chest with a renewed interest.

Glendale knelt down, opened the chest, and began pulling out a collection of faded letters, carefully folded uniforms, and other relics of the past. "These belonged to Marros—my husband," she said quietly, holding up a worn military uniform. "He fought in the Thorrin War too."

Razma, still reeling from everything he'd just learned, watched in silence as Glendale sorted through the items. She pulled out old letters and handed them to him, her eyes soft with the pain of remembrance. "He wrote these during the war. Maybe they'll help you understand."

Razma took the letters, his hands trembling slightly as he unfolded the first one. The paper was fragile, crinkling softly under his touch, and the ink was faded, but the words were still legible. He hesitated for a moment, steeling himself before his eyes began to scan the worn page.

"My Dearest Liliah," the letter began in shaky handwriting. *"The fighting grows fiercer with each passing day. I hardly recognize the men I once fought alongside. Belazar is different now. They call him The Sliverfang, and there's no mercy left in his eyes. He fights like a beast, like something far more dangerous than any man. I don't know how much longer I can follow him—how much longer I can stand by as we become something we were never meant to be."*

Razma's breath caught as his father's name leaped from the page. *Belazar…* The man who had raised him with steady hands and gentle words had been feared, not only by his enemies but by his comrades. He kept reading, the words of the letter wrapping around him like a cold wind.

"Even Warden and Dalmon, men of strength and power, are uneasy around him. Warden, who has faced death more times than any man should, watches Belazar like a predator, waiting for the moment he'll strike. And Dalmon—gods, even a Slivdhe fears him now. Dalmon once respected Belazar, but now his sister, who once followed him, cowers in his presence."

Razma blinked, confusion swirling in his mind. Dalmon… a Slivdhe? He had never known that about Dalmon—how could he have missed it? He had always assumed Dalmon was human, just like him. But a Slivdhe? His shock mingled with disbelief as he looked up from the letter, trying to make sense of it all.

He stared at the page again, trying to absorb the information. His father, *The Sliverfang*, had been feared by everyone around him—even Warden. And Dalmon, someone Razma had always thought of as a mere shopkeeper, was a Slivdhe—a being of elegance and magic.

"Tomorrow, we march to the keep. Tor'valis says we fight the Bazel forces there, but the place reeks of something far worse. It feels as though the darkness has seeped into the very stones of the keep. I fear it, Liliah. I fear what will happen there. Belazar—no, The Sliverfang—says he will lead us, but I fear him more than I fear the enemy. I fear that, in the heat of battle, he will turn on us. I've seen it in his eyes, the hunger for blood that can't be sated. I pray to the gods that we make it through this night."

Glendale shot him another glare. "Warden, will you sit down already? You're making me dizzy. And what are you waiting for? Sit down!"

Warden gave her a weak smile but remained standing, his eyes still flicking toward the door.

Glendale's frustration mounted. "You keep looking at that door as if something's about to happen," she muttered.

As he lowered the letter, Warden's pacing resumed, the rhythmic sound of his boots against the floor echoing through the room. Each step grated on Razma's fraying nerves, as if Warden's restlessness mirrored his own turmoil.

Warden's eyes flicked toward the door every few seconds, his movements sharp and agitated. He was like a caged animal, unable to settle, waiting for something to happen.

Razma's fingers tightened on the letter as he reread those words. His father wasn't just a soldier —he had become something far more terrifying. And Dalmon, someone Razma had trusted for years, had been part of it all, even if he feared what Belazar had become. Anger flared in his chest. How had they all kept this from him? His father, Dalmon—even Mrs. Glendale. They had all known, and yet no one had told him. How had he been kept in the dark for so long? How could they have lied by omission, pretending he didn't deserve the truth?

Mrs. Glendale, sensing his growing frustration, sighed softly as she set down an old document. "Razma, we wanted to tell you, but the past... it's complicated. It hurts." Her voice was low, weary. "Your father and I have a history. And *Sliverfang*... that's a dark part of it. People think of him as a hero, but it's so much more complicated than that. It's not a simple story to tell."

As Glendale spoke, Warden's pacing slowed. His eyes flicked to the chest with a dark curiosity. "Hmm," he muttered, catching sight of something within. Leaning forward, he pulled out an old journal, its cover worn and tattered. As he flipped through it, he quickly realized it was a copy, with several pages torn or missing.

He glanced at Glendale, who was still showing Razma old documents, and slipped the journal into his coat without a word. No one noticed as he continued pacing, though now with a quiet sense of purpose.

Glendale, who had been watching Razma carefully, finally had enough. "Warden," she said, her voice cutting through the tension, "sit down before you wear a hole in my floor."

Warden didn't respond, his pacing growing more frantic. He rubbed a hand over his face, clearly torn between the conversation at hand and whatever thoughts gnawed at him. His fingers brushed against the journal he'd pocketed earlier, but he didn't draw attention to it.

"Warden!" Glendale snapped, her eyes narrowing. "Why do you keep looking at the door? You're making everyone nervous."

Warden gave her a tight-lipped smile but remained silent, his eyes dark with unspoken thoughts. His pacing didn't stop, and every time he circled the room, his gaze would flick to the door, as if expecting something—or someone.

A knock echoed through the quiet room, pulling Razma from his thoughts, and immediately, the air thickened with tension.

Lilah's instincts kicked in as she rose, hand drifting to her dagger. She crossed to the door cautiously, her heartbeat drumming in her ears. When she opened it, the familiar figure of Vil'elm stood before her, silhouetted in moonlight with blood splattered across his clothes.

"Vil'elm?" Her voice was laced with confusion and alarm. "What are you doing here... and is that blood?"

He offered a cold, unsettling smile. "Yes," he replied smoothly, as though it were a trivial detail. "I had a run-in with an old friend. But I come with news, Lilah—news I thought you'd want to hear." He stepped inside, his gaze briefly flicking to Warden, who waited with a steely, expectant calm.

Warden's hand hovered near his weapon, his eyes never leaving Vil'elm. "Finally," he murmured with a dark satisfaction, "it was only a matter of time."

Razma, oblivious to the sudden shift in atmosphere, brightened at the sight of Vil'elm. "Vil'elm!" he called, relief flooding his face. "Did you know my father was the Sliverfang?" He took a step toward the storyteller, the admiration and excitement clear in his gaze.

Vil'elm chuckled, his voice carrying a false warmth that masked something sinister. "Yes, I did, kiddo. I could tell you many stories about your father. Come with me, and I'll tell you all about it."

But as Razma moved forward, Lilah's instincts screamed. She recognized the look exchanged between Vil'elm and Warden, a silent, shared understanding. Her hand tightened on her dagger. "Razma, stay where you are," she commanded, her tone sharp.

Razma stopped, confusion and hurt crossing his face. "What? Why?"

Lilah's gaze stayed on Vil'elm, disbelief and betrayal evident in her eyes. This was a man she had trusted, a friend with whom she had shared countless memories, meals, and stories. He had even once hinted at loving her, despite her devotion to her late husband. She took a steadying breath, her voice a painful blend of anger and sorrow. "Why, Vil'elm? After all these years—after all those memories—why betray me now?"

Vil'elm's smile vanished, replaced by an expression devoid of any warmth. His eyes narrowed, and his voice dropped to a chilling monotone. "The journal, Lilah. That's all this was ever about."

Warden's grin turned cruel as he flipped through the pages of the old journal in his hand. "What, this?" he sneered. "You thought it was just nonsense from your husband's work?" He laughed, low and mocking. "It's a cipher, Lilah. I've watched Dalmon and Belazar for years, waiting for them to lead me to it—and all this time, you had it right here."

The realization struck Lilah like a blow. Her heart raced, fury rising as she gripped her dagger. Every word, every act of friendship from Vil'elm had been nothing but a lie, a careful manipulation.

Razma, still clutching the letter in his hands, felt the weight of betrayal bearing down on him. The stories Vil'elm had told, the admiration he had instilled—they all unraveled, leaving him feeling exposed and disoriented.

The warmth drained from Vil'elm's face entirely, leaving only a chilling indifference as he turned back to Lilah. "It didn't have to be this way," he said softly, the hint of regret in his voice twisted and false. He looked to Warden, giving a curt nod. "Get the boy… and kill her."

The words hit Razma like a punch, his eyes widening in horror as he glanced between the two men, disbelief etching into his young face. "What…?" he stammered, his heart pounding with confusion and terror. "What's going on?"

Lilah watched Razma's face crumple in shock and grief. She didn't have the time to explain, nor could she soothe him now. With fierce determination, she drew her dagger, her eyes blazing as she faced Vil'elm. "Razma, run!" she shouted, her voice filled with raw desperation. Without a second thought, she lunged at Vil'elm, every ounce of her strength channeled into the strike.

Vil'elm's smirk returned as he lifted his hand, sending a wave of dark energy that slammed into her, throwing her backward. "Really, Lilah?" he mocked, his tone dripping with scorn. "You're as predictable as ever."

Warden laughed, his voice cold and ruthless. "You think you can stand against us?" He drew his sword, the firelight glinting off its edge. "You couldn't stop us then, and you won't now."

Razma's heart shattered as he watched the people he had trusted reveal themselves as enemies. His hands shook, and the letters he held slipped from his grip, scattering across the floor.

"Why?" he whispered, his voice thick with betrayal.

But Lilah didn't let her pain stop her. She staggered to her feet, her voice fierce and unwavering. "Razma, run!" she yelled, her gaze fixed on his. She planted her hands on the ground, sending a powerful shockwave through the room, momentarily forcing Vil'elm and Warden back.

Warden stepped forward, his smile widening with malicious delight. "Listen to her, Razma," he sneered. "Run. It'll be the last advice she gives you."

The urgency of Lilah's voice struck something deep within Razma, and before he knew it, he was sprinting for the door, his heart pounding and his breath ragged. Behind him, the last sounds he heard were the clashing of magic and steel and Lilah's fierce, defiant cry echoing in the darkness.

Outside, Razma tore through the deserted streets, the cool night air sharp against his face. Every familiar landmark now seemed twisted, distorted by the lies that had been laid bare. His world was shattered, but he didn't stop—he couldn't. He had to escape, to survive.

As he fled, Warden stepped into the doorway, his eyes narrowing as he watched Razma disappear into the distance. His smile grew even darker as he turned to Vil'elm. "Shall we catch up to the boy?"

Vil'elm laughed, a gleam of satisfaction in his eyes. "Yes, she'll want him."

Warden's laughter followed him into the night as he broke into a run, his footsteps relentless as he pursued the fleeing Razma.

Inside the dimly lit room, Lilah Glendale braced herself, her stance firm as she faced Vil'elm, who now wore an expression twisted by malice. They circled each other, his once-familiar face now a cruel mask, the friend she had trusted for years transformed into a stranger wielding dark power.

"Why are you working with Thorn?" Lilah demanded, her voice sharp and unyielding. She could feel his magic pressing against her like a suffocating fog, seeping into the air around them. "What could she possibly offer you?"

Vil'elm's smirk deepened, his eyes cold and calculating. "Thorn?" he laughed darkly, as if she'd spoken nonsense. "Thorn is a pawn in a far greater game, Lilah. You still don't see it, do you?"

Lilah's heart pounded, her fingers curling tightly around her dagger. Magic pulsed through her veins, ready to strike, but something about the subtle menace in Vil'elm's voice kept her on edge. "If not Thorn," she said, her voice tense with disbelief and anger, "then who? Who do you serve?"

Vil'elm took a slow, menacing step forward, his voice lowering to a dangerous whisper. "If only you knew, Lilah. If only you had any idea." His laugh echoed through the room, chilling her to the core.

The realization hit her like a wave of ice, betrayal slicing through her. This was the man she had shared countless nights with, laughing, telling stories, forging a bond she'd thought unbreakable. She held his gaze, her heart cracking as she demanded, "Why, Vil'elm? After everything—after all those years of friendship and trust—why betray me now?"

His smirk twisted into something cruel. "Friendship?" he scoffed, his voice dripping with disdain. "You were nothing more than a stepping stone—a means to an end. Your husband, your precious loyalty to his memory—blinded you to the truth unraveling around you." His magic coiled around him like a living shadow. "While you clung to your grief, I watched, I waited, and now, the Lost Queen will rise… because of me."

Lilah's face twisted with shock and anger. Forcing herself to steady, she met his gaze, her voice defiant. "Who is this queen?" she spat, daring him to answer. "Whose journal is that? What could be worth tearing everything apart for?"

Vil'elm's eyes flashed with impatience, his hand tightening around the journal he had stolen from her husband's belongings. "The journal, Lilah, holds knowledge—power beyond anything you could comprehend. Your husband was nothing more than a tool, just like you, recording secrets he never understood. And with this cipher," he held the journal up like a trophy, "the Lost Queen will reclaim her throne."

Her blood turned to ice. She had kept that journal close, believing it was just a collection of old notes. Now, the terrible realization of its importance dawned on her. Vil'elm noticed the horror in her eyes and sneered.

"Thorn is nothing compared to her," he said with a cold, condescending tone. "This queen isn't some forgotten relic, Lilah. She is power. She is permanence."

Without warning, he thrust his hand forward, and dark tendrils of magic erupted from his fingertips, rushing toward her like a storm of shadows. Lilah moved instinctively, raising her dagger and murmuring an incantation, summoning a shield of light that flared to life between them. The tendrils struck her shield, crackling and hissing as they tried to breach her defenses.

"Still fighting?" Vil'elm laughed, his voice mocking, as he pressed harder, his magic pouring down on her barrier like a wave threatening to drown her. "You always did cling to hopeless causes."

Lilah's arms shook as she pushed back against his dark energy, her shield straining under the relentless pressure. Gritting her teeth, she channeled every bit of strength she had left into her defenses. "I'll fight until there's nothing left," she snarled, her eyes blazing with defiance. "I'd rather die than see you twist everything we built."

Vil'elm's mocking expression faded, his gaze hardening as he summoned more magic, his next attack striking with brutal force. Lilah felt the shield tremble, cracks splintering through the barrier like glass under strain. Before she could brace herself, a final surge shattered it entirely, and the impact sent her crashing backward into the wall.

She hit the ground with a pained gasp, her body aching as she struggled to pull herself up. Her vision swam, and she clutched at her side, her fingers brushing against the hilt of her dagger— a small comfort amid the chaos.

But Vil'elm was already advancing, his eyes gleaming with ruthless intent. He raised his hand, and dark tendrils of magic coiled around her throat, lifting her off the ground as they burned into her skin. Her fingers clawed at the invisible bonds, gasping for air, her vision dimming with each passing second.

"Who is she?" she managed to choke out, her voice barely audible as her strength waned. "Why… are you doing this?"

Vil'elm leaned in close, his gaze cold and unfeeling, his breath brushing against her cheek. "The Lost Queen does not suffer rivals," he hissed, his tone low and menacing. "You, Dalmon, Belazar—all pawns." He tightened his grip, his voice dropping to a chilling whisper. "Pawns fall, bishops fall, even kings… but queens… queens never die."

With a final twist of his hand, the tendrils tightened, and Lilah's body went limp, her hand falling away from the dagger as her eyes lost their light. Her body slumped to the floor, a final shudder passing through her as the room settled into silence.

Vil'elm stood over her, savoring the victory, his gaze dark with satisfaction. Taking a deep breath, he whispered, as though to the shadows themselves, "Long live the Lost Queen."

Chapter 31: The Weight Lifted

769, 10th Day Of The Ninth Moon

Today, the twins took their first steps. I should have been filled with pride, joy swelling in my chest. Instead, there was only the sharp ache of absence.

They toddled forward, clumsy and wide-eyed, their laughter echoing through the room. But as they stumbled, each tiny footfall a triumph, it struck me—these steps, their first... taken in worlds so divided.

If only they could walk on a path that's whole, with no rifts or chasms between lands, and without the weight of the worlds pressing upon them. But that is not our fate. So, I watch them and I hope, perhaps foolishly, that in their lifetime, the ground will be steady beneath their feet.

✳✳✳

Ky'len fell in step alongside Dalmon, his thoughts churning so heavily he barely registered the winding paths beneath his feet. Belazar and A'nara led the way, conversing in the gentle, flowing cadence of Slivdhe, their words colored by shared concerns. By keeping pace with Dalmon on one side of Belazar, Ky'len effectively left the two women—A'nara and Yvonne—on the far side, a subtle arrangement he seemed intent on maintaining.

They walked in a loose line through the ruin-strewn outskirts of Sergora, each footstep echoing with the memory of fires and screams. Yvonne's glance flicked briefly in Ky'len's direction, but the moment he felt her eyes, he quickened his pace, refusing to meet her gaze.

Dalmon broke the hush with a musing thought. "Lilah Glendale's a sharp one," he said. "If anyone can help us figure out our next move, it's her."

Belazar gave a small nod, though his stare remained distant. "I hope so… for all our sakes."

Ky'len said nothing. He couldn't banish the image of Sergora aflame from his mind, and the unspoken weight of their mission pressed heavily on his chest. They needed more than allies, more than goodwill—they needed to end the darkness at its root.

And so they pressed on, a quiet knot of travelers bound by shared purpose, the soft language of Slivdhe weaving through the air as they set their sights on Grey Leaf Village—and the answers Lilah Glendale might yet provide.

Dalmon's gaze shifted to the distant mountains, where Halzor's Keep lay hidden among the shadows. His brow furrowed, and he murmured in Slivdhe, his words carrying a weight that made the air around them feel heavy. "Mara'tor fin Halzor Falir?" he asked quietly, his tone laced with unease. *"Shall we face Halzor's Keep?"* The question hovered, evoking memories of battles, foes conquered, and old dangers now perhaps rising again. The others fell silent, each recognizing the danger and the answers they hoped—and feared—awaited at the Keep.

Belazar's expression tightened as he shook his head, his voice somber. "Valdis en falor sath, araedr fin var Halzor Falir. Ienor veron'na. Ethis harl, ser'dan vor sathir." *"Strength of the heart must be great for the Keep of Halzor. It will take more than memory—it demands all we are."*

Ky'len followed the conversation as best as he could, recognizing only the name Halzor's Keep. The ominous tone of Belazar's voice was unmistakable, a testament to the danger ahead.

A'nara, her tone steady though tinged with concern, spoke in Slivdhe, "Halzor Falir vel'tir vorn valdis. Vor den faris en'thal, mara yel'thir krados ni'thal. Tal Slivar Fang men'tir hin thalor?" *"The Keep awaits strength. Will our path endure, or will the Sliverfang overcome?"*

Belazar's shoulders tensed at her words, replying in a voice shadowed with quiet dread. "Mutt, Thorn, Warden… en'thal Slivar Fang. Fin varan tel'tir. Mara vor hin'thar var'tor? Mara vor tel'vir ni'rath vor hin—ni'thal en aliir?" *"Mutt, Thorn, Warden… and the Sliverfang. They test us all. Can we stand against it? Or will it consume us?"*

A'nara met his gaze, her tone firm yet soft, grounding him. "Falir voth onra; voth fin'thal or'hira. Mara'tor fin ther'thal. Vor ni en'tor talir." *"The heart binds, and we are stronger together. Let us not fear, but press on."*

Dalmon nodded solemnly, his gaze shifting between Belazar and the others. "Thalor vor'ri, Belazar. Mara'voran en'thor, vor'voth vor'athar, maran fal'vor or'hara, veth en'thar vor'ri." *"Strength will guide us, Belazar. We are each other's anchor in the darkness, and that will save us."*

Their exchange, steeped in the Slivdhe language's poetic cadence, resonated with unspoken fears and promises. Ky'len observed, feeling the gravity of their words even without fully understanding. Yet, he recognized they were wrestling not just with strategy but with past wounds, lingering doubts, and the weight of choices yet to come.

Dalmon, his voice gentle but filled with conviction, looked directly at Belazar and said, "Falir ver'thal hin ther, Belazar." *"Let strength be your guide, Belazar."* He paused, his gaze steady. "Razma vel'thal, vor mara'tor hin en'thal. Vor ni mara or'thal mara vor ri." *"Razma's safety lies with us all. We must face this together, side by side."*

Belazar nodded, his gaze softening with a rare vulnerability. "Ienor veron'na… Fin mara'varan," he admitted quietly. *"We are not alone… strength carries us."* His tone dropped as he continued, "Vor ni en'thal, mara'thal Slivar Fang… mara ni tel'vir en'thal. Mara vor'tor en krados fin tharvor." *"We stand united, against the Sliverfang… against darkness. We will endure and remember our promise."*

Sensing the depth of his struggle, A'nara stepped closer, her voice gentle yet resolute. She stood on her toes, placing a soft kiss on his cheek, entwining her arm with his as a gesture of solidarity. "Vor mara'tor hin," she said softly, her conviction unwavering. *"We will walk together."* She gave Ky'len a knowing smile and added in Slivdhe, "Vor ni'thal en'tor talor'ri. Dalmon, Yvonne, mara fin'thal vor'ri… ara vor hin Ky'len var'thal." *"Ky'len will aid us in finding Razma and in the fight ahead."*

Realizing his name was mentioned, Ky'len looked at her in confusion. A'nara chuckled softly, switching to Common. "Sorry, Ky'len. I said that you'll help us find Razma and fight with us."

The mention caught Ky'len by surprise, but he nodded, meeting her gaze with determination. "I'll fight too," he replied steadily. "We'll bring him back."

As they pressed forward on the path toward Lilah Glendale's home, Dalmon noticed Ky'len's struggle to follow their Slivdhe conversation. With a glance at A'nara and Belazar, he cleared his throat and addressed Ky'len in Common, his voice carrying a soft lilt. "Forgive us, Ky'len," he said. "We'll speak in Common, so you're not left out. Slivdhe takes time to learn, and it's best taught in small steps."

Ky'len offered a small, grateful smile. "Thanks. I'm trying to pick up some words, but it's… not easy."

A'nara chuckled warmly. "Slivdhe isn't the easiest language, but we can teach you a few phrases as we go. It might be useful, especially if you meet more of our people."

Belazar gave Ky'len a steady look. "Let's start with something meaningful. 'Valdis' means strength, heart, and spirit—it's a word we value greatly."

Ky'len nodded, repeating the word to himself. "Valdis. Got it."

A'nara grinned, a hint of mischief in her eyes. "Another you might like, especially in battle, is 'ther'thal,' which means 'fight together.'"

Ky'len tried the phrase, stumbling slightly, "Ther'thal."

Dalmon chuckled. "Close enough. You'll get the hang of it."

Belazar, his gaze thoughtful, added, "When you greet someone, say 'velin.' It's our way of saying 'hello' or 'greetings.'"

Ky'len repeated it, feeling a little more confident. "Velin."

A'nara's expression softened as she added, "And if you want to say 'I trust you,' it's 'lenar fin'theran.' Trust is essential to us."

Ky'len looked at her thoughtfully and then repeated the phrase carefully, "lenar fin'theran."

"Perfect," A'nara praised, nudging him playfully. "You're learning fast."

Belazar's voice, though quiet, held a reassuring warmth. "These words will serve you well, Ky'len. We'll teach you more as we go."

Ky'len nodded, feeling a deeper sense of connection to the group. Though he didn't yet speak Slivdhe fluently, their efforts to include him resonated. The path ahead was uncertain, but with each word he learned, he felt a little more prepared for what lay ahead.

The four of them walked side by side, laughter bubbling up as they shared stories from days past. Yvonne threw her head back, her bright laughter filling the air as Dalmon recounted a tale of narrowly avoiding a disastrous encounter with a wayward spell. "Och, Dalmon, ye didn't!" she exclaimed, her accent slipping into a little that hinted at her childhood, eyes gleaming with mirth.

"Believe me," Dalmon said with a hearty laugh, "I was nearly vor'ri—turned into a heap of ash!" He clapped his palms together for emphasis. Nearby, A'nara gave him a playful nudge, though a smile lit her face.

"You've always had a taste for danger," she teased, an affectionate edge to her voice, "but I swear Belazar here outdoes you sometimes."

Belazar raised an eyebrow, a hint of mischief playing at his lips. "What can I say?" he replied, dropping into a fluid Slivdhe phrase, "Ther'thal with a strong spirit."

Yvonne, standing close by, leaned in to gently bump her shoulder against Belazar's. "More like pulling us all headfirst into trouble," she teased, laughter sparkling in her eyes. A low chuckle rumbled in Belazar's chest, the sound mingling with the warmth of the campfire as though this small circle of friends and family were a world unto itself.

Moments later, as the reminiscing deepened, Yvonne aimed an impish grin at Dalmon. "I'm still not over that time you tried befriending a wild bear—only to end up fin ther'thal, flat on your back!"

Dalmon threw up his hands in mock surrender, the grin never leaving his face. "I was young," he admitted. "And a little too eager to prove myself. Next thing I knew, that bear had me pinned —didn't even see it coming."

A'nara shook her head, exchanging an exasperated-yet-fond glance with Dalmon. Their bond showed in the way she managed to both roll her eyes at him and smile like no one else in the world could. A comfortable hush settled, punctuated by the crackle of the fire and the lingering echoes of laughter, as the four of them savored a moment of rare peace on the long road ahead.

A'nara chuckled, her voice softening. "Ah, but some things never change, *mara'varan*," she said, slipping a hand through Belazar's arm. She gave him a fond smile, her eyes warm with an affectionate glow that only time and shared history could bring. "Like Belazar's stubborn streak. Remember that siege in Tantora?" she asked, eyes twinkling as she looked to the others.

"Oh, aye," Belazar chuckled, nodding. "Nearly cost me a *falor* or two." He lifted a hand to tap his forehead where an old scar traced down, a testament to one of many battles fought side by side.

They shared a hearty laugh, each word of Slivdhe slipping easily into their Common, as though each language carried its own memories and moments. Their laughter felt like an embrace, pulling them closer and offering comfort, even here on this uncertain road.

As they walked, Ky'len lingered behind, each laugh and shared memory driving a wedge deeper between him and the others. Their camaraderie felt like a taunt, emphasizing the isolation that seemed to cling to him, fueled by memories he couldn't outrun. His fists clenched, nails biting into his palms as resentment simmered, each step toward Bazel feeling heavier, hotter.

Up ahead, Yvonne's laughter trailed off when she glanced back and noticed his tense posture, the anger hardening his face. Her smile faded as she slowed, drifting back to match his pace. She reached out, placing a light hand on his shoulder. "Ky'len," she began, her voice soft, concerned. "What's on your mind?"

Ky'len shrugged her hand off, his voice sharp. "What's the point, Yvonne?" he snapped. "How are we supposed to stand a chance against her? She has beasts—monsters that can tear through us without a thought. And you all talk of trust, unity?" He laughed bitterly, the sound hollow. "It's hopeless. None of that will stop her."

Yvonne's gaze softened, her tone steady as she tried to soothe him. "I know it feels impossible, Ky'len. Anger... it can feel overwhelming, but it doesn't have to define you."

"Do you?" he interrupted, his voice dropping as the hurt spilled over. "You knew what he was like—what my father did. I watched him hurt her, Yvonne. My mother couldn't take it, and she left. And then you—you left too. And I was left to face him alone." His voice cracked, years of pent-up pain rising to the surface.

Yvonne's face fell, guilt clouding her expression. She looked away, voice trembling. "I'm so sorry, Ky'len," she whispered. "I was fifteen. My mother had just died, and I was... I couldn't stay."

Ky'len didn't let her finish. Pulling up his sleeve, he revealed faded scars on his forearm, his voice raw. "This is what I was left with," he said. "When you left, he didn't hold back anymore. You were all I had." Vulnerability cut through his voice, yet his expression was steeled, forged by years of buried pain.

A tear slipped down Yvonne's cheek as she met his gaze. "I failed you, Ky'len. I didn't know. I'm... I'm sorry."

Ky'len turned without another word, breaking away from the group as he stormed off, leaving her standing alone, her face etched with remorse. As Yvonne tried to compose herself, wiping her face, she rejoined the others with a forced smile. But Dalmon noticed, his brow furrowing as he glanced at Ky'len's retreating figure, then back at Yvonne's stricken expression.

Without hesitation, he strode up to Ky'len, grabbing his shoulder. "What did you say to her? Why is Yvonne crying?" he demanded.

Ky'len shook him off, his eyes blazing. "Ask her yourself! Ask her why I had to grow up alone with him!" His voice cracked with anger, words thick with pain.

Yvonne's head bowed, fresh tears slipping down her cheeks, and A'nara slipped a comforting arm around her, quietly urging Belazar, "You need to talk to him."

Meanwhile, Dalmon's face had hardened, his voice stern as he faced Ky'len. "Go apologize to her. Now."

Ky'len's own fury ignited as he shoved Dalmon back, fire in his eyes. "I'm not a boy! I had to become a man because of what she left me with!"

Dalmon, taken aback, recovered quickly and pushed him again, his tone cold. "Respect your elders, Ky'len."

Before things could escalate, Belazar stepped between them, his tone calm but firm. "Dalmon, cool off. I'll handle this."

With one last glare, Dalmon turned back to the others, muttering under his breath as he returned to Yvonne and A'nara. Belazar turned to Ky'len, meeting his gaze with an unflinching expression. "Let's talk, kid."

Ky'len scowled, his breathing ragged from his frustration. "What do you want, Belazar?"

Belazar's voice was steady, unshaken by Ky'len's fury. "I'm here to help. You've got everyone worked up. Dalmon might not have held back if I hadn't stepped in."

"Let him hit me," Ky'len spat bitterly, turning as if to follow Dalmon, but Belazar's hand shot out, gripping his shoulder with a quiet warning.

"You've got spirit, kid. But Dalmon's tougher than you know. And so am I," Belazar said, his voice low.

Ky'len stopped, his shoulders rigid as he choked out, "My father… he beat me after she left."

Belazar's brow furrowed in confusion. "Your father? I knew he was… stern, but I didn't know—"

Ky'len's voice quivered with old hurt. "No one knew. No one was there. My mother left, and Yvonne… she left too."

Realization dawned on Belazar's face as he pieced it together. "Yvonne… she was your father's handmaiden, wasn't she?"

Ky'len's expression was bitter. "Yeah, until she left me to his anger."

Belazar took a deep breath, his voice gentle but firm. "I know she let you down, Ky'len. She was young, too—she'd lost her mother, never knew her father… and she left, like you said. But she's here now, trying to make things right."

Ky'len's voice was a mix of rage and desperation. "I was five, Belazar! She should have stayed! We could have faced him together!"

Belazar's gaze remained steady. "You're carrying a lot of anger, Ky'len. But I don't think it's just for her. I think some of it's for yourself. You feel like you're becoming him, don't you?"

Ky'len's voice cracked, his hands clenching as he fought back tears. "What if I am? What if I turn into him? I want this anger out!" He pounded his fists against Belazar's chest, sinking to his knees as the weight of his emotions overtook him.

Belazar crouched beside Ky'len, his hand firm on the young man's shoulder, grounding him with a quiet but unshakable support. The air between them thickened, carrying the weight of words unspoken, as if the world itself paused to listen.

"Ky'len," Belazar began, his voice soft, carrying a rare gentleness that seemed to cut through Ky'len's anger. "You know the legend of the Sliverfang, right? But the truth is darker than any story you've heard."

Ky'len's scoff held a bitter edge, though curiosity softened his expression. "I know the tales. Everyone does—the monster who tore down armies, the unstoppable warrior."

Belazar's gaze darkened, shadows flickering in his eyes. "The tales are what people chose to remember. But no one ever talks about the cost, the destruction, or the lives that anger consumed. I became a danger to everyone I cared about… and I lost one of my best friends because of it."

Ky'len blinked, the weight of Belazar's words slowly sinking in. He'd never seen Belazar this vulnerable, and it stirred something deep inside him. "You… killed him?"

Belazar nodded, his expression clouded with old, haunting memories. "It sent me into a rage I couldn't escape from. Dalmon barely pulled me out of it, and I nearly tore apart everything that mattered to me."

Ky'len's throat tightened at the revelation, but Belazar continued. "It was after one of the bloodiest battles of the war," he said, his voice low and laced with pain. "I was lost in the aftermath, in the madness that followed the rage. My hands were stained, my mind frayed. And then I stumbled upon a creek at the edge of a shattered village."

The image formed vividly in Ky'len's mind as Belazar spoke. "There was smoke in the air, the kind that clings to your throat and makes breathing hard. Bodies lay scattered, some in pieces, remnants of lives torn apart. And there, half-hidden in the reeds by the water's edge, was a small bundle." Belazar's voice grew quieter, almost reverent. "At first, I thought it was debris—a scrap of fabric caught in the current. But then it moved. I saw tiny hands, clutching at nothing, fighting the cold."

Belazar's eyes glistened with the memory. "I waded into that freezing water, pulled him from the mud. He was barely alive, blue from the chill, his cries too weak to echo. But he was there, and when he opened his eyes, it was like seeing light for the first time in days."

Ky'len listened, his expression softening as he pictured the fierce warrior cradling a baby amidst the wreckage, a moment of fragile hope in a scene of devastation.

"Razma was just a baby," Belazar continued, his voice heavy with emotion. "But in that moment, he became my reason to fight differently. To control the beast inside me, to protect rather than destroy. I couldn't save his family, couldn't change what I'd done, but I could make sure he had a chance. That's why I raised him as my own, why I became the man he needed, not the monster I feared."

A flicker of realization crossed Ky'len's face. "Wait… you're not Razma's real father?"

Belazar's expression softened as he nodded, glancing into the distance as though recalling faraway memories. "No, I'm not. I told him his mother died in childbirth. It's a lie I've carried to protect him, and I'd ask you never to speak of it to him. He doesn't need to know."

Ky'len stared at him, the layers of Belazar's hidden past unfurling before him, mingling with his own pain. "You… lied to him, kept that secret, all because of… this rage?"

Belazar's gaze remained steady, his voice both weary and resolute. "It was my way of shielding him from what I'd become. He gave me purpose, something to fight for that wasn't just revenge or rage. I learned, Ky'len, that anger can't simply disappear. It has to be tamed, given something to hold onto." His hand on Ky'len's shoulder tightened. "Dalmon helped more than I can say. He's better at raising kids than I ever will be, even with his past. He knows what a father needs to be—that's all I'll say on that."

Ky'len looked at him thoughtfully before speaking, "You seem like a good father, Belazar. Razma's a good kid. A bit cocky, sure—taking on a noble and all that—but he's solid."

Belazar chuckled, a rare warmth lighting up his eyes. "He gets that from Dalmon," he said with a smirk, the corner of his mouth twitching up in amusement.

Ky'len laughed, casting a teasing glance at Dalmon. "Oh, sure, not from you, Belazar? Definitely all Dalmon's influence, right?"

Dalmon, who had been listening from a short distance away, raised an eyebrow, crossing his arms with mock indignation. "Oi, leave me out of it, lad," he called, but a grin tugged at his lips.

The tension between them eased into laughter, lifting some of the shadows they carried. For a brief moment, their burdens felt a little lighter, and the path ahead seemed less daunting.

Ky'len looked down, his hands loosening as he absorbed Belazar's words. "It feels impossible, though. It's always… there."

Belazar's tone grew firmer, a quiet strength in his words. "It'll always be there. But you have us —Dalmon, A'nara, Yvonne. People who will stand by you when that anger feels like it's going to swallow you whole."

Ky'len looked up, meeting Belazar's gaze, a glimmer of hope breaking through the storm inside him. "Thank you," he whispered, his voice barely audible.

Belazar smiled, helping him up. "One day, you'll look back on this moment and realize just how strong you are."

Together, they walked back toward the others. As they approached, Yvonne's tearful eyes met Ky'len's, a shared understanding passing between them without words. For the first time, he felt a little less alone, and with Belazar's guidance, he was finally beginning to see a way forward.

Yvonne's gaze found Ky'len immediately, her green eyes shimmering with understanding. Without a word, he approached her, the turmoil of their recent conflict still fresh, but something new driving him forward. He took a steadying breath, and in Slivdhe, the words fell, resonant and true.

"I'm sorry, Yvonne… for the anger, for the way I acted. You deserved better."

Her expression softened, a smile playing at her lips as she clasped his arm warmly. "Thank you, Ky'len. I know it wasn't easy for you." She squeezed his arm, melting the final shards of his bitterness. Then, her eyes sparkled with a touch of amusement. "You know, I'm not cleaning up after your mess anymore—that's on you now, young man."

A small laugh escaped him, easing the tension as he nodded. "I suppose I deserve that."

Dalmon gave him an approving nod, his usually guarded expression softening. A'nara offered a slight smile, one of acceptance that spoke to her own silent battles. Their support stitched together the broken pieces Ky'len had carried alone for so long.

Belazar clapped him on the shoulder, his voice low but filled with pride. "This is where it begins, Ky'len. Lean on them. Lean on us."

Ky'len nodded, finally letting himself feel the warmth of their presence, the power of not having to carry his burdens alone. As the group set off together, he knew that whatever lay ahead, he wouldn't be facing it on his own.

Chapter 32: Gardens and Journels

788, 18th Day Of The Second moon

_ *"The winds grow restless, whispering of an old power stirring, and the earth feels heavier underfoot. The tribes speak of visions, shadows rising from beneath, and roots binding stone with ancient wrath. There is talk of a queen—a specter some have claimed to see, her form twisted yet fierce, eyes as black as night. Many dismiss these tales as ghostly murmurs, but I feel the weight of something more.*

I have sealed the journal's cipher with a ward of blood, hoping it binds what must stay hidden. If she rises, may the ones who bear our blood remember the pact we forged in the fires of old, for darkness is clever, and if left unguarded, it consumes."

Razma's legs carried him through the doorway and into the night, his breath coming in ragged bursts as the clash of magic and steel echoed behind him. He didn't dare look back; the weight of betrayal, heavy as lead, drove him forward. Every instinct screamed one thing: survive.

Outside, Grey Leaf was a vision of destruction. Streets he knew as familiar and safe were warped, ripped apart by tendrils of thick roots and debris from splintered homes. The earth heaved beneath him, the buildings quaking as Warden's magic ripped through the town, tearing up gardens, walls, and fences with malicious ease. The terrified cries of villagers echoed around him, underscoring his own desperation as he sprinted through the chaos, ducking beneath shattered awnings and stumbling over loose stones.

Razma's lungs burned, his legs weakening with each frantic step, but he forced himself onward. He ducked into a narrow alley, hoping for shelter, his heart pounding like a war drum in his chest. Yet, as he rounded the corner, he stopped dead—a towering wall of twisted vines awaited him, each root coiling and shifting like a serpent. They seemed to pulse with life, moving almost as though they could sense his presence, as if mocking his every attempt to escape.

Trapped.

Warden's footsteps, calm and deliberate, echoed through the darkness. The faint crackle of branches and roots crept closer, each step marking the slow tightening of a noose around Razma. "You won't outrun me, boy," Warden called out, his voice tainted with a sick satisfaction. "You never could."

As Razma's legs carried him onward, the village of Grey Leaf unraveled around him, transformed from a quiet town into a nightmare of collapsing structures and splintering wood. The ground beneath him buckled, sending fresh waves of dirt and stone into the air, stinging his eyes and filling his mouth with grit. He stumbled, hands scraping against the jagged earth as he regained his footing, his mind racing with a single, primal command—survive.

The air was thick with the acrid scent of woodsmoke and earth as buildings collapsed in every direction. Roots, thick and serpentine, erupted from the ground, tearing through homes and sending walls crumbling down like children's toys. Screams pierced the air, desperate and raw, as families scrambled to escape the relentless force that Warden's magic wielded over the town.

He darted down an alley, narrowly avoiding a cascading rain of bricks as a shopfront caved in, the roof crashing to the ground in a cloud of dust and shattered timber. The walls around him trembled, seeming to pulse with Warden's sinister magic. Rubble lined his path, jagged and unforgiving, and every step became a frantic, uneven scramble to stay ahead of the destruction.

With a desperate gasp, Razma spotted a doorway barely visible beneath a blanket of shadows. He slipped inside, pressing himself flat against the cold stone wall, hoping—praying—that the darkness would shield him from Warden's wrath. His breaths came fast and shallow, his heart pounding as he tried to still himself in the silence.

Outside, Warden's footsteps drew closer, slow and deliberate. The building trembled with his every step, the roots around it creeping like snakes over its structure, their rough surfaces scratching against stone and wood. Razma tensed, his breath caught in his throat. Then came Warden's voice, dark and honeyed, almost a whisper but laced with cruelty. "Come out, come out, little mouse," he murmured, as if savoring every syllable.

The seconds stretched into an eternity, each heartbeat thunderous in Razma's ears. Then, with a deafening crash, Warden's roots tore through the walls. Everything shook as if seized by a violent storm, debris spraying in every direction. Razma ducked, covering his head as chunks of wood and stone rained down. A cloud of gritty dust filled his nose, making each breath burn.

He burst out the back of the building just as another wall collapsed, stumbling onto a narrow path. Up ahead, he glimpsed the dim outline of Jeff's house. Razma's mind screamed at him to keep going, but his limbs dragged with exhaustion, lungs aflame. He managed to sprint past Jeff's home—only to spot Warden looming behind him, the towering silhouette flickering with malicious glee.

With a languid wave, Warden summoned a swarm of roots that tore through Jeff's carefully tended garden, uprooting vegetables and splitting the small wooden fence like kindling. Hearing the commotion, Jeff appeared in the doorway, eyes widening at the devastation. A woman—a neighbor or friend—tried to dart forward, some wild instinct telling her to help, but Jeff caught her arm, pulling her back.

"Not now," he hissed quietly, shooting her a cautionary look. "I'll handle this."

The woman stifled a sob, torn between terror and concern for Razma, but Jeff held her in place, stepping out onto what remained of his porch. He let out an outraged huff, squaring his shoulders at Warden.

"Hey—hey now!" Jeff barked, waving his arms in protest. "I've spent years getting that garden just so, and you come along, tossing vines around like you're the grand wizard of weeds?" He pointed accusingly at Warden. "Look, I'm all for a green thumb, but maybe try re-landscaping somewhere else!"

Warden pivoted toward him with an irritable glare, the air turning oppressive. "You're interfering," he snapped, flicking his wrist again. More vines erupted, cracking the porch beneath Jeff's feet. The woman he'd held back gasped, nearly rushing forward, but Jeff shot out an arm to keep her behind him.

"Alright, I get it—you're big on botanical mayhem," Jeff said, raising his voice to be heard over the splintering wood. "But next time, do a fella a favor—send a memo first. I'd at least move my begonias!"

His flippant tone drew Warden's full attention; for a moment, the towering figure nearly forgot Razma's presence as he advanced on Jeff with a dangerous gleam in his eye. "You'd do well to hold your tongue," he warned, power radiating from his stance.

Jeff puffed out his chest, though the tremor in his voice betrayed his fear. "Never been good at that, sorry to disappoint. You see, I'm not partial to strangers wrecking my livelihood." He lifted his arms in a halfhearted shrug, stepping back just beyond the threshold. "But if it's that important to you, I'll let you do your root-and-ruin show without me getting in the way."

Behind him, the woman watched, hands trembling, as Jeff continued to distract Warden with his cheeky commentary. Freed from Warden's immediate focus, Razma seized his chance. Gritting his teeth, he broke into a run, ignoring the dull ache in his legs. Buildings lay fractured, beams and roofs collapsed, acrid smoke curling from the remains of what once was a peaceful village. Every second, he expected Warden's roots to burst forth and cut him off again.

Suddenly, the ominous echo of Warden's voice rolled through the night, low and venomous. "Come out now, boy, or I'll show you just how serious I can get."

Razma froze behind a crumbling wall, heart hammering. He pressed himself into the shadows as the quiet thickened around him, Warden's presence looming.

"So be it," came Warden's silken whisper, and the air seemed to shiver.

A moment later, a door creaked open, followed by a muffled scream—someone being dragged out into the street. Another voice, that of a frightened woman, rose in frantic protest. And then the trembling cries of children from inside.

"Mama!" The shrill call of the frightened youngsters cut Razma to the core.

Warden's chilling voice sliced through the darkness. "Come out, Razma, or I promise you—this will end poorly for them."

Razma clenched his teeth, hands flying to his ears as if to block out the horror. Each echoing sob stung like a blade. He couldn't stand it any longer. "No! Leave them alone!" he shouted, voice raw.

For a moment, silence reigned, cruel and suffocating. Then came a drawn-out sigh, filled with malevolent satisfaction. "Razma," Warden said softly, his tone almost affectionate, "you made me do this."

A sickening crack tore the air, thunderous in the hush. The children's sobs became the only sound, their ragged cries spiraling into Razma's soul, filling him with sick dread. He gasped, horror constricting his chest, the weight of his decision crushing him.

From Jeff's porch, where he still clutched the terrified woman's arm, Jeff's bravado melted into silent disbelief. And as Razma reeled, consumed by guilt, the world seemed to grind to a halt—proof that even all the sass and bravado in the world wasn't enough to stand against the darkness unleashed by Warden's power.

He stumbled backward, his legs weak beneath him, and took off again, determined to escape Warden's wrath before anyone else paid the price. His vision blurred, fear clouding his senses, but he forced himself to keep moving, stumbling over debris as he ran.

Turning a corner, he found himself trapped by another wall of roots, towering and impassable, cutting off his last route of escape. Every instinct screamed for him to flee, but he was surrounded, nowhere left to turn. The sound of Warden's slow, deliberate footsteps echoed down the path, each step heavy with purpose.

With one final burst of desperation, Razma darted down a narrow alley, his heart pounding as he rounded a corner—only to confront another wall of twisting vines. These were thicker, darker than before, writhing as though they possessed a malevolent will of their own. Every potential escape was blocked.

He was truly trapped.

The unhurried rhythm of Warden's footsteps echoed along the stone, growing louder with every step. "You won't outrun me, boy," Warden called, his voice gliding over the silent alley with dark confidence. "You never could."

Razma pressed his back to the wall, chest tightening, his eyes flicking from one impossible route to the next. But the vines had woven themselves into a living barricade, sealing away any hope of escape. He could almost feel them shifting beneath him, tightening around his ankles in anticipation.

Warden stepped closer, curling his fingers with casual malice. With a flick of his wrist, the vines surged forward, snapping around Razma's arms and legs. Razma fought to pull free, but they only dug deeper, rooting him in place.

"You never could outrun me," Warden murmured, the words brimming with dark satisfaction. He paused within arm's reach, twisting his fingers again until the vines' hold on Razma became absolute. "Nowhere left to run," he added softly, and the finality in his tone left Razma's heart pounding in fear.

Razma struggled, panic choking him as he thrashed against the relentless grip, but it was futile. The more he fought, the tighter the vines coiled around him, squeezing until he could barely breathe.

"Quiet, kid," Warden sneered, leaning close, his voice a dark whisper. "The queen is waiting for you."

Razma's eyes widened, a faint glimmer of confusion breaking through his terror. "Raelle?" he whispered, barely able to speak.

Warden's smirk deepened, his eyes gleaming with cruel amusement as he leaned even closer. "No… the Lost Queen."

The words echoed through Razma, each syllable laden with implication. *The Lost Queen?* He didn't have time to process the revelation, though, as the vines constricted further, choking off his breath. His vision wavered, the edges darkening under the crushing weight around his chest and limbs. Darkness began to close in, dragging him under, suffocating him.

Somewhere beyond Warden's looming form, Razma's eyes caught a flicker of motion in the dimness. Through the dust and swirling debris, he glimpsed Jeff trudging down the road, carrying the small, limp body of a boy in his arms. Urgency etched across his features, Jeff urged the nearby villagers to run for safety. Then, just as Razma's consciousness began to slip, he saw the boy stir—a faint cough escaping the child's lips. Jeff let out a long, shaking sigh of relief, gratitude and hope passing over his face before they both disappeared into the chaos.

As Razma's gaze unfocused, a hauntingly surreal sight overtook him: red rose petals drifting downward like soft, crimson snowflakes. In the midst of this eerie display, Vil'elm's silhouette emerged, outlined starkly against the falling petals, his expression a mystery. The last of Razma's strength ebbed away, and with it, the world dissolved into darkness.

Vil'elm's smile was thin, his gaze fixed on Razma as he approached. With a practiced bow, he murmured, "Long live the Lost Queen."

Warden's expression softened, the malice in his eyes replaced by something almost reverent. Reaching into his coat, he withdrew the old, worn journal he had taken from Lilah's belongings. He held it up, his thumb brushing across its leather cover, before a pressed red rose slipped from its pages, landing softly at his feet. He began to read, his voice quiet but filled with a deep, twisted satisfaction:

"Shadows return, in silent creep,

Rise from roots, from deep to deep.

When lost queen stirs, heed the call,

May old king's blood not let us fall.

The stone will quake, the forge go cold,

As tribes must gather, fierce and bold.

Hold fast the ward, and bar the gate,

Or all we've built succumbs to fate.

Where roots bind stone, we make our stand,

Or darkness claims both kin and land."

As he finished, Warden's gaze lingered on the fallen rose, his smile growing with a slow, dark satisfaction. His voice softened, as if whispering a promise to himself. "Mama," he murmured, his tone almost tender. "I am coming home."

Epilouge

"So it be, it begins,

Our heroes must bring the kin,

Races to gather, rise, and stand,

While Sliverfang prowls the land.

Young Razma, oh, poor Razma,

Off to meet the queen,

With Tala bold and Ky'len keen—

Their fate lies yet unseen."

He chuckled, pausing as if searching for something, then continued, a little softer:

"The stars may guide, the earth may quake,

But a bond unbroken they must make.

Through danger dark and shadows deep,

Their promises to keep."

He patted his pockets and frowned, then laughed:

Afterword

To the Stranger Who Finds This,

Seventeen years have passed since I first pledged myself to him, and still, my heart remains tethered by a love as fierce as it was on that first day. I came to him in defiance of tradition, with vows that sought to bridge two worlds my kin believed should never mix. Our union was always destined to stir doubt, yet I thought love alone might be enough to hold us together. But now, as I write these words, I feel the weight of a secret I have guarded fiercely —a truth I have withheld from the man I swore to stand beside.

Our children were born into joy and fear, twins bound by blood yet marked with a fire I could never extinguish. I believed my love could shield them, but the choices I made have brought unbearable burdens. My kin, ever watchful, saw something dangerous in our son. His anger, they said, was a threat, a force that would consume him. They took him from me, molding him in their ways, and though I still feel his presence, it is distant, as if he belongs more to them now than to me.

Today, my husband—Halzor, king in name, warrior at heart—rides to war, and the council we once called friends now tears us apart. They have turned against him, fracturing what was once united under a common cause. Where once we stood together, they have left us in ruins, each grasping for power amidst the crumbling remains of our kingdom. The violence that now looms over us seems inevitable, as though war has been etched into our fate.

I had hoped for a future without bloodshed, a future where our children could grow without the burdens of war. But that dream has withered, as all things do. My son marches to battle beside his father, and I fear that the darkness I tried to protect him from will consume him. My daughter's gift, hidden for now, is the only thing I can still shield.

Mira, once my closest friend, now spends her nights with my husband, poring over ancient texts, drawn to the same dangerous knowledge. I love Halzor, but I fear his growing obsession with that which should remain untouched. He looks for answers in the forbidden, chasing the same shadows that once consumed others in our line. I see it in our son too, that pull toward the darkness. And it is because of that fear that I took matters into my own hands —when my father-in-law grew too curious, too close to unraveling secrets that could destroy us, I... ended it. I did what I had to, for my family. And I will not hesitate to do it agai

I sometimes think of confessing everything to Halzor, but fear holds me back. He does not understand what we truly face, the dangers within our very walls. His mind is set on ruling, on battles with distant enemies, blind to the war I fight here. I've tried to warn him about

Mira, about how her loyalty to him blinds him to her true intent. She, too, once followed our line with devotion, but now she serves another purpose, one I cannot fully discern. Still, her presence unnerves me, and I suspect she knows more than she lets on.

The burden of these secrets is crushing. I long to unburden myself, but I fear his sense of justice, his pride, and most of all, his hurt. Would he still see me as his wife if he knew what I've done to protect our children? Or would he see me as the keeper of a legacy that defies his understanding? How would he react if he knew I commissioned the crystal rose for our daughter, the one designed to drain her magic and temper her light? It was the only way I knew to keep her safe—from our kin, from the world, and perhaps even from herself.

If you are reading this, know that I acted out of love. I have fought to protect my family from the shadows that cling to us, even when it meant making choices that tore at my soul. And still, I cannot regret the life we have built, fractured as it may be. I only pray that, one day, Halzor will understand why I kept these secrets, and that our children will forgive me for the burdens they now bear.

I hope that, when all is revealed, they will see beyond the secrecy to the love driving each decision. For our daughter, I see both his courage and my kin's resilience, and I am filled with both pride and dread. She is a reminder of all I cherish, but also of the bloodline's secrets that could undo us all

So I write this, stranger, to tell you that my actions, however painful, were born of love. I have done what I must to protect those I hold dear, even if it means betraying the trust of the man I lov

May those who read these words find the strength to forgive, and may they see in my story a love that was as fierce as it was-Lyrith

Character List

Ky'len -A young squire from Bazel, determined to prove himself and redeem his kingdom's name. Ky'len is loyal, brave, and torn between his duty and the rising tension between Bazel and Seragora. As he uncovers the truth behind the attacks, he finds himself thrust into a conflict much larger than he expected.

Iszell -Ky'len's childhood friend and fellow squire. Iszell is intelligent, strategic, and always looking out for Ky'len. Though often more cautious, he plays a key role in uncovering Mrs. Thorn's schemes and helps balance Ky'len's impulsiveness with logic and reason.

Razma -The son of Belazar, Seragora's stable master. Eager for adventure, Razma stumbles into a plot far more dangerous than he could have imagined. As he seeks excitement, he is pulled into the chaos surrounding his homeland and discovers more about his family's past.

Belazar -A former war hero and now the stable master of Seragora. Belazar's past as a fighter haunts him, and with the growing unrest, he is forced to confront old enemies and allies alike. As his son, Razma, gets drawn into danger, Belazar must once again take up arms to protect what he holds dear.

Tala -Daughter of Chief Arak, a brave muckspawn warrior determined to save her people from the corrupting influence of Mrs. Thorn. Torn between her loyalty to her tribe and the dark magic that has twisted them, Tala teams up with Ky'len and Iszell to stop Thorn's sinister plot.

Flin-Quiet and practical, Flin'thor's broken Common and Vek'smed rhythm give him an earthy, wise presence. He values action over words and respects strength, grounding those around him with his steady, no-nonsense demeanor.

Flak-A mischievous instigator, Flak'tin delights in stirring up trouble, with his sharp wit keeping friends and foes alike on their toes. Loyal but provocative, he's never afraid to prod others just to see their reaction.

Dalmon-A shopkeeper in Seragora, Dalmon is sharp-witted and resourceful. He has connections to many of the kingdom's secrets and is often the first to know when something's wrong. As old wounds resurface, he must navigate past grudges to help stop Thorn's plan.

Warden-A mysterious wanderer with a troubled past. Warden's motives are unclear, and though he initially operates on the fringes of the conflict, his ties to the unfolding events soon become undeniable. He must reconcile with his own past to fight against Mrs. Thorn's growing threat.

A'nara-A Slivdhe warrior and Dalmon's sister, A'nara is deeply connected to the magic and history of her people. Proud and resilient, she fights to protect her kind from being drawn into the darkness spreading across the land. Her bond with Dalmon and her loyalty to their shared legacy drive her to face the challenges ahead, even when it means confronting her own people's secrets.

Yvonne-A skilled human ranger from Seragora, Yvonne is pragmatic and fierce. She often works independently, guiding those in need through dangerous lands and scouting threats before they strike. Though she seems hardened by her experiences, her loyalty to her kingdom runs deep, and she becomes an invaluable ally in the fight against Thorn. Her bond with the natural world and her ability to track and fight make her a formidable opponent.

Mrs. Thorn-A powerful and manipulative figure orchestrating the attacks on Seragora, making it appear as though Bazel is to blame. Thorn uses dark magic to corrupt the muckspawn and push the kingdoms toward war. Her thirst for power knows no bounds, and her sinister influence is felt across the land.

Mutt-Mrs. Thorn's brutish enforcer, Mutt is a terrifying figure obsessed with power. He follows Thorn's orders with ruthless efficiency, though he harbors his own ambitions. As the conflict escalates, Mutt is determined to rise higher, no matter who stands in his way.

Iggy-Mutt's younger brother, often a source of trouble and frustration. Iggy is more reckless than his brother, but his loyalty to Mutt remains, even as they both get drawn deeper into

Thorn's schemes.

Lord Darth- A merchent lord in Bazel and father to Ky'len. Leader of a large mercnay force that montors Bazel amking him effecttly a king in eveythign but name.

King Tor'valis: The ruler of Seragora, struggling to maintain peace between his kingdom and Bazel while dealing with internal conflicts. He strives to keep the kingdom united but faces threats from both within and outside his borders.

Queen Raelle: The queen of Seragora, known for her wisdom and strength, having earned the trust of the people despite her mysterious past. She is key in maintaining the fragile peace within the kingdom.

Lord Cedric: A stubborn and proud noble, wary of the tensions with Bazel and critical of Ky'len. He represents the more conservative and distrustful faction of the council, resisting change.

Lady Kira: A strategic and politically savvy council member, she is cautious about the rising tensions with Bazel and constantly weighs the risks to Seragora's stability.

Lord Aric: A pragmatic and level-headed member of the council, he supports King Tor'valis and advocates for peace, seeing the bigger picture beyond old rivalries.

Clive: A captain in the king's guard, who is loyal to King Tor'valis and tasked with keeping the peace within the city during the chaos. He is more of a soldier than a politician but understands the need to keep the people calm.

Chief Gruk'thar (deceased): Former Chief of the Boar Tusk Tribe, known for their fierce and relentless nature. He was defeated by Mutt.

Chief Rak'tan (deceased): Former leader of the Owlbeak Tribe, cunning and wise, specializing in ambush tactics. He was defeated by Bea'ranti.

Chief Bea'ranti: Female Chief of the Wolffang Tribe, known for her strategic mind and loyalty to her people. She defeated Rak'tan to gain her position.

Chief Arak: Leader of the Wolfclaw Tribe, Tala's father, with a strong but conflicted leadership, reflecting the strength and dominance of wolves.

Chief Scor'jan: Chief of the Scorpiontail Tribe, ruthless and feared, with a venomous bite that is both literal and political, much like the scorpions his tribe represents.

Chief Zra'ka: Leader of the Webshroud Tribe, known for their mastery of dark magic and webs, using manipulation and fear to dominate, akin to spiders weaving intricate traps. Zra'ka killed Urshak.

Vark'nal (deceased): Former Chief of the Venomfang Tribe, specialists in poison and deception, feared even among the muckspawn. Defeated by Mutt.

Urshak (deceased): Former Chief of the Crowfeather Tribe, a dark figure known for his agility and flight-like abilities. He was defeated by the human Ky'len, then killed by Chief Zra'ka.

Kraggor: Chief of the Stonetooth Tribe, embodying the raw strength and defense of bears, his tribe is resilient and steadfast.

Zarnok: Chief of the Serpentcoil Tribe, agile and lethal, his tribe excels in stealth and poison, much like the snakes they revere.

Vruk'tal: Chief of the Thunderhoof Tribe, swift and aggressive, channeling the speed and strength of wild stags in battle.

Mara'kis: Female Chief of the Briarthorn Tribe, her tribe is resilient and tough, resembling the thorny plants of the jungle, using their environment to set traps and protect their lands.

Made in the USA
Monee, IL
06 April 2025

b1ca0324-65b3-44f1-b975-b9d1f69fe1b5R01